PRINCE

of

SECRETS and SHADOWS

BOOK TWO OF *THE ORDER OF THE CRYSTAL DAGGERS*

C. S. Johnson

C. S. JOHNSON

Dedication

First off, this is dedicated to my incredible family. My love of reading and fun and functional dysfunction comes from you.

Second, to Sam. Wherever you are, you are always in my heart, mind, and prayers. I still hope to see you again one day.

Third, to the wonderful people who made my writing time possible: Ryan, my beloved; Gabby, our new friend; Joy, our special aunt; Dr. Jon and company, down at my local coffee shop; and to Barry and Joann Benningfield. Every word I write, I write with the joy, wisdom, and time afforded to me.

And finally, to my fans. I can't believe I am lucky enough to have you as fans, and I am certain your generosity in being my friends, too, is even a less warranted miracle.

To Get *Awakening* (A Special Christmas Episode of The *Starlight Chronicles*) as a bonus for picking up this book,

Click Here

Or Download It At:
https://www.csjohnson.me/awakening

1

◊

"Ella."

The whisper of his voice inside my mind was enough to jolt me free from any dreams and propel me into the waking world.

I gasped as I woke, gripping the fine sheets I found surrounding me. The silken softness beneath my fingers was a foreign feeling, one that became clearer as I sat upright on the bed. I blinked, glancing around as moonlight glowed outside the window in front of me.

Squinting, I saw the view was completely unfamiliar.

Where am I?

My nose wrinkled, as the scent of lavender and mint wafted around me, and I began to feel a pounding pain in the back of my head. Reaching under my loosened curls, I felt a small bump.

The pain seemed to spread as I became aware of it; my muscles were sore, and my body ached. I took careful inventory of myself, finding a bandage wrapped around my right leg, just above my knee, and another around my shoulder. I was still in my stealth habit, with its short skirt, black bodice, and armored sleeves, tucked between fine sheets in a bed that was not mine.

As my eyes finally adjusted to the night, I could make out my surroundings.

My hand covered my mouth in shock.

I was in a bedroom, alone, seemingly surrounded by every creature comfort imaginable. The bed was grand, with intricate carvings and covered in delicate drapery. There were rugs on the floor from the East Indies, and a messy bookshelf tucked beside a window seat. Other items—chests and chairs and lamps of all sizes—dotted the room, shining in the retreating moonlight.

Despite the glory of the room around me, my gaze went immediately back to the window.

The dwindling starlight reflected through the glass as morning rapidly approached. Outside, the remaining walls of Prague Castle gleamed, taunting me with their unmoving stasis as my last memories trickled into my mind.

"The fire," I whispered hoarsely, struggling to orient myself to reality's bitter welcome. I did not know if the sound of my voice against the emptiness of the room would keep me from going mad or send me there sooner. There was a singed quality to my throat, and the taste of smoke was suddenly on my tongue.

I licked my lips and cleared my throat. Then I shifted out of the bedsheets and forced myself to find a cognizant starting place.

The last I remembered, I had been at the Advent Ball, the yearly event hosted by King Ferdinand V and his wife, Empress Maria Anna. It was the first time in over a decade I had seen the former rulers of the Austria-Hungarian Empire, which included my home nation of Bohemia, and it proved to be just as devastating as the last time.

"If not more so," I whispered, as my head fell into my hands. I rubbed my forehead and raked back my hair, the dark curls feeling frayed and knotted between my fingers.

It was almost like a bad dream, and my current surroundings did nothing to make it less surreal. The room I was in was crowned with high ceilings, the walls were decorated with splendid paintings and lined with silk wallpaper, and books of all sorts were scattered around, while

THE ORDER OF THE CRYSTAL DAGGERS

a half-open wardrobe and several unlit, half-melted candelabras leered at me from the shadows.

On a nearby table, there was a basin filled with lavender-scented water. The fragrance caught my attention before I saw the folded dress beside it.

After only a second's hesitation, I went over and picked up the gown. The fabric felt as soft and pliant as liquid when I held it up to me, surprised to find it was my size. There was even a new set of matching combs on the table beside it.

Is this for me?

It was too much. Everything about the room was too much, I thought, spying a copy of *Morte d'Arthur* on the floor, splayed upside down, carelessly forgotten. I picked it up, briefly noting it was a different copy than the one my father used to own before I clutched it to my chest and looked around again.

The elegance of the castle room was something my stepmother would have sold her soul to have, even if it was just for a day.

I looked back at the dress, noting the fine stitching and the ornate design. My fingers fiddled with some of the ruffles, marveling at the elegance.

Cecilia would probably sell the souls of both her children for this dress.

Not that the devil would take them, I added, allowing myself a small giggle despite my uncertainty.

As I made my way back to the bed, my eyes scourged over everything; the room was elegant and beautiful, resplendent with treasures I had never seen and could never earn. But it was a kind of illusion—just like the heavenly city of Prague outside my window.

The room was still a prison, and I was its prisoner.

THE ORDER OF THE CRYSTAL DAGGERS

I was *his* prisoner.

I slumped back against the pillows as the onslaught of memories ran through me. I relived those last moments of terror all over again. In many ways, they kept me captive more than the sturdy locks on my door.

Fresh wounds scraped against the flesh of my heart, as I drifted back to that night, to that moment—the last moment before everything fell apart, and nothing seemed like it would ever be the same again.

I remembered running as fast as I could through the hallways of the castle, my breath coming in small pants. I knew I only had a limited amount of time before the walls would fall, thanks to the wine cellar collapsing. The castle's cellar had been set afire, and it was only a matter of time before it spread and wrecked its way through the castle.

It was an act of treachery courtesy of Lord Maximillian, the Duke of Moravia, his nefarious henchman, and possibly Karl Marcelin, the secret heir to the throne of Bohemia.

On the other side of the ballroom, guests were quickly evacuating the castle under the orders of the King, aided by the oversight of my grandmother, Lady Penelope Ollerton-Wellesley, the Dowager Duchess of Wellington and the leader of the Order of the Crystal Daggers. My brother, Ben, and our small team of spies were working to save as many people as possible.

I had been sent to find the second heir to the kingdom—only to discover I already knew him.

"Ferdy."

In my mind, I heard myself speak his name. I saw him, standing in the hallway outside the ballroom. He was regal and serious, nothing like the boy I had fallen in love with. We sparred verbally, fighting with our feelings, arguing over

THE ORDER OF THE CRYSTAL DAGGERS

secrets and lies, before the castle rooms behind me echoed with oncoming destruction.

The last thing I remembered was grabbing onto him and trying to pull him away from danger.

There was a small part of me that felt him grip me back, that heard him call my name.

I clutched my arms, trying to force myself to distinguish between dreams and reality after that. It was too much to hope for that he would call to me, after everything else that had happened.

My shoulder shifted against the pillows. I saw it taped up, covered with medical bandages. Carefully, I reached up and began to unwrap the wound, flinching as the bandage tugged at my skin.

I was prepared for the worst, so I was surprised when, underneath it, I only saw a small cut across my skin. Immediately, my eyes squeezed shut, trying to ward off the memory.

It was hard—there were a million moments I wanted to forget, but they were all still there.

Ferdy dancing with me in the ballroom. He had worn a lord's jacket and combed back his coppery hair. There had been a distinctive shine on his boots and a twinkle in his eye. He was utterly irresistible, and never more so when he told me he was in love with me.

Ferdy kissing me with grand and growing passion as I unremarkably admitted I loved him, too.

Ferdy overhearing me discuss marriage with his brother, before confronting me, assuming I was only after Karl because he was a prince.

Ferdy trying to run from me before I could explain. Then him struggling as I tried to speak before he finally pushed himself free of me. I had scraped my shoulder at the time, causing it to bleed.

I barely registered the pain then, and now there was none left as I carefully touched the clotted blood scabbing over in a thin line and a patch of red, roughened skin.

But the bandage was soaked with herbs and medicine, and it had been tied back with care so evident it could have been a silent apology.

Does this mean he still loves me?

I could not stop myself from hoping he did.

For several moments, I allowed myself to indulge in my feeble hopes. I wondered if he would come and see me again. As the eerie light of dying night transformed into blossoming day, I finally shook my head.

I was being foolish—a lovesick servant girl and spy, pining for a prince.

"I shouldn't even want to see him," I said to myself. "He *lied* to me! And about so many things. Who's to say he was even telling me the truth about loving me?"

My memory tried to contradict me, and it was at its rebellion that I pushed myself out of bed and began to get ready to leave.

I *had* to find a way out of there.

"I still have a job to do," I reminded myself.

I needed to find out what happened to Ben and Amir, and the others, too. Admittedly, I was not as worried about Lady Penelope. My grandmother was a spymaster, no doubt one used to dangerous situations. She was probably used to finding a way out of a mission's complications, even ones like half of a castle collapsing. She might have been used to losing people, too.

THE ORDER OF THE CRYSTAL DAGGERS

After all, she had lost my mother.

Deep down, I knew it was possible Lady Penelope would be happy to see me when I returned to my father's manor. But I could already hear her chiding me for even needing to recover as I washed my face and brushed out the knots in my hair.

As I contemplated changing into the new gown, the locks behind me chimed, and the door opened.

A shadow stepped forward. "Good morning, my lady."

Disappointment crushed me. It was Philip, the servant I had originally believed to be the Prince of Bohemia. For the first time, I recognized the smothered accent of the streets, the hidden Bohemian harmony, tucked underneath his proper tone.

There were other things I noticed now, too; Philip was close to Ferdy's height, only a little taller than myself. He had a similar color of hair, but his eyes were brown rather than silver, and even in the darkness of the morning hours I could see the string of light freckles on his face.

I could also see the hesitation in his gaze as he looked at me.

Carefully balancing a silver tray in his hands, he cleared his throat, clearly embarrassed to be caught staring. "How are you feeling, my lady?"

It was hard to give him an answer when I did not know myself. "What is today?" I sidestepped the question altogether.

"It's the seventh of December," he said. "Two days after the Feast of St. Nicholas."

Two days since the attack on the castle.

"How did I get here?"

"His Highness and I brought you here after you fell unconscious," Philip replied. He cautiously made his way to a bedside table and set down the small tray. My stomach grumbled at the smell of freshly baked bread and herbal tea.

"Can you tell me what happened?"

"After you found us and argued with His Highness," Philip began slowly, "the floor in the ballroom collapsed in on the castle's underground hallways while some of the nearby walls and ceilings fell."

He looked up me, clearly overwhelmed with gratitude. "You pushed His Highness out of the way and protected him. Some debris fell on your head."

The small bump on my head twanged with remembered pain, as if in agreement.

"I see. So then you brought me here."

"Yes, my lady."

One of the lessons Lady POW had taught me was to observe things, and knowing how traumatized I was by Ferdy's deceit—how I failed to realize he was a prince in disguise, I would never fully understand—I vowed to be extra careful in the future. As I watched Philip, eyeing his quick and careful movements, I saw no immediate reason to distrust the freckled servant who apparently served as Ferdy's royal stand-in.

Admittedly, I was not willing to distrust him when I was as desperate as I was for news.

"What happened to my brother? And what about the ballroom? Did everyone... survive?"

Philip stood, straight and rigid, as he informed me of what he knew. There was no way for him to answer some questions, but even then, I already knew some of the answers.

As Philip remarked on the damage, the Empress' pain, and the king's proclamation of sorrow regarding the loss of life, worry for Ben started to override my concern for Ferdy. I had to get back to my home, find Ben, Lady POW, and my other friends. Then, if I was still allowed to help after all of my mistakes, we had to find out what to do next.

Lady Penelope will be upset with me when I see her again.

I decided I would welcome her ire, if it meant Ben was alive and the Order would allow me a chance to redeem myself. And then Lord Maximillian would pay, I vowed, gripping my fingers into fists as my failure tormented me.

"Please," Philip said, stepping forward as I began to pull on my boots. "You are not well."

"I'm fine," I insisted. It was at that moment I realized my dagger, the one that marked me as a member of the Order of the Crystal Daggers, was missing. "Where is my dagger?"

Philip hesitated again. "Please, just rest for now, my lady. His Highness only wishes for you to recover."

"I am feeling fine," I repeated angrily, shooting him a threatening glance. "Give me back my things. I need to be on my way, and I won't let you—or him—stop me."

Philip did not seem to be very brave—or at least, he was not willing to anger me. As displaced and determined as I was, I supposed I could not fault him for that. He gulped and nodded slowly. "As you wish, my lady. I shall return."

He paused briefly when he opened the door. "I know I should not tell you this," he said quietly, "but His Highness wishes for you to stay here. You are safe, and so are your secrets. We are indebted to you for what you have done."

Heat poured through me. As Philip left, relocking the doors, I finally caught sight of myself in the mirror. My

THE ORDER OF THE CRYSTAL DAGGERS

cheeks burned bright crimson as my heart began to beat faster inside my chest.

He wants me to stay.

But a long moment later, I forced myself to move. I could not stay. I had my family to find, my work to finish.

My dignity to salvage, my honor to restore.

I grabbed at the dress left out for me and tugged it over my head. With the stays laced loosely, I could easily wear it over my stealth habit. I hurried to secure it, grateful it would be a suitable disguise. Just as I was contemplating how to get home, even if it meant walking the whole way there, the lock clicked again.

The door opened as I pulled my hair free and tucked my hood down beneath a line of ruffles.

"You can put my dagger down on the table, Philip." I tugged the sleeves down off my shoulders, grimacing as the lower neckline brushed over the small cut. "I'll get it in a moment."

"I suppose it shouldn't surprise me that you hardly pay attention to me when we meet like this."

My spine tingled with sudden awareness, and my heart began to race at the sound of his voice. It was not Philip who had come.

It was Ferdy.

2

◊

Ferdy's voice stilled me. My body felt paralyzed as he moved behind me.

"But then," he drawled, "you've never seemed to recognize me for who I am."

I whirled around to face him. He was leaning against the door, dressed in a new ensemble of princely clothes. His brown hair was brushed back and styled so I could not see any of the hidden red, although there were hints of it in the shadow of a beard on his cheeks. There was a faint smirk on his face as I studied him, trying to see the Ferdy I knew: the street urchin who had set out to save me from trouble, the footman who stole me away from ballrooms … the simple boy who had loved me as a simple girl.

"You look well." Nervously, I fiddled with my sleeves, smoothing out all the wrinkles as I called on my failing courage. I could feel Ferdy's eyes linger on my bare shoulder, the one he had bruised. "Are you going to Mass?"

"As a matter of fact, I am. Mother has called for special masses this week for the victims of the incident, and I am to attend them with her."

"I suppose Karl will be there, too," I said. "He assured me that he was dedicated to your mother's happiness."

Ferdy's breath released sharply. "I was hoping we could avoid talking about him."

"Why should we?" I snapped. All my courage and patience was gone, and only my anger was left. "You *lied* to me. About *everything*."

"Not everything."

11

THE ORDER OF THE CRYSTAL DAGGERS

A new thought struck me as I stood there. "I don't even know your real name!"

His confidence faltered, ever so slightly. "My name *is* Ferdy. Well, Ferdinand. I was named after my father and the king. I wasn't lying about that. I only … neglected … to mention that my father and the king were the same person."

When I crossed my arms over my chest, he gave me a sheepish look. "The name goes back several generations," he murmured, still attempting to defend himself.

My chin jutted forward defiantly. "I suppose Karl's does, too?"

"Even you should know Bohemia's history." Ferdy shifted his stance, moving away from the door to stand tall, his temper kindling in response to my own. "Karl was named after the first crowned king of our people. I was named after the last crowned king, which, thanks to my cousin, is still my father."

"You should have told me Karl was your brother."

"I told you enough about him!" Ferdy argued. "I even said he had a brother, the night I tricked him with the note from the footman. Remember?"

It took me a moment, to recall the scene at the Hohenwart Ball, where Ferdy had appeared out of the shadows to come and see me. The scene became clear in my mind as I stood there, still attempting to rein in my remaining arguments. Underneath all my inner fury, I saw that night. I remembered Ferdy telling me Karl had been summoned away to go and retrieve his brother.

"You were the one fooling around with an actress?" I arched my brow at him.

THE ORDER OF THE CRYSTAL DAGGERS

"I did not know how accurate it was at the time." Ferdy's eyes roamed down my body, unable to hide his appreciation. "You clearly had some secrets yourself."

"Secrets are one thing," I said, blushing. "Lies are another."

"I agree." He glowered at me. "There's enough of an overlap in this case that I find it offensive."

"Offensive enough when it's done to you, but you don't seem to have any trouble offending me."

"I also hate accusations."

"This from the man that has lied to me from the beginning!" I waved my arm around, gesturing toward the room around us. "Should I be flattered or insulted that after all your lies and secrets, you've kept me here like a prisoner of war?"

"You were the one who accused me of being an assassin before. But you saved me, so I think we should consider ourselves even," Ferdy said.

"You had a handkerchief from the assassin's place of employ," I said.

I thought of the handkerchief Ferdy had handed to me, the one he offered to me to stop the bleeding on my shoulder. It was just after he left me at the Advent Ball after Karl had run off, trying to find Lord Maximillian, in hopes of renegotiating their terms for the kingdom takeover. Ferdy had carried the handkerchief in his pocket.

"There was a man who worked for the Szapira household who attacked Tulia," I said. My head throbbed as I tried to keep my focus, but I was not going to let Ferdy see me cry.

Never, I vowed.

"Tulia was attacked?" Ferdy's anger quickly transformed into surprise.

13

I barely noticed his concern or heard his question. "Why else would you have it, if you were not in league with him?"

"I had to borrow the ensemble from Karl, if you must know," Ferdy said. "The handkerchief must have been a mix-up. He has been staying at the Szapira household since he returned to Prague. A simple mistake, that's all."

"Your lies are no 'simple mistake.'" I put my hand to my forehead, rubbing it in irritation. "You let me think you were nobody!"

"You kissed my brother."

"*He* kissed *me*."

"You didn't stop it."

"I was trying to stop him from possibly killing a bunch of people. It seemed like a decent gamble at the time." I turned away again, looking for some way to distance myself from him.

"That's all you have to say about it?" He came up to me and put his hand on my arm.

"Of all people, you should know that when you gamble, sometimes you lose," I said, sullen at my own poor luck.

"You told me that you loved me."

This time, Ferdy's words came across as an accusation more than a reminder, and they cut deeply into my already floundering heart.

His hands took hold of my shoulders and forced me to face him. I refused to look at his face; I did not want to witness the fun-loving Ferdy I had fallen in love with fade into nothingness.

Another illusion, I told myself bitterly. "After all the lies you've told me, I'm sure we can forget about that."

"I never lied about how I felt about you."

"Well, I never did, either," I snapped, trying to step back from him. I came up against a wall, and suddenly I was trapped.

"Prove it." He pulled me close, and I felt helpless as the angry heat between us transformed into desire.

My arms were already twining around his neck as his mouth came crashing down on mine.

There were endless lies surrounding us, but as he embraced me, I knew there was also one very important truth between us: I wanted him, and he wanted me.

I almost laughed as Ferdy held me tightly, his hands pressing on the small of my back; I remembered Lady POW telling me once before that men liked to grab onto hips during intercourse. Then his body pressed even more into mine, and I stopped thinking altogether.

Our kisses grew hotter and harder as I gripped onto him, unable to stop myself from wanting the moment to go on, even though I knew it had to stop.

"We can't do this," I whispered, nearly out of breath.

"I want to," Ferdy murmured, as his lips found my throat, and then my shoulder, where he lovingly lingered over the cut he had caused. My former pain was replaced by pleasure, and a small moan escaped me, as if to give him absolution.

"I know." I hugged him, gripping him for balance as much as to keep him close. "But we can't."

"Why not?" His eyes had clouded over with passion.

"You know why not." I waved my arm toward the window, gesturing at the broken kingdom outside the room. "You're a prince."

"I'm not a real prince."

THE ORDER OF THE CRYSTAL DAGGERS

"Yes, you are," I said. "And you just can't be with someone like me." I wanted to burst into tears, telling him that he could hardly marry someone who used to scrub the floors of her own home, let alone someone who was part of secret order of spies and protectors.

It was just not proper.

I pushed him away from me, determined to put a safe distance between us. "That's why I have to go."

"Ella."

The vulnerability in his voice made my knees weaken. "The kingdom needs both of us," I murmured, forcing myself to keep moving. "You have a duty to the kingdom, and I … I have to protect you."

"But—"

Outside of the room, the church bells rang. We went silent in the room, letting the solemn joy of the music interrupt us for the moment.

When the bells quieted, I shook my head. "Your mother will be worried for you. You should get to Mass."

"My mother can wait," Ferdy said with a dismissive snort as he turned to look out the window. "She thinks I've been in Silesia for the past several months and that I came home to celebrate Christmas with the family. Do you remember the invitation to the Advent Ball? The one I gave you?"

The one I had used as a bookmark for my reading as well as marker for my daydreams. The one I had run my fingers over many times, even the ragged, ripped edges at the top, where Ferdy had torn off the official greeting. Yes, I remembered it.

"That was the invitation she sent out for me," Ferdy said. "I stole it from the mail carrier one day while Jarl distracted him. Philip is the one who has been serving as the prince in my place, staying with the Duke of Silesia, disguised as a cousin to the Empress. He came back to report to me this past week. When he is gone, I will be free to go into the city while he goes back to studying and attending lectures in my place."

"So your mother thinks you've been at school instead of running around the streets of Prague dressed like a homeless person?"

For a brief second, Ferdy grinned, and I had my beloved rascal back. "*Absolument.*"

I grinned in reply, and we stared at each other for a long moment. It was so strange, I thought. I knew him so well, even though I knew nothing about him at all.

The moment between us passed, and then he came up to me, threading his fingers into my hair before he kissed me again, softly and sweetly.

No, I thought. There was one thing I knew for sure. We could not be together. Not now—not when there was nothing lasting between us, no real truth, and certainly no trust. Without that, the tidal wave of our passion, a tumultuous and rapturous thing, would end up destroying both of us.

"Ferdy," I whispered, with both wanting and warning.

"You're safe here, in my room," he whispered back. "Let me keep you."

I knew what he wanted. I knew I wanted it, too. Already, half of my mind was mentally calculating the days of my monthly courses, anything to give me a reason to stay, while the other half was scolding me for even considering it.

"How do I know you're telling me the truth?" The last thing I wanted to do was hurt him, but if I did not find a way to break free of him, I would risk doing even more harm.

Ferdy met my gaze with his. "I promise you this, Ella, that as of now, I will never lie to you again." He leaned forward and kissed me again, and I stood there, letting him, desperately debating whether I could trust him or not. His promise burned through me, his words scorched into my being. It was so tempting to believe him, more tempting than anything else I had ever faced in all my life.

Freedom was only freedom if I could trust it to be true.

"Will you let me keep you?" Ferdy whispered against my lips.

I was floored. The pleading in his voice, though disguised by pride, was clear; Ferdy was begging me to stay. He was a prince. Even while he played a beggar on the street, he never had to worry about his next meal or fear that he would be denied anything he wanted. But as he kissed me, I could feel the raw, burning desperation inside of him, the kind that only came with true risk. He knew he could make me stay. But he also knew it would mean nothing if I did not want to.

"I have to go back to my family." His humility, juxtaposed against my own humiliation, allowed me to pull back once more. "I don't know what happened to my brother or the rest of them. Ben is too important to me."

Ferdy held onto me more tightly, and I felt my breath catch. I did not want to have to remind him there was a murderer on the loose.

But as he held me in his arms, still and unmoving, I had a feeling we both knew he could convince me to stay, and I would not object so long as I had his kisses to keep me content.

It seemed both too long and too short of a time had passed before he nodded, letting me slide out of his embrace. "You saved my life, despite my attempts to negate it, perhaps. I am indebted to you. And I know what your brother means to

THE ORDER OF THE CRYSTAL DAGGERS

you, even if my own brotherly affections have been stymied over the last years."

I bit my lip, curious all of a sudden. "Why don't you and Karl get along?" I asked. "He seemed nice enough to me. I know Ben and I have our differences, but we still love and care for each other."

"It takes an extraordinary amount of kindness and courage to love someone who hates you. Karl and I don't appear to have much patience for that." Ferdy smiled at me. "That's something I've always loved about you. Your kindness and bravery were endearing to me, even at the beginning."

"The beginning?"

"The first time I saw you, at your father's funeral." Ferdy looked out the window again, where dawn was starting to peek through Prague's elaborate streets. "When the king heard about your father's death, he was unusually determined to go. He said he never owed a man more of a debt than he did Adolf Svoboda."

It felt strange to hear Ferdy speak of my father. "*Táta* served as one of his bodyguards during the Revolution of 1848."

"While my mother was pregnant with Karl, and later after he was born," Ferdy said with a nod. "I know. My father made your father a knight and gave him land before my cousin took over as Emperor."

"That's the only real reason I'm a lady," I said. "Is that how you knew who I was, the day we met in Prague?"

Once more, the flirtatious grin appeared. "Among other things. It wasn't the first time I'd seen you in the city. I know you were upset at losing your book, but I was quite glad for the excuse to rescue you."

THE ORDER OF THE CRYSTAL DAGGERS

I did not tell Ferdy that Amir had been the one behind the theft, and I had forgiven him for that day.

"I remembered the funeral," I said. "I didn't realize you and Karl were there until… "

Until I learned the truth. Until I learned the truth about the secret heirs of Bohemia.

"Karl would have gladly neglected the funeral. I am the younger heir, but I am my father's favorite. That is a large reason for the animosity between us. I doubt Karl has ever forgiven Father for such an insult."

I bit my lip, tempted to tell Ferdy he was my favorite, too. I kept to the relevant topic instead. "That is hardly your fault."

He paused for a moment, studying me closely.

"You were your father's favorite, too, weren't you?" Ferdy asked, startling me with the abrupt question. "You don't know what it is like, to feel the pain of being rejected by a parent."

I thought of how *Táta* had treated me, and then how he had treated Ben. Even before Ben fell off the barn roof and shattered his right leg, our father had been less affectionate toward him.

I have never thought about that before.

Was it possible I had ruined his life even before I had caused him to break his leg?

"I don't think Ben hates me for that," I said, forcing myself to focus on Ferdy.

"He has likely thought about it, even if he does not hate you for it." Ferdy shrugged. "Karl and I have many differences, but most of them come from our father's favoritism. He hates that he is still ordered to watch out for me, too."

THE ORDER OF THE CRYSTAL DAGGERS

I nodded blithely. From what I knew of him, Karl was a proud man.

When Ferdy had tricked Karl into leaving the Hohenwart Ball, Karl reacted furiously. He was irritated at the interruption of our time together, but it was also clear he hated the task he was called to perform. It would anger him to be obligated to chase after his younger brother, especially while facing the neglect of his father. Such a slight would have been devastating.

No wonder Karl was so accomplished for his age, I thought. He would have wanted to stand out in other ways, almost as a way to punish his father for his lack of faith and favor.

"When I said I wanted to go to your father's funeral with him, Karl changed his mind," Ferdy said, continuing with his tale.

"Why did you want to go?" I asked. "You couldn't be much younger than Ben. Even *he* didn't want to go."

"Any boy who has ever wanted to be a man looks to his father first," Ferdy replied.

I thought about Ben's own disdain for our father's memory, but how quickly he would defend *Táta's* legacy as a soldier for the kingdom. Ferdy was right, as much as I might have wished to disagree with him.

"I know my father has his mental limitations and he is not what anyone might consider a prize. But as a child, none of that mattered quite as much to me as it did to others."

I knew that still did not matter to Ferdy. He had always been the one who saw the worth of others before he saw their capabilities or labels. He acknowledged his father's shortcomings, but clearly, he did not see them as a barrier to a relationship.

"When I found out what going to the funeral would mean to my father, I was determined to go."

"That must be why we get along so well," I said. "We are both determined creatures at heart."

"You more than me. When I saw you—when you smiled at me as I helped my father through another one of his seizures at your father's funeral—I felt unusually uncomfortable. I was there because I wanted my father to be proud of me. You were there because of your father's death, and even in your sadness, you had enough goodness to offer a child your kindness."

He came up to me again, clasping my hand in his and caressing it affectionately.

"So you must know, Ella," he whispered, "this idea that you are not of my station is true. But you have it wrong. I do not deserve you."

I shook my head. I did not believe him.

"There are other reasons we can't," I whispered, looking down at my new dress, the one that covered the stealth habit Lady POW had commissioned for me. "It's too dangerous."

Ferdy straightened and took a small step back from me, allowing the tension between us to lapse ever so slightly.

"That reminds me." He reached behind himself and pulled out my sheathed dagger. "I kept it safe for you. Here."

"Thank you."

"I have heard of the Order of the Crystal Daggers," Ferdy said. "I'll admit, I do not know how I feel about you being part of that assassination group."

"It's not an assassination group," I insisted.

He ignored me. "I feel better knowing you're a beginner."

My eyes narrowed at him. "What makes you think I'm a beginner?"

"You've had the younger prince of Bohemia in front of you for weeks now, and you only learned the truth two nights ago," Ferdy said pointedly, clearly trying to hide a smirk.

My fists clenched angrily at his remark, as true as it might have been.

Before I could defend myself, he shook his head. "I will not fight you on this now. You saved me when the ballroom walls fell, so I know, for the moment, you are on my side. I know that might change, but I do not feel like that should preclude you from my attentions."

There was nothing I could say. There was just too much between us, and that moment, the moment back in the castle, right before everything was destroyed, only proved our fate. We were too far away, and even if we were to work to bridge the chasm between us, one of us—or both of us—would end up hurt.

And I did not want to hurt him. I was not willing to risk his life or safety, even if it meant we would be together.

I glanced back at the door, eager to escape.

"If you are determined to leave me, I've already said I would let you go," Ferdy said in a resigned voice.

He knew I was not going to choose him. His voice was too much like before when I first met him, and he asked if we could see each other again.

Too much had separated us back then. Even more kept us apart now.

"Thank you," I said. That was the only thing I could think to say. I put my hand over his before I added, "Your Highness."

THE ORDER OF THE CRYSTAL DAGGERS

He frowned, before leaning close to me. I thought for sure he was going to kiss me again, and I could not stop myself from wanting him to do so.

But he only touched his forehead to mine, lightly and softly, staying there for the most bittersweet moment of my life. "Goodbye, Ella."

The way he said it, I wondered if he would ever call me that again.

Before I could find the courage to ask, he turned around and left the room, leaving me alone with my many scrambled thoughts.

The door was left open for me.

I did not move as I listened to the sound of Ferdy's footsteps fade across the castle hallways. I was finally free to leave; I did not know if I had ever been free to stay.

3

◊

The journey home felt painfully interminable.

Philip arranged for me to travel by coach, so I did not have to sneak through the city. Even in my state of sadness, I could see why Ferdy trusted him; Philip took care of everything, down to the smallest details. He even brushed my hair, pinning it back with new combs. When I commended him on his work, he lightheartedly confessed that men could be even more difficult than women when it came to styling hair.

It was only when I promised to send the combs back to the palace after I arrived home that he refused to accommodate me.

"His Highness gave them to you as a gift." A slight flush peeked out from under Philip's freckles, and I had the feeling he was telling me the truth against his better judgment. "The prince would like you to keep them."

It broke my heart, but I allowed it. If it was Ferdy's gift to me, and I turned it away, he would be even more hurt.

As Philip drove me home, I looked out from the coach windows and saw the small portion of Prague Castle that had caved in and fallen over.

I felt as though my heart had done the same.

What could I do in the face of such evil?

The rest of the city seemed just as wounded. The people, usually so jubilant and colorful, wore heavy-hearted, careworn expressions as they wandered through the wintery streets. The church bells chimed, but this time there was a bleak, tinny quality to their music.

The sun was shining through the last layer of morning fog as we pulled up to my family's manor. I looked back at the city skyline long enough to see that nothing had changed from this far away. The dullness of the buildings struck me as strange; the heart of the kingdom seemed wearier than ever as it stood against the passage of time.

What could I do against such sadness?

"Thank you for the escort, Philip," I said, as he helped me out of the coach.

"It was an honor, my lady. The prince and I are glad you are safe."

I sighed, looking around my family's home. It was a smaller manor, made of stone and wood. It had been built and refurbished over the many years, starting as a small keep itself and then, as peaceful times came, it blossomed out into a home instead of a fortress. Hallways were added even as the battlements were maintained. It was surrounded by plenty of farmland, and even a few tenant cottages dotted the edge of our property.

Thankfully, there was no one outside; no one was there to witness my shameful entrance. "I don't know if I will get to see you again, but please tell Ferdy—I mean, His Highness— that I am grateful."

"Thank you. I know he will be very pleased."

Recalling Ferdy's earlier sadness, I doubted that. Ferdy would be happy to hear I kept his gift, but he would have preferred that I let him keep me.

I did not even know what he meant by that, exactly.

"My lady."

The sudden look of worry on Philip's face surprised me. "What is it?"

THE ORDER OF THE CRYSTAL DAGGERS

"You won't tell anyone else about His Highness, will you?"

It was the first time I had even thought about that. Lady Penelope would have known about Ferdy, wouldn't she? I thought of the night of the Advent Ball when Empress Maria Anna sent me off to find Ferdy. It was possible, I realized, Lady POW would not have known about him. She had gone off to help others escape the castle before the empress said anything about her younger son.

I have to find out, and I have to be careful.

I did not want to think about what Ben or Lady POW would say about Ferdy, especially since I had fallen in love with him without knowing his real identity. It would only make my failure even worse in their eyes.

I shook my head. "No."

"Thank you." Philip smiled. "Empress Maria Anna has spent a good deal of the younger prince's life hiding him from others, including those in the Order of the Crystal Daggers and the League of Ungentlemanly Warfare. Now that you know the truth, she will be glad when I tell her you have given your oath of silence."

"Why would it be a problem if they knew?" My hands curled around the dagger I kept at my side. Surely the Order would have protected Ferdy if they had known the truth.

"Years ago, the Spring Revolutions brought change, but there is much corruption and self-service among the aristocracy. This is not something unique to Bohemia, but if another upset comes, it may lead to bloodshed, as it nearly did last time. Both King Ferdinand and Empress Maria Anna know it could just as easily come from within our own borders as it could the outside."

My mind wandered back to the Cabal, where Ferdy had taken me. It was a small tavern beside the Jewish Quarter that housed a small group, one that met to discuss everything from local news to culture, religion, and politics.

Maybe that was the real reason Ferdy became friends with them—to make sure he was safe.

But as I thought of his carefree smile, of the friendliness shared between Ferdy and Clavan, Jarl, and Faye, I quickly discarded the idea. It might have been a benefit, but Ferdy did not stay with them to protect himself; he clearly enjoyed them as much as they enjoyed him.

"Currently, there are certain parties—more than most would prefer to believe—that are very glad for His Highness' brother speaking up against Emperor Franz Joseph," Philip continued. "The princes have taken on their mother's family name to ensure they are hidden."

"Is Ferdy in danger?" I asked, suddenly afraid for him.

"He easily could be," Philip said. "Fewer know of Prince Ferdinand than his brother, but with Prince Karl's political ambitions, Empress Maria Anna is worried he will cause the wrong attention. Especially since, as Bohemia's history will tell, we have only survived so long because of the benevolence of God and the friendships we have with our foreign neighbors, as precarious as they are at times."

It was at that moment I realized how little I actually knew about Ferdy. Why would he be running around Prague disguised as a homeless person? Was he hiding? Did he have a plan of his own?

There were suddenly a million questions I had never allowed myself to ask, and even more, I did not know if I would ever have the chance to ask him.

The former empress had been willing for me to go and protect Ferdy. She could have sent someone else. *Why send me? Why admit to me at all that she had a second child?*

When I asked Philip, he smiled at me. "From what I understand, your mother made quite an impression on her. Lady Eleanor and the other gentlemen who came to her aid during the Revolution of 1848 vowed to keep their silence."

Other gentlemen?

Was Philip talking about my father? The League? Or someone else?

It seemed I would have to figure that out, too. It would not be an easy task, especially where Lady POW was concerned.

"Her Imperial Highness no doubt trusts you will live up to your mother's legacy," Philip said.

"I will," I promised. "I'll protect him."

Even if I cannot trust him.

"Thank you. Prince Ferdinand is a good man, and Bohemia would certainly suffer at his loss."

I agreed with Philip. Bohemia would never be the same without Ferdy. Neither would I.

Philip said his goodbyes again, bowing before he climbed up to the carriage perch once more. He flicked the reins and then sped off, leaving me all alone, standing before my childhood home.

My family's manor seemed different. The same farmland still surrounded it, the same morning sky watched over it. But the world had changed, and so had I.

I looked toward the city again. The world would have to move on, and so would I.

The entrance opened, and I heard a familiar voice cry out to me.

"Nora!"

Ben's greeting welcomed me like nothing else could have, and I hurried toward him at once. "Ben!"

He ran up to me, his crooked leg perfectly balanced in its brace, and we collided into each other as he gripped me in a tight hug. He was as strong and solid as he had ever been, smelling of home and mischief and a familiarity that absolutely blindsided me in all of its mysterious wonder.

It was such a contrast to the lavender and mint of Ferdy's room, and such a departure from the careless mix of fun and longing I found in Ferdy's embrace.

Tears started to swell behind my eyes.

"We were so worried for you," Ben said.

"I'm so glad to be back." I whimpered out solemn worries and my apologies as Ben wrapped his arms around me, whispering back assurances that everyone else was fine. But I ignored him, and soon he realized I was crying for other reasons.

"What is it, *ségra?*"

At his old endearment for me, I felt so young and helpless; I would have wished for my mother if she was still alive. I swallowed the rest of my tears, taking a deep breath, desperately forcing myself to regain control.

"It's nothing," I managed to choke out.

Ben knew me well enough to know I was lying. "Nora."

For the first time, hearing Ben call me "Nora," shocked me. It was so strangely different from Ferdy calling me "Ella," and it was unnerving to realize how odd I felt at the distinction.

"What is it?" Ben pressed.

"It's Ferdy," I mumbled. I breathed deeply and swallowed the rest of my sobs. I had hoped to distract Ben away from my weakness, but saying Ferdy's name proved to reveal it even more.

It was bad enough I had failed in so many ways to prevent disaster, but it was even more embarrassing to admit I had made a complete fool of myself in the process.

"Did something happen to him?" Ben asked. I shook my head, and then he pulled himself back from me, allowing me to see the sudden spark of fury in his blue-green eyes. "Did he hurt you?"

By his tone, I knew Ben was ready to defend my honor. "Not exactly," I admitted. "But I shouldn't see him anymore."

"Why not?"

"Just because," I muttered. I took a deep breath, trying to steady myself. "There are plenty of other things demanding our attention now. We can worry about him later."

"Tell me."

I sniffed again. "Later."

"Does he know about the Order?"

All of my bravado left me as Ben guessed a significant part of the truth. I nodded and looked away, hoping that would end the conversation.

"Well, if he thinks that you're beneath him for that, he was never worth your time to begin with."

At his anger, I wanted to cry all over again. I could not tell Ben that it was not because Ferdy did not want me that I was upset; it was more upsetting that Ferdy wanted me anyway.

Thankfully, Ben only patted down my curls and kept me close. "I'm sorry."

THE ORDER OF THE CRYSTAL DAGGERS

Ben was the one person who knew me, the one person I could trust without hesitation. I leaned into him, briefly glad he did not have to carry his crutch any longer; since Amir had come, Ben had designed a new brace using our new companion's medical expertise, and he was able to go for longer periods of time without using it.

As I stepped back from him, I knew I was not willing to trust him with the full truth. I did not want to admit I had fallen in love with Ferdy, thinking him to be a pauper, only to find out he was a prince, and I did not want my brother to know how damaged my pride was despite all the desire Ferdy and I felt for each other.

Ferdy was mine, and that meant my heartbreak was mine, too.

Sniffing loudly, I wiped my eyes again, determined to show strength. "I'm glad to be home."

"You might not say that after you see Lady POW." Ben's voice was soft and playful, and I knew he was trying to make me feel better. I was glad for his support, especially since his joking meant he was not asking for more answers.

Together we made our way toward the library. While we walked, Ben told me how, back at the castle, he had hurried to meet up with Amir before the ballroom, and the adjoining wings caved in. Several hallways, the kitchen, and two more sections of the castle had imploded, including the hallway beside the east library. They both helped guide people to safety and even rescued a few people caught under some of the debris afterward.

"Not that they were that grateful for our efforts," Ben said. "They were more upset at their fancy clothes being ruined than they were happy to be alive."

My laugh was dry, too bogged down with despair.

THE ORDER OF THE CRYSTAL DAGGERS

"Some of the king's guards have told us that the fires are still burning underneath all the rubble in the wine cellar," Ben said. "They have been working to account for as many people as possible while they try to extinguish them. Harshad is waiting to hear the final count of casualties. The latest estimate was six."

I hung my head. "This is entirely my fault."

"Please." A new voice broke through our conversation. "There's no need to be so narcissistic and melodramatic about the whole situation, Eleanora."

Glancing up, I saw Lady Penelope standing in front of the library. The look in her eyes, the same deep blue as my own, suggested she was relieved to see me, but her arms were crossed, and her face was pinched into a disapproving frown.

A small bubble of pride swelled up inside of me; I had been right about her reaction. She was glad to see me, but she was rightfully suspicious of my sins. She was likely just as eager to expose them to the rest of the world, too.

I swallowed hard. "Lady PO—I mean, Lady Penelope."

"We have been waiting for you, Eleanora. You're late."

"Apologies, Madame," I murmured humbly, knowing it was the best way to irritate as well as appease her.

Her frowned deepened, before she whirled around, her dark skirts snapping in the air as she walked into the library.

My grandmother is definitely unique, I thought. In all my life, I had never met anyone so inclined to win, yet so irritated when she won without a fight.

Ben nudged me in his brotherly manner as we entered the room behind her. "She hasn't rested much since we heard you were missing."

"I knew she would be difficult about seeing me again."

THE ORDER OF THE CRYSTAL DAGGERS

"She is difficult with nearly everything."

Amir, Lady POW's medical consultant and an honorary member of the League of Ungentlemanly Warfare, looked up at me first. In his chestnut eyes, I could see his visible relief, and I welcomed it.

Harshad, my grandmother's other colleague, also glanced over at me. I was not sure what to expect from him, but when he only turned away, unaffected, I felt that was a logical response.

Briefly, I had to wonder if the two of them were thinking of *Máma* instead of me. Both Amir and Harshad had known my mother, Lady Eleanor Svobodová, for many years. She had been a member of the Order of the Crystal Daggers before she resigned her post and married my father. She never contacted them again after her last mission in Prague.

Amir admitted to me before that he had been in love with *Máma*, but Harshad's exact feelings were harder to deduce.

I only knew for sure he objected to Lady Penelope's orders to train me; of course, he objected to plenty of her other decisions, too, but this was the only order he had successfully managed to avoid. Seeing how he turned away from me now, I wondered if the nature of his objection was rooted in my mother's memory.

"So." Harshad's attention remained on the papers strewn across my father's desk. "You are back."

Amir inclined his head. "It is good to see you, Eleanora."

"Thank you," I said, giving Amir a quick curtsy. I ignored Harshad. I never thought he was impressed with me, and I never expected him to change his mind—least of all now, as I returned from a failed mission.

Before they could ask me any questions, Ben cleared his throat. "What is the latest news?"

Amir and Harshad looked to Lady POW as she settled herself behind the desk.

It was such a simple movement, but it was one that summed up my life since Lady Penelope, and her small group of spies and secret guards, had arrived in my father's manor in Prague. It not only changed my present and my future but my past, too. Thanks to learning the truth about my mother and the Order of the Crystal Daggers, the ideas I had about my family and my childhood had faded into illusions.

"Well, what has happened?" I asked. "Were we able to catch Lord Maximillian?"

Lady POW wrinkled her nose. "Unfortunately, no."

"What?" I put my hands on my hips, allowing my right hand to rest just above my dagger. Having it so close lent me courage, and I knew I would need it in standing up to my grandmother. She was not called the Iron Dowager for nothing. "He orchestrated the attack on the castle."

Ben gave me a rueful look. "Since the man who attacked us by the wine cellar is dead, there is no way to prove Lord Maximillian was involved."

My breath left my body in a rush. I did not know why I was surprised to hear our attacker was dead.

From the sympathetic look on Ben's face, he had been anticipating my reaction. He knew I was not prepared for death, let alone one I might have caused.

"We are back to where we started, with Dr. Artha's unresolved murder," Lady Penelope said, as Amir slipped around the desk and made his way to stand beside Ben and me.

At the mention of Dr. Artha—my father's former doctor and a consult to King Ferdinand V, as well as a former politician—another wave of weariness washed over me. A lifetime had passed since the Order's arrival, and I was still reeling from my losses.

It seemed like just yesterday when Ben and I had been working to prepare a grand engagement celebration for my stepbrother, Alex, and Lady Teresa Marie, Lord Maximillian's daughter. I remembered that night vividly—Lady Penelope, my indomitable grandmother, commanding the entire dining hall as I floundered in the kitchens with my friends and fellow-servants; Cecilia, my stepmother, unable to whine her way out from Lady POW's thumb. There was also Ben's initial disgust at meeting our spymaster grandmother, my early arguments with the reserved but determined Amir, and hearing Harshad speak with such daring against my grandmother, even while going along with her wishes.

Everything about that night became a fixed anchor in my life, a point where time stopped, and the direction of my life forever altered.

"That is not entirely true, Pepé," Harshad insisted. "We know that the political system has been compromised by a powerful coup, with foreign players and native members alike. The doctor's death has allowed us to discover this connection."

We knew Dr. Artha had been murdered just outside the Church of Our Lady of the Snows. as he researched the mysterious deaths that were happening around Bohemia, especially after finding out several had been poisoned.

Upon arriving in Prague, Lady Penelope had set out to find out why. Then she found Ben and me, and she began to train us as members of the Order. As we slowly uncovered an organized plot to take over the kingdom, we discovered the truth about King Ferdinand's secret heir.

Heirs, I silently corrected myself.

THE ORDER OF THE CRYSTAL DAGGERS

"Eleanora, I knew you were caught in the castle when you did not return here after the ball." Her eyes looked up and down my dress before she narrowed her eyes at the combs in my hair. "I heard Karl Marcelin was at *Tynem* today with the empress and King Ferdinand. Did you see him at all after the wine cellar collapsed?"

I shook my head. "No."

"The empress sent you after him, did she not? And you were unable to find him?"

"No, I didn't see him. He had left earlier, remember?"

"I remember." Lady Penelope's eyes flicked over me again before her brow furrowed. "Are you quite certain that you did not meet with him?"

There was something almost sadistic in her voice, strangely threatening. She knew I was keeping secrets from her.

"Anything at all could help," she added slowly, as if she knew each second her gaze burned into me left me more anxious than the last. "Bohemia's heir could still be in danger."

Ferdy.

Recalling what Philip had said earlier, I blanched. "Why do you think that?"

"Karl Marcelin is at the center of the coup," Lady Penelope said. "He might have initiated it, but it could easily get out of hand. Despite what fairy tales might tell you, there is no honor among thieves. I know that well enough from my own experiences."

I was confused for a moment before I realized Lady Penelope did not know about Ferdy.

Thank you, Lord.

THE ORDER OF THE CRYSTAL DAGGERS

One of my biggest questions had been answered, and one of my biggest fears had been allayed. While I was happy she did not know the extent of my humiliation and failure, there was something else that kept me back from trusting Lady Penelope with the truth about Ferdy. I did not know what it was, or at least, I did not know how to describe it; maybe it was because of my promise to Philip, and by extension, Empress Maria Anna, or maybe it was because of Lady Penelope's own reluctance to share her past. Either way, my nerves rattled as her eyes stared at me, watching me with her cool, unblinking gaze.

"Well, Eleanora? Is there anything else?"

"No." I shook my head fiercely. It was time to ask my own questions. "Why do you want to know? Do you think Dr. Artha was the one who told Lord Maximillian about Karl? Would he have known about him?"

"We do not know that for sure," Lady Penelope admitted. "I am not inclined to think so, but there is no way to verify that now."

Amir cleared his throat. "There are others who could have informed Lord Maximillian of the Bohemian heir. The League has a history in Prague."

"I have already considered that, Amir," Lady Penelope snapped brusquely. "I do not wish to discuss it. We are discussing Dr. Artha's death, not the Revolution, and not heir to the Bohemian—"

"I fear there are other connections to the past we cannot ignore, Madame," Amir interrupted his voice oddly laced with impatience.

At the abrupt interruption, I blinked. For the entire time I had known him, Amir had always allowed Lady POW an impressive amount of deference, even when she did not reciprocate. His hardened tone caught me off guard as much as it did Lady POW.

Amir glanced my way as he added, "And you well know."

Lady Penelope's jaw tensed, and Amir remained steadfast as he weathered her wrath. As they glared at each other, silence paralyzed the room. I dared not even breathe as Amir, and Lady POW faced off against each other in wordless rage.

Finally, Lady Penelope sighed. "Jakub is dead."

"Jakub?" Harshad repeated. "Dezda's father? He died fifteen years ago, shortly after he retired from the League."

"One does not merely 'retire' from the League." Lady POW's lips pursed, wrinkling her face and souring her whole demeanor like a slow poison.

"Wait." I stepped forward. "You mean my grandfather is a member of the League of Ungentlemanly Warfare?"

"He *was*." Lady POW could not hold back her small, cruel smile. "He is dead now, likely fighting the devil for his throne in hell."

"After being dead for fifteen years, it is unlikely he has influenced our current situation significantly," Harshad said.

"But he had friends and contacts," Amir said. "Tulia is one of them. Her codename is *Mira*. And there are others. I reached out to some of them for information last week, and that was how we discovered Mr. Marcelin and Lord Maximillian were working together."

Lady POW shot up out of her seat. Her anger was palpable as she faced down Amir. I worried for him, but his face remained calm. He was not afraid of her.

That did not comfort me as much as I hoped.

"Jakub is dead," Lady Penelope repeated, briefly narrowing her gaze at Ben and me. "He was a liar from the start, and I was a fool to believe anything he said. You would do well to do the same, Amir."

"Amir, you know Pepé, and I do not agree on much," Harshad said, "but there is no telling how much, if any, of his old followers can be trusted."

If Amir interrupting Lady POW had been a surprise, it was nothing compared to seeing him shake his head at Harshad. I had never seen the two of them disagree about anything, especially something this important.

"I believe there are some we can trust," he said. I watched as he clasped his hands together before him, his fingers curling over the bright white scar on his fist. "Our current information from my source has been proven true."

Lady POW snorted disdainfully. "They always give you some truth so the lies will be more easily believed. In the future, Amir, you will cease contact with your sources from Jakub's councilors. We are in a tenuous enough situation."

"There is no need to make it worse, Madame."

"I am glad you agree with me, then. You should have no trouble ceasing your communications with them. Even Tulia was reluctant to give me more information. I cannot imagine what would compel them to make our jobs easier."

"I know there are friendly—"

"You're fortunate enough that I can trust Harshad and you, Amir, but I do not trust your so-called friends." Lady POW glowered at him, and Amir, in realizing he would not win, fell into a disgruntled silence.

I found myself wishing Lady POW would argue with him in another language, like she usually did with Harshad. At least then I would have some idea of the level of vitriol between them. Both of them seemed to accept the impasse between them, but neither regarded it as a good position. It was too quiet for Lady POW to bow out of a fight, and it was unusual that Amir stood up to her in such a direct and disrespectful manner.

A knock at the door interrupted us. A footman materialized in the doorway with a note in his hand. Lady POW broke off her taciturn war with Amir as she took the message, allowing the rest of us a moment of peaceable reprieve.

When I first met Amir, Lady POW had expressed the utmost confidence in him. Now, he wore a deadly expression, one that marked him as a man who was very capable of hurting others, and one who was possibly eager to do so. I saw his fingers twitch before curling around the hilt of his curved dagger, the one he always carried at his side.

Beside me, Ben looked worried as Lady POW returned.

"It seems that we have some more complications to deal with in addition to figuring out Lord Maximillian's next steps," Lady Penelope said. She had a tired look in her eyes as she sighed. "John has just informed me that Lady Cecilia has completely disappeared."

I wrinkled my nose in disdain at the mention of my stepmother. "I don't know if I would call that a complication."

"It is still suspicious," Harshad said. His brusque tone made me flinch. "She is Lord Maximillian's cousin, and, by your own admission, one of the only few who knew of his plans."

"It is even more suspicious because she knows we are here," Lady Penelope said. "She and her offspring have refrained from going out into Society since our arrival. But she could easily do much damage in undermining my authority and our reputation."

"But she doesn't know about the Order," I said. "Does she?"

41

"Not to my knowledge. But she has always been trouble, and she sees us as her enemies. You know this better than anyone."

I did not want that to be true; it was too uncomfortable. I looked away and straightened my skirts, brushing some imaginary dust off the finery Ferdy had given me.

"If she has been kidnapped," Amir added somberly, "her life could be in danger, too."

I wrung my hands, torn because I did not care much that Cecilia was in danger, but I felt like if I were a better person, I might have felt more sympathy for her.

"I have instructed my footmen to keep searching for clues to their whereabouts," Lady Penelope said. "There is no one here to tell us where she might be."

"I'm still happy she is gone," I muttered, more to myself than anyone else.

Amir reached out and put a hand on my shoulder, unsettling me. "I know you did not get along, and I even know to say that is an extremely poor understatement. But Cecilia is also a source, one who might be able to give us the connection between your father's murder and the current political killings."

His remarks made me curious. "Why would my father's death matter after all this time, Amir? Lady Penelope said before it was unlikely that it was the same person," I reminded him.

"It was not likely the same person." Lady Penelope interrupted our quieted conversation through gritted teeth. "But it was clearly done under the same direction."

I frowned at my grandmother, who shot an angry glare at Amir. "What do you mean?" I asked.

THE ORDER OF THE CRYSTAL DAGGERS

Before Lady POW could dismiss the issue, Amir cleared his throat. "The Order of the Crystal Daggers has a disturbing connection to these murders, Eleanora, and not just because they threaten to upset the political order and possibly damage the British relations with India," he explained. "The silver thallis herb was a mixture that was originally concocted by a member of the Order. Since the Justinian era, the Order has used it as a silent killer."

"Our secret weapon is poison? Not our daggers?" My hand involuntarily went to my own weapon, hidden in the pockets between my stealth habit and my new dress.

Lady Penelope groaned loudly. "You see, Harshad? This is why you need to instruct her!"

I felt my cheeks flush over in embarrassment. "What is it? What did I say?"

"Daggers are a poor choice of weapons," Ben told me in a hushed voice, as Harshad and Lady POW began one of their famous fights. "They can do quite a lot of damage in skilled hands, but it is easier to kill with a sword or a pistol."

"Or poison," Amir added.

I nodded slowly. "Oh."

"Poison is not considered an honorable weapon." Despite his avid disagreement with Lady Penelope, Amir gave me a kind smile, one that tugged at the ends of his neatly trimmed mustache. "It is not a topic Society would consider proper."

"Propriety be damned, right?" I replied, making a small laugh break free from him.

At the sound, Lady POW broke off her argument with Harshad to turn and snap at me. "You would not know such things, Eleanora, because Harshad has been reluctant to teach you anything."

"I have been learning other things," I said. Harshad had made it clear he wanted very little to do with me, and I doubted he wanted to instruct me any more than I wanted to learn from him. "Surely it takes more than a fortnight to learn everything."

"It takes a lifetime." Harshad scowled as he looked at me. "And even your mother stopped well before then. Perhaps she gave up even before she left."

I felt my mouth drop open in surprise, but before I could say anything, Lady Penelope shook her head.

"Harshad." Lady Penelope stepped between us, as I tried to recover from my shock. "That is enough. Eleanora is young yet. She questions these things out of ignorance, not impudence."

Harshad tucked his hands behind his back and turned to face the fireplace. There was no evidence of remorse in his demeanor.

"We have let enough time go by, Harshad. Especially now that we will have to locate Cecilia and her household."

"The whole household is gone?" I asked, surprised.

"Of course." Lady Penelope arched her brow at me. "Did you fail to notice there is no one in the stables? All of the servants and your stepsiblings are gone, too."

"That is … strange." I blushed at my mistake; while I did not care much for Cecilia, Alex, or Priscilla, several of the other servants, including Betsy and Mavis, were friends of mine.

What could have happened to them?

Another concern rose up from inside of me. "Is Tulia still here?"

THE ORDER OF THE CRYSTAL DAGGERS

Silence once more descended on the room as no one stepped up to answer me. From the stoic expressions on Harshad and Lady Penelope's faces, to Amir's sympathetic look, and even Ben's clear resignation, I knew the answer.

She was gone.

My breath rushed out of me in a huff, as though I had been kicked in the stomach. My mother's companion was gone. My head fell into my hands as another part of my heart collapsed.

"We have to find her." Tulia had been attacked the previous week and was making a slow recovery. She was older, too, and I knew she would not be able to last long without proper care.

The sickness inside my stomach transformed into anger. When I looked back up, I saw everyone quickly divert their gazes.

"We will do our best," Lady Penelope said, surprising me with her patient tone. "It is not an easy situation in which we find ourselves."

"Do not forget," Amir said, "they disappeared under our watch, too."

My fingers clasped around the hilt of my dagger. "Lord Maximillian must be behind it. We may not be able to prove he was behind the attack on the castle, but we know he was the one who supplied the wine. Cecilia would have known of his guilt. Maybe he took her to live with him."

"He has been staying with the Hohenwart family," Lady Penelope reminded me. "He does not need servants for a household."

"Perhaps he is moving?" I suggested. "Surely staying with them is temporary."

THE ORDER OF THE CRYSTAL DAGGERS

She considered the idea, tapping her fingers together as she thought it over. "We will need to investigate."

"I don't think that will be too difficult," I said. "When can I go back out into Society? Surely someone will be able to tell us something."

Ignoring my question, Lady Penelope began her habitual pacing. "Since the Advent Ball, King Ferdinand and Empress Maria Anna have let it be known that there was an accident that started the fire, which in turn destroyed different parts of the castle."

"But we know it wasn't an accident," Ben said. "The king knows that there's danger, and the Order was sent to protect the kingdom."

"He might know that, but the royal family doesn't want the people to know the truth," Lady Penelope said. "Which is why I did not appreciate your appearance in the ballroom that night, Eleanora. Others have seen you, and now there will be whispers about a secret coup."

"I had my mask up," I argued.

"That might work to our advantage." Amir picked up a sheet of parchment off my father's desk. "If there are rumors of a coup, our enemies will be on high alert and more inclined to make mistakes."

Lady POW waltzed around the library in moving thought. "It is still not ideal."

Harshad gave her an uncharacteristic smile. "What other choice do we have, Pepé?"

I was a little surprised to see Lady Penelope smile coyishly at his words. There were likely years of shared moments between them, and at any given second, any random memory could manifest itself between them.

"The same one we always do, of course. But giving up has never been our style," Lady Penelope replied.

"We can spread other rumors about the coup to make it more confusing if that will help," Ben offered, clearly cheered by the thought of making his rounds.

"Or more convincing," Amir added.

Lady Penelope glanced over at Ben. "You can take care of that, Benedict, while you are out looking for the other seller of the silver thallis herb. We still need to find the merchant if we are to make an antidote and possibly find out more about Dr. Artha's murder."

"I can help with that, too," I said. "It would give me something else to talk about at any parties. I have been introduced to quite a few gossips. If we head out tonight, we might even be able to learn about Lord Maximillian."

I was not excited about the thought of dancing again—especially knowing that Ferdy was unlikely to come and "rescue" me as he had before—but I was eager to prove myself again.

Lady POW shook her head. "You will be staying here, Eleanora."

"Why?" I put my hands on my hips, and from Amir's sudden smirk, I had a feeling my nostrils were flaring. He had told me before that *Máma* used to do the same thing when she was angry. I ignored him as I tried to stare down my grandmother.

Lady Penelope was not about to let me win, any more than she had been willing to let Amir defeat her earlier. "Calm down. You can use some time off from Society while Harshad starts training you."

"Excuse me?" Harshad whirled around and frowned at her. "Pepé, I must object."

"I do, too!" I stepped forward angrily, cringing as my leg, the one Ferdy had bandaged so carefully, ached with momentary pain. "If you remove me from Society, people will talk."

"People *always* talk." Lady Penelope sniffed. "If you do one thing, they'll talk, and if you do another, they'll talk. And if you do nothing or speak out or anything, they will talk. There is no stopping it. The trick is to get them to talk about what you *want* them to talk about."

"So what would you have them say about me?"

"I will tell them you were injured in the castle incident. We can say your leg was injured—which appears to be true." She looked down at my leg. There was nothing preventing me from applying pressure to it, but Lady Penelope had apparently noticed my injury. "It is a decent excuse, and it will give Harshad the chance to train you in basic fighting techniques."

"What about Cecilia?" I asked. "And the others? How am I going to find them if I stay here?"

"And how are you going to stop an assassin or prevent a castle from imploding if you don't have the correct training?"

Shame instantly silenced me, while Lady POW turned to Harshad. "There are times when expediency allows for flexibility. This is not one of those times. We have a responsibility to Eleanora. No objections, Harshad. We have made too many mistakes already. The coup is clearly very astute, and we need to make sure Eleanora is ready to face them next time. You will begin her training in the morning. No excuses."

She glanced over her shoulder at me, as though she was daring me to object. There was a familiar, critical look in her eye, and I knew she was analyzing me for weakness.

THE ORDER OF THE CRYSTAL DAGGERS

Remembering my failure again, I knew it was not a hard calculation to make.

Harshad and I exchanged glances and then briskly looked away.

"Amir," Lady Penelope called. "You will continue with your assignments."

"Yes, Madame." Amir nodded, but at his bitter exasperation, I realized Lady POW was punishing him. As Lady Penelope issued Ben his orders, Amir gave me an enigmatic glance.

When I arched my brow in return, he shook his head, but I saw his fingers twirl and flick, just the way Tulia did when she wanted to tell me something.

Later.

A rush of curiosity and dread ran through me at his signal. As Ben left the library, trotting at Lady Penelope's heels and Amir excused himself, I realized I was not the only one who was keeping secrets.

49

THE ORDER OF THE CRYSTAL DAGGERS

50

THE ORDER OF THE CRYSTAL DAGGERS

4

◊

Much to my dismay, Amir was gone for the rest of the day. It seemed I would be left wondering how long it would take to hear what he wanted to say in addition to wondering what it would be.

I could not say if my ignorance made it easier or harder to fall asleep, as a hundred little things kept turning over inside my mind. Everything from leaving Ferdy, to Lord Maximillian's success, to Amir fighting with Lady POW—all of it shifted through my mind as I lay in bed, waiting for sleep to come and free me.

I learned too late it was a false freedom. When I slipped into sleep, I dreamed of *Máma*. I saw her, I ran for her; my arms were wide open. I desperately wanted to embrace her, but I somehow managed to run right past her, before she faded away entirely. I was despondent, left with my father as he lay dying in his study. *Táta* looked over at me as he cried, and I wondered if he saw me as a ghost of sorts—a shade of my mother, always present but never there.

A loud knock at the door sounded behind me, and I blinked awake. My eyes opened to see my bedroom, and I was instantly torn between what was real and what was true, unable to see the difference. My dreams were filled with terror and longing, and so was my reality.

"Wake up, Nora. Harshad sent me to collect you. He expects us in the west wing parlor at once. You're already late for your first lesson."

Ben.

His voice pushed back the fog inside my mind, reminding me of our former lives—days full of chores, ranging from frivolous to dangerous to monotonous, evenings together as Ben toiled away with his tools and I fled reality with the help of my stolen books. I could have been happy with that life, if it were not for Alex. Over the years, my stepbrother's leering grew more licentious, and I began to feel more nervous. While she was intolerably proud, I welcomed my stepsister Prissy's haughtiness to Alex's predatory gaze.

"Harshad is waiting," Ben called from the other side of my bedroom door. There was more impatience in his voice this time.

How long has it been since he came to wake me up? It could not have been more than a minute or two.

"You don't want him to give Lady POW a poor report, do you?"

"Of course not." I finally sat up in bed, reluctant to leave my bed even if I was eager to run from my dreams.

"We should be there already."

I rubbed my eyes, slightly irritated by his persistence. "Why are you coming?"

"Harshad asked me to help with your lesson today. Lady POW thought it was a good idea for us to train together."

It took me a moment of consideration, but I eventually decided the decision made sense to me, even if it caught me off guard; after all, Ben always did his best to make sure I could protect myself, whether I was fighting against Alex or my own doubts and despair.

That was how Liberté was born.

THE ORDER OF THE CRYSTAL DAGGERS

I smiled at the thought of our old dream. By the time Lady Penelope had arrived in our lives, Ben and I had a fully-conceived plan to own a bookshop, and we only needed a little more time to get the money to finance it. We were going to name it Liberté, all in hopes it would bring us the freedom to escape Cecilia.

There were many times, I remembered when Liberté was my only light in the darkness of my life.

Ben knocked on my door again, calling me back to the present. "Harshad is a demanding teacher. You don't want to do anything to make it worse."

"Tell him I will be down shortly," I said as I got out of bed and reached for my stockings.

There was no reply, but I could hear Ben's uneven footsteps echoing softly down the hall; there was an eagerness in them that made me pause. My brother had a good deal of respect for Harshad. When Cecilia called us to work, Ben would only hurry if we were going to be punished. He never did more than he had to for her.

If Lady Penelope had not shown up the night of Alex's engagement, what would Ben and I be planning now?

Not getting dressed for an early morning training session with the most surly man on this side of the empire, that was for sure, I thought. I pulled back my hair with a tie before taking a quick moment to examine myself in the mirror.

My breath caught at the sight of the twinkling gold and glimmering gems behind me.

The combs Ferdy had given me for my hair were lying on my night table, next to my mother's locket and my father's

THE ORDER OF THE CRYSTAL DAGGERS

pocket watch. I had pulled them out last night, clinging to them like talismans as I let myself mourn over my losses.

At the sight of them, shining so innocently in the small light of my room, I hurried to put them away.

I did not want to lose the ones I loved or the treasures they left behind. But for now, there was nothing I could do. I shut them inside my drawer firmly, reminding myself of that truth before I made my way down to the west parlor.

The west parlor was a room usually kept for the master of the house and, as far as I knew, his brandy collection. When I was much younger, Ben and I used it as a place to play on rainy days, wrestling with each other and climbing on the tabletops, pretending they were mountains, while our father watched.

After *Táta* died, I never returned to that room, or to the idea that life could be carefree and fun.

When I arrived for my lesson, I did not recognize the room at all. From the strange rearrangement of the furniture and the potent smell of sweat and leather, nothing fit with my previous memories except the small fire crackling cheerfully in the fireplace. I stared at it, seeing the light was unable to penetrate into the farthest reaches of the room, slinking around the strange equipment.

"Good morning, Miss Eleanora."

Harshad was seated on the floor in front of the fireplace, his back facing me, sitting so still I had missed him entirely.

THE ORDER OF THE CRYSTAL DAGGERS

He was wearing a loose shirt and a strange pair of pants, ones that were printed with bright colors and stitched with golden thread. His feet were covered with tight leather shoes, vastly different from the Hessians he usually wore.

At his tone, I could not tell if he was irritated or not, so I decided if he could be matter of fact, I could too.

"My apologies for the delay, Mr. Harshad, sir."

"Allow me to formally introduce myself to you." He stood up. "My name is Harshad Prasad, and I am a longstanding member of the Order of the Crystal Daggers, as well as an honorary member of the League of Ungentlemanly Warfare under Her Imperial Majesty Queen Victoria."

At his introduction, I started to curtsy to Harshad, offering a proper greeting, more out of habit and manners than anything else. "How do you—"

"You need to work on your observation skills, Miss Eleanora," he continued. "Lady Penelope has never properly addressed me in your company. If you are going to work with us, you must do better."

"I noticed that you call Lady Penelope 'Pepé,'" I said. From the other side of the room, I thought I heard Ben chuckle softly.

Harshad arched his brow, seeming to hide a smile. "What good does that do you?"

I felt my cheeks flush over in embarrassment. "I know you are friends that way," I said, attempting to salvage my pride.

Ben signaled to me from the corner of the room. I did not know what he wanted to say, but Harshad did not give me time to figure it out.

THE ORDER OF THE CRYSTAL DAGGERS

"'Friends' is hardly the proper term," he scoffed. "Colleagues, yes. Friends? We have known each other too long for that."

"But—"

"But nothing. You will need to pay very close attention to what I am saying and what I am doing, starting with two basic skills. As you know, your brother is here to help in these matters."

Ben gave me a quick, self-assured smile. I thought about giving him one back when I caught sight of a small, empty plate on the desk. The sight of it made my stomach rumble uncomfortably.

Someone had his morning tea already, I thought, torn between hunger and jealousy.

As if he knew I was already distracted, Harshad cleared his throat. "You're not dressed properly. Where is your stealth habit?"

"I didn't see why it would be necessary," I replied, unable to stop my cheeks from burning. I had not thought of what I would need to wear before I left my room, but Harshad had already made me feel uncomfortably hapless. I tried to dismiss his worries. "I can work fine in skirts. Ben and I have been brawling with each other and battling our way around the manor since we were born."

"That's true," Ben said. "She has a lot of promise as a fighter."

Harshad glared at Ben. My brother fell silent, but I was heartened that he did not recant his words.

"For our first area of instruction, Miss Eleanora," Harshad began, "what I will be teaching you includes different techniques and styles of fighting."

"Will we work with weapons, too?" I asked, pulling out my dagger. It was still in its sheath, the violet blade hidden by the ancient leather.

Harshad took it out of my hands so fast I only blinked and then it was gone. "Pay attention to what I am telling you now."

"But—"

"You would have been able to move better if you had been in your habit. If you are going to work with the Order, you should know right now, you will face opposition. If you are to stand for something, you will find yourself standing against something else."

"That sounds like one of Newton's Laws," I murmured, thinking back to one of my father's books on science I had once stolen from the library.

"It is similar," Harshad agreed with a small sigh, and I felt a small spark of hope inside of me that I might be able to impress him, if only a little. "You will find it is easier to fight the more you prepare for to face backlash on multiple fronts. You will find it is necessary to stand for something, because other people will not only stand against you, but their ideas will come up against yours. Ideas cannot be destroyed—they can only be controlled."

I nodded in easy agreement. What he was saying seemed to make sense. As much as I might have loathed the instructor, I lauded the content.

THE ORDER OF THE CRYSTAL DAGGERS

"Chaos is never as chaotic as it seems. You will see that in each struggle. And that is where we will begin."

"How is Ben going to help?" I looked over at my brother, watching him as he stepped forward.

Harshad frowned. "I thought I made myself clear earlier. Do not interrupt me when I am talking, Miss Eleanora."

I narrowed my eyes at him; I had a feeling I was not going to like Harshad any more than he appeared to like Lady POW.

"You must focus your mind and learn to balance your body. Where your attention is, where your focus lies, that is where the rest of you will follow."

"Why would that help—"

"Following that," Harshad continued, interrupting me, "you will learn to direct your strength in mind, body, and spirit in order to fight effectively.

"Not all battles are physical. Many are fought in the worlds beyond this one, and many are fought inside of us—in our need for purpose, to understand, to be loved and accepted and understood. The heavenly and hellish wars, we cannot do much for; but the battles inside of us we must learn to fight, especially if we are to win."

I nodded, figuring there was no way he could object to that, so long as I remained silent. Before I could find out, the door opened.

"Amir," Harshad barked. "You are late."

"My apologies, sir." Amir stayed at the edge of the room, standing with his arms folded, serving as a guard and silent audience. In the bleak harshness of the early morning light, I

THE ORDER OF THE CRYSTAL DAGGERS

could see the weariness etched into his face, which made him look much older.

What is Amir doing here? Does Harshad think I will need medical treatment after this morning?

I sincerely hoped that was not the reason.

From the expression on Ben's face, I knew he was curious as to why Amir had come, too.

"It seems you are working well enough with the first rule, Miss Eleanora," Harshad said, forcing my attention to return to him. "Now, let us begin. We will be working with a form of western boxing, mixed in with more eastern martial arts."

"What is the difference between the East and the West?"

"It is the same difference between power and persuasion, between truth and authority," Harshad murmured, clearly pleased by his own mercurial answer. "Both have their advantages and disadvantages. They start at the same point— your form."

With Harshad's instructions and Ben's help, I began to work through different fighting stances. Before long, I forgot about Amir, and a good deal of the rest of my troubles, as my mind was overrun with descriptions and positions and reasons, exceptions and metaphysical meanings, all while my body was tasked with working through several motions and movements.

"From now on," Harshad muttered, as I wobbled around on the balls of my now-bare feet, "when you come to train with me, you will wear the outfit Lady Penelope has commissioned for you. Skirts are hardly advantageous for these sessions. I would send you back to change, but Lady Penelope insists on hastening your instruction."

In other words, he is content to make me suffer from my own poor choices.

Beside me, Ben worked at a steady pace. The more tired I felt, the more calm he looked. In many ways, he reminded me of Amir, and I both envied and hated him for that.

Eventually my legs, unaccustomed to the peculiar exercise, began to twinge in pain. It had been several weeks since I worked as a servant, and my muscles resisted the old, familiar movements of chores, even those of a different sort.

At least Harshad is still someone I can trust more than Cecilia, even if he is less hospitable.

So far as I knew.

"Your brother never complained at the pain," Harshad said, catching me secretly trying to massage my leg cramps.

"I didn't say anything," I said, as I noticed Ben straighten with pride.

"One does not need to say something in order to communicate."

"I wasn't thinking of physical pain," I lied. My fists clenched, and my chin shot forward defiantly. "I was thinking of what my mother would say. These sessions are hardly proper."

"I taught your mother, too, if that makes you feel less improper." Harshad waved away my dishonest objection while Ben raised an eyebrow at me.

At their simultaneous dismissal, I sighed. "I did not mean to insult you, Mr. Prasad."

THE ORDER OF THE CRYSTAL DAGGERS

There was nothing reverent or polite in my tone, but I thought an apology might help smooth over our relationship—that approach usually worked with Lady POW—and, as much as I might have hated to admit it, I owed it to him. I had already learned from my time with the Order that I would be expected to do any number of inappropriate actions. Society's civilized manners were maintained through sacrifice. I did not have to think of anything other than Advent Ball to know this, where my attempts at saving everyone had done nothing to prevent disaster.

"I do not need your false apologies," Harshad replied dismissively. "And for the sake of time, you should just refer to me as Harshad."

He was right about the fake apology. Every time I opened my mouth, I only seemed to get into more trouble.

I shouldn't have said anything at all.

The time passed more slowly as I remained silent. Ben joined in with me, always careful to show more dedication and discipline. As I watched Ben work, I sincerely hoped Lady Penelope did not want him to come train with me because he was behind in his own espionage instruction.

Ben had already had close to a month of training with Harshad and Amir, but he had been at the castle when its ballroom walls collapsed, and Lady POW would likely blame him for the destruction as much as she blamed me.

Well, she likely blamed me more.

But I could see where Ben would have trouble. His right leg was crooked, and his stance was still uneven. With the special brace he had built with Amir, he wobbled without his crutch on occasion.

THE ORDER OF THE CRYSTAL DAGGERS

Twelve years had gone by since his accident. I was only a little over seven years old when it happened. *Máma* had been gone for two years, lost at sea, and *Táta* was just starting to come out of perpetual mourning, staying at home for longer periods of time. Tulia admitted to me a few years later that my father found it easier to pretend my mother was still alive while he was away.

The day Ben broke his leg, *Táta* had just arrived home from Vienna. He often reported between the king and Emperor Franz Joseph, passing along information and making requests to politicians from the different branches of the empire. One of my kittens had found a way to slink through the barn rafters, and I had cried for help. The maids were sympathetic but unwilling to leave their work; the stable hands dismissed my needs; my father was exhausted and ordered no one to pay me any mind.

But Ben came to my rescue. He patted down my curls, gave me a brotherly hug, and headed up to the top of the barn to rescue my kitty.

She was such a sweet little kitten, with her large green eyes and black fur. I loved her as my own, and I was terrified when she ran away from me and seemed to be stuck on the roof.

Ben quickly climbed up next to her; I cheered as he reached for her and scooped her into his arms, only to end my celebration in horror as she wriggled free and Ben lost his balance.

I squeezed my eyes shut against the memory of my ten-year-old brother's scream and the distinctive *crack!* of his leg snapping.

"Miss Eleanora, are you paying attention?"

THE ORDER OF THE CRYSTAL DAGGERS

"What?" I blinked, only to see Harshad in front of me, staring down at me from below his thick, pristine-white eyebrows. I blushed, feeling the drops of sweat on my forehead simmer. "What were you saying?"

"We were discussing the breath. Breathing is very important."

I nodded blandly, following through Harshad's orders as I tried to focus. Ben stood beside me, working through the same fighting motions, and I gave him a smile.

He gave me a worried look, glancing back at Harshad. In his own way, he was telling me Harshad was serious, and it was best if I adopted a similar demeanor.

I resisted the urge to roll my eyes, but only barely. If Ben knew I had been distracted by the memory of his accident, he would be angry. Ben had forgiven me, but he never wanted me to feel sorry for him.

"You will be able to sense your body through your breath," Harshad intoned, drawing my wandering attention back to the present moment. "It moves through your blood and touches every part of you. As you move between your inner self and your full self, breathing will help you focus. It can also ease your pain as you stretch."

As I reached down for my toes, I exhaled, and the tension inside of me broke. I did not know why I was so surprised that Harshad's advice continued to prove itself true.

"You will need to breathe while you keep your stance; for balance, always find something to focus on in the distance. Your focus will determine your perception, and your perception will influence your decisions."

THE ORDER OF THE CRYSTAL DAGGERS

Breathing while balancing was difficult, but it did allow me to forget about Ben and my other troubles.

"The world presses into us at every moment." Harshad's lilted words poured over me like a waterfall, both soothing and terrifying as they spouted down wisdom and beauty.

"You must learn to quiet your mind as it takes in everything around you. Once you quiet your mind, you will be able to better pinpoint the exact issues you need to consider."

My legs varied between numb and cramped from all the stretching and standing. I said nothing still, allowing myself to cheer at the ease of this part of my instruction. I had grown up in church, where prayer and meditation were encouraged, and it had a similar process; my weakness was in collecting all the right information, not in determining what to do once I made up my mind.

"Whether it is a matter of belief, action, or destiny," Harshad said, "you will only be open to answers when all of your questions have ceased."

At that, I was done being submissive. "That doesn't make any sense."

"Discipline, Miss Eleanora," Harshad remarked, making me squeeze my eyes shut in irritation and shame.

"Eleanora is fine," I said. "If I don't have to use formalities with you, you don't have to use them with me."

"How very democratic of you, Miss Eleanora."

I did not like the annoyance in his voice. "Are you going to call Ben, 'Mr. Ben?'"

Harshad was momentarily stunned by my question. "My logic makes sense," he finally replied, ignoring my interruption, "because questions do not answer themselves."

"But you're still asking questions."

"Nora, be quiet," Ben hissed. "You need to—"

"There will always be questions, Miss Eleanora," Harshad interrupted, "and only once you are done asking them will you be able to receive answers."

I mumbled out a wordless reply, unhappy he was right.

"It seems suffering in silence is not your strength, Miss Eleanora."

It seemed he was just as capable as Lady POW was when it came to hearing my inward thoughts.

I frowned. "I guess suffering is easier for you and Ben."

"Being a cripple does not tend to make life easier, no matter the task," Ben grunted, and I flushed over in shame. I silently vowed to say nothing further.

Ben's life was much harder, and I knew it. Whether it was because he loved me enough to go and retrieve my kitten off the barn roof, or because of our father's scorn, there was nothing noble about wondering if he had an easier time at training than I did.

"Envy ruins everything, Miss Eleanora," Harshad said. "That I know far too well."

His words echoed Lady Penelope's own words from the day before, and I suddenly wondered what Harshad's past was like, what made him play the spymaster alongside my grandmother. His sentiment seemed very personal. I stared at him for a long moment, trying to imagine the sort of life he had lived, the things that led him to make the choices that he did.

He cleared his throat, and I blushed, realizing I was caught up in my own imagination. I must have made him uncomfortable because his footsteps were very distinct against the floor. "If silence will not stay with you, maybe it is time for you to show me your fighting."

The room fell quiet. I heard only the rapid beating of my heart, the slick dripping of my sweat, and the faraway crackle of the fire.

THE ORDER OF THE CRYSTAL DAGGERS

5

◊

"Fighting?" I repeated cautiously, hoping I would still be able to talk my way out of it.

Much to my displeasure, Harshad ignored me and turned to face Ben. "Are you ready?"

Ben hesitated for only a second before he nodded.

"Wait, Ben is going to fight me?" I stood up, forcing myself not to scream as my numbed legs swayed. "Why?"

"It is just a beginner's battle," Ben said. He gave me one of his friendlier smiles, his earlier frustration still there but buried. "I won't hurt you."

"I'm not worried about that," I said, fighting off the urge to rub my legs again. I managed to give Ben a teasing look. "I'm more concerned with how easily I'll win."

Harshad sighed at our verbal sparring before he began snapping out orders and directions.

"This is a test," he told me, "to see what you can do with what you know and what you've learned."

"Ben and I already defeated the assassin at the castle," I reminded him.

"But it was not enough to stop the henchman from carrying out his work. You will have other enemies, and you will need to learn how to stop them more quickly."

I went back to stewing silently, angered at his remark and frustrated with myself once more. Harshad talked with Ben,

THE ORDER OF THE CRYSTAL DAGGERS

discussing their previous instruction on different stances, attacks, and counterattacks.

"Why are you helping Ben?" I crossed my arms. "That's not fair."

"Life is not fair," Ben reminded me.

"Your brother is the better trained between you," Harshad said, stepping between us. "This is unavoidable for now, and there are two potential issues. One is that his affection for you will affect his performance. The second is, as the better trained fighter, he will be in a position to protect you, should he feel the need to do so."

"The second part is negating the first," I said.

"Contradictions are not the same thing as paradoxes, Miss Eleanora."

Before I could say anything else—likely an objection—I heard a small cough from the other side of the room.

Amir caught my gaze with his own using Tulia's gestures to sign his message.

Go along.

I traced a few of my fingers in the air, asking a question of my own, and he nodded. I relaxed at his response. In his silent response, Amir promised he would help me later.

Ben let out a small grunt, and I was surprised to see him glare angrily at Amir. I did not know what Ben was so upset over; he worked with Amir all the time, and Harshad was the one helping him now.

"Ready?" Harshad called the two of us to attention. After checking our stances and listing some rules, he nodded, and Ben and I faced each other.

It was at that second that it all seemed too strange to me, to be fighting Ben. I did not like it—not like this. Ben was my brother, after all, and the one person in the world I would never want to hurt.

"Work on your focus, Eleanora," Harshad called, as I brushed a few stray hairs out of my eyes.

At his words, Ben lunged forward; I caught his attack with a block, before twisting my left arm and hitting him back.

He retreated, and I gave him an apologetic look. "Sorry."

"It's fine, Nora," Ben said, giving me an aggravated look. "We have done this before, remember?"

"Not properly," I murmured, and Ben sighed. He glanced back at Harshad, who was watching us with his hawkish gaze. Ben moved in front of him, blocking Harshad from my view.

"Why are you always so worried about propriety?" he asked, launching out a series of punches. "It's not like you will ever truly be accepted into the polite world."

I ducked and twirled away, frowning in concentration as much as frustration. "I still have to pretend to fit in with them, if I'm going to help the Order."

Ben caught my arm and pulled me in close, trapping me with a headlock. "If you really want to help the Order, you're going to have to fight me. I can handle your attacks, Nora."

I said nothing, partially because I was struggling to breathe, and partly because I knew Ben was right. I would have to learn how to fight, and Harshad was going to see to it that I did it, regardless of how emotionally difficult it was going to be.

"Would it help you if I pretended I was Alex?" Ben asked. I laughed as I slipped out of his hold.

"We can try," I said, stepping back. "But I don't think you could ever be as evil as Alex. Or Lord Maximillian, come to think of it."

THE ORDER OF THE CRYSTAL DAGGERS

"What about Ferdy?" His voice was soft enough that I knew Harshad could not hear.

I stumbled, nearly falling over as my heart skipped a beat. "Leave Ferdy out of this."

Ben groaned. "You can't be opposed to hurting him, after all he put you through."

"Balance, Miss Eleanora," Harshad snapped.

"Yes, Harshad," I muttered back, suddenly angry he was here at all. I turned back to Ben. "I don't want to talk about him, Ben."

"Why? Afraid Ferdy will keep you from winning?" Ben ducked down and managed to land a blow to my legs, sending me crumbling down to my knees.

I forced myself to swallow my heartbreak. I did not want to think of Ferdy any more than I wanted to fight Ben.

"Good, Ben," Harshad said. "Find the weakness and use it."

A flicker of sympathy crossed Ben's face. "Please, Nora," he whispered as we locked blows again. "Fight me."

"I am," I insisted.

"Do it better, then. I don't want to have to bring up Ferdy every time I need you to attack." Ben shook his head. "You don't still love him, do you?"

The question struck me hard, leaving me stunned and still. My hand flew to my chest, pressing into my heart as it beat furiously. Ben's words cut like an accusation, containing such a level of vitriol and disgust.

I knew that Ferdy and I could not be together. He was a prince, after all, and he would be expected to marry someone politically beneficial—someone with a standing well above

THE ORDER OF THE CRYSTAL DAGGERS

my own, someone whose life was not tainted by abuse and poverty, not to mention the scandal of espionage.

But I was not able to completely forget Ferdy. Not yet. The worst part was I did not know if I wanted to forget him, either. It was a legitimate weakness.

I fell to my knees, slumping over as I shook my head. "I give up. Ben wins."

At the long sigh, I looked up to see the disappointment on Harshad's face. I expected to see it on Amir's, too, and I was right—but he was looking at Ben, not me.

"That is enough for today." Harshad scowled at me. "I have seen what you and your brother can do. From your years of service under your stepmother, it is clear you have a good deal of flexibility and endurance. Your balance and focus need work in addition to your fighting form. We will spend the next weeks working on building up your strength and then work on technique."

"I told you Nora would be a good fighter." Ben reached down a hand to help me up.

The self-satisfaction in his demeanor was repugnant, and even more so because I was suffering. Before I could stop myself, I reached out and jerked him hard, forcing him off-balance. His brace clattered as he fell to the ground in front of me.

"Ouch!" Ben grabbed his right leg, hurrying to check on his brace.

For the first time in a long time, I could see the terrible bend in his limb; his lower leg jutted out to the side from the knee, more curved than crooked from where he had grown over the years. There was a small indent in his calf where the temporary splint had cut into his skin for weeks after the fall.

A spring had shaken loose, and there were several shimmers of metal on the floor beside us as the other parts began to bend and twist out of sync.

"Well, that is one way to use weakness," Harshad said. "A point for Miss Eleanora."

"I didn't mean to do it," I sputtered, feeling sick as Ben glared at me. "I didn't, I promise. It was just an accident. I didn't mean—"

"Stop it," Ben snapped, already retreating from me. "It's over. There's no need to pretend anymore."

He found a way to stand using his other leg. Without the brace, I could see his limp was much more exaggerated and painful. As he stood, I hurried up next to him, grabbing his arm to help.

"Get away from me." Hatred burned in his blue-green eyes. "I can do this myself."

My hands fell to the side as my mouth dropped open, stricken as if he had struck me across the face. "Ben—"

"That's enough," Harshad said. "It appears that you both have significant work to do. While you are strong, you must work on your weaknesses."

"Ben doesn't have a weakness," I insisted. "He can use his leg to fight just fine. I caught him off guard, that's all."

Ben huffed. He exchanged a few words with Amir before he left, but I was too far away to hear. All I could see was Ben's deepening scowl and Amir's hardened expression.

Harshad had me clean up the room as my final task. I had to put the equipment away, mop up the floor, and wipe down the room.

I did not want to; it was something that reminded me of my days as a servant, something I was as eager to escape for my

THE ORDER OF THE CRYSTAL DAGGERS

dignity as much as my bitterness. Eventually, I resigned myself to the task, taking it on as a punishment for hurting Ben.

Amir stayed behind to help. We worked in silent harmony, our movements smoothly synchronized, as if we were working on our waltzing.

It was only after Harshad left the room that Amir finally said anything. "You did well for your first lesson, Eleanora."

I shook my head. "It doesn't feel like it."

"You are not the judge of this matter. Harshad is, and I can tell he was satisfied."

"If this is what it is like to win his approval, I'm not sure I want it." I hid my gaze, focusing on scrubbing scuff marks off the floor. "I did not want to hurt Ben."

"His weakness is not his leg."

"I know." I lifted my chin proudly. "It's not going to stop him from being a good fighter. He can do anything he wants, just like anyone else."

"That is not quite true," Amir said. "If he is to be a good fighter, he has to acknowledge his shortcomings. That includes his physical ones as well as his emotional ones. Ben is able to compensate for his injured leg. He has done it for years, and he is able to work through our exercises with accommodations."

"You just said that his leg was not a weakness."

"And it is not. *You* are."

I stopped moving, my eyes wide. "I am?"

"He loves you, as much as a brother can love his sister, and he cannot easily forget that connection." Amir gave me a wistful smile. "I know that from my own sister."

"You have a sister?"

He nodded, and I blinked in surprise. It was not just Ferdy who I did not know as well as I should have.

"There is a reason that Lady POW requested that he fight you. He is clearly worried for you, but he did not say why."

"Lady POW wanted him to fight me?" My voice raised in anger and surprise. "I can't believe—"

Amir gave me a warning glance. "Things are not always as they seem. She talked with him after your return."

"I know that. I thought she was sending him out to find Tulia and others."

"Your grandmother is not worried about Tulia. She was injured, but she has lived a long life, and she knows how to take care of herself." Amir crossed his arms. "Lady POW wants to know more about you. She knows you are keeping something from her."

I wrinkled my nose. "Well, that would upset Lady POW. She does not mind keeping her own secrets, but she is quick to seek out others'."

"Is your brother right to worry for you, Eleanora?"

Before I could think through it, I shook my head. I had promised to keep Ferdy's secret safe, and I did not know yet if telling my brother was a good idea or not. He would be furious that Ferdy had lied to me, and then there was the fact that Ferdy knew more about Karl than he had revealed.

With no substantial proof leading us to Lord Maximillian and our only other leads missing, Ben would not hesitate to confront Ferdy.

"Are you certain?"

At the note of sympathy in his voice, I was unable to brush aside his concern. Lying to Ben to keep Ferdy safe was

THE ORDER OF THE CRYSTAL DAGGERS

necessary, and lying to Lady POW, knowing she had her own secrets, was nothing. But lying to Amir, a man my mother had loved and trusted, felt very different.

I will have to tell him something.

I sighed. "I'm coming to the conclusion that I will have to let my friends go if I am going to succeed as a member of the Order."

It was not the complete truth, but it was not a complete lie, either.

"Knowing what I do know of you, Eleanora, I would suspect it is more than that." He gave me a small smile. "What about your beloved?"

I blushed at his perceptiveness. "I don't want to talk about that."

"I already know about him, and I've kept that information from the others," Amir reminded me gently.

"Why?" I narrowed my eyes.

"Because I know firsthand how difficult it is to face scorn from your grandmother for young love." He shifted his stance, clearly uncomfortable. "You have my sympathies, Eleanora. Heartbreak is never easy. It was not meant to be, for either side."

He was likely right; I knew Ferdy was not happy with the situation between us. My chest constricted at the thought of him, alone and hurting, and all the more so knowing it was my fault.

I shook my head, clearing away all the images of Ferdy suffering. He had his friends from both the Cabal and the castle to help stave off his loneliness and disappointment.

Glancing up at Amir, I saw his eyes had blurred over with memories, too.

THE ORDER OF THE CRYSTAL DAGGERS

"What are you thinking about? My mother?"

Amir shrugged, a crimson color lighting his amber cheeks. "It is hard not to, with you around. But there are others who I have caused to suffer. Your mother is not alone in that regard."

"You had another beloved beside *Máma?*"

"I have had some passing fancies in my lifetime. I promise Naděžda was the only true love of my life, but there were others who were heartbroken by my devotion to her."

Other women would have loved Amir, I thought. While we had been at odds the first several times we met, I knew he was a gentle, virtuous man, one who was knowledgeable and insightful, and even after all these years, he remained loyal to my mother's memory.

"Of course," Amir continued with a small smile, "no one was more disappointed in me for loving Naděžda than my father. That one continues to sting the most."

He glanced down at his right hand, where his old scar scorched through the warm brown of his skin, an inch above his knuckles.

"Does it hurt?" I asked the question before remembering it was not proper to do so.

Amir did not seem to notice. "The scar itself? No. The pain of rejection it represents? That is a different matter."

"What happened? My mother didn't do that, did she?"

"Harshad was right. You do ask a lot of questions."

I could feel my nostrils flare as I made a face at him, but Amir only laughed.

"You did say before you would tell me more about her. Why not tell me now? It'll give me something else to think about while we clean. I could use the distraction." I held up

THE ORDER OF THE CRYSTAL DAGGERS

my rag. "This brings up bad memories. I hated cleaning for Cecilia."

"If you make it a point that I owe you for the years of your pain, it is a poor argument."

"I have been told I am quite determined. Ben, Tulia, and plenty of others have said so."

Even Ferdy had noticed that, seeing my determination and kindness at my father's funeral. I faltered for a moment, wondering if it was as much of a gift as he thought it was. My determination to find truth and protect others seemed to erode my kindness of late, and I could not say if it was a good thing or not.

Maybe I was more kind when I was a child.

"Tulia was the one who could have told Lady POW about you and your brother. She is more at fault for your pain."

"I have forgiven Tulia for that."

"Have you not forgiven me, then?" Amir's voice was slightly teasing, but I worried that he was sincere. Before I could say anything, he nodded slowly. "I suppose you are right. I did say I would tell you more. I will start by saying Naděžda was not the one who gave me the scar, but she was part of the reason for it."

He turned away and went back to helping me clean. I saw the scar, a strange, dotted loop on his hand, gleaming white against the warm tan of his skin.

I had seen the shape of it before, and I said so. "That's the same symbol that's on the journal you have—the one you took from me when we first met in Prague."

I saw his mustache twitch at the mention of the journal. "What is it?" I asked.

"There is another reason Lady POW is not afraid for Tulia," Amir admitted. "She thinks she is the one behind the disappearance of your stepmother and the rest of the household."

"What?" My mouth dropped open in surprise. "Why?"

"Tulia is Jakub's half-sister. She had connections to the League, even if she was not a full member. Dr. Artha's priest sent out a message to her, remember?"

To Míra, and the Light.

"He sent word out about the threat to the League then," I said. "But Dr. Artha was one of the Order's correspondents."

"Yes." Amir's forehead creased with worried lines. "There are plenty of us who work for both the League and the Order, but it seems strange he would send for only them."

"Perhaps it was because they were close friends?" I suggested, remembering the endearment from the letter, saying word had been sent to "my sweet *Míra*."

"That would confound Lady POW," Amir agreed wryly.

"What does this have to do with the journal?" I wondered why the mention of my mother's journal had sparked the change in topic. As I waited for him to say something, I knew it could only be something bad.

"The journal is missing," he admitted. "I have not seen it since the ball."

"It's gone? Where? Did someone take it?" I was stunned. I could well believe others would want to read my mother's journal, but I was not sure who would have recognized it.

"Those are my questions, too, I can assure you."

"Did you finish reading it?" I asked. "Before it disappeared?"

"I finished reading up to where your mother admitted to running into Jakub while she was on her mission, and that is it." Amir gave me an apologetic shrug. "I would have read it faster, but seeing Naděžda's writing again is a joyful sort of pain."

I decided not to chastise him for that. I would have lingered over every word myself if I knew how to read Arabic.

Instead, I shook my head. "This is terrible. We have to get it back."

"I would appreciate your continued silence to Lady POW in this manner," Amir said. "She might have taken it too, but Tulia is the more likely culprit."

I did not know what to say. Tulia was hardly a thief, that I knew of, even if she did not like my grandmother. But I was coming to trust Amir.

I did not know what to think.

"Finish telling me about your scar," I said. We could worry about the journal when we found Tulia. "What does that symbol mean?"

"It is an Arabic letter, the *noon*, one that marks the *nassara*, the Nazarenes," Amir said. He paused for a long moment as if he was trying to calm himself, before he finally continued. "One of my cousins gave it to me at my father's orders, after I told him of my conversion to Christianity."

"Your father had you marked for converting?" My mouth dropped open in surprise.

"It is the mark of the deepest betrayal, for a Muslim to convert," Amir replied. "We do not only betray our upbringing, we dishonor our families and taint all the good we have been given in the name of Allah and his prophet. Religion is a way to understand and demonstrate the best life has to offer, from honor and truth and compassion, and for both the Muslim and Christian, rejecting it cuts sorely into the heart of those who believe.

"I was my father's only son, so my cousins took on the task of restoring honor to the family. My father gave them this dagger to take care of it. They carved it into my skin and then prepared to kill me."

He reached down to his side where his dagger, the *Wahabite Jambiya*, was carefully secured.

Eying the mark once more, I grimaced. "It must have been painful."

"It was," Amir said with a nod. "Your mother was working with Xiana at the time, and it took both of their skills to stop me from bleeding out or losing full function in my hand."

"Xiana?" I barely managed to recall her name, horrified by Amir's experience. "Oh, the lady who taught you about herbs?"

"Yes. She is part of the Order, too, and hopefully you will get to meet her soon. Harshad has sent for her to join us here in Prague."

"If she helped save you, I am sure I will like her. It was fortunate that she was there with my mother so they could save you."

"My sister was not so fortunate."

At his remark, I did want to know what happened. As I had learned before, there was a cost to knowing the truth, and I was quickly finding out that cost was both freeing and sobering.

"Halal was my older sister. She distracted my family so Xiana and your mother could smuggle me out of my family's estate, so I could escape. Halal did not want me to die. She tried to understand why I did this to our family, even if she did not agree with my decision. She worked hard to foster peace between me and my parents. But when I escaped, she was killed."

"She was killed because she did not want them to kill you?" I barely felt my lips move at the question. I felt my heart ache in pain for Amir and his sister.

I knew Ben was angry at me, but I suddenly wanted to go and hug him, reassuring him, and myself, of our affection for each other.

"You are young yet, but even you know there are things worth dying for."

"Dying for something is different than killing for something," I said slowly.

"The first time I killed a man, I did it to protect your mother." Amir tried to give me a small smile. "I considered that a matter of deep honor and love, even though it was gruesome. But that is another story, of course."

Amir slipped into silence. I reached over and patted his hand, covering his scar with my hand.

"I'm so sorry," I whispered.

"Do not be sorry for me. I ask that you do not judge my family. I have known deeper betrayals than theirs, but it is good of me to forgive them."

"Who could betray you more than family?"

Amir's lips twitched into a wry smirk. "Those who would become family, of course."

I wondered if he was talking about my mother, but he shook his head before I could ask. "Forgive my grievances, Eleanora. It was one of the hardest things I ever had to do, to first leave my family, and then forgive them. In spite of the

THE ORDER OF THE CRYSTAL DAGGERS

pain between us, I still love them, and there are many values we still share. There is much good we can affirm."

"You are a better person than me. It is too easy to hate people." I thought of Cecilia, and how she had treated both me and Ben over the years. As cruel as it was, it was nothing compared to Amir's sorrow. I clenched my fist, struggling not to hate Amir's family for him. "I'm sorry I asked you about it."

"It is better to remember," Amir said. He turned his hand over and patted my hand gently, the same way my father used to. "We must remember, too, that blessed are those who mourn, for they shall be comforted. And we can only mourn properly when we remember the depths of our losses."

At his own words, I thought of my own faith, and how much it was a cornerstone of my own life. I had been born into it, but Amir had given up his entire childhood and his family to gain it. I silently prayed for his comfort, but I already felt like he had been further cheated with the loss of my mother.

As if he knew what I was thinking, Amir said, "It is much better for me to remember Naděžda than forget her, too."

It was hard to speak at the sudden lump in my throat. "I wish she was still with us."

"She is," Amir replied. "She is here, even if she is not. We will see her again one day, Eleanora. Some people say that religion only causes pain, but there is much pain tied to goodness. If all truth is God's truth, then all goodness is his, too."

When we first met, I had envied Amir's time with my mother. Now, as we stood there, having lost so much, I wondered if I had been strangely spared from missing her even more than I already did. I clung to Amir's certainty that he would see her again, with the further hope I would, too.

THE ORDER OF THE CRYSTAL DAGGERS

"I should have asked a question about fighting instead," I said, resuming my cleaning.

"Religion and fighting share something very significant, and that is why it is actually good to consider matters of faith and its practices alongside battles."

"What do they share?" I asked.

"Truth." Amir gave me a smile. "And, by extension, love."

"Love?" The word might as well have been one of the Arabic words inscribed on his dagger. "What does that have to do with truth?"

"True truth is unable to be separated from love, and you know as well as I do, that God is love. If I were allowed to guess, Lady Penelope and Harshad's teachings have failed to serve you because they have lost that connection."

I snorted. "You are likely correct. I didn't know love had anything to do with any of this."

"They are set in their ways, and they are not used to having their authority, or their intentions questioned, let alone by you."

"Me?"

"You look so much like your mother," Amir said. "When they look at you, with your dark locks and your bright eyes, I would not be surprised to find they see her looking back at them. It is a hard thing, to live between times."

"You said before I looked like my father."

"You have the narrow facial structure of a Bohemian, as well as the curls your mother wished for all the days of her life." Amir shrugged. "But your expressions, and even the way you flaunt authority, surely reminds them of happier... of the past."

I did not disagree with him. Lady POW had called me "Eleanor" several times before, and it always seemed hard for her to acknowledge her mistake. I suddenly wondered if Lady Penelope had offered me the chance to join the Order of the Crystal Daggers to relive her days with my mother as much as I had accepted in hopes of connecting with my mother's memory.

"I suppose it is hard to live between times, but it is even more difficult being a conduit for it," Amir added.

I profoundly appreciated the sympathy in his voice, but only nodded at his conclusions.

"I am glad she has convinced Harshad to work with you. His lessons will serve you well in the weeks to come."

Amir changed the subject, and I let him.

"I might need your help understanding them," I said, laughing a little.

"They are a good distraction from thinking of your beloved, too," Amir added, making me cough. "And if they do not, and you need someone to talk to, I would—"

"I'll come and find you." I cleared my throat. "Hopefully, my heart will be all mended before too long."

Even though I doubt it.

"Thank you. But that is not what I was going to say," Amir said, his voice quiet and grave. "I was going to say, I would not say anything to Ben. Do not forget, he wants to prove himself too."

We did not say anything else after that. Amir and I finished cleaning the training room, working together in amicable silence.

After he left, I thought there was likely another reason
Amir kept his knowledge of Ferdy to himself. Undoubtedly,
he wanted me on his side as much as I wanted him on mine.

86

THE ORDER OF THE CRYSTAL DAGGERS

6

◊

"Eleanora."

At the sound of my name, I looked up from the book in my hands, only to see Lady POW standing in the doorway before me.

A week had passed since the Advent Ball, and I had finally made it back to the library. Cecilia had forbidden me from using the library after discovering my love of books, and I found peace in having full access to them once more—even if I was consistently distracted. For the last hour, I had been looking past the words while my mind drifted off to other places in search of comfort.

"What is it?" I asked. "Ben and I finished with Harshad today. He said I could rest up for tomorrow."

"I am not here about Harshad's lessons. You and I have things to discuss. Come with me."

From the tone of her voice, I had a feeling I was in trouble. As Lady Penelope guided me out of the library and propelled me down the hallways of my home, I mentally prepared myself for another lecture and stinging letdown. It had to come, did it not? After all, I had already woken up to a world filled to the brim with disappointment last week. Why would Lady POW refuse to add her own distinct flavor to my sadness? Her displeasure was not a question of what, it was a matter of when.

So I was surprised, after several hallways of silence, she pulled out a chatelain and used one of the dangling keys to unlock a door.

"Go inside."

THE ORDER OF THE CRYSTAL DAGGERS

Her tone was still frigid. I walked inside, unsure if I would be locked in the room as a punishment. It would not have been unearned, I thought sadly.

The room was dark and musty; I wrinkled my nose at the smell. There were only little strings of light slipping through the curtains to brighten the room.

"What is this place?" My voice echoed into the dark shadows.

I almost expected Lady POW to snap at me for daring to ask a question. Instead, she struck a light and walked around the room, lighting some candles.

Slowly, the outline of another broad desk, several bookshelves full of books, scrolls, and papers, came into quiet view. In the other corner, I could see a large chair covered in mothballs, and a large globe tucked awkwardly behind the entrance.

"This room was your father's study."

I went cold at her words.

This is worse than a punishment.

"Why are we here?" I asked, unable to stop myself from gaping at the room around me.

My father had died there, alone, sitting at his desk. At the time, there had been no reason to suspect anything other than natural causes.

But now, Ben and I knew the truth. Our father had been poisoned by someone using the same silver thallis herb mixture that was unique to the Order of the Crystal Daggers.

My fingers tingled as I remembered touching *Táta's* hands at the funeral, unwilling to believe that he was truly gone.

"I wanted to ask you what you know about your father." Lady POW waved her arm out. "I understand you were quite young when he died. After Eleanor married her Dolf, I did not hear much from her. Of course, I did receive her dagger, and the later request for money to buy out the manor's debt. But I did not endeavor to know him on a personal level. Eleanor could take care of herself, after all."

The bite in my grandmother's words reminded me my mother had left on unpleasant terms with Lady POW.

"So you did not know my father at all?" I pressed, hoping to find out more from her reaction.

"I did not try to learn much about her life after she left the Order. Eleanor left for her last mission to Prague at the end of 1847," Lady Penelope admitted. "I knew there was a certain risk in sending her. Bohemia was her first home, but because of her talent for taking care of delicate matters, I decided to allow her to go. I never met your father in person. What I know is what she told me, and even that was limited enough."

From the way she spoke, so carefully precise, I knew there was something she was keeping from me.

Everyone lies. Everyone has secrets.

Lady Penelope's own teachings were working against her.

Ben had warned me about this at the beginning, I thought, remembering his own apprehension and disgust at the thought of being at our grandmother's mercy. After meeting her, he had seen her as a woman who put business over family, a relentless fighter in pursuit of her preferences.

Thinking of my brother's current eagerness to please her, I almost groaned at his complete reversal.

"Ben would be the better person to talk to," I said slowly, keeping an eye on Lady Penelope. "He was older when *Táta* died."

"I have already talked with him. He has seen this room, too."

"Why do you want to know what I think?"

"Because you are different from your brother, and you might know something that will allow me to see him in a different light." Lady Penelope held herself steady, keeping her eyes focused on me. "I want to know why someone would want to kill him."

My father was almost as elusive in my mind as mother was, but it was hard to dispel his ghost when I stood in his study. I thought about the reasons he had to die, and I could not think of personal ones.

"He worked for the king, mostly as a court ambassador and then later as a soldier," I said. "He was knighted at the end of the Revolution, before King Ferdinand abdicated in December."

"Your mother would have been in Prague for about a year at the time," Lady Penelope said. "Thanks to Tulia, we know that your mother knew about the king's son. They helped hide and protect him."

"They?"

Lady Penelope grimaced, ever so slightly. "Tulia and your mother, of course."

There it was—she was lying. There was someone else who had been helping my mother. Philip's earlier comments echoed in my memory, and at Lady POW's irritated hesitation, I wondered if my grandfather had worked with my mother on her mission.

Why would Lady POW hide that from me? He was dead, after all, even if she did not want to remember him.

Looking at her now, and recalling her vehemence before, I decided I would ask Amir. He had contacts from the League

THE ORDER OF THE CRYSTAL DAGGERS

who might be able to tell us what happened when my mother came to Prague.

That was not the only thing she did not want to discuss, I thought. Lady POW had been loath to admit the Order of the Crystal Daggers used the silver thallis poison, and someone was using it now to poison politicians, and someone had used it to kill my father.

A new thought suddenly struck me. *Was it possible the Order was responsible for* Táta's *death?*

Ferdy's voice, the one voice I tried to muffle more than any other, called to me at that moment. His assertion that the Order of the Crystal Daggers was a group of assassins ran through my mind. While I did not agree with his perspective, I was suddenly very aware that I was floundering in a sea of confusion and distrust.

If I was going to protect my kingdom, save others, and restore my honor, I would have to find out the truth about the past, and how it connected to the present, and I would have to do it before anyone else was injured or killed.

"Well?" Lady POW put her hands on her hips, clearly irritated I had slipped away into my own world. "What do you think?"

"My apologies." I glanced around the room, trying to think of how to describe my father. "Well ... *Táta* was a very kind man—to me, at least. He would travel for long weeks, but he always came home. Before *Máma* died, he would hold small parties here occasionally."

I had been too young to understand many things; I was only five when *Máma* had been lost at sea, and nine when my father followed her to the grave.

"What was his temperament like?"

THE ORDER OF THE CRYSTAL DAGGERS

"He was a quiet, studious man, but still very tough. He always had time for me. He would dance with me sometimes, and he read to me at night." I lowered my eyes to the ground. "He was very upset when Ben broke his leg. He had been training Ben to be a soldier for about two years when it happened. After that, they were never close."

"I see." Lady POW frowned. "So you were his favorite, then?"

Hearing her echo Ferdy's earlier observation made me even more uncomfortable.

"I think so," I admitted softly. "But I'm not sure it was because of my own merit. He told me once I was proof of *Máma's* love, since I looked so much like her. He said he could enjoy her for two lifetimes instead of just one."

The room seemed to settle from our earlier intrusion. I stood there, watching the last of the dust dance around in the dim lighting, waiting for Lady Penelope's next question.

"I can understand his feelings on that particular matter," she finally said, a small smile forming on her wrinkled face.

I looked around the room again, eying the framed items on the wall. There were maps and a few documents, but no pictures. "There was a portrait of my mother hanging in the library when I was younger. I remember after she died, he looked at it quite frequently. Cecilia removed it after she married him."

"It was in here when Benedict came in with me," Lady Penelope said. "I am having it restored by one of the footmen. Hopefully you will see it again in the library soon, where it belongs."

"Really?"

She nodded, and I beamed with pleasure. "Thank you. I appreciate that."

THE ORDER OF THE CRYSTAL DAGGERS

I had agreed to work with Lady POW because I wanted to know my mother more. Having her portrait restored was an added blessing, one that would help exorcize Cecilia's harsh memory from the manor.

"Nonsense, Eleanora. You should know I loved your mother, too, even if … " Her voice trailed off, and then she sighed. "What else do you remember about your father?"

Renewed by her revelation, I looked around the room once more. "He had dark eyes," I murmured, sinking into my own past, shocked at how much I had let myself forget. "I think they were hazel. He was a tall man, too. Or so it seemed, from the shortness of my age. I knew he collected a lot of things from the different places that he went for the king."

"Books?"

"Most of the ones I remember are books," I said. "Cecilia has made me trade them or sell them off over the years. The day I met you, I had just sold his copy of *The Prelude*."

I did not mention that Cecilia had wanted me to sell my mother's journal, too. Amir had stolen it from me, and I was more grateful than ever that he had. Not only had I met him, and by extension Lady Penelope and the Order, but that was how I met Ferdy, too.

"Ella."

Impossible yearning momentarily devastated me. It seemed in allowing his voice to speak inside of me, there was no longer any hope of suppressing it. I would go from suffering of one sort and then slide into another too easily, all while I was compelled to further hide my true self from everyone around me.

"What is it?" Lady Penelope asked. "Do you remember something else?"

I had to force myself back into the moment, back into my father's study, facing my grandmother as she watched me along with the rest of the room.

"He has been gone for several years now, and I knew him as a daughter, not as an equal. Maybe when we find Cecilia, she will be able to help you answer more questions about him."

"I'd rather not rely on her completely, given the choice." Lady Penelope shuffled her skirts toward the desk. "But you are right. She will be a good source. You can really only trust the people you don't trust at all."

"That can't be right." The absurdity of her statement almost made me laugh. "That's irrational."

"Haven't you realized it yet, Eleanora?" Lady Penelope hissed. "People are far more irrational than rational. You can't trust *anyone*. We are loyal to our mission, but our allegiance is to the truth alone, and that includes the realization that other people will fail you—sometimes purposefully."

At her temper, I felt my own anger stir. "Is that why you and Harshad work together?"

"Yes." Lady POW's lips pursed, souring her expression even more than her tone. "We know each other's worst traits, and we are well aware of our capacity to betray each other. That means he will be prepared to make sure I stay in line, and I him."

I gaped at her. "That is madness! How could anyone ever have any normal relationship?"

"Why do you think your mother left?" Lady Penelope shook her head. "This is part of the price you pay to protect others, Eleanora. You only trust people you know well enough, and once you know someone well enough, you know exactly how they will fail you in the end."

"That's not true," I insisted.

"If you truly believe that," Lady Penelope warned, "you will only be more disappointed when it happens."

Another chill ran through me at her words.

"Right now, we must work to find Lady Cecilia," Lady Penelope continued. "We know the disaster at the Advent Ball was meant to inflame the public. The former king has managed to quell a lot of conflicts. Since it failed, we can be sure that there will be another attempt to upset the kingdom."

I thought of waking up in Prague Castle, in Ferdy's room, seeing the damage done to the city; a sense of determination renewed inside of me. I was allowed to mourn, but there was still work to do.

"While you are training, I will keep making my rounds in the city. It likely won't be long before there is another plan we will have to foil. Christmastime and the weather may offer politicians a break, but there is no vacation for insurgents."

"What else would you like me to work on?" I asked, crossing my arms over my chest. If there was danger, and Lady POW wanted to keep me at home, I would place the blame for any incident on her.

"Keep focusing on your lessons with Harshad for now. We are still working to find more information, but the weather and Society's stagnancy has slowed our resources in that regard." She paused. "You should know Benedict is worried about you."

I squared my shoulders at the sudden change in subject. "Ben knows I am sad that we failed to protect the people at the castle."

"Forget about that." Lady POW snorted delicately. "People die all the time. We do what we can. You clearly did what you could, and it did not save everyone. That happens. Now we must work to prevent it from happening again."

I said nothing, stunned by her brusque tone. Lady Penelope had been quite adamant before that we had to do something to stop the kingdom from crumbling. Now that it had fallen apart, she seemed much more cavalier.

"Ben does not think that there are other reasons you might be distracted, does he?"

I thought of Ben's antagonism toward Ferdy and quickly shook my head.

"I don't know what he thinks," I said, unable to disguise the growing irritation in my voice.

"Perhaps Ben is the one who is distracted in his observations, then?" Lady POW shook her head. "And here I was, thinking he was doing so well, too."

"I think Ben is doing an excellent job." I knew from just looking at my brother how much he had changed in the last several weeks. I had to credit the Order, and even Lady Penelope's own efforts, for Ben's happiness.

"Maybe I should make him step down from the Order for now. If he is wrong about you, then there is no telling how wrong he is about other things. He knows you so much better than the rest of us, after all."

"No." I balled my fingers into a frustrated fist. "He really likes working with you. He would be upset if he had to stop."

"Should I put the rest of our team in danger, all to spare his feelings?" Lady Penelope asked. "There is much more at risk than one person's comfort, if I need to remind you."

She was not just talking about Ben. She was talking about me, too.

I tried to relax and succeeded only in the smallest degree. I did not want Ben's position with the Order to be jeopardized. After my father's rejection of him as heir, Ben had carried such a burden. I did not want to be the reason, again, that he would suffer.

"Ben is just overprotective of me," I insisted. "Even when we were fighting the assassin in the wine cellar, Ben was more concerned with me."

"I see. I will note your thoughts on the matter." Lady POW folded her hands together thoughtfully. "Very well, then. Get some rest, Eleanora. Harshad will send for you in the morning."

"Where are you going?"

"I will continue making my own inquiries. Before Tulia disappeared, she gave me some information, and I must check her reports."

I felt another chill at her words. *Tulia knows about me and Ferdy.*

Even if Tulia did not know he was the younger Prince of Bohemia, she might have been able to tell Lady Penelope about the boy I loved. "What did she tell you?"

"Always so curious," Lady Penelope murmured crossly. "You will find out when you need to know. For now, go and rest. I'd hate to think I've spent a good deal of time harassing Harshad to instruct you only to find he was correct about what a poor student you would make."

My fingernails scraped into my palms as my fists clenched, and I watched her disappear down the hall. I fought the urge to scream.

Instead, my hand went to the dagger at my side. I had earned the right to carry it, even if I did not know how to wield it. I was a member of the Order, and I was only loyal to the truth.

And the truth was, I had little to no idea of what that could be. I only knew for sure that the illusions I had grown up with were gone, and I had to monitor their remaining influence.

Visions of those lies passed before me as I made my way to my bedroom. I saw my mother's life and my father's death; I saw my grandmother and her colleagues; I saw Prague in all of its glory, stained by the sadness I was now intimately acquainted with. I even saw Tulia for who she was, as my grandfather's half-sister; and there was Ferdy, too, with his roguish grin and his princely stature.

What do I have left?

I clasped my hands together, no longer able to carry my anger and frustration. "I still have you, Lord," I whispered, leaning my head down in prayer. I begged for his help, for his patience, for his comfort. "Please help me."

After several long moments, my heart steadied. I still had my faith, and I still had Ben. I could trust Ben.

I bit my lip, looking at the door to my father's study one last time.

I can trust Ben … can't I?

THE ORDER OF THE CRYSTAL DAGGERS

7

◊

As much as I worried about Lady Penelope, I did listen to her advice and focus on my work. As the days passed, I worked on becoming a more skilled warrior, learning how to be invisible, to move in silence and stealth. The effort was demanding but engrossing, and I was largely able to hide my worry from myself.

That was part of the real trick—finding a way to put fear aside for the moment, before forgetting it altogether.

Of course, just because fear is silenced, that does not mean it truly goes away. It bides its time, waiting for a moment of weakness, before it pounces again, twisting itself into sudden sickness.

I discovered this the hard way when Lady Penelope called for me the following week.

"Eleanora!"

Ben and I had just finished up another session with Harshad. When I heard her voice, I jumped, whirling around to face the door to the west parlor as my sweat-soaked towel whipped through the air after me.

"Careful." Ben ducked around the sudden movement.

I glanced over at him apologetically, but he only gave me a spiteful look in return. He was absent the last few days of Harshad's lessons, but I had not missed him much.

Perhaps it was because of his festering irritation I only noticed at the end of our session that his one eye was shadowed by darkened puffiness.

Immediately, I forgot all about Lady POW.

"Ben!" Examining his injury, I could tell he had been hit very hard, and very recently. "What happened to you? Your eye—"

"I don't want to answer any questions, Nora," he hissed. "Amir already told me I would be fine. He even assured me that I was deserving of it, thanks to you."

"What?" I tried to reach for him, but he slipped away from me. "What are you talking about?"

"Eleanora!"

Lady Penelope's voice cut through the air between us, this time much more sharply. Ben wrinkled his nose at me. "Lady POW is calling. You should see what she wants."

"Ben—"

He shook his head and left the room, leaving me with my mouth open in hurt shock.

Why was he being so harsh? I knew Lady Penelope was trying to get him to tell her my secrets, but for the first time, I was more angry than hurt by Ben's attitude.

Ben should be on my side, not hers.

Ben did not tell me about Lady Penelope's inquiries regarding my secrets, but he should have, just as she should have talked about the League or about the past. I had my own secrets, but I had good reasons for keeping them. I could see no reason Ben would hide something from me.

Something has to be done.

My fists clenched angrily. Over the past weeks, I had focused solely on my work with Harshad with very limited interruptions and manageable relapses. In many ways, it was necessary. What else could I do to stop myself from thinking of my failures? Between Ferdy's loss, Ben's antagonism, and the Order's demands, I was overwhelmed with pain, sorrow, and shame.

I knew in coming home from Prague Castle, I would need to redeem myself. That meant becoming a better fighter. My fighting, while still rudimentary, was now more nuanced and fluid; my muscles were stronger, my endurance increased, and, no doubt much to Lady Penelope's glee, my midsection was even flatter. I could do several rounds of pushups, lunges, and sit-ups; I ran and jumped, moving until my breathing came in erratic patterns as I panted, feeling sticky in my stealth habit.

There was no hint of Lord Maximillian's next move, or Karl's, or anything else suspicious. There were no more murders for us to solve or activities to investigate. We were still stuck at the same unanswered questions, and I was tired of waiting for an absolution that might never come.

As I stood there, watching my brother willingly ignore me after an uneventful Christmas, after weeks of no word of Cecilia's whereabouts or Tulia's fate, my resolve only strengthened. Being a better fighter was obviously important, but it was only part of what was required of me. I had worked through my pain only to find more pain waiting for me when I was finished.

It was time to change my focus. It was time to go look for answers myself.

"Eleanora!" Lady Penelope's voice was much louder as she burst into the room. "There you are. Thank the Lord I've found you."

"What is it?" My voice was edged with bitterness, but I was genuinely curious at her overwhelming pleasure.

"Something has happened, at last," Lady Penelope cheered. "You have a visitor."

"I do?"

THE ORDER OF THE CRYSTAL DAGGERS

"Yes, and we need to hurry!" Lady Penelope grabbed me by the wrist and pulled me out of the room, nearly running into Amir. She brightened at the sight of him. "You should come, too, Amir."

"Yes, Madame," he replied, careful to keep his tone respectful. But as we headed out, I caught the glimmer of defiance in his eyes and knew he was still frustrated with her, despite his façade.

It seemed that Amir was growing tired of playing along with Lady POW's lead as much as I was.

"I heard you did well enough in your sessions this week. I am glad to hear the mostly positive results." Lady Penelope in exuded an excited energy as she pulled me along, belying the seventy-some years old she had to be.

But then, maybe I was just too tired by comparison.

"Should I say thank you?" I almost pulled myself free before noticing Lady POW forcing me to move was actually a reprieve from my own efforts.

"Training with Harshad has been very good for you, Eleanora." I saw her glance down at my midsection for a quick second. "It has helped significantly with your figure."

Normally, I would have said something at her condescending remark, but I was too tired, and I did not want my rudeness to give her a reason to further reprimand me. Beside me, Amir gave me a silent look of teasing approval.

"Who is here to visit me?" I asked, deciding it was time to change the topic.

"A certain gentleman has come to call," Lady Penelope replied with a cheery grin. "He gave me his card."

"Let me have it," I said, snatching it out of her grasp. *It can't be ...*

THE ORDER OF THE CRYSTAL DAGGERS

My heart sank as I read the card. Karl's name stood out in bold lettering. I crumpled up the paper in my hand, angry at myself more than anything.

Of course Ferdy is not going to come and see me.

Ferdy could play the gentleman, as I now knew thanks to the Advent Ball. But that did not mean he would. He had let me go, and it was not like he was going to show up at my home and demand I change my mind about us.

Even if I might want him to.

"Eleanora?" As we stopped in front of my bedroom door, Lady Penelope cleared her throat. "What is it?"

"It's Karl," I said. "Karl Marcelin. He's here."

"I know that. Why do you think I went to go and find you? What is wrong? After these last few weeks, I thought you would be happy to see him."

"It's nothing," I murmured. "I am just too tired to be surprised, pleasantly or otherwise."

Another thought hit me hard. What if the empress or King Ferdinand had said something to Karl about my role as a member of the Order? Was he here to confront me?

The earlier, unpleasant feeling in my stomach morphed into pure dread.

"I was hoping he would visit sooner, but now I am just glad he is here at all." Excitement laced Lady Penelope's words as she burst into my room, opened my wardrobe, and began tossing me towels. "Amir, you stay outside. Eleanora, come. Karl is expecting you."

"What?" I gestured down my body, where my sweat-soaked outfit hung limply and my body odor eagerly announced itself. "I can't see him."

THE ORDER OF THE CRYSTAL DAGGERS

I did not want to mention that I did not have any strength left to fight Karl in the event he attacked me for my deception.

"Amelia and the others will take care of you while I distract him," Lady Penelope promised. "I heard some interesting rumors a few days ago, and I would love to hear them confirmed."

"What rumors?"

"Just hurry. Mr. Marcelin is our remaining link to Lord Maximillian, and we cannot alienate him. Not yet, anyway. We must use charm to get information, and that means you need to be ready."

"If Karl and Lord Maximillian are working together, why don't we just confront Karl?" I asked.

"Karl is the king's son, and Lord Maximillian has significant status as a duke, and we can't forget he is a cousin to Emperor Franz Joseph," Lady Penelope reminded me. "In our position, we need proof, not just what appears to be a coerced confession, and that means we need to find out who is financing their nefarious deeds if we are going to protect Bohemia and the surrounding nations from further danger."

"Oh."

"They are never going to admit to murder, let alone attempting to take over the kingdom, without damning evidence," Lady Penelope said. "We are fortunate that the empress trusts us, or we could easily be imprisoned ourselves."

Lady Penelope gathered her skirts as she bustled out the door. "So that is why you cannot fail us now. Change your clothes, fix your hair, and wash up. In ten minutes, Amir will carry you into the front room and you will sit there, like the invalid I've reported you as being. No objections."

"Ten minutes?" My mouth dropped open in disbelief.

"Did I not just say you were to have no objections?" She sighed heavily as she left the room, brushing past Amir. "I am pleased with your progress this week, Eleanora, but you must realize this does not make up for your mistakes at the castle."

I nearly stopped breathing at her words, chilled at the edge of disappointment in her voice.

"Go and do what she says." Amir broke through my momentary despair as he reached over to close my door. "The rest of us are here to help you."

Even if Karl knows about me and the Order.

I relaxed, but only by the slightest degree. "I'm going."

"Not eagerly," Amir replied, attempting to coax a smile out of me; I obliged, if only a little. It was hard to resist Amir's kindness. Before I could say anything else, Amelia, Jaqueline, and Marguerite appeared to take charge of the situation.

Lady POW's seamstresses were a team of frightening efficiency. Their movements blurred together, perfectly synchronized as they pushed me into a new outfit and cleaned up all evidence of my training session.

"Your hair needs work," Marguerite said. "Here. Let me put it up in turban so we can hide it."

"No, leave it down," Jaqueline said. "It is much more intimate, *non?* The gentleman will appreciate it."

"If we leave it down, we will need to comb it with oils. That will help cover up the smell of the sweat. I think it is better if we put it up." Amelia spoke with a kind smile on her face, but I forced down a grimace before letting the three of them take over.

"Here you are, miss," Marguerite said, as she handed me a large swath of bandages.

"What is this for?"

"Your leg. Madame instructed us to wrap your leg in extra bandages. The rumor is that you've injured it."

"Oh. Well, it's not broken." Before I could say anything else, new bandages were drawn tight and warm against my skin, firm against where the bruise on my leg had once been. I tried not to compare the sense of cold detachment to how I felt before, when my leg was wrapped in Ferdy's kindness.

When everything was done—when I was dressed in a modest house gown, my hair was clean and pulled back into an ornate bun, and my body was covered in multiple layers of soap and perfumes—Amelia, Jaqueline, and Marguerite handed me over to Amir.

I saw Amelia grab a thick blanket. "Hurry, sir," she said. "Madame will be waiting for us."

"What are you doing?" I asked as Amir picked me up, surprising me. His strong, gentle embrace, combined with his careworn expression, reminded me of my father.

"No need to worry, Eleanora," Amir said. "I have you."

"This seems unnecessary."

"It is all part of the plan. There is no telling what Karl will see while he is here. It is better we give him a show."

I sighed as I hooked my arm over his shoulder, embarrassed more than anything else. I felt like a little girl again—and in some ways, I reveled in it. The world had seemed like such a different place when *Táta* was alive, and it had been so long since I relied on someone to take care of me. The death of my mother had ripped the world out from underneath me, but the loss of my father had left me without any sunshine in my skies.

I shrugged off my yearning as we entered the front room from the back way. I could hear Lady POW talking with Karl

THE ORDER OF THE CRYSTAL DAGGERS

in the adjacent room. Amir set me down on the couch, while Amelia and Jaqueline hurried to tuck the blanket around my skirt. Marguerite appeared with a wet rag to lay on my forehead a moment later.

"For added effect," she explained quickly.

The instant she turned away, I let it fall to the side. I already felt silly, like a bedridden child or an overly-dressed grandmother. "I'm glad it's winter. This is getting hot."

"You should be fine while Mr. Marcelin is here." Amir tucked the cover in around me. "Lady POW will likely only bring him here for a few moments to talk to you. She'll need you to get as much information from him as possible."

"I'll try. I don't think he will confess to anything." I thought of my brother, too. He did not want to tell me about his injury, and he had managed to keep that hidden from me. What were the chances that Karl would confess anything important?

I glanced up at Amir. "Do you know why Ben has a black eye?"

Amir must have been expecting that question, because he waved it aside. "He has other orders from Lady Penelope. That is all he told me."

The answer was vague enough to make me suspicious. "He is still angry with me. If he didn't tell you what he was doing, he might be upset with you, too."

"I am certain he is," Amir admitted. "He was not happy with me the other day, after your fight."

I remembered that day Ben fought with me, after Harshad's first lesson with me. "What was it that you said to Ben on his way out of the parlor?"

"Nothing of importance."

"If it's nothing of importance, you should have no issue telling me."

"There is no stopping you, is there?" Amir sighed. "That day, I told him that he deserved it when you knocked him down."

"What? Why?" I slapped his arm. "That's awful."

"He was proud of his victory when you gave up," Amir said. "That's not right, Eleanora. Ben has his own struggles to overcome. You are a weakness of his, but you are not the only one. He needs to watch for his own flaws, and winning can show them as much as losing."

"That's still cruel."

"The truth is often upsetting. If Ben is to improve, he must understand the difference between not only failures and victory, but victory and false victory." His eyes met mine as he added, "It is the same for you. There is a difference between freedom and false freedom."

It was hard to push my sudden discomfort away, almost as hard as it was to hide my fear. "I suppose you are right."

"Well, if you say so," Amir replied, and I saw the smirk under his mustache appear briefly.

"Thank you for telling me." I folded my hands, unsure of what else I could say. I was not happy with the truth, but there was nothing I could do to change it.

"You are welcome, Eleanora. I'll look forward to seeing what you can find out from Mr. Marcelin."

"I just hope we can discover something that will help. I know we haven't been able to discover much since the castle incident."

THE ORDER OF THE CRYSTAL DAGGERS

"I hope so, too." He gave my hand an affectionate squeeze, allowing me another look at the scar on his fist before he left the room.

I bit my lip. Obviously, Amir had known his share of suffering. I did not want to add more anguish to his life. But as I heard Lady Penelope's formal remarks and eager footsteps coming closer, I had a feeling that neither of us would be able to avoid it.

"Ben told me that we have to find a physical connection to Lord Maximillian and the castle's attack," Marguerite said as she pulled one of my curls out of its pin. "So please, Nora, see if you can find a connection."

"Why were you talking to my brother?" I asked, frowning.

"We are all concerned about the mission, miss." Marguerite blushed, no doubt sensing she had overstepped herself.

"I'm sorry," I said. "I was just curious, that's all."

It did not make me feel good knowing I had gotten better at hiding the truth in the last few weeks. Deceit might be required for a spy, but it was disheartening to see myself fall so easily into sin.

"Of course. Hopefully this will not take long," she replied. "It is not proper for a gentleman to be in a lady's presence when she has taken ill or if she is injured. But Lady POW wants to give him the chance to slip up, and this is a clever way to surprise him."

"Surprise him?"

"Yes. When you surprise an unsuspecting foe, he will have a harder time hiding the truth." Marguerite patted my hand in a friendly way, while I just sat there, dumbfounded.

I had never been very good at asking Karl to give me information. It did not help that he was as much of a liar as Ferdy was.

THE ORDER OF THE CRYSTAL DAGGERS

If not more so.

Secretly, I hoped Karl would decline an audience with me. He knew I was indisposed, and I did not think he would push to make me even more uncomfortable. When he came through the door a moment later, I stifled back a groan.

It's really a good thing I never learned to like gambling. Ferdy would be appalled at my luck.

"Eleanora is, of course, delighted to have you as a visitor," Lady Penelope was saying, and I had to bite my cheek to keep from arguing with her. "Goodness knows the poor dear needs something to lift her spirits. She has been rather down since the accident."

"I am pleased to be of service to my lady."

I had to bite down even harder at the sound of Karl's voice. I had never noticed before how much he had the same lyrical undertones as Ferdy, the same cadence to his proper tone. All that was missing was the heart of a rogue beating underneath it.

My cheeks grew hot as he took my hand.

In truth, Karl looked very little like his younger brother. They were of similar height, and they shared the same jawline and pointed nose, but Karl's eyes were a darker gray, giving him a more hawkish face. And while I could nearly always make out a smattering of fuzz on Ferdy's cheeks, Karl was cleanshaven. His ebony hair was brushed back from his face, emphasizing his steadfast demeanor. He was clearly a man with a serious and settled nature, strong willed and focused. While I had witnessed Ferdy's temper before, I did not want to know what Karl's was like; I had a feeling it was just as resolute as the rest of him.

"Mr. Marcelin." My voice was low and weak as I greeted him, and I suddenly wondered if Ferdy also used Marcelin as his surname. My eyes watered at the thought.

"My lady," Karl replied. He bowed over my hand and kissed it, just as gallantly as he had the night of the Hohenwart Ball. There was nothing in his demeanor to suggest he thought I was a traitor and a liar; if anything, I could feel his eagerness beneath my palm. "I am glad to see you again."

Empress Maria Anna did not tell him.

The thought struck me hard and fast, and I was relieved and disappointed at the same time. What kind of mother did not tell her son he was courting a spy?

Then again, what kind of mother *was* a spy? Philip had said *Máma* had impressed the former empress, and I was starting to see why. They must have had a lot in common.

Karl sat down on a chair close to me. I gave him a teasing look. "Even if it is in this condition?"

To his credit, he blushed a little at my banter. Karl had impeccable manners. "I heard the tragic news of your injury, but I did not want to inconvenience you or hinder your recuperation. Lady Penelope was kind enough to allow me to see you."

"You are most welcome, Mr. Marcelin." Lady POW held her position at the doorway as Amelia, Marguerite, and Jaqueline all filed out of the room. When they were gone, only Lady Penelope loomed over us, as any proper companion would.

Of course, the situation was already inappropriate, since I was supposed to be indisposed. We were courting scandal as it was.

"I am glad to see you are being taken care of so well. I miss you dreadfully, and I fear I will continue to do so while you recover," Karl said.

THE ORDER OF THE CRYSTAL DAGGERS

"I am sure there are other ladies who would be willing to dance with you in my stead."

"There is no one like you, Ella." His words were soft and quiet, hushed enough to hide the intimacy from Lady Penelope.

"Eleanora, you should know that you need not worry much about that," Lady Penelope said. "There is not much amusement to be had in the city with weather such as this."

She looked toward the windows, where a small layer of powdery snow was lying on the grounds.

"That is correct, Madame." Karl nodded. "While Emperor is in Vienna, he has granted Empress Maria Anna's request for a political recess while the castle undergoes repairs."

"It seems that we must continually suffer boredom as well as inconvenience because of the incident." Lady Penelope narrowed her gaze. "What a shame anything happened at all. And those poor souls who died. I am so fortunate that my Eleanora only injured her leg."

Karl nodded solemnly. "I should have stayed with you that night."

"Forgive my upset, Mr. Marcelin," Lady Penelope replied. "It is not as though you caused the ballroom walls to collapse."

Karl clenched his jaw at the sudden silence between us.

"I did not hear much of the official story while I have been recovering," I said, feigning delicacy, drawing Karl's attention back to me. "Do you know happened at the Advent Ball?"

"There was a fire in the wine cellar of the castle that night." The smoothness of his voice made me wonder if it was practiced.

But then, I thought, Karl was an excellent politician.

THE ORDER OF THE CRYSTAL DAGGERS

"Roman is very upset by the news. As the architect who restored the wine cellar, he feels responsible for the design's failure. He is offering to oversee the rebuilding and repair of the castle."

"I see."

"I have also offered to help. In fact, I have moved out of Roman's house to stay in the castle itself while it is repaired." Karl straightened, clearly eager to share his news.

I nodded and smiled. "So you are staying with the king?"

"Yes," Karl said, clearly enjoying the prestige of his position. He would welcome the attention, and I had to admit, it was a nice cover story for staying with his parents. "From the castle, I will be easily able to attend to the needs of the Bohemian Diet and the *Reichsrat* Congress as sessions resume. The Minister-President is also not far away, should he require my attention."

"I have heard that Count Potocki has decided against retiring his position," Lady Penelope spoke up from behind us.

Karl's subdued expression further soured. "Yes, Madame. That is true. Since the accident, Alfred has decided to stay on until the repairs are organized and Emperor Franz Joseph has taken care of Bohemia. Should the emperor decide to do anything about it at all, of course."

"If Count Potocki is not retiring, what will you do?" I asked. "Will you campaign for his position while he remains in office?"

"Such a venture is risky," Karl murmured, clearly flustered. "It is not polite or honorable."

"It would be a political move." I almost expected Karl to laugh at my observation, but he did not.

"I have not conferred with Alfred about the matter," he said. From his serious tone, I would have said he was lying, but there was no way to know for sure. "I am, for now, content to remain where I am."

At that, I *knew* he was lying. Since I had met him, Karl had talked eagerly of moving into the count's position, and now he was trying to come across as a man with solid connections. I commended Karl on his attempts at humility, and even his success at deception, but I did not believe him.

"If you are not running for his office, is Lord Maximillian still insistent on your arrangement with Lady Teresa Marie?" I asked.

It was too hard to sound hopeful.

"The immediacy of our mutual discussions has stalled for now, if not indefinitely," Karl replied. His eyes went dark as he looked away from me. "However, I believe this gives us some time to discuss our own future, my lady, especially considering our last conversation."

"Oh." I thought of the Advent Ball again, remembering he was in agreement to marry me. Panic nearly choked me, as I remembered I never gave my own specific approval, but I had allowed him to think that I was in agreement. We had shared a private moment, even a kiss, and Karl had run off to make arrangements.

I could not even remember Karl's kiss; all I could think of was Ferdy, and the taste of his lips on mine as we grasped onto each other in his room, each breath between us crying out with fervent desperation.

Lady Penelope cleared her throat, making me blush even more. "Mr. Marcelin has informed me of his intentions, Eleanora. For now, I have only consented to consider his offer. My life experience with husbands has brought me a fortuitous amount of wisdom when it comes to arranging a

THE ORDER OF THE CRYSTAL DAGGERS

marriage, and I feel it is appropriate to exercise it in this regard."

Karl cocked an eyebrow at me, and I nearly laughed. He was no doubt recalling Lady Penelope's hasty wedding and short marriage to the Duke of Wellington before he passed away several years ago. They had been rumored to have a scandalous affair and a difficult marriage.

Thinking of the Order, I could not stop myself from wondering if he had been poisoned, too.

"I would also prefer to wait for your full recovery to give my final answer." Lady Penelope's condition seemed to give Karl a renewed sense of hope, and he cheered at once.

"I am certain of your knowledge in this matter, Madame, and I am glad for the opportunity to embrace it," Karl said. If I did not know him so well, I would have believed his sincerity.

"Well," I said, "you know what happened to me the night of the Advent Ball. What happened to you?"

"I went looking for the Duke of Moravia as soon as we parted," he said. "I was hoping to renegotiate the terms of our agreement, as you know. I was informed that he had left. The footman I spoke with told me that one of his business associates had summoned him."

"Business associates?"

"The Duke is a very wealthy man with many connections," Karl said. "He no doubt had to discuss his latest investment pools or company stock. He is quite diligent in personally overseeing these matters. From what Alfred and Lord Hohenwart have told me, he does not follow the accepted practice of hiring a man of affairs for such activities."

So Lord Maximillian is personally involved in the scheme to take over Bohemia, I thought. It made sense, from what I had heard Cecilia say before. He had several foreign backers that were invested in his project, too.

"Grandmother?" I nearly gagged at the strange title. While Lady Penelope was indeed my grandmother, it was difficult to think of her as such. If it was not for her blue eyes, the blue eyes shared by both my mother and me, I would hardly believe we were related.

"Yes, Eleanora?" Lady Penelope's eyebrow twitched in irritation. I did not think she liked the title either.

"Would you call for some tea?" I asked. "Please?"

I saw her gaze from me to Karl in that calculating way of hers.

"I shall return momentarily." She narrowed her gaze at Karl in warning, but I knew she was secretly pleased.

"Thank you, mum," I said, making her smile even more twisted.

The second she was gone, I turned my full attention on Karl. "I am so glad to see you, Karl. Thank you for coming."

Pleasure radiated from Karl's face. "It is hard talking candidly with your chaperone present."

I nodded. I was ready to ask him my questions when he slipped down on his knees in front of me.

"Ella, I know your grandmother has denied me consent to marry you for the time being, but might I at least ask a promise of your fidelity?"

"My fidelity?" I stared at him blankly.

"I understand a formal engagement is a big step, especially for your grandmother," Karl said. "But the matter of a pending engagement is different."

THE ORDER OF THE CRYSTAL DAGGERS

As he explained the nature of differences between this—which I did not understand at all, thanks to my ignorance in Society's demands—I felt my stomach twist into several knots. A pending engagement between Karl and me would allow people to believe he was courting me, with the intent to marry. Those people would believe that I was in agreement as we appeared in public together.

In other words, I thought glumly, it was the engagement without the announcement.

I would be lying every step of the way.

Everyone lies about something.

Ferdy's words, so close to Lady Penelope's, skipped cheerfully across my mind, and I hated Ferdy in that moment. I hated that he could not be mine, that I was too proud in my rags to have him, that he would too easily discard his worth to gain me.

I hated that everything had happened in such a way that I could not trust him to stay beside me, nor could I assume I would not push him away.

And Karl, whether he realized it or not, was just making me feel worse. The one thing I never wanted to do when I started working for the Order was marry for the sake of a mission. I clearly remembered fighting with Lady POW about it.

And yet, here I was, about to lie and sacrifice everything for my kingdom and my heart's desire for answers.

But, true to form, I would not do it senselessly.

"I will agree to this," I said slowly, hating myself for every word, "if you make me a promise in return."

"What is it?" Karl asked impatiently, clearly startled and displeased by my request. He cleared his throat and corrected his tone. "Anything for you, my lady."

"I want you to promise me that you will not ever lie to me."

"Done."

"About anything," I emphasized the words very carefully, and Karl narrowed his eyes. I knew he had his own secrets, and he would not enjoy sharing them with me.

But a moment later, as he met my gaze with his own, I saw him relent. His gray eyes softened, and I felt a sting of shame at my manipulative demands. I had to remind myself that Karl, no matter how nice he might have been to me, was working with Lord Maximillian to take the Bohemian monarchy, that he was connected to a plot to kill people, and that no matter how noble he thought he was, Karl had to pay for his unhealthy ambition.

"You have my word, Ella," Karl took my hand again and bowed over it. "I was so worried you would completely retreat from me."

Not while I have a murder mystery to solve and a coup to uncover.

"I will not allow myself to keep anything from you that would hinder our relationship," he said, standing up straight and puffing out his chest proudly once more. "And I will begin working on a way to change your grandmother's mind immediately."

"Thank you," I said. "I believe your oath. Now, I would like you to tell me about your brother."

He dropped my hand, reeling back on his heels as his face blanched and his cheeks burned with fury. "What?"

The disbelief on his face was almost amusing. I doubted I could have said anything else that would have made him feel less surprised, even if I accused him of blowing up the castle himself.

"I apologize for my impudence," I said, feigning sudden discomfort. "But since you knew about my brother, I thought

THE ORDER OF THE CRYSTAL DAGGERS

it would be nice to know about yours. After all, my brother is my closest family, and I am glad to know we have such a blessing in common."

There was a long moment of silence as Karl's expression became more embittered. I said nothing, holding my breath nervously.

"I regret I will not be able to share in your joy. My brother is a nuisance and a plague to my family's legacy. I prefer to forget about him altogether if possible."

"Oh?" My hands folded in my lap, as I watched him with sudden curiosity. "Why is that?"

"My brother has been suspended from any number of schools across Europe. He spent several years in Paris, and some in London with me, and I can attest to his brawling, his gambling, his … numerous indiscretions."

I blushed, thinking of Ferdy with other women. Anger flared inside of me, even as a very small part of me held onto that memory of our first kiss.

"I see," I said very quietly. "I can see why such a reputation would upset you."

"All I have worked for is the future of Bohemia," Karl said. "My brother has spent his life dedicated to fun and frivolity. He is not anything like me."

"Not by the sound of it," I said. "Where is he now?"

"He is currently staying in Prague, but just for a little while longer," Karl admitted. "He is finishing up his education in Silesia. Until his return, I will keep watch over him and make sure he does not get himself into trouble."

"It sounds like he has a talent for it." I had to muffle a giggle. Ferdy was much more trouble than Karl could have ever guessed. "Would I be able to meet him?"

"No." Karl's sharp tone was quick and fierce, and it took the rest of my daring to ask him another question. "Please, Ella, he's hardly proper. My family prefers I do not tell anyone about him."

I could believe that, from what Philip and Ferdy had both mentioned before. "What is his name?"

"I'd rather not tell you, if it would keep you from finding out his trouble," Karl said. "I know I promised to tell you the truth, but this is something you are better off not knowing."

"I am only curious," I insisted. "If I wish to know you better, it would be best to do it on more intimate terms. Indeed, I would like to know more about your family."

Karl's mouth twisted again, and I could see he was getting more frustrated with me. "His name is Ferdinand. He was named after the king, of course."

I pretended to brush a stray curl out of my eyes as I smirked. "Of course."

"May I ask how you learned about him?" Karl asked, suddenly rounding on me. "No one knows of him here in Prague, not even my closest companions."

"I learned about him the night of the Hohenwart Ball," I said. "Was that not what was written on the note the footman gave you? That you had to go and attend to your brother?"

Ferdy had thrown that in my face before, and as I watched Karl for a negative reaction, I suddenly wondered if that was what the note truly said.

No, Ferdy would not have lied about that.

He was too pleased at his cleverness, that he had told me the truth without me realizing it.

Before I could say something else, Karl's fists clenched at his side. "I did not realize that footmen could be bribed so easily. You are correct. I was called to go and extract him from another potential scandal."

"I am sorry for my curiosity," I said once more, noting his frustration. "I did not mean to make you upset. I would prefer to have no lies between us."

Outside my room, I could hear Lady POW approaching, and I was relieved my time alone with Karl was nearly over. As much as I was excited to learn what I could, there was still nothing to prove that he was behind the attack on Prague Castle—at least, not that I could see.

"It is understandable that you are curious." Karl gave me a hardened look. "And I am happy to satisfy your need for answers, so long as your loyalty is to me."

He certainly did not look happy. My earlier concerns resurfaced in my stomach, and I felt it twist into more uncomfortable contortions. Had I just risked Karl's favor, in order to find out about Ferdy?

"Of course my loyalty is to you," I lied. "I did not mean to cause trouble. What a burden you must bear over this. After all, you are an honorable man."

If my flattery was excessive, Karl did not seem to notice. He took my pity in stride, only nodding. "Thank you. Ferdinand has long been a thorn in my side. Maybe it is good you know about him. There are not many I can admit my frustrations to when it comes to him."

"If he is as deplorable as you say, I can certainly sympathize."

"It is not just his personal choices, Ella. It is his whole approach to life. When one is blessed with privilege and opportunity, one is responsible for the betterment of other people."

THE ORDER OF THE CRYSTAL DAGGERS

At his remark, I was intrigued enough to risk a daring question. "Even if the people don't want it?"

"Of course," Karl said. "It is the best way to ensure only good choices are made. When there are too many options, a man chooses whatever one benefits himself first. What of others? Ferdinand believes that freedom matters more than order, nobility, and education. His own choices in these matters have led to his life of chaos, a disregard for the Bohemian aristocracy, and a disdain for the knowledge found in the best universities."

He sighed. "It is better that those who know best lead the way, even if compulsion is necessary. This is the only way for civilization to progress."

As Karl stood there, I felt a little afraid of him. He was a proud man, and he would not take being found a fool lightly. I did not know how he would react in discovering I was attempting to use him to find connections between several recent murders and an ongoing political coup.

It would be even worse when he realized I was in love with his brother.

"Here is the tea, Eleanora," Lady Penelope called, entering the room with Jaqueline close behind her. Thankfully, Karl quickly resumed his respectful demeanor.

"Thank you, Grandmother," I called, straightening up against the couch. "Would you like a cup, too, Karl—I mean, Mr. Marcelin?"

I gave him a sheepish look as I said his name. It was proof enough that I was becoming closer to him. He gave me a small smile before he shook his head. Behind me, Lady POW frowned. She seemed to understand I did not find out anything relating to our mission.

It was hard to feel bad about that. I did want to find a way to trap Lord Maximillian. We needed to understand his role and Karl was our best lead. But just as Karl felt some relief in confiding to me the truth, however reluctantly, I was pleased to hear Ferdy was alive and well, even if he was annoying his brother.

"I must decline for now, Madame. I believe I must be going. I have numerous meetings to attend today, some of which I have forgotten. But I would love to call upon you in the near future." Karl's hand tightened in mine almost painfully, and I knew he was looking for reassurance from me that I would receive him again.

I gave him a brilliant but false smile back. "I would certainly hope so."

"Would you be well enough to attend a concert this week, my lady?"

I glanced over at Lady POW, looking for her permission. I already knew she would want me to go, but I was still disappointed when she nodded her approval.

"A concert would be lovely, though I regret we will not be able to dance." I gave him a small, modest smile. "It would be an honor to join you, sir."

"Thank you. I will send out the formal invitations after the arrangements are made," Karl promised before he turned to Lady Penelope. "A pleasure, as always, Madame."

"I will see you out," Lady Penelope offered.

Jaqueline handed me a cup of tea as Karl gave me one last lingering gaze. I smiled brightly at him as he left, pretending to believe a lifetime of bliss was before us.

The bliss only came when he was gone.

"Well, miss?" Jaqueline asked. Her eyes, a light mix of green and brown, glittered with excitement. "Were you able to find out his secrets?"

THE ORDER OF THE CRYSTAL DAGGERS

"No," I said, thinking of Karl briefly before turning my thoughts to Ferdy. "But I at least had him admit to a few of them."

Lady Penelope poured her own cup of tea. "Well, then, tell me what you learned. I hope you didn't disappoint me."

I sipped my tea carefully, hiding a snort of laughter. I was already a disappointment. While I wanted to redeem myself to Lady POW, I knew I could not do it at the expense of Ferdy's safety, and I was not willing to lose Ben over it.

I stirred the spoon in my tea slowly. I decided I could keep Lady Penelope distracted while I tried to fix everything.

So I gave her a short summary of what had transpired between Karl and me—leaving out any mention of Ferdy. At the end, I was surprised to see Lady Penelope smile.

"Excellent," she said. "We can expect to see him more in the near future. And in the meantime, he sounds like he genuinely likes you."

"He barely knows me."

"He knows about Ben," Lady Penelope pointed out. "And there is no telling what Teresa Marie might have told him. Nobody can give you information like a scorned rival."

"That still doesn't mean much." I sniffed, thinking of Lady Teresa Marie, Lord Maximillian's spoiled daughter. It was not hard to picture her, shaking her amber locks back from her young face.

One of the conditions of Karl getting financial support from Lord Maximillian had been agreeing to marry her. Karl was not interested in that, even though he wanted the support for the Minister-President position. Lady Teresa Marie, who had been previously set up to marry Alex, was not happy the secret heir to the Bohemian throne had turned her down.

THE ORDER OF THE CRYSTAL DAGGERS

She was especially not happy he had snubbed her in favor of me, especially since I was Lady Cecilia's stepdaughter and former servant.

"Ben is not a dark secret of our family," I said. "There's a perfectly good reason he is not moving in Society. He has chosen to stay away because of his leg. And he seems to be good at working for the Order."

"Amir has been doing well with him."

I was glad to hear her compliment both Amir and Ben. My brother's progress meant a lot to him, and it was nice to see Lady POW held Amir in high esteem, even if they could not entirely trust each other.

"One hopes," Lady Penelope murmured, "that you will one day do as well with Harshad."

I nearly dropped my tea, cut deeply at her sudden derision.

She excused herself before I could say anything in return.

As she marched away from me, I glared at her back, hoping she would be able to feel my displeasure. "One hopes that one day I will be able to prove you wrong," I muttered, knowing she was unable to hear me.

126

THE ORDER OF THE CRYSTAL DAGGERS

8

◊

The rest of the week passed uneventfully, as if it was allowing me time to recover from Karl's visit. After he left, I did not think much of anything again, allowing myself to fall into a daily routine of working instead of waiting. Ben was still avoiding me, Amir was never around, and Harshad was his usual quiet self. Lady Penelope was moody and distant, and I did not know whether I preferred her that way or not.

Days later, I was lying on my bed, staring up at the ceiling, when I finally decided I had waited long enough.

Previously, after working with Ben and Harshad, I would retire to my room, throw myself onto my pillows, and allow rest to come. My body screamed for relief, and sleep was usually kind enough to answer it at the end of each day.

Until now.

There was a sadness inside of me, one I both recognized and did not recognize. I could have blamed Karl for my troubles, but I decided more responsibility belonged to Lady POW. She had interrupted my session with Harshad earlier, barging into the room only to announce Karl's formal invitation had arrived.

"Karl Marcelin has sent a personal invitation for you," Lady Penelope told me. "He requests your attendance at a concert at the *Stavovské divadlo* tomorrow night."

"Why is it such big news?" I asked, using her arrival as an excuse to catch my breath—for all the good it did. As if he knew, Harshad motioned for me to finish the various fighting sequences before giving Lady Penelope my full attention. "He said he was going to send out an invitation."

"That was *two days* ago." She emphasized the words carefully and slowly, as if I was struggling to learn a new language or understand basic arithmetic.

When I frowned and kept punching the bag in front of me, she only sighed.

"You still don't know much about Society, do you?" Lady POW shook her head. "If his interest in you wanes, we will have a harder time finding information. There is also the matter of your reputation."

I stopped moving as Harshad gave me a nod of approval. I was finished with his assigned work. "I don't care about that."

"You might want to. The *Stavovské divadlo*, the Estates Theatre, is hosting a special concert to celebrate the new year. If Karl shows up with you, especially for your triumphant return to Society, he will be showing the people that Prague can return from disaster. He will be seen as an inspiration, and he can use that to transform into a leader."

"I think you are giving him too much credit. I can't imagine why that would be inspiring." I wiped the dripping sweat off my forehead with the leather of my stealth habit's small skirt. "But it will be nice to get out of the manor."

Even if I have to join Karl for the evening.

"I will send out your acceptance and get Marguerite to prepare your dress at once," Lady Penelope said, already skipping out the door.

Once she was gone, Ben snorted. "She sure can be frustrating at times."

"I know." I gave Ben a smile, but he ignored me and went back to working on another round of fighting sequences. I looked over at Harshad.

He wore his usual unreadable face, the stoic expression more enigmatic than ever as he turned away from me, looking toward the window. Harshad was content to ignore Lady Penelope, and at the time, I wished I could, too.

Hours had passed since then, but my sadness only increased. I glanced over at the drawer where Ferdy's combs and my parents' heirlooms were tucked away.

I missed him.

I missed all of them.

My life was very different from the previous year. Last Christmas, Ben and I had been ordered to help Cecilia prepare for an extravagant dinner for several of our rich neighbors. I was certain that, while she believed Alex's marriage arrangements were settled, she was hoping to find someone for Prissy to marry, too.

At the last moment, a large winter storm had come over the area, and no one was able to come. Rather than allow the staff to celebrate the holidays, we were ordered to throw out the food and stay in our rooms.

But despite Cecilia's anger, Betsy and Mavis, my closest friends, had made little gifts for me and Ben. We celebrated together in the barn. It was freezing but huddled around the fire, we were content. Ben and I took turns reading from the books I had pilfered from the library, and Betsy, at Ben's prodding, brought us food she had saved from being thrown out.

This year, Betsy and Mavis were gone, Ben was ignoring me, and I spent my free time working with Harshad and pretending to read. I barely noticed the cold winter days as snow began to fall and accumulate.

I am alone.

129

THE ORDER OF THE CRYSTAL DAGGERS

I wondered, briefly, what Ferdy would think of me if he saw me at that moment. At the thought of his gloating, or more likely the thought of his sympathy, I sat up.

There was no reason I had to lie here and wait for things to happen, I decided. It was time to go and make things right, starting with Ben.

Squaring my shoulders, I made my way out of my room and headed toward Ben's. My brother had ignored me for long enough. I had apologized and given him some time alone, and he was still begrudgingly diffident.

Thankfully, we had a mission, just as Amir and Lady POW did, and if he would not reconcile with me in one area of our lives, he would still work with me on another. I could certainly force him using that leverage.

Still, I said a silent, desperate prayer as I knocked on his door.

"I'm coming!" he called enthusiastically.

I was about to tell him it was me when he opened the door. His excitement faded at once. "What are you doing here?"

"Who did you expect?" I pushed past him, walking into the room.

Before I could press for an answer, Ben groaned.

"Why are you here?"

I gave him my best smile. "I have a favor to ask of you, *brácha.*"

"My answer is no."

"I didn't even tell you what I wanted," I objected.

"I know you, Nora. I'm not helping you go see Ferdy." He crossed his arms. He narrowed his eyes at me; his black eye, still slightly puffy, made his acerbic expression more comical than aggravating. "I'm a cripple, not your caretaker."

"You're both," I snapped back before I remembered I was here to make amends. I did not appreciate his attitude, but we were not going to be able to get along if I reciprocated.

"I'm sorry." I took a deep breath. "I came here to say I'm sorry, about everything. I was upset the other week, and you were right. I still … I still don't want to think about Ferdy."

"Then why do you want to go see him?" Ben asked.

"I'm not here to go see him. I wanted to go to the Cabal. I thought if we can go see Clavan and Eliezer, we might be able to find a lead on where Cecilia and everyone else is."

"I've already been there a few times. I didn't learn anything. Why don't you go with Amir, since you're his favorite now?"

"His favorite?" I paused for a moment, and then I shook my head. "That's not true, and Amir is friends with both of us. Even if it was true, that has nothing to do with this."

"So you say." Ben rolled his eyes. "Either way, I'm not going with you."

"It's been a few weeks," I pressed. "Surely there's something new for us to find. Come on, please? I'm tired of just training. You've been able to see our friends there and I haven't, and we do need to find out what we can. Even if we don't find anything, we can at least say we tried."

There was a long minute of silence before Ben softened and sighed, ever so slightly. "Harshad will be upset if we are tired in the morning."

"Maybe Clavan can give us some tea to take home." I smiled brightly. "I know you want to find Betsy and Mavis as much as I do. I'm worried, especially since they disappeared with Alex. There is no telling what happened to them with him around."

"That is true. I haven't thought about what might have happened to Alex." He shook his head. "I'll go with you, but you have to follow my lead. If we do run into Ferdy while we're out, I don't want you causing trouble."

"Me?" I laughed. "You were the one who looked like you wanted to kill him the other day."

"He hurt you."

Ben's voice was conflicted, and I paused. All of my life, my brother had been the one to protect me. Even though I knew he was angry at me, I knew he would have felt responsible for my pain—even if it had nothing to do with him and everything to do with a roguish prince.

"That doesn't matter now," I said quietly. "Betsy and Mavis, Tulia, and the others all need our help. And as for Ferdy … I don't think we will have to worry about him at the Cabal."

"Why?" Ben asked.

Amir had warned me Lady POW was pressuring Ben for my secrets, but it would have been amusing to tell him that Ferdy was Karl's younger brother, playing the part of the good prince with his family for the holidays, instead of running around Prague dressed like a pauper. I could picture Ben's reaction—the initial shock, the eventual anger, and then the list of questions I would not be able to answer.

The thought of those questions, and the certainty of my complete humiliation, prevented me from saying anything.

Instead, I turned toward a window. "It's cold outside. He's probably not going to be walking out in the winter this late at night."

Ben's gaze followed mine, where the ground was still sprinkled with a small layer of white powder. "You have a point, but you could just as easily be wrong. What if we do run into him?"

If Ferdy did dare to show his face to me, knowing my heart was tender and my mission was dangerous, I would likely kill him out of frustration. I might have wanted him, but I still wanted him to be safe more.

I did not tell Ben what I was thinking. Instead, I shrugged. "Thanks to all of Harshad's training, I can take care of him."

When Ben laughed, even though it was a small one, I knew I had won.

"I don't want to tell Lady POW about this," I added, as Ben reached for his shoes.

"You might as well tell her," Ben said. "She finds things out anyway. Remember how she caught us coming back from the Cabal last time?"

"I know, but she's got secrets of her own. I should be entitled to a few myself." I reached out and took his hand. "And, for now, Ferdy is one of them. I don't want her to know about him."

"What happened with him, exactly?" Ben asked. "I know you saw him at the castle."

"He knows about the Order," I said. That was the truth.

"And?"

"And he did not want anything to do with me after that."

That was a lie. My mind taunted me with the memory of Ferdy's embrace, the beautiful horror of our fiery passion, a self-sentenced penance far worse than any I could have been given.

Once we made it to the stables, I watched as Ben made a few adjustments on his brace. "Is that new?"

"Yes." Ben did not look at me. "After it broke the other day, I decided to try out a few ideas to help with our new activities. See? I added some padding at the joints to help with the clacking sound, and it fits inside my boot better."

"Can you ride using it?"

"I can, but since we're going to go into the city tonight, we should walk."

"Walk? It's going to take more than an hour to do that," I groaned.

"Lady POW is more likely to notice we are gone if there's a horse missing," Ben said. "And Dox is getting old. Let him rest."

"He's not that old. *Táta* bought him the summer before *Máma* died," I remembered. "He called him 'Dox,' for doxology since it was a miracle he had gotten such a good price on a horse in his prime."

"That was fifteen years ago. See? He is old."

I said nothing in reply. Although Ben was right, even though I was attempting to get along with him, I did not want to give him more accolades than he needed.

"*Otec* did always have a strange way with names," Ben added, almost as if he sensed my reluctant concession. "'Benedict' was short for 'benediction.'"

"It seems to be appropriate, on both accounts."

Ben brushed off my teasing. "Well, I suppose it's a miracle now that Dox has managed to survive this long."

"We survived, too," I reminded Ben gently. If I had been younger, I might have reached over and hugged him in comfort. As it was, I was still tempted to reach for him.

THE ORDER OF THE CRYSTAL DAGGERS

Instead, I buried myself into my cloak, already blistering against the chill as we made our way toward the heart of Prague.

The city was not far from our home. Riding in the carriage or up on Dox, I could cross the Vltava within thirty minutes, and that usually included a stop at Tulia's cottage. We passed by her former home, and I could still see a few of the remaining walls. The fire had devoured the small house weeks before, and now the snow covered a good portion of the scorched wood.

In the background, Prague's city skyline glowed with lamplight from within and moonlight from without. From where we were, I could not see the broken, collapsed castle walls, nor could I hear the city's chatter.

As I studied the castle walls, I saw a few rooms lit up with light, and I wondered if Ferdy was there. Karl was staying there, too, I recalled, and I chuckled at the thought of them forced to dine together. I knew it was wrong to laugh at another's misery, but if I could find no joy in my own despair, laughing at someone else's did not seem so unnatural.

"What is it?" Ben asked. "What is so amusing?"

"Oh … I was thinking of Karl," I said, scrambling to think of something else. "He said he was staying at the castle. I thought … I was thinking it would be amusing if we just kidnapped him."

"We could do that." Ben's tone was serious as he considered my jest. "You know him, so we would be able to get close enough. If he is there without Lord Maximillian, he would not be able to call for help. And we could likely get around the guards. King Ferdinand already knows about the Order."

"I do know that Empress Maria Anna trusts me, at least enough she did not tell Karl about me," I added. Philip had told me that before, and Lady Penelope confirmed it. "You know, she trusted *Máma*, too, during the Revolution."

"Did she?"

"*Máma* was the one who protected her, along with *Táta*." I glanced back at the castle, thinking of Karl. "She was pregnant at the time."

"Well, I was born just after the Revolution," Ben said.

"I meant the Empress, not *Máma*."

"Well, she was pregnant, because I was born just before 1849." Ben shrugged. "I guess they were both pregnant at the same time."

It was strange to think that. I had never thought about it before, but Ben was right. My mother and the former empress had both been pregnant at the same time.

Maybe that was the real reason they were able to trust each other, I thought. There had to be something to motherhood that bound women together, the same way that my life was connected to Karl and Ferdy, in that I could understand the uniqueness of a sibling's love, or the lack thereof.

"Ben?" My voice dropped to a whisper, as though I knew it was treachery to even think such a thing. "Do you think we made the right decision to join the Order?"

"Of course." Ben's answer was immediate and certain, and I could not stop myself from envying him. He had all of his doubts answered at the beginning.

"Why do you ask that?" Ben pressed, stepping closer to me as we crossed the Vltava, heading toward the Jewish Quarter where the Cabal was located. "Don't you like it?"

"Well, I've failed at it," I said. "And … what about *Táta*? He was poisoned with the Order's secret weapon. Who could have done that, other than a member of the Order?"

THE ORDER OF THE CRYSTAL DAGGERS

"There are always traitors on every side."

His answer did not give me comfort. It sounded too much like a scripted answer, something he had overheard and decided to believe until a better theory or certain proof came along.

"I've been thinking … maybe we should find out what happened when *Máma* was here before," I said. "I know Lady POW does not want to talk about it, but she says she knows that our father's murder and the current political coup are related."

Ben sighed, his steps slowing down as we came up to the entrance of the Cabal. "I don't know, Nora. If Lady POW does not want to reach out to the League, she likely has a good reason."

"Amir and Harshad are both part of the League, as is Lady Penelope herself," I pointed out.

"She would know firsthand how treacherous some of the members are then."

"Stop making excuses for her. We should learn about that ourselves. And besides, if Lady POW is keeping secrets, she might be lying to us as well."

"She's been a good leader so far. What could she be lying about?"

"Plenty. She's a woman who puts business before family, remember?" I bit my lip, not sure what else I could say. Ben's disinterest made me worry that I could not trust him with my doubts, and as much as I knew it was true, I hated to think that I was right to keep Ferdy's secrets from him, too.

"Maybe we can learn some things about the past when we get back," Ben said, clearly conflicted. I saw him avoid my gaze as I looked over at him. "But first, we are here to look for Betsy and Mavis."

THE ORDER OF THE CRYSTAL DAGGERS

I sighed. He was right about that. We could worry about multiple things at one time, but we could only do one thing at a time, too.

"I feel so useless sometimes, Ben," I confessed. "There is so much evil in the world, so many questions that will always be unanswered. And there are so many other people who don't seem to care."

He gave me a scrutinizing look. "Do you want to quit the Order?"

I bristled, feeling like he had missed my point. "*Máma* did."

And she kept her own mother from learning about us, too—maybe to protect us.

Philip said before that Ferdy had been kept a secret from the Order and the others who protected the king during the Revolution. Was it possible that in joining the Order, while I was able to learn more about my mother and who she truly was, I was actually working against her wishes?

"Nora." Ben tugged on my cloak. "We can't leave the Order now. There are people we need to save."

Even if I did not feel good about it, I knew Ben was right. I could almost hear Harshad's voice inside my head, telling me to focus. We were here to find information on Betsy and Mavis, and the rest of our former household.

I did not have time for doubts.

But ... but there would likely *always* be people to save, countries to help, maybe even rulers to protect.

"I don't know if we will ever be able to leave," I whispered. "Do you think we can?"

"Why would you want to?" Ben said. When I only shrugged, he sighed. "Leaving is one thing that Lady POW never did mention to us. We know she has been doing this for decades now. I suppose it's possible she doesn't know how to quit herself."

That was a distinct possibility, I thought. Lady POW did not seem to give up, and she would see quitting as giving up.

We fell into silence, as the Cabal came into sight.

It was time to see if we could find some answers to my many questions. I straightened my shoulders, determined to remain hopeful.

THE ORDER OF THE CRYSTAL DAGGERS

9

◊

The Cabal seemed different as Ben and I entered. Last time, the warmth of the atmosphere had leaped out to greet me, to pull me in and absorb me into its setting. This time, I felt more like a stranger, as though I had walked into the wrong building by mistake.

It was mostly empty, like it had been the day Tulia and I visited for the first time, and I could not stop myself from wondering if I had imagined it differently with Ferdy by my side.

The long, wooden bar at the back of the room was polished to a shine. Several tables cluttered the room in front of it, while a few large chairs were arranged in front of a fireplace. The embers burned low, already spent from the cold weather; I saw the small fires blink at me from among the soot, like demon eyes pulled out of the past.

Ben hesitated more than once as we made our way through the pub. My stomach briefly clenched, wondering if it was possible Ferdy would come. I could easily see him stealing away to see Clavan and his other friends, breaking away from his time at the castle with his family.

But as I walked closer to the bar, I knew Ferdy was nowhere to be found; his absence was as noticeable and as tangible as his presence.

"Ben." A familiar voice, coupled with a cloud of pipe smoke, called out in greeting from the far end of the room.

"Jarl." My brother instantly cheered. We shuffled over to his table, where I could see he was reading a book and sipping from a glass of beer. With his smoker's coat and a pair of thick, half-moon spectacles perched on his nose, Jarl looked much older than me and Ben, even though he was in his late twenties.

"I cannot tell you how delighted I am to see you," Jarl said. "Faye is working with her mother, and Clavan is seeing to the business side of things tonight."

"There are not a lot of people here," I said.

"Which is good for me, and possibly bad for you." Jarl stood politely, giving Ben a nod.

I glanced around. There was a priest reading his Bible alone, and a pair of travelers who settled into a corner at the far end of the bar.

One of them caught my gaze and gave me a brilliant smile. He was wearing a greatcoat, while his bright blonde hair, curled and styled high, twinkled under the bar lights. I was first embarrassed at the exchange, and Ben, seeing my discomfort, stepped between us. But when Ben turned his full attention to Jarl, I saw the man's piercing green eyes settle and stay on me.

I tried to shake off the ominous feeling of being watched. It was only when Jarl pulled out my chair that I managed to forget about the man at the bar.

"Thank you for joining me," Jarl said.

"Of course." Ben gave him a friendly clap on the shoulder before he took his seat. "I know you enjoy having an audience, and the options are limited tonight."

"Usually Ferdy helps me out in that regard, but he hasn't been here for a few days."

At Ferdy's name, spoken so casually, my world broke. My previous embarrassment shifted into something more morose; I felt the fear of upcoming mortification, the terror of a confrontation I did not want, and the fervent wish for a divine reprieve.

THE ORDER OF THE CRYSTAL DAGGERS

"Where is he?" Ben gripped his hands together, and I could hear him cracking his knuckles. I frowned at him, hoping he would calm down. I did not want to make a scene, and this was the wrong place for Ben and me to hold a rematch to our earlier battle with Harshad.

"He frequents the Cabal but goes missing from time to time." Jarl took off his glasses and tucked them into a pocket on the front of his coat. "But since you're here, I can assume he is coming? He owes me some money from our last bet."

I shook my head. "I haven't seen him lately, either. My apologies."

Jarl waved away my regret. "If I didn't know he was good for it, I'd hunt him down. But no matter. Now, keep me from perishing from boredom. Tell me of the excitement around town. Working as much as I do, you always hear the good gossip last."

"We are quite bored ourselves," I said. "We were hoping Clavan and Eliezer would be here."

"Clavan's in the back, and Elie might be here later. My Uncle Rhys came into town, and the two of them can talk for days, if they can find the time, and I know Elie would be quick to do just that. Zipporah's been keeping Elie busy with all the babies she's been tending to of late."

"Zipporah?"

"Elie's wife is a midwife." Jarl took a long puff from his pipe before grinning. "I'm surprised you didn't know. Eliezer repeats it quite frequently during our meetings. I think he wants to remind us that at some point in our lives, the difference between life and death might come down to how nicely we've treated him over the years."

I had heard that before, I realized. But it was not because of Eliezer; Clavan was the one who had mentioned it. Eliezer's wife had worked with Dr. Artha before.

THE ORDER OF THE CRYSTAL DAGGERS

Inspiration struck. "Has she seen a lot more patients because of Dr. Artha's death earlier this year?" I asked.

Ben glanced over at me in surprise, while Jarl merely nodded. "I don't imagine it is much different. They worked well together, but some patients do not want to be tended to by a Jewess. She is more than a midwife, working with herbs and other medicines."

"That reminds me," Ben spoke up. His voice had an eager tone to it, one I shared as much as I recognized. "I need to buy some special herbs for our companion, Tulia."

"Zipporah's likely got it," Jarl said. He chuckled. "She has everything. Ferdy's been looking for better pipe tobacco for me for weeks, trying to prove she doesn't have better connections than he does."

"Did he prove himself the victor in that bet?" I asked, unable to stop myself.

Laughing, Jarl blew out a stream of smoke thick enough I had to swallow back a cough. "Honestly, I'm not keeping score. He gives me plenty for free, while Eliezer insists Zipporah keeps raising her prices so I will stop smoking in here. He insists it is not kosher and I only laugh at him, knowing Clavan would easily smoke one along with me."

"Would she happen to be around?" Ben asked, drawing the focus back to our mission. "I'd love to see about buying some of her stock."

"She only comes in here every once in a while, but Clavan can always send word if you need an order filled."

At that moment, the door behind the bar opened. A bald man came out, carrying a pair of cups in each hand. The light reflected off his head and the small pair of rimmed glasses precariously balanced on his slightly crooked nose. He smiled in greeting as he made his way to our table.

THE ORDER OF THE CRYSTAL DAGGERS

"My ears are burning more than my eyes, so I am not surprised to hear my name, and I am especially not surprised to find it coming out of this knucklehead," Clavan said, nodding his regards to Jarl. "What lies is he spreading about me now?"

Ben and I laughed congenially as Jarl and Clavan chatted, exchanging barbs and insults with the familiarity of a close-knit family. Their easy conversation reminded me of Ferdy even more. It was not until Jarl mentioned him again that I remembered I was supposed to forget about him.

"Ella's wondering where Ferdy has been lately," Jarl said.

Clavan turned and glanced at Ben. Before he could say anything, Ben shook his head.

"She doesn't want to talk about Ferdy," Ben insisted. A second later, he winced as I stomped on his foot. With Harshad's training, I knew it had to hurt, but he really did not need to announce to everyone that I was upset.

"I'd much rather talk about the local gossip," I declared, struggling to put on a brave face. "What news can you tell us? Are any important things happening? Any more murders?"

"The weather has slowed the trickle of news somewhat," Clavan said, giving me a smirk as he adjusted his glasses. "Surely you can't be so bored that you want to hear about murder, Lady Ella?"

I ignored his question. "Were you able to find the man who murdered Dr. Artha, Mr. Clavan?"

He stared at me for a few seconds, likely weighing out whether or not I should be indulged. But he relaxed a moment later with a shrug. "No."

At his solemn expression, I felt a rush of shame at my insensitivity. Dr. Artha had known my father, just as he had known Clavan. I remembered Dr. Artha as a decent man, and even if I was uncomfortable at my own loss, I did not have a right to cause further despair. "I'm sorry. I was hoping for better news."

"He was a good man, and he made peace with God and his life," Clavan said. "There is no better news than that."

"It would be better knowing justice has been done," Ben said.

"Better for us, maybe, but not much different for Sigmund." Jarl puffed his pipe a few more times with a tepid smile.

We dipped into a remorseful silence. Ben took a sip of the drink Clavan had brought him, and I just stared at the table top, briefly noting the title of Jarl's book. From the small amount of German I knew, I saw it was *The Evils of Revolution*.

If revolution was evil, I thought, it was good to prevent it as much as possible.

I glanced back at Clavan. "Jarl mentioned that your friend's wife sells herbs and medicine. Do you know if she is around? My companion, Tulia, is in need of some for her health."

I did not like lying to Clavan. He turned to me with that ageless look on his face, the one that made me wonder if he could listen to my mind as well as speak to my most ardent desires.

"She is not here right now, but I can arrange an introduction for you. If you leave me your direction, I will send word when I can to you."

"That would be wonderful."

"Do you know what you need? I can give her a list. Sickness waits for no one in this world." Clavan pulled out his glasses and put them on, the small round frames adding a touch of whimsy to his character.

THE ORDER OF THE CRYSTAL DAGGERS

Ben began rambling off a varied list, starting with sage and rosemary. He slipped the silver thallis in along with thyme and nutmeg and cinnamon.

Clavan paused as he wrote. He said nothing until he was done, and then he looked over at Ben's eye. "She should have all of this. None of this is because of your fight, is it?"

"No." Ben's reply was too quick. When I looked over at him, concerned, Clavan only laughed.

"I know Ferdy suffered some damage, too," he said. "Elie told me he came by his house and interrupted their Hanukkah celebration after you were finished with him."

"Fight?" I repeated.

Ben groaned, and at once, everything became clear: Ben had gone into the city, found Ferdy, and they ended up fighting.

I grabbed Ben's arm and hauled him up out of his chair. "Excuse us," I said, my teeth ground together forcefully as I struggled to maintain my manners. I pinched Ben's arm to keep him from saying anything. He likely already knew I would refuse to let him escape my anger, whether we left or not. "I do believe we must be going now. I will look for your note."

I did not wait for Clavan and Jarl to extend their own well-wishes or wave goodbye, but as I passed by the bar, the man with the green eyes spoke to me.

"I'd go easy on him, *chérie*. Why, Society would be horrified to see a temper such as yours unrestrained."

I whirled around to face him, watching as he laughed. For the first time, I noticed his companion. While Prague held its share of traveling foreigners, I had only ever seen a few dark-skinned men before, and I faltered at the sight of them together.

THE ORDER OF THE CRYSTAL DAGGERS

"Oh, dear, I do believe you've shocked her, Didier." The man with the green eyes shook his head, still smirking. "No need to worry, *chérie*, we are just strangers in town having a bit of fun. I mean, of course we are having fun at your expense now, but still, we are quite harmless, I can assure you. You can run along home in peace."

At his teasing, Ben shuffled free of my grip. "Don't talk to my sister."

The man cheered even further at his new audience. "You're a gem of a brother, I'm sure, and a handsome one at that. But you need not worry about me, good sir. If anything, I was on your side, was I not? I'd hate to see her beat you. Women with incorrigible tempers are such nasty creatures, aren't they, Didier?"

The man beside him gave him a disapproving look, and I took the moment of silence to grab Ben's arm again. I tugged him out of the Cabal.

The men had disrupted my anger, but the minute Ben and I were outside, I felt it return in full force.

"What was that all about?"

"I don't know," Ben said. "I've never noticed that man before."

"I'm not talking about him!" I put my hands on my hips. "And you know it. Why did you attack Ferdy?"

"That's none of your business."

"Of course it's my business!"

"It's my job to take care of you, whether you like it or not. That's why I stood up to that obnoxious man in there for you, too."

"It's *my* job to take care of myself."

"Please. You couldn't even fight me before. At the mere mention of Ferdy, you lost."

I glared at him. "So you went to take care of him for me?"

"Yes." Ben returned my glare with one of his own, one without any hint of remorse. "Sort of. I didn't know I would run into him."

I turned away and started walking back home, struggling to keep my voice down. "I can't believe you did that. I wish you would've just left him alone. I didn't want you to hurt him!"

A new thought struck me hard and fast. What if Ben had hurt Ferdy, and that was why he had stayed away from the Cabal? *How can Ferdy ever forgive me for this?*

"He hurt you," Ben said.

"Well, now you've hurt me, too, all because you stuck your nose in my business where it doesn't belong," I snapped. "I didn't want you to bother with him at all. Now he probably hates me."

"What does that matter? You told me he hated you before, because of the Order."

My cheeks flushed red. "No, he didn't. Oh, goodness. Did he say something to you? What did you tell him?"

The thought of Ferdy admitting the truth terrified me. I did not want him to be in danger, and I did not want the former empress to lose her faith in me. I was supposed to be protecting him, and thanks to my brother, I had failed once more to do my duty.

"Tell me what he said!" I gripped Ben's collar hard, astonished at the sudden rush accompanying my strength and fury.

"Oh, now you want to fight me?" Ben shook his head.

"I will," I warned. "I will, and I won't stop until you tell me everything."

Ben and I stared down at each other for a long moment, and I felt the world crumble between us. If my mother had been my sunshine, and my father the earth, Ben was my moon, and I felt darkness fully overtake me in that moment.

Lady Penelope was right. She was right. I can't believe she was right.

Ben had failed me. He had failed me, and I had never seen it coming.

I stepped back from him, shaking my head. "I can't believe this."

Behind me, Ben shrugged. "If you must know, and I suppose you must, he didn't say anything useful. He commended me on being a good brother. Even after we fought, he tried to make nice with me. He said he never meant to hurt you, but that's what anyone would say after a fight."

I did not think Ferdy would tell Ben the truth; it was good to hear it confirmed, even if I still hated Ben's role in the whole situation.

"If you want to be a good brother," I said, "just stay away from him from now on."

"Why do you even care? Ferdy doesn't care about you."

Ben's words were soft but angry. I gave him the only answer I could.

"It doesn't matter what I feel. He knows about the Order, Ben, and scuffling with him in the back of an alley is not going to make him stay quiet. If we want him to keep our secret, it's best to leave him alone. Don't tell me you didn't think of that."

Ben said nothing, and I scoffed. "You didn't think anything through at all, did you?"

"I'm not the only one with weaknesses," Ben shot back.

I crossed my arms over my chest. "I'll work on mine by myself, and you can work on yours alone, too."

We fell into a bitter silence as we made our way home. The journey back seemed so much longer and harder. There was much less of a chill in the air, or maybe I had grown accustomed to it. It was also possible that I was just numb from everything. That I was too afraid to let myself feel anything.

It was only when I fell back onto my bed that I allowed myself the freedom to cry, to let the tidal waves of my loneliness and sadness flood over me.

THE ORDER OF THE CRYSTAL DAGGERS

152

THE ORDER OF THE CRYSTAL DAGGERS

10

◊

I had been hoping that the trip into the city would close the rift between me and Ben, but it only made it worse. That night, I did not sleep well at all. Getting up for Harshad's training sessions the following morning went against every natural instinct I possessed. Dread crept through me as I made my way down to the parlor.

But when I entered the room, Ben was nowhere to be found. I did not know whether I was more grateful or upset, and if I was upset, I did not know if it was more because of Ben or because of myself.

It was almost as though he suspected my thoughts on the matter, I thought bitterly. Especially since Ben was the one who had been so concerned we would upset Harshad with our late-night outing.

"There you are, Eleanora," Harshad said. True to his usual self, he was sitting at the desk in the corner of the room, working on some notes in a foreign scrawl. "I have been waiting for you."

I studied him, watching as his aged hands moved his pen swiftly across the stationary, transforming his thoughts into symbols I could not decipher any more clearly. With Ben's absence, I had a sudden appreciation for Harshad's consistency. I might have had reservations about him, but I could see why he would stay with someone like Lady POW for so long; he was a man who knew how to dismantle chaos, and it was possible he even looked forward to the job.

Before I could ask Harshad if Ben was out on assignment for Lady POW again, I saw there was a new presence in the parlor.

153

The figure stood in front of the fireplace, wearing a hooded cloak, much like the ones I had seen Harshad and Amir wear when I first met them. Before I could say anything, Harshad looked up from his desk.

"Eleanora, I am pleased to introduce you to another member of the Order."

The hood fell away, revealing another foreign face, this one of a warrior maiden. A looped braid of pure black hair settled on her head before it fell away, hanging down her back. Her slanted eyes were dark, closer to black than brown, as she watched me. It was impossible to guess her age; she seemed timeless, too wise and watchful, too still to be a part of our world.

"This is Xiana," Harshad said. "She is the Order's leading expert on herbs and medicines, as well as one of our best fighters. She has agreed to come here and assist us with our inquiries."

"You make it sound as though I had a choice," Xiana murmured, and I was astounded to see Harshad smile.

"Xiana, this is Miss Eleanora Svobodová, Dezda's daughter." Harshad cleared his throat, quickly wiping away any trace of emotion. "She is our newest member."

Xiana gave me a bow, bending her body forward. She was clearly from the Orient, and I wondered if that was really how they were allowed to address each other. I curtsied in reply. At Xiana's wry smile, I knew I had amused her with my manners.

"A daughter for Eleanor at last, I see, along with her son," Xiana murmured. Her voice was so precise, almost as if it were constrained to each perfect syllable. Her gaze never wavered as she smiled. "How wonderful it was that she was able to keep you."

THE ORDER OF THE CRYSTAL DAGGERS

"I certainly think so," I replied, mustering up a smile at the mention of my mother and Ben.

I saw a glitter of laughter in her gaze. "It is nice to meet you, Eleanora. I am sure I will enjoy teaching you while I am here."

"You're going to be teaching me?" I glanced around the room. "And Ben, too?"

"Benedict has been given a new assignment by Lady Penelope," Harshad said, and I knew at once it was no coincidence that Ben was not here. After we had returned home, Ben went to see Lady Penelope. I could understand why he would ask her to be free from me, but I hated that he had severed more ties between us.

Xiana cleared her throat delicately. "I understand you need a new sparring partner."

"Xiana is a fine tutor," Harshad replied behind me. "She will allow me to help you with some more complicated moves, Eleanora. She will begin to assist us tomorrow since she has only arrived."

"What about Ben?" I asked. "Will I still have to fight him? What is he supposed to do now?"

"Lady Penelope has reassigned him, and that is all you need to know for now," Harshad said.

"Why?"

Harshad's brow furrowed in irritation, but he answered me nonetheless. "Do not forget, we are still looking for Lady Cecilia and the others. Amir has not been able to find any leads in this regard."

"Amir? Amir Qureshi?" Xiana asked.

Harshad and I both turned to see the startled look appear briefly on her face.

THE ORDER OF THE CRYSTAL DAGGERS

"Yes," Harshad answered. "Yes, Amir Qureshi. He will be glad to see you again. I am surprised he is not here already."

The point of her chin jutted out a second later. "I did not realize he was here, too. It has been many years since I have last seen him," she murmured, her tone shifting toward apologetic.

I remembered Amir's story from before. *So this is Xiana, the woman who helped my mother save him from his family.*

Amir had spoken of Xiana highly, especially her expertise with herbs and plants, and I told her so.

She nodded once, firmly. "It is good to hear he remembers me."

"We will get reacquainted in good time," Harshad said. "Eleanora is working on the basics of fighting."

"Not that I've mastered them, of course." It was better that I told her the truth than allow him to, I thought.

"All masters begin the same as the student, and eventually return to their beginnings," Xiana said, coming up beside me. She pushed back her cloak a little, enough to where I could see she was clad in a close-fitted outfit, one with long black pants and sleeves allowing her to blend into the shadows completely. From what I could see, the fabric reminded me of my own stealth habit, only her set was cut differently.

Her mouth curled into a smile as she caught me staring. "I was never very good at fighting in any skirt, even one as short as yours."

"I can understand that," I said. I liked my habit, but I did not think I would ever get used to the thin, short skirt that went down to my knees.

I was just about to ask Xiana more questions when the door opened. Amir slipped inside, clearly arriving from his nightly rounds of collecting and dispersing information in the city. He never faltered as he saw Xiana, but I saw her balance shift ever so slightly.

"Amir."

"Xiana. It is lovely to see you again." Amir gave her a quick but respectful nod. I knew him well enough to know there was nothing in his movements to suggest he was being false. He was glad to see her.

Amir gave me a quick smile. "Are you going to be fighting with Xiana today, Eleanora?"

"We will start tomorrow, as I have only just arrived in Prague." Xiana straightened. "I wonder if she will give me as much of a fight as Naděžda used to?"

I did not pay attention to them too much as they talked; I was too surprised to her Xiana use Amir's name for my mother. She had allowed Harshad to call my mother "Dezda," but she herself had called me Eleanor's daughter. I glanced over at Harshad, remembering what he had taught me about names, and the names people give each other.

At my glance, his mouth hardened into a straight line, one I could not be entirely certain of, but it almost made me smile. Harshad had noticed the change in my mother's names, too, and it seemed as though I was growing in his esteem.

I was glad for that. It was not just physical battles I was supposed to learn how to navigate.

Harshad cleared his throat a moment later, interrupting Xiana as she mentioned her recent trip to Paris. "Amir, would you show Xiana to her quarters? She just arrived this morning and I imagine she is eager to settle in."

"Yes, Master." Xiana gave him another nod and then turned to face me. "It was nice meeting you, Eleanora. I look forward to seeing what you have learned."

When Amir and Xiana were gone, I glanced over at Harshad. He waited for several long moments before he nodded to me.

"Thank you for your patience, Eleanora," he said. "Welcome to your first official day of training."

"What?" My mouth dropped open. "What do you mean? I've been in here working nearly every morning since the Advent Ball."

"You have been learning how to fight, how to protect and prepare yourself," he conceded. "I did not think you would agree to continue for so long and I applaud you for your efforts."

"I don't think I should thank you for that, by the sound of it," I grumbled.

He did not seem to hear me. After all our time working together, he was likely used to ignoring me. "But what I have taught you so far, any street fighter could have. Now that your brother has been reassigned, it is time for us to officially begin."

"Why did you teach me to fight at all, if it was not for real?"

"Because Ben has to learn, and he thrives when faced with a competitor. You were our only option, and indeed, the best option."

"He's been mad at me ever since we began," I said. My cheeks burned, and I struggled to hold back my tears. "You destroyed the trust between us, and on purpose!"

"Of course. Life does this, on a regular basis," Harshad said, his flattened tone somehow much more harrowing than any anger could have been. "You were instructed to find your weaknesses."

"Which is apparently trusting the wrong people, and failing to trust the ones I should," I muttered.

THE ORDER OF THE CRYSTAL DAGGERS

"Trust was already a weakness of yours," Harshad said. "Your parents have both died and you were left with your stepmother to raise you. But she did not do that, did she? She used and abused you and your brother. While Lady Penelope and I are now here, we cannot undo her damage. We can only work you through it, and that is often times more painful."

"Well, what else is my weakness, then?" I put my hands on my hips and frowned. "If you're going to be torturing me to teach me, I might as well be prepared for it."

"You are too stubborn and too easily distracted. You are far more compassionate than you should be. You lie quite a bit, possibly for the wrong reasons. You have trouble with authority, and you are concerned with appearances much more than realities."

He clasped his hands behind his back. "That is just a preliminary list, Eleanora, and as we work on diminishing those, others will appear. It is the nature of things."

I did not know what to say. There were plenty of things I would not argue with him, if only he had been a little nicer about presenting my flaws.

Harshad turned his back toward me. "We will also work on your strengths, if that is any comfort to you. You are a stubborn, curious soul, and that is something we can harness as a strength as much as a weakness."

I wonder what my other strengths are. I tried to think of what else Harshad would say, but recalling that he had just dismissed me as too easily distracted, I tucked the question away for another time. I consoled myself with the knowledge that even if he did tell me my strengths, he would do it in the same backhanded manner Lady POW did.

A new idea popped into my head. Lady Penelope's teachings had worked against her, and I wanted to know if Harshad's had that same capability.

THE ORDER OF THE CRYSTAL DAGGERS

"Harshad?" Despite his teaching, and all the time we had spent together in the recent weeks, his name felt strange coming out of my mouth.

Perhaps that was why he did not reprimand me right away.

"What is it?" he asked.

"What is your weakness?"

He was silent for a long moment, and I was sure he was going to refrain from answering. But then he sighed. "Several of your own," he admitted. "But there are others, too."

I put my hands on my hips, a sinful sense of satisfaction coursing through me. "It is good to know you're not perfect."

"Your mother is one."

At the mention of my mother and his admission, I froze. I had not been expecting him to admit any specific weaknesses, let alone one that seemed so personal.

"Amir says you are curious about her most of all," Harshad said. "Is that true?"

It was suddenly very hard for me to swallow. "Yes," I whispered.

"I thought as much." Harshad's eyes lost their hardened quality, and he seemed much older all of a sudden. "If you do well with your sessions, I will tell you more about her."

I pursed my lips. "Does that mean you'll tell me something about her today?"

"I have already admitted she was a weakness of mine," he reminded me. "That is enough for today, is it not?"

"Well, you said she was a weakness, but you didn't explain how." I crossed my arms over my chest. "That seems like a fair follow-up question."

"Fair, but foul as well."

THE ORDER OF THE CRYSTAL DAGGERS

"Paradoxes are not the same thing as contradictions," I reminded him.

"It is good to see your wit is quite a weapon." Harshad nodded. "But it also shows that I was right. When you want something, you are much more focused."

I blushed, unsure as always if it was a compliment or an insult or even both. Harshad had been merciless in forcing Ben to admit to his hidden resentments and his insecurities, and now I was sure he was going to do the same with me. Harshad was focused, too, and I had to give him credit for it. I saw now that he was willing to do anything to see that I became a better fighter.

He sat down, crossing his legs on the floor. He motioned for me to follow, and I did.

"Why did you join the Order, Eleanora?"

"To help save others," I answered.

Nothing changed on his face, but his tone softened ever so slightly. He closed his eyes and breathed in deeply. "There is more to it than that."

"Well, I wanted to be free from Cecilia," I admitted. "And I thought … my mother …"

My voice trailed off as I thought about my mother. *Máma* had been a beautiful ghost of sorts, a memory never real enough to satisfy me. I wanted to grow up to be a true lady, as she was, and make her proud; I had no idea how to do that. In meeting Lady Penelope, I had been hoping for some way to capture that ghost, to make the memory more real, to resurrect the dead long enough to find my way in life.

How did someone admit to that? How could I put into words that I was on a strange, illogical quest for my mother, looking for approval and acceptance I feared I would never find in anyone else?

"I met Dezda for the first time when she was very small," Harshad said, jolting me out of my introspections. I blinked to see he was watching me intently, and I wondered if he was able to make sense of my own confusion. "Your grandmother was still working with Jakub and his best friend, Louis Valoris, at the time."

"You knew my grandfather, too?"

"I knew him before I met Pepé," he said. "She was his mistress when I met him."

An involuntary blush heated my cheeks and I coughed, choking on air.

Harshad sighed. "You are old enough to not be surprised."

"According to Society, I'm supposed to be horrified," I said. "Surprised is much more mild."

"Society is so strict with youth. And in many ways, I can understand it. So many people suffer needlessly when people are careless. Rules are there for reasons, even if those reasons might seem strange to others. But there are exceptions in every case, and you need to watch for them."

"I've already noticed Lady Penelope makes up her own rules," I said. "You don't need to tell me that."

I was surprised to see the smile on his face. The little lines on either side of his lips tightened together in little batches, wrinkling his face as much as humanizing it.

"Exactly. But that was something she picked up from Jakub, and something that she only enacted when he grew increasingly uncomfortable with her involvement with the Order. She had an aunt who was a member of the Order before her, who ran a brothel in the streets of London. When Pepé's father died, she was sent there to work, learning how to coerce gentlemen into giving up their secrets."

THE ORDER OF THE CRYSTAL DAGGERS

I did not say anything, this time too shocked and horrified. The truth seemed too awful for words, even though I was suddenly very glad Lady POW did not teach me the full curriculum on sexual manipulation. I had a feeling it was even larger than I originally feared.

"Dezda, by Lady Penelope's own words, was a … miscalculation," Harshad continued. "But … But I certainly never saw her as such, and as Her Majesty Queen Victoria took more interest in my work and Pepé became her close acquaintance, I made it my mission to convince Pepé that Dezda was a blessing to us. She was the next generation of our legacy, working for the Crown and helping maintain the order of the world."

The rest of the story's outline fell into place as I listened to him. Amir had told me before that he had met my mother in Agra, in India, when he was on business with his father. They were there with Harshad. Lady Penelope and my mother had come along with him in order to escape Jakub and begin a new life.

Lady Penelope had been irrevocably disillusioned with men and relationships, and as proud as she was, she would not allow Harshad to rescue her from her disappointments. My mother might have been repulsed by Amir at first, but when she fell in love with him, she found there was nothing she wanted more.

Well, almost nothing, I recalled. *Máma* wanted her freedom, and she wanted a family of her own.

"Do you know why I am telling you this, Eleanora?" Harshad's voice, always so strict and brusque, was almost calming.

I shook my head. "No."

THE ORDER OF THE CRYSTAL DAGGERS

"I have two reasons for doing so. The first is practical in our lesson. Your mother is the key to your focus. I was hoping she could also lend some help with your balance."

"I'm not sure how learning about her would help with balance."

"Balance must be inward as much as outward," Harshad explained. "There are too many lies and too many secrets that surround us."

"You could just get Lady POW to admit to her secrets," I pointed out. "That would help."

"That is the second reason for my explanation. Secrets are different from lies," Harshad said. "When we lie, that is when we inflict damage to ourselves and others. Secrets, even the ones we keep from ourselves, sometimes protect us as much as they can hurt us. It is much harder to calculate the risk when it comes to secrets."

"But they hurt others, too," I said. "Just look at Lord Maximillian and Karl. And even Tulia, too. She kept me and Ben a secret from Lady Penelope for all these years. We have a duty to find out the truth."

"Sharing secrets is a sign of trust," Harshad said. "Your duties for the Order do not need to supersede your relationships; the wisdom you learn should inform your decisions, not dictate them. And that is the slippery part of free will."

He gave me a knowing look. "You have your own secrets, Eleanora. You know this is true. Secrets offer us freedom from the world, but they can enslave us, too. They let us draw close to some and push us farther away from others."

I did not say anything, slipping into a thoughtful silence as Harshad gave me another assessing look. "That is why the search for truth must be an ongoing process."

THE ORDER OF THE CRYSTAL DAGGERS

"What do you mean?"

"Do you know what will be even more perfect than our first day in Heaven, Eleanora?"

The question was unusual and seemed to be misplaced, but luckily, Harshad did not wait for my answer.

"Our second day."

I understood. "You can't have something 'more perfect,'" I said. "Perfect is perfect."

"I both agree and disagree. This seeming complication did not stop the Americans from putting it in their Constitution," Harshad said. "But it is not poor learning as I assumed before. Perfection is not a state of stagnation, though we use the word as such."

I thought about what Lady POW had said before, about not trusting anyone, especially the people who would fail her. I realized before that it was an absurd premise, but she was not seeing the same thing I was. She was looking at the paradox as stagnant, and I had known, instinctively, that it was malleable.

"I told you the truth about your grandmother's past, including some of the secrets she carries," Harshad said. "But you are still not any more inclined to trust her with your secrets, are you?"

I blushed at his perception and shook my head. "No."

He nodded. "I thought as much. Trust is a process, especially in a fallen world."

Perhaps for once, I understood why Harshad wanted me to remain silent while he talked. Everything he said was intentional, designed to tantalize the mind. I was suddenly appalled when I realized how much I had likely missed in our sessions before.

THE ORDER OF THE CRYSTAL DAGGERS

I hoped I would be able to make up for it, after our mission was over.

When he did speak again, it seemed as though ages had passed. "You really are so much like Dezda. I wanted to see for myself how different you are, and that required time." His voice was much more of a whisper, and I knew he was taking a risk, and letting me know one of his secrets. "I know you are different enough that I can freely admit that I came to regret training Dezda. I did not want to make the same mistake with you."

"This is not a mistake," I said, but I felt my resolve weaken. I remembered how Ferdy told me that the Order of the Crystal Daggers was full of assassins, and I had nothing to say in return. He was likely right. I did not know if I was comfortable having the talent to kill someone.

Harshad seemed to agree with my unspoken concerns. "Fighting is contrary to your nature."

"Being stubborn and contrary is not." A wry grin appeared on my face, and I was suddenly determined to change the subject. "Besides, Lady Penelope says that Society can only exist when people do things that are unacceptable to save it."

"That does not mean you must be such a person."

"I do not agree," I said. "I am free to see the truth of such a calling, even if it is uncomfortable."

"This is not what you want."

I did not know how to respond; Harshad was right. I had my doubts about the Order, about working with people who, as Lady POW said, would fail me.

But I was at the castle when Karl and Lord Maximillian's attack commenced. If I had done nothing at all, if I had backed away from Lady Penelope's offer, if I had jumped at the chance to travel abroad and find a husband, or if I had taken enough of her money to start up Liberté with Ben, I would not have been able to save Ferdy.

And he was worth it. Protecting Ferdy was worth it.

As if to prove myself, I stood up and moved back toward the center of the room and took a fighting stance. "If you're going to help me win against Xiana, I'm going to need to learn more advanced moves than you've been having me and Ben go over."

Harshad turned around, reverting back to his solemn, unreadable self as we remained content to let the topic drop. "You are correct; Xiana is quite the skilled fighter. That is certainly no secret."

167

THE ORDER OF THE CRYSTAL DAGGERS

168

THE ORDER OF THE CRYSTAL DAGGERS

11

◊

Later that evening, I stepped down from Lady Penelope's coach and made my way into the *Stavovské divadlo*. I was dressed in the extravagant gown of a socialite, a member of Society. The weight of the gown surprised me, after days of working in my stealth habit and loose clothing, but I had to admit, it was beautiful. My dress was a deep amethyst lined with mink, with matching ruffles of silk and muslin. I had a matching fur stole and even some jeweled combs in my hair. I was tempted to wear the ones Ferdy had given me, but when Marguerite had shown up with silver combs, dazzling with tiny diamonds, I made no objection. Because I loved my outfit, the inconvenient frivolity of it was much more enjoyable. I was happy enough that I had an assignment that would allow me to sit down for several hours, even if I had to entertain Society and spend time with Karl.

Underneath my gown, I wore a new pair of kid boots. The soft covering of winter snow had slushed over near the theatre, and the boots protected me from the cold as much as the mixture of horse manure and other dirt from the streets.

Not that I was thinking about that when I arrived; I was ready to observe my environment, pick up on all the important details, and search for the information I needed. I was still here on a mission.

This thought marched through me, almost skipping to the sound of music as it poured out of the *Stavovské divadlo*, the Estates Theatre, as Lady Penelope and I walked inside.

Even Lady POW was in brighter spirits. I learned from Amir that Ben told her about Zipporah, and they were waiting for Clavan's summons from the Cabal.

Any progress was progress, and after weeks of wintery solitude and monotonous training, we were both excited to be back, looking for clues while we dazzled the crowds.

"This is wonderful," Lady Penelope murmured as we arrived. I could practically feel her enthusiasm beside me as we were escorted to a box at the side of the theatre. "I have missed the theatre quite a bit since we left England. I wish we were here to see a play, but this is lovely, too."

"Aren't you always a player on the stage, as a spy?" I asked. "Why would you miss something you have to live through every day?"

"Watching others perform is much more enjoyable."

She is a complicated woman, I thought, *but she is right*.

I sat down in my seat with my own sense of wonder, mostly awed that I was able to be seen as much as I was able to see everyone else. There were several lords and ladies all around us, enjoying the concert—or pretending to enjoy the concert, while they indulged in gossip.

Even a month ago, such a sight would have been unimaginable to me. The golden gilt of the theatre shined, the warmth washing over the audience along with the sound of music. The silk-covered walls and the velvet stage curtains hinted at their highest glory, adding to the magic of the performance as I sat there.

The magic did not last long.

I glanced over to see Karl come into the box. He made his formal greetings, both to me and Lady POW, and then he took the seat beside me, a rare privilege allowed to a gentleman. Lady Penelope, resplendent in her own gown behind me, waved her fan of feathers, signaling to me to get to it.

I could almost hear her thoughts.

THE ORDER OF THE CRYSTAL DAGGERS

Get on with it, Eleanora! We need information.

We might be enjoying ourselves, I thought with a smile, but we were still working, too. "This is a wonderful performance. Don't you think so, Karl?"

"I am eager for the finale," he said, but I wondered if he was telling me the truth. Karl was dressed elegantly for the evening. He watched the crowds, as if waiting for his cues to wave or appear deeply invested in the music. I saw him nod gallantly to several others who were looking our way. He seemed to enjoy the attention he was receiving, and he loved to have the chance to gain more later.

"Well, I am glad to see you are eager to leave me," I teased, batting my eyelashes at him. My stomach twisted, and I decided I did not like flirting with Karl.

"It's not that," Karl quickly assured me. He reached for my hand, and I allowed him to take it. "I requested a special number in your honor."

"My honor?"

"Of course. You have enchanted all of society, Ella."

I did not know what it was, but suddenly hearing him call me "Ella," Ferdy's name for me, made me feel sick. Maybe it was because of Ben, fighting with Ferdy over a misunderstanding or maybe it was realizing I would likely never see him again. Ultimately, I did not want to be reminded of Ferdy anymore.

"Eleanora, if you please," I murmured, pulling my hand out of his. I glanced back to see Lady POW frown at me and hurriedly set about adjusting a hairpin to cover for my quick movements.

I hoped she would not question it. I did not need her snooping into my personal life. I counted it as a blessing that I did not have to reveal anything to her at all about Ferdy, romantic or otherwise, and I was praying I never had to. I did not want to admit I had a broken heart, and I desperately missed someone I had no business loving in the first place.

"My apologies … Eleanora." Karl took my hand again, and I relented.

As the music continued, I looked down at the crowds where Karl was watching.

"Are you looking for Lady Teresa Marie?" I asked. "I don't believe I see her here tonight."

"She and her father have been busy of late, moving into their new townhouse," Karl said. "My parents were able to help get them a residence in the city for the rest of the Season."

"Oh?" I arched my brow. "Does this mean he is still interested in supporting your political ambitions?"

"Yes. Lord Maximillian and I have reached an understanding. He has been preoccupied these last few weeks, but in the meantime, I am free to attend to you."

He glanced over at me, giving me an affectionate look. "Not that I have much of a choice, of course. One look and you are enough to enchant even the hardest of hearts."

"Thank you," I mumbled, trying to hide my irritation under the guise of pleased modesty. "It is good your parents approve of Lord Maximillian, especially if His Grace is still supportive of you."

Which was strange, when I thought about it. Empress Maria Anna was very concerned for Karl and Ferdy. Why would they help Lord Maximillian set up a household here, especially when he had been behind the fire at the castle?

Maybe they were watching him, I thought. That made sense.

THE ORDER OF THE CRYSTAL DAGGERS

"Max is grateful, too," Karl said. "He has some extended family in the area, and he is eager to spend more time with them."

"I see." I was getting tired of trying to find ways to circle around to information I wanted, without seeming suspicious.

Before I could find a way to see if Lord Maximillian had been talking about Cecilia, there was a shuffle of movement behind us.

The curtain parted, and a footman stepped forward.

My heart clenched. I peered closely at the footman's face, half-hoping, half-dreading that Ferdy was up to his old tricks. When I saw the footman's young face, clearly several years younger than myself, I exhaled. I was still not sure if I was more disappointed or relieved.

"A note for you, m'lady," the footman said, bowing to Lady Penelope. "From Lady Hohenwart. She is visiting Lord Taafte's box and has requested you come and join them."

"I see," Lady Penelope replied. She glanced over at Karl. "I shall return shortly, Mr. Marcelin. Do take care of my darling granddaughter for me until then."

"As you wish, Madame," Karl replied with a grin.

He waited until Lady POW was out of our box before he inched closer to me.

"I am greatly honored you were able to come tonight," Karl said.

I mostly ignored him, waving out into the crowd. I was hoping some of the many people who came to fawn over me at balls and parties would wave back. I got my wish and smiled, noticing Karl was suitably impressed. But it also helped to remind Karl we had an audience.

173

THE ORDER OF THE CRYSTAL DAGGERS

"Things have been rather lonely since I have returned from London," Karl said, surprising me. "Now that I am staying in the castle, I am, of course, very grateful, but I have not had much time with the people I love."

"I imagine you have more friends abroad, considering you studied there."

Karl nodded. "I am hoping some of them will come and visit."

"Will you have time for them when they do?" I pressed. "I mean, you have your duties to the Diets, after all."

"I am certain once our sessions resume, there will be more time for revelry."

For the next several moments, I half-listened as Karl laid out his plans to introduce new bills for the Diets to consider.

"If you can see that Emperor Franz Joseph has no concern for us, even after the fire incident at the castle, then surely others do, too."

I did not have to feign ennui anymore; I had to hide it. "I'm sure."

"He should not be allowed to ignore us," Karl said, his jaw hardening in anger. "He is supposed to take pride in his empire, and he has not even come to Bohemia for a formal coronation. Don't you think that the nation feels his neglect? And we still suffer for it, too."

"But it's not so bad, is it?" I thought of what I had learned at the Cabal. "The Bohemian Diet remains in power, and the German Diet has allowed us to celebrate our roots to a much more liberal degree of late. The people are more free than ever, and we have hopes for more representation."

"The German Confederacy has fallen in stature since the time of King Ferdinand," Karl replied. The bitterness was creeping into his voice as he railed against the established

THE ORDER OF THE CRYSTAL DAGGERS

governments. "And the Bohemians should be represented properly with a king, not one of these republics the Americans are celebrating. Look at what that brought them. Only civil war. Millions have died for a republic that will one day fall, too, and all because they could not trust in their leaders."

"Plenty of kingdoms have experienced that," I reminded him. "Even King Ferdinand was forced to abdicate because he was unable to lead his people. I do not think you would be able to convince the people that separating Bohemia from the empire would be good for us."

"They only need a strong leader who is unafraid to stand up for his nation," Karl said. He tightened his fingers around mine. "Not one like Franz Joseph."

"What about the people?"

Karl frowned. "I know Empress Elisabeth has made democracy look attractive, but it only leads to mob leadership in the end. And if there is a stalemate, war comes without mercy, Ella."

"Eleanora, please."

"Why?"

I blinked. "Why what?"

"Why do you prefer I call you Eleanora?" He frowned, and for the first time, I saw the two little stress lines in the middle of his forehead, as he crinkled his face into an angry, thoughtful expression. "Ella is a perfectly lovely name."

"I just do," I said, trying not to grit my teeth. "A name is very important, after all. Ella sounds like a silly girl's name. Eleanora is my proper name, and propriety is very important, as you well know, sir."

When his frown only deepened, I tapped my fingers against his arm playfully. "It is no different for you and Bohemia, is it

THE ORDER OF THE CRYSTAL DAGGERS

not? You wish to give it a leader and a vision with a good name, so it can have a prosperous future."

Karl brightened at my comparison. "Yes, I do. I want to make Bohemia a great nation once more. Even if it means breaking free from Austria and Hungary."

"That would be treason," I said, exaggerating my shock.

"Treason against slavery," Karl argued. "Surely you know of the freedom of which I speak."

I thought of my own freedom from Cecilia. I had wanted that freedom, to determine my own life's course.

"There is freedom," I said, "and there are false freedoms, Karl. It is important to know the difference."

He did not seem to realize I was looking past him, seeing if I could find a glimpse of Ferdy in his gaze.

Karl reached out and took a hold of my other hand. "Which is why I am very glad you are here with me. It is no small task to turn the tide of history, to fundamentally change a nation. A man who wishes to do just that needs a strong woman behind him."

I did not know what to say to that. I did not think I was that strong, and I knew as a member of the Order, my missions were to be carried out in the shadows.

"Speaking of the country," Karl said, "there is a special dedication ceremony this week most of the Diet members will be attending. It is at the *Nàrodni muzuem.*"

"I see. Does this mean the Diets are resuming their sessions?"

"Not quite. There is still a little more time before that. But I would love to have you accompany me to the ceremony." Karl gave me a smile. "I want to show them a vision of a brighter future."

THE ORDER OF THE CRYSTAL DAGGERS

"I will be happy to join you," I said, "but I don't see what your vision for Bohemia's future has to do with me."

"You're the daughter of Adolf Svoboda, a man who saved King Ferdinand from certain death at a critical time," Karl said. "You're beautiful and charming, and everyone here loves you. Just look around at all the people who are watching us."

I hated that Karl had a point. Society in Prague was small, and many had seemed to approve of me. Or at least, they approved of the picture I made. Between Lady Penelope's dowry, and my own performance, several spyglasses settled on our theatre box throughout the evening.

"You are the embodiment of everything I could hope for," Karl said, his voice softening. "A lady who was fashioned from adversity, one who is determined to make her way in the world while making it more blessed along the way. There is nothing that could make Bohemia greater than you."

I blushed at Karl's praise, even if it stung. The first time he had wanted me, it was for my money, and now, it was for my influence. He might have liked me enough to believe I was perfect for him, but I almost wished he would just marry Lady Teresa Marie. Her father wanted power and the throne, and it seemed that they were so well-suited to each other in that goal that they would be reasonably happy together—but, I thought, only if they succeeded.

"Thank you, Karl," I murmured, suddenly desperate to get away. "You must also thank my grandmother. She is my inspiration. She was married to the Duke of Wellington."

"I know that," Karl agreed, "but—"

"My goodness. I did not realize until this very moment how thirsty I am. Would you be kind enough to fetch me a glass of lemonade?"

THE ORDER OF THE CRYSTAL DAGGERS

Karl narrowed his eyes at me as he stood up. My attempt to distract him was not smooth, and even he knew I was uncomfortable. "I will alert a footman at once, my lady."

He knew I was uncomfortable, and he did not like it. I let out a sigh as he walked away, feeling a reprieve for the moment, even as I knew Karl would make me pay for it later. If he wanted me to be his wife, and a perfectly enchanting one for all of Society to see, he would have to find a way to get me to agree with him.

Isn't it bad enough that he got me to agree to a pending engagement?

The other side of the curtain fluttered, and I heard Karl's voice rise briefly.

I frowned. *What happened?*

"Karl?" I called. The music from the stage made it difficult to know if my voice was loud enough for him to hear me. "Is something wrong?"

He had stepped outside the box, out of my sight. I sighed and went after him, hoping I could sneak away with an excuse. Maybe I could tell him that my grandmother had signaled to me from the Taafte's box—anything that would allow me to escape that conversation.

All of my plans disappeared as I pulled back the curtain.

Karl was standing there, arguing in an angry, hushed voice. His back was turned to me, and I was just about to interrupt him when I saw who he was talking to.

It was Ferdy.

THE ORDER OF THE CRYSTAL DAGGERS

12

◊

I never considered myself to be the type of lady who was prone to fainting. After years of serving as Cecilia's chimney sweep, I was used to more difficult and dangerous situations than the delicate ladies of the city's social circles, and the idea of fainting at the least provocation was laughable. But at that moment, watching Ferdy as he stood there, I felt my knees wobble, and my heart stop. A lightheaded feeling took over me, and I could not tell if I was dizzy from pain or pleasure, or some heady mix of both.

Ferdy, by contrast, seemed undeniably pleased at the sight of me. He was dressed in his proper gentlemen's attire, down to the ruffled shirt and the fitted coat, formal enough to make me feel underdressed, even in my elaborate gown. His hair was brushed back properly, and he wore a smug smile on his face. He stood at ease as Karl faced him, meeting his brother eye to eye, deliberately being as provocative as possible. His insufferable self-satisfaction and the resulting anger it stirred inside of me were the only reasons I did not swoon.

"Why do you insist on making things difficult?" Karl's tone was harsh against the musical background. I might have even felt badly for Ferdy if I did not want to ask him the same thing.

Karl's authoritarian tone did nothing to deter Ferdy. He heaved a large, dismissive sigh. "Why, brother dear, we only have so much time before I will be on my way back to Silesia. I thought it prudent to spend *some* time with you. When I found out you had gone to the theatre, I could hardly resist, now could I?"

"Do not call me 'brother,'" Karl hissed back.

179

"Oh, would you prefer 'cousin,' then? I remember that is how all of your teachers described our relationship back at Oxford, especially as they lectured me on dishonoring my family's heritage and denigrating its obvious potential."

"It is not my fault you insisted on wasting your years of education causing nothing but trouble for your headmasters."

"A man is not a true leader unless he can get others to follow him," Ferdy replied. Then he glanced over at me, and it was then that I realized my mouth had dropped open in surprise and outrage. My heart raced with fear and a sudden desire for revenge. "Isn't that right, Ella?"

Karl whirled around. I heard him inhale sharply as he caught sight of me.

I froze. *Why is Ferdy jeopardizing himself, and me, too?*

Did he hate me that much? Was this revenge for Ben's attack?

"Eleanora," Karl said. "I must beg your pardon. Please, do not concern yourself with … this unfortunate interruption to our evening."

Ferdy rolled his eyes at Karl's attempt to dismiss him. My own anger flared again, but my curiosity compelled me to speak up. "What is going on?"

Karl scowled. "Nothing."

I arched my brow at Karl, silently attempting to remind him he had promised not to lie to me.

While I could not tell if he was able to decipher my thoughts, Karl relented a moment later. "Fine. May I introduce you to my brother, Ferdinand? He has decided to grace us with his presence. Much to my dismay, of course."

THE ORDER OF THE CRYSTAL DAGGERS

Ferdy stepped around Karl swiftly, knocking him out of my direct path. Ferdy reached for my hand and kissed it gallantly, letting his fingers slip into mine.

I was unable to stop the flush on my cheeks, remembering our more intimate kisses. An unstoppable wave of longing flooded through me.

"It is a pleasure to meet you, Miss Eleanora," Ferdy said. "You must be the one that my brother calls 'Ella,' even though it is more of a name for a silly girl, don't you think?"

All my embarrassment transmuted into rage.

So, he has been listening to us, waiting to make a move.

My fingers gripped his in warning. I knew Ferdy loved to play games and take risks, but I was in no mood to join in on his fun.

"A pleasure to make your acquaintance, Mr. Marcelin," I said through gritted teeth. "Karl has told me much about you."

"I can assure you all of it is true, even the worst of it. Karl would never lie to you, my lady. I doubt you would allow him, either. You are clearly as smart, charming, and beautiful as he says." Ferdy's voice dropped to a softer, more seductive tone. "Even without the introduction, I recognized you."

At his tender, familiar words, I dropped my hand from his, breathless at the wound as much as I was with wanting.

"When exactly are you leaving to go back to Silesia, Ferdinand?" Karl asked. "I would hate for you to miss Eleanora and I announcing our engagement."

I did not want to look at Ferdy in that moment; I forced myself to remain still. I tried to let him know it was part of the game, but I saw the pain flicker across his face.

THE ORDER OF THE CRYSTAL DAGGERS

"So good to know that Lord Maximillian has allowed you to step out of your previous arrangement with his daughter, brother dear," Ferdy said, recovering quickly. "I assume he has made other plans, too?"

"Who told you about that?" Karl scowled before he stood tall. "And why would you even care? Are you looking for a bride yourself?"

"I'm sure it would be something to consider, even though you know I am a dedicated bachelor." Ferdy's smile went cold as he looked at me. "I would not want a wife to worry while I make my rounds about the city, looking for all sorts of lively entertainment. And I am sure Ella here would not want to be such a wife, either."

"I'm sure your wife would search the streets just to make sure you were safe," I retorted. "Not that you would ever know of her sacrifice."

He arched his brow playfully. "It is almost worth kidnapping Karl, just to see if you would come after him."

"From what I have heard of you, it is better that I not come if he was with you. I shudder to think of where he would end up with you at his side," I snapped.

Karl cleared his throat. "I believe it is time to end this conversation. Ferdinand, please, you are causing Eleanora undue duress with your ... impropriety."

Karl was right about that, even if his reasoning was wrong.

"Eleanora, let us return to enjoying the concert, if you please," Karl said.

As much as Ferdy was upsetting me, I felt everything inside of me call out to him as I was forced to retreat. The past weeks' worth of missing him broke through me, and I could only look over my shoulder at him as Karl pushed the curtain aside.

THE ORDER OF THE CRYSTAL DAGGERS

Karl turned back to face Ferdy. "I trust you will find someone else to bother? Ella and I are presently occupied."

"Eleanora," I whispered.

Karl halted his departure to glare at me, and I flinched at his impatient frustration. "My apologies, my lady."

Ferdy cleared his throat. When we looked back at him, I saw he had finally stopped smiling.

"I will be leaving for Silesia in the morning, Karl," Ferdy said. "It appears you will be in better company until then."

"Allow me to extend my heartfelt wishes for a safe journey." Karl held out his hand, solemn but still disdainful. "The Diets resume their sessions this week, and I have other commitments. I regret I will be unlikely to meet with you before your departure."

"Unwilling, or unlikely?" Ferdy stepped forward and shook Karl's hand, though there was no evidence of brotherly affection or goodwill between them. "Never mind. Farewell, *brother.*"

At his taunting, Karl swung around, angry, and brushed past me. Ferdy gave me one last look, nodding down the hall; it was a signal of sorts, letting me know he wanted me to find a way to follow him before he disappeared into the crowds.

It took everything I had not to run after him at that moment—I could not honestly say if I wanted to kiss him or strangle him more—but I knew I had to see to Karl first.

I headed back over to my seat next to Karl.

"Well, you were obviously correct. It was a waste of time to meet your brother," I said, forcing myself to say something. I knew he would like the reassurance I was not enchanted by Ferdy, and that I was on his side.

THE ORDER OF THE CRYSTAL DAGGERS

"I call him my cousin to help with the embarrassment," Karl admitted. "I do not know how we are brothers at all."

"Of course. You care about Bohemia's future, and he only cares if he is having fun."

Karl took my hand, clutching it affectionately with a flooding sense of relief. "I am glad you see the differences, my dear. They are quite stark, I assure you."

I nodded, even though I disagreed. Ben had made similar remarks regarding both of them before, noting Ferdy's carelessness and Karl's ruthlessness. I held onto Karl's hand, thinking how his deep devotion to the country had led to destruction, and how Ferdy's careless lies had left me broken.

"Did you know, Eleanora, in some countries they execute family members who bring dishonor to their families?" Karl sighed remorsefully. "What a shame that we do not adopt that custom. Disownment will only go so far in certain circles here. Fortunately, my parents are supportive of our estrangement."

Karl's statement jolted me out of the stupor of my own thoughts and ignited my rage.

He was obviously upset. I watched him as he anxiously tugged at his collar, straightened his cravat, and smoothed out his jacket. He was fidgeting, and Ferdy had rattled him to the point he was making lighthearted comments about situations like the one Amir faced, comparing Ferdy's embarrassment to an act of family dishonor punishable by death.

Karl always seemed very refined, always very courteous—a gentleman to his fingertips. But his remark, as careless and thoughtless as it was, revealed the more grotesque truth inside.

Disgust ran through me, and I knew it was time for me to escape. My heart felt hollow at the thought of staying where I

THE ORDER OF THE CRYSTAL DAGGERS

was, for so many reasons, and there really was nothing I wanted more than to go and find Ferdy again.

"I do believe my grandmother is signaling to me from Lady Hohenwart's box," I said, struggling to keep my voice from breaking. "Please excuse me. I will return shortly."

Before Karl could offer to escort me, or worse, question my decision, I hurried away. I pushed past the velvet curtain and made for the stairs, heading in the direction Ferdy had indicated before.

"Where did he go?" I muttered, frustrated as I had to smile and weave through the crowds. I caught sight of a darkened staircase at the far end of the hall and hurried onward. Navigating the stairs in my gown slowed me some, but I finally found an exit.

Just as I slipped outside, a hand reached out and took hold of me from behind. I almost fought back, but then I heard his voice.

"I was wondering if you were going to come at all."

Ferdy.

My knees buckled, and I fell back against him briefly. Then I remembered how upset he had made me by showing up and pretending we had never met before.

"And miss getting the chance to chastise you for your impudence? Never." I turned to face him. "What were you thinking, showing up here? Were you trying to make me upset?"

"You cannot make me feel guilty over making you upset," Ferdy replied tartly. He drew me back against the side of building. The alleyway behind the theatre was dark, but we were safe and out of sight. "Especially after promising Karl you would consider an engagement."

"I only did it to see if I could trap him," I said with a huff. "He promised me if I agreed to it, he would never lie, and I was trying to get him to by asking about you. I didn't think he would admit to being your brother."

"We need to work on your gambling skills."

Despite my anger, I almost laughed. "I've been too busy learning how to fight to worry about gambling."

"I am relieved to hear that. Philip and I agreed that your injured leg was an exaggerated excuse to stay out of Society while Karl figured out what to do next."

"How is he? You'll have to give Philip my regards." I crossed my arms over my chest. "And speaking of Society, why are you here?"

"Why, to see you, of course." My eyes were gradually adjusting to the darkness in the alleyway, and I could see his smile against the shadows. "Karl is not the only one who has missed you."

"Ferdy—"

"Don't worry," he said. "We don't have time for a proper reunion right now. I am here because I wanted to see you, but I also wanted to give you this." He reached inside of his coat and pulled out a folded sheet of paper.

"This isn't another invitation, is it?" I asked, taking the paper.

"No, it's not," Ferdy replied with a quick grin. "It's a letter my brother sent out to Lord Maximillian, the Duke of Moravia, this morning. I had one of my informants intercept it."

"You have informants?"

"Of course I do. I've been running around the streets for nearly a year, and since then I've come to learn the value of

THE ORDER OF THE CRYSTAL DAGGERS

having the right information." A sly glimmer appeared in his gaze. "How else do you think I knew to come and rescue you tonight, *chérie?*"

I refrained from slapping him at his teasing remarks, but only barely. Instead, I unrolled the paper, but it was too dark to read it. "What does it say?"

"He was formally rejecting Lady Teresa Marie as his future wife," Ferdy said. "He says that he is pursuing you instead, since you have expressed your interest, and his friends in the League would approve of his choice because of your father, and of course, your other 'most excellent qualities.' Karl also offered the Duke a seat on his council and considered it a 'gracious' and 'generous' act, considering the nature of their recent disagreements."

"The League? The only league I can think of is the League of Ungentlemanly Warfare," I said. "But that's based in London, and Lady POW is a member. I don't know why they would care what Karl was planning."

"I was more surprised to see your name," Ferdy said. "I am sure you've noticed I am disgusted by your position."

"You can take heart in knowing that it's a lie." I did not want to tell Ferdy, but I agreed with him. I crossed my arms, remembering I was supposed to be upset with him. "You're pretty familiar with those, if I recall."

"I'm working on making it up to you. Since you told me you only allowed Karl to get close to you in order to save people the night of the Advent Ball, I am keeping a closer watch on my brother."

"Ferdy." I felt my earlier ire soften as I shook my head. "The Order knows Karl has reached out to Lord Maximillian and they are trying to restore Bohemia to a full monarchy. They were going to use the death of the politicians and aristocracy back at the castle to leverage Karl back onto the throne."

"Fortunately, their plans were foiled by a clever young lady." He brushed his hand against my chin, and I hurriedly turned away.

"I still failed," I murmured, torn between shame and pride at his remark. "The Order suspects there are contingency plans."

"You are right to do so. I've known Karl has wanted to free Bohemia from the empire for some time. But I did not realize until recently he was intent on following through." His gaze dropped to the ground. "I should have."

"It's not your fault," I assured him, surprised by the amount of guilt I heard in his voice. "You were the one who told me he is very smart."

"He is," Ferdy said, "but I should have known something was wrong. With the Duke of Moravia and now the League of Ungentlemanly Warfare, he has the right connections, and after the Advent Ball, he no longer seems to exhibit any moral restraint."

I bit my lip momentarily. I did not want to encourage him, but I did not want to miss out on any important information, either. Finally, I gave in. "What do you know?"

"Enough to know we have to stop him."

We?

The day that I left him at the castle, I thought Ferdy was letting me go. But now, as I held the letter he had given me, as he looked at me with such concern, I saw he wanted to help me and the Order—even though he believed we could turn on him.

THE ORDER OF THE CRYSTAL DAGGERS

That was not the only risk he faced, either. Going up against Karl would mean that he was putting himself at risk from his brother's ire and possible retaliation.

"Ferdy." I took his arm. "Your mother is worried for you."

Ferdy balked. "What does that have to do with this?"

"I appreciate the help. I really do," I said. "This letter is a good clue. Maybe Lord Maximillian's foreign backers include members of the League. But I can't have you looking into this. You need to stop. This is dangerous."

"You told me that the kingdom needs me," he said, and I felt a rush of anger; he was trying to use my own reasoning against me. Before I could object and fight back, he stepped even closer to me, trapping me between his body and the building. "And as much as you might not like it, I need you."

His hands cradled my face, and I ached for him. My heart was thundering loudly between my ears as we stood there. All of my being was torn inside—duty and love fought a dizzying battle inside of me, leaving me unable to move.

"You need me, too." Ferdy's voice was soft and full of wonder, sending shivers down my spine. "I can tell."

"This is madness," I whispered.

"Madness or magic?" Ferdy's gaze fell to my lips, and I felt my heart fall out of my chest and into his hands all over again.

I barely managed to find my resolve. "My life is nothing, Ferdy. You have to be protected. I can't have you involved in this."

"It's not your job to take care of me," he said. "I can protect myself. What do you think I've been doing for the last year, playing the pauper for all of Prague to witness?"

"I'm not sure how that helps." I eyed him curiously. "Why were you living on the streets, exactly?"

"I may not be a true prince—"

"Yes, you are." I jutted my chin forward. I did not want to debate the technicalities of his title, but I would if I had to. "That is the truth, and you promised me you would only tell me the truth."

"Fine." The reluctance in his voice was palpable as he drew back from me. "I am a prince. But my father was king and emperor, and eventually, he was forced from his throne because he did not know his people. He was lucky he wasn't killed. And now, Karl is following in his steps to the same end. He is too focused on his own ambition to see that the people simply will not support him."

"There is a strong Nationalist movement. And he could easily garner support after the fire, even claiming it was an accident."

"The Nationalist support will disappear when they see Karl wants power for himself. The people want to be free, as free as they can be in a fallen world. Karl doesn't think they are smart enough to know the difference, but I know they are."

I felt my own heart push back at me, telling me Ferdy was right. Clavan had recognized it in me, too—the desire for freedom, for liberty. That was another reason I had agreed to join Lady POW, too. Freedom required power.

"I have chosen to live among the people, as one of them, so I could know them again," Ferdy said. "I can assure you, it was more educational than going off to school, too, especially considering what Clavan and Eliezer have taught me."

"I can imagine," I said. "But Karl—"

THE ORDER OF THE CRYSTAL DAGGERS

"Karl doesn't know Bohemia the way I do. If there is a way to stop him from destroying himself and the kingdom, I will find it."

"Even if you're the one who is destroyed in the end?"

He shrugged. "He has protected me my whole life, and while we disagree on many issues, I would not have him killed. Mother would be more than distraught, especially after the hell she went through to have us."

"Ferdy …"

Ferdy gripped my hands. "And I can't have you in danger, either. I know of the League, and the Order, Ella. So does Karl. We heard about it years ago, first from our mother and then while we were at school. Karl might not know that your grandmother is a member or that you are part of it, but we both know of its deadlier capabilities."

"We're not assassins."

"Your enemies would not agree," Ferdy argued, giving me a pointed look. "And that might include Karl's friends in the League."

My breath caught in my throat. I thought of my mother's mission and my father's murder. Amir, Harshad, and Lady POW were not enemies of the Order. But there were other members, too—like my grandfather—and Lady POW was against utilizing them, even to help our mission.

"Do you think it's possible there are members of the League who would want to betray the Order?" I asked.

"There are always traitors on every side."

His answer unnerved me, both at its truth and timeliness.

Ferdy did not seem to notice my discomfort as he continued. "I'm sure it's possible, just as I am sure it is possible that the League is using Karl as much as his thinks he is using them. And that's why I won't let you face this alone."

"I'm not alone."

"Oh, yes, I've almost forgotten your brother." Ferdy laughed as he patted the right side of his torso, just above his hip. "He bruised me up quite a bit the other day."

"I'm so sorry about that," I murmured, embarrassed. I reached out and touched him, feeling him shiver through the layers of clothes. "I did not tell him to go find you."

"Oh, I know. You've never been one to have other people fight your battles." He placed his hand over mine, tracing his fingers over my knuckles, where days of Harshad's instruction had left them red and slightly swollen. "I was wondering if you were learning how to box. Maybe one day I'll get a chance to show you how to fight like a beggar."

I blushed. "We aren't discussing that now."

"Of course not," he said, giving me one of his irreverent smiles. "If it makes you feel better, I was actually glad to see Ben. Even fighting him was worth it."

"You gave him a black eye. Why would it make you happy?"

"Because it meant you were upset." He pulled my hand up to his cheek before grazing his lips across my palm. Even through my glove, the sudden, searing heat between us taunted me, urging me closer even though I knew it would burn me in the end. "Over me."

"I'm nearly always upset over you," I whispered, unable to stop myself from leaning closer, basking in the smothered scent of mint and lavender on his formal jacket.

"So you have missed me, too?"

THE ORDER OF THE CRYSTAL DAGGERS

The playful tone reminded me of how much I did not know him, of how I had allowed myself to be dazzled by him before—of how I wanted him anyway.

I stepped back from him and smiled, even as I felt his disappointment. "*Absolument.*"

For a long moment, one of those moments that burns through time more sweetly, we stared at each other, and I was allowed to bask in the wonder that I loved him, and he loved me. Even if there was no trust between us, even if there was only danger ahead—I loved him, and there was nothing more freeing than feeling secure in that love.

In the distance, the *Pražský orloj* chimed, and the magic of the moment was gone.

"I will have to wait until next time to kiss you," Ferdy said, making me both angry and grateful. "Karl and your grandmother will be worried for you if you don't return soon."

The thought of Lady Penelope and Karl waiting around for me anxiously was enough to break the spell surrounding us. I swallowed hard. "You're right. I have to go."

With a quick nod, I started back toward the entrance of the concert hall. Just before I turned the corner, Ferdy called out to me again.

"Ella."

I turned around. "What is it?"

Even in the shadows, I could see the sparkle of silver in his eyes. "It gets harder to leave you, every time."

I felt the lump in my throat return before I tried to smile. "Parting is such sweet sorrow," I reminded him.

"With all due respect to the Bard, Shakespeare was never so wrong as he was about that," Ferdy said. "I don't feel any

THE ORDER OF THE CRYSTAL DAGGERS

sweetness in my sorrow. Desperation, anxiety, and longing—even anger and suffering—but no sweetness."

"It's supposed to be sweet in knowing it won't be long before a reunion."

"Do I know that we will ever meet again?"

I laughed. "Of course we will. How else will you kiss me?"

His sad smile came back briefly. "Will you let me keep you?"

"Ferdy." I took a step toward him, unsure of what I could say, or even what I would do, but he shook his head.

"No. We do not have time right now. My brother will ask you too many questions as it is."

I patted my pocket where the letter he had given me was safely tucked away. "Thank you."

"*Absolument, chérie.*" The cheeky grin fluttered on his face, and then he sank further back into the shadows, disappearing completely.

After the past weeks of trying to forget Ferdy, it was clear I had failed spectacularly. I headed back inside, making my way back to the theatre box, completely overwhelmed.

I could not stop seeing his face inside my mind. His eyes swam before me, silver seas of emotion and intelligence. He was broken by our separation, and I seemed beyond repair without him.

It was only when I bumped into a man that I returned to the world once more.

"Pardon me," I murmured. I glanced up to offer an apologetic curtsy, but as I saw the man's face, I stopped and stared.

THE ORDER OF THE CRYSTAL DAGGERS

It was the man from the Cabal—not the obnoxious green-eyed man, but his companion, Didier. He was wearing the formal suit of an aristocrat, with his black hair cut short, the same shade of ebony as his boots, and a few shades lighter than his skin. He smiled kindly at me; even in the shadows of the theatre hall, I could see his gentleness. "All is forgiven, Lady Ella."

It was the first time I heard his voice, and it startled me. He offered me his gloved hand, and I blinked again. Even with the name and outfit of a Frenchmen, his manners and accent were distinctly American. I glanced at his coat, where a small revolver was peeking out from his inner pocket.

"There she is!"

I nearly jumped at the sound of Lady Penelope's voice. She came up to me, and I briefly saw Karl was not far behind her, before she smothered me into an awkward hug, smooshing me up against her bosom. I saw Karl behind her, looking frustrated.

"What is wrong with you?" Lady Penelope hissed in my ear. "Where did you go?"

"Uh ..." I glanced back and saw Didier was gone. He had slipped away, falling back into the shadows, much as Ferdy had done only moments before. "I was just looking for the ladies' withdrawing room."

"I still can't believe you got lost on your way to see me, Eleanora," Lady Penelope nearly shouted, as she turned to smile at Karl. "Can you imagine!"

She held me tight against her once more. "There's no need for you to go to the withdrawing room if you told Karl you were going down to join me."

"I was trying to escape the marriage talk," I muttered back, hoping she would not inspect my reasons for leaving too closely.

THE ORDER OF THE CRYSTAL DAGGERS

"We will have another discussion about this later," she hissed before Karl stepped up next to us.

"I am just as glad as you are, Madame, that we have found her," Karl said.

He might have been trying to reclaim the kingdom as his own, but I was grateful for Karl's interruption in that moment. It was very fortunate timing, and I could only hope and pray Lady Penelope would forget all about discussing anything later with me.

"The finale is coming," Karl said. "Please, Eleanora, we need to get back to your box. At my request, *Kde domov můji?* Is the last song of the night. The song and its composer have ties to the theatre and remind Bohemia we are united in this place we know as home."

I eagerly abandoned Lady Penelope's false affection, practically leaping onto his arm; we just made it back to our seats as the music began to play.

Karl's eyes widened in excitement as the music began to swell; the crowd was full of mixed reactions, but many people seemed unsure. Some of them stood up to cheer, and some began to leave.

But then, the music stopped, and trumpets began to sound from behind the crowds.

"What is going on?" Karl asked. Over the blaring horns, I could not hear him very well, but I heard him enough to know he was furious. "This is not part of the concert."

I stood up, angling myself over the railing in front of me. Down in the center of the crowd, two lines of servants, strangely dressed figures in bright French livery, touted out on trumpets.

THE ORDER OF THE CRYSTAL DAGGERS

At the sight of them, I turned to Lady POW. Her jaw was rigid with anger, and I did not know what to make of that; I could only hope this had nothing to do with Ferdy.

The trumpets continued, as a pair of dark-skinned performers suddenly appeared between them. I quickly looked away; they were dressed in grass skirts and flowered ornaments, hardly what I would call clothes. Their chests were bare, and their faces were covered with masks as they juggled sticks.

From around the concert hall, I could see half of the ladies in the theatre boxes scrambling to get away while the other half tried to look demure and embarrassed as they secretly stared at the spectacle.

It was a strange sight, the sort of thing I always pictured when I tried to imagine Vauxhall Gardens in London. I almost smiled at the performance before I noticed Lady Penelope's face crinkled with disapproval. Before I could ask what was wrong, the trumpets went silent, and a man's voice called out to the crowd.

"Good evening, my lords and ladies! As God said, 'Let there be light,' it was so, and he saw that the light was very good. I am Lumiere Valoris, and as I was named for the light, I can say, it is very good that I am here!"

The voice was coming from a pallet, carried by six more muscular men, as it made its way in front of the room. There was a man at its center, sitting on an ornate chair, as though he were a king; surrounding his feet were brightly colored flowers and a large array of peacock feathers. Flames flickered up from hollowed-out coconuts.

Fully fledged rage lined Karl's every feature as he turned to me. "Excuse me, my lady," he said, bowing over my hand quickly. "I do believe I must depart for tonight. I will send a formal invitation for you for the ceremony at the *Nàrodni muzuem.*"

197

He left before I could say anything else, and I was more than a little relieved. Karl had been upset at me when I left him to go after Ferdy. If he was too distracted to ask questions about my earlier disappearance, I was content.

I turned my attention back down to the man who had usurped the concert finale, watching as he descended from his throne, shook hands, and nodded cordially to all the ladies. I was confused at his performance, but I did enjoy it much more than the rest of the concert.

But then the man looked up at me directly, catching my eye, and I felt my skin grow cold.

It was the man from the Cabal, the one with the green eyes and the sneering smirk. And while I did not know him, he clearly knew me.

THE ORDER OF THE CRYSTAL DAGGERS

13

◊

Lumiere seemed to be in his natural element, though whether it was chaos or the spotlight, I could not say. Several of the theatre's musicians ceased their playing, and it appeared Lumiere had anticipated their response. His own small troupe of footmen took up the lapse, using an array of different instruments to send out a stream of music I had never heard before. Judging by the small drums and hollowed flutes, I would have said it would have been at home on an island, perhaps on in the Caribbean or among the more distant East Indies, perhaps as far as the island of Hawaii.

"What's going on?" I whispered to Lady Penelope. "Who is that?"

"Lumiere," she muttered. "I haven't seen him in years. I always assumed he would die on some island, hung for his deviant crimes or incessant foolishness. It is a testament to his cunning he's still alive, just as it is sign of his immaturity that he's still undertaking obscene spectacles like this one."

"I heard his name. I was wondering who he was that you would know him."

Lady POW did not seem to hear me. The crowd in the theatre was undergoing a mass exodus at this point, while only a few lingered behind, including me and Lady POW.

"This is all Louis' fault," she whispered, shaking her head. "Come, Eleanora. We should return to the manor. I have things I need to discuss with Harshad."

"I'm a member of the Order, too," I objected, watching as some of the policemen attempted to get near Lumiere. Up on his pallet, he only smiled and signaled to the officers that he did not hear them. "Tell me who he is."

She pursed her lips together thoughtfully, before she sighed. "Years ago, before Eleanor was born, your grandfather was the leader of the Eastern division of the League. Lumiere's father, Louis, then the Viscount de Beaumont, was his second in command. Until Jakub met me."

I remembered what Harshad had told me before; Lady POW would have known Louis while she was still my grandfather's mistress.

"So?" I frowned, frustrated. "Why are you worried?"

"If you're going to stop the destruction of civilization, you should be worried," Lady Penelope snapped lightly, her eyes never leaving Lumiere's dawdling figure.

I had a feeling she was more upset I had witnessed her worry than she was perturbed by Lumiere's appearance. She did not say anything else to me; instead, she remained focused on moving through the crowds, her ageless grace suggesting none of her irritation.

We were near the theatre's main entrance when she slowed. I nearly ran into her at the sudden change of pace, but before I could ask her what was wrong this time, I saw the answer in front of us.

Lord Maximillian was at the entrance to the theatre. I could hardly believe it. He was standing there so effortlessly, even though he was the man behind all the plotting and all the disaster that had run through my home and my city.

He was dressed in his usual finery, with a golden sash and a pristine white vest, underneath an elegant coat. While I had met him several times before, I had never seen him so meticulously sadistic in his appearance. His mustache, thick and full of black and white hairs, twitched with perverse delight as he saw Lady Penelope, and the toes of his shined boots seemed to tap with anticipation. I stumbled as we approached him, but she only met his gaze with cool interest.

"Lady Wellington." He reached for her hand. She eagerly stepped forward. So, Lady POW did not want to avoid him as much as I did.

"Your Grace," she said, inclining her head in an elderly curtsy. I wanted to ask her why she insisted on using manners, why we did not just capture him there and demand answers, but I knew she would not welcome such a question.

"It is lovely to make your acquaintance once more." Lord Maximillian's gaze went to me. "I have heard of your recent upset, and I am relieved to see Miss Eleanora has made her recovery. I am one of the many who are celebrating her return to Society tonight."

"Yes, we have just had the pleasure of your friend's company," I said. "Mr. Marcelin speaks very highly of you, sir."

"I am flattered to hear so." Lord Maximillian's eyes narrowed only slightly. "I know he is beholden to you."

"Yes, he certainly is," Lady Penelope agreed. "I have heard he was considering marrying your own lovely daughter before he met my Eleanora, so you must know Mr. Marcelin has excellent judgment."

Lord Maximillian might have been a leader in a coup determined to overthrow the empire, but he was still able to be flustered by a matchmaking grandmother. I watched as his cheeks fluttered with a rosy glow as he narrowed his eyes at Lady POW.

"It may be unfortunate for me and my daughter that we did not act quickly enough," Lord Maximillian said, "but that does not mean we will not get another chance in the future."

THE ORDER OF THE CRYSTAL DAGGERS

Lady Penelope and I both caught the underlying threat, and she was just about to reply when Lumiere's voice once more rang throughout the theatre.

"Max!"

We all turned at once, only to see Lumiere break away from a team of police. He hurried forward toward us. Now that he was standing, I was able to see his outfit more clearly, and I had a hard time not staring. He had a cloak trimmed in ermine and peacock feathers hanging on his back like a robe, while his suit was cut in classic lines. There were several watch fobs hanging on off the chain of his pocket watch. The little glimmering fobs caught my eye, and I noticed the watch looked very similar to my father's.

Glancing back up at Lumiere's face, I suddenly wondered how old he was. He seemed young and foolish, as Lady Penelope had asserted earlier, but his jovial milieu, along with carefully placed makeup, only hid his age better.

I need to get better about estimating ages.

After another careful look, I realized he likely had to be close to Amir's age, though perhaps a little older. Early-to-mid forties, at most.

"Max!" His voice carried a distorted amusement, as if he knew he was causing trouble. Lumiere came up and placed a greeting kiss on each side of Lord Maximillian's cheeks, before he shamelessly embraced the man in a hug.

Lord Maximillian was clearly not expecting that. "Come, now, Lumiere," he grunted. "That is enough."

"*Tsk, tsk.* Ever so straight-laced, *mon ami.*" Lumiere ran a hand through his golden hair, letting the theatre lights catch on his many rings. "God gave us everything for our pleasure, remember? It is only sin that keeps it from being so."

He glanced at me with a smile. "Speaking of pleasure, mademoiselle, may I introduce myself?"

"I do believe you have already done so, back in the theatre, Mr. Valoris."

At my wry tone, I saw I earned his respect, though whether or not it was a good thing, I could not say.

"Your mother would be pleased to see you have become a woman who pays attention to 'the least of these,'" he said, quoting the gospel of Matthew in such dulcet tones that it made me wonder if he was the devil himself in human form. "The daughter of such a lady deserves the proper introduction."

I stiffened at the mention of my mother, and I turned to see Lady Penelope was appalled as well. She clamped her lips together tightly, as if she was too outraged to risk allowing herself to speak.

"You needn't worry about my sensibilities when it comes to propriety at this point, sir." I stepped forward and reached out my hand, allowing my grandmother a moment to collect herself.

For that small, pitiful, prideful moment, it heartened me to see Lady Penelope had to recover from a secondary attack. I had come to notice Lady Penelope was a superb fighter, but on occasion, she still needed time to switch tactics.

"Oh, of course not, mademoiselle. But I would be remiss if I treated you in such a nasty manner, especially in such a public place, with the finer members of Society around to witness. Perhaps another place would be better for informalities."

At his provocative gaze and his deliberate choice of words, I knew he was referencing our first encounter back at the Cabal.

THE ORDER OF THE CRYSTAL DAGGERS

"I would have you call me Lumi, if we are to be friends," he continued, taking my hand. "It is my pleasure to formally meet you, Lady Eleanora. After all, any previous meetings are not official until names are honorably given, *ne c'est pas?*"

"The 'honorable' aspect would be the part in question," Lord Maximillian interrupted. "It seems the police are still waiting for you to leave after your disruption tonight."

I turned to see he was right. The police were looking on our small group, waiting anxiously. They knew they could not do much, not with the higher-ranking members of Society around Lumiere, but they seemed prepared to wait.

"You and my father know very well that I have always been good at inconveniencing people with my mere existence," Lumiere replied with an impish grin. "Undoubtedly you remember him well, do you not, Lady Penelope?"

It was an interesting sight to see Lady Penelope's cheeks fluster over. She composed herself quickly, but I still saw the glimpse of irritation in her eyes.

"Who could ever forget your father?" Lady Penelope's tone turned deadly as she gritted her teeth behind her snakelike smile. "Is he joining you in town?"

"Shortly." Lumiere grinned. "I consider myself playing John the Baptist to his Jesus, of course. Quite an honor, you know."

"If you are comparing your father to Jesus, it must be a high honor indeed." Lady Penelope arched a brow. "Should I expect to see him arriving on an ass?"

Lumiere laughed uproariously, drawing even more uncomfortable attention to us. "He's more likely to part the waters, considering our recent acquisition of a fleet of clippers. They're sadly going out of style, but now is the time to buy. I've just had the loveliest time on the Vltava in one of my own. I'm sure Max here can tell you how hard and time

THE ORDER OF THE CRYSTAL DAGGERS

consuming it is to find good accommodations when traveling. Of course, you know how I jump at the chance to take on any hard task I can."

Lord Maximillian's face blotched over in annoyance. "Give my regards to him, please. For now, if you will excuse me, ladies, I do believe I will retire for the evening."

"Wonderful. I will accompany you, as we have business to discuss," Lumiere said.

Lord Maximillian, finally out of patience, blinked and frowned. "I beg your pardon?"

"Come, Max. We might have had our differences the last time we met, but I insist on the chance to make amends." Lumiere gave me a wink. "Business is so unfashionable, and even more so on holidays. I was unable to make the Advent Ball because of you before, and I was much saddened to hear I missed the excitement. Surely you owe me for that. Or perhaps I owe you?"

He turned to Lady Penelope again, and then nodded to me. "If you will excuse us, Madame. It was so lovely, so absolutely lovely to meet you again. Your daughter spoke highly of you before, and I am glad to see after all these years, her assessment remains astute."

"I'll kindly ask you to refrain from discussing my beloved Eleanor," Lady Penelope snapped. "She has passed, and I would not have my granddaughter's sensibilities maligned by your thoughtlessness."

For the first time, Lumiere looked somewhat contrite. "A thousand apologies," he said, bowing to me. Behind him, Lord Maximillian was trying to slink away unnoticed. Lumiere gave me the same self-satisfied smile he had worn before, when I saw him at the Cabal. "Perhaps I will see you again soon. Perhaps in a more quiet environment, one that allows

THE ORDER OF THE CRYSTAL DAGGERS

for thoughtful discussion? There are so many good places to meet in Prague, after all."

"Perhaps," I muttered, unable to say anything else. I did not want him to mention the Cabal to Lady POW. "Good night, Mr. Valoris."

"Lumi, please, *chérie*. There is no need for us to be strangers."

He might have thought that, but I was not convinced. My fingers clenched into a fist as he walked away. He stepped up beside Lord Maximillian.

If he was a friend of Lord Maximillian's, and the son of a League member, he was somehow connected to our mission.

"What do you know about him?" I asked Lady Penelope. "He's part of this. He more or less just admitted to it."

"Come, Eleanora," Lady Penelope hissed. "We must get back to the manor quickly."

"Why?" I glanced around into the night, wondering briefly if I would be able to find Ferdy among the crowds. I did not see him, but I did see a shadow slinking around the columns of the theatre, and it reminded me of Didier. Was Lumiere's companion following us, too?

"Just hurry," Lady Penelope snapped, waiting on me as I climbed up behind her into the coach. I heard her give directions to the footmen, and I had only just sat down when she rapped on the roof and we sped off.

"I don't see why you're in such a hurry," I said, rubbing my knee. The sudden lurch forward had sent me tumbling, and I banged my knee on the hard edge of the seat.

"Now that Lumiere has made his appearance, I have a feeling I know who attacked Tulia."

THE ORDER OF THE CRYSTAL DAGGERS

"What?" I glanced out the window, watching as the city's twilight scene rushed past us. "You think Lumiere did it?"

"I'm almost certain of it," Lady Penelope said. "Lumiere is Louis Valoris' son—and he is a trickster to the very end. The fact that he was meeting with Lord Maximillian before only makes everything more precarious. I have no idea what kind of trouble he has managed to create."

"Are you going to tell me and Ben about Louis now?" I thought of what Harshad had said to me before, about Louis working alongside my grandfather. "And Grandfather Jakub, too?"

"There is no need to know all the details of the past," Lady Penelope insisted. Even in the soft moonlight, I could tell she was blushing. I did not know my grandmother was still capable of shame. If I was not as curious as I was, I might have laughed. "Suffice it to say, you only need to know Louis was a troublemaker then, and he has clearly remained one after all these years."

"You were the one who told me before that there is a cost to learning the truth," I nearly shouted, irritated beyond measure. "Why are you trying to protect me now?"

She ignored me. "Thank the good Lord that Xiana is here. Now that I know Lumiere is in Prague, we must be even more cautious. I must speak with Harshad, and I will have to find Amir, too. We need to see everything all over again, starting with Dr. Artha's death."

"What about Ben?" I asked, suddenly curious as to what my brother was doing. While Harshad had mentioned he had a new assignment, I still did not know the exact nature of it.

"Ben is working," Lady Penelope said. "I'm having him spy on a few people in the city, if you must know."

"Why?"

"He needs the practice." She waved her hand through the air, brushing the matter aside. "As you will learn, if you haven't already, there are many tasks one must master in order to protect others. Stealth, fighting, understanding strategy, and finding the right information are all imperative skills in our line of business."

"And keeping secrets, too?" I crossed my arms.

Lady Penelope wrinkled her nose. "Partially. But we are more concerned with discovering others' secrets than keeping them. Tonight, you will get a full demonstration of just such a skill."

I gulped, immediately trying to hide any trace of guilt. "I will?"

"Yes." Lady Penelope steepled her fingers together, while a sadistic form of pleasure came over her face. "My patience is at an end, and there is too much riding on this, now that the reasons are becoming clear. I have been waiting for this day, really."

"You have?" I tried not to let my voice crack. Lady POW was a forceful presence, but after all the hard work she had put me through, and the anguish she had caused between Ben and me, I hated to think she would try to find another way to break me.

"Oh, yes. I knew he was just waiting for the right moment to betray me." She seemed to be talking to herself more than me. "Now that he has found Eleanor's children, it was only a matter of time."

"What?" My skin began to hum with eerie uncertainty.

"What are you talking about?"

"Tell me, Eleanora," Lady Penelope said, her voice deadly and dangerous.

THE ORDER OF THE CRYSTAL DAGGERS

For a second, I worried she was going to ask me about Ferdy, and I would be unable to face her. But her next words sent an even deeper chill through my blood.

"Tell me what Amir has been keeping from me."

"What? I don't know of anything." I shook my head, somewhat relieved before I remembered that Amir had agreed not to mention Ferdy to Lady POW.

"This is not the time to be playing favorites," Lady Penelope snapped. "Your mother never won against me either, not even when it came to him."

"Clearly," I replied bitterly. "But Amir has nothing to do with Dr. Artha's murder. You weren't even here when it happened, were you? Frankly, I fail to see what Amir has to do with the rest of the coup, either."

"That is not something you would know. Lumiere is the missing piece in all of this, and his father is behind it. There is not just a coup that is happening in Bohemia, but one happening within the League of Ungentlemanly Warfare. Everything makes sense now."

I twisted my hands into my skirts, trying to force myself to remain strong against Lady Penelope's reasoning. The letter Ferdy had given to me earlier brushed against my hand. My earlier question about the League called to me, and I was beginning to realize the danger of our situation.

If I am going to protect Ferdy, I need to be careful.

I took a deep breath. "I still don't see how Lumi fits into all of this."

"But you know he *is* a part of this. You just said the same thing only moments ago!" Lady Penelope shook her head. "Do not allow your stubbornness or your loyalty to Amir blind you."

"Tell me how Amir's betrayal fits into everything, then." I covered my hidden pocket, shielding Ferdy's letter further from detection. "If you think I know some of Amir's important secrets, then you'll have to do better to convince me to part with them than just because you order me to."

"Insolent child," Lady Penelope roared. "Need I remind you that I am your leader?"

"Trust is earned, not forced." I glared at her. "And you're in no position to order me around in this regard. You won't tell me any of your secrets, either."

"There is a difference between us. I am not obligated to tell you anything. I am charged with keeping certain secrets of history, for the kingdom of Britain and for others as well. You accepted me as your authority. You owe me your allegiance."

"My allegiance is only to the truth!"

It was hard to remember the last time I rendered Lady Penelope speechless, if it had ever happened. But as she stared at me, her expression aghast, I gloried in a small victory against her.

I reveled in it even more when she sighed in defeat.

"It seems I have taught you too well," she murmured. "Well done, Eleanora. You have managed to learn your lessons, and much more proficiently than I thought."

I bristled at her reluctant praise. "It doesn't do me any good if you won't tell me the whole truth."

"The whole truth is not yet known," Lady Penelope admitted. "But there is no denying Lumiere's presence, and I must consider the evidence. And I need your help to do that."

"I can only help you if you tell me what you know."

Lady POW's eyes went soft. "We will have to compromise."

"Then you can go first. You need more practice with humility."

She dropped the sympathetic act. "I should have known you would avenge Eleanor, too."

I took a deep breath, inhaling sharply. I did not know if Lady Penelope had been meaning to insult me or not, but I knew *Máma* had always called me to be brave, and that meant being brave enough to be kind, too.

We were discussing delicate matters, and it was easy to see kindness as a sort of cowardice in this case.

I did not want to fight my grandmother, and as much as I doubted Lady Penelope was anything like the average grandmother, that was who she was. We were both disillusioned and damaged by the world, and it was my duty—my freedom, my choice, but my duty nonetheless—to help bind up the broken wounds inside of us.

"She would not need to be avenged if things had worked out differently," I pointed out quietly. "But it's like you said before, about the fallen castle walls. There is nothing to be done about it now. We can only go forward."

"Yes." The terseness of her voice suggested Lady Penelope was, indeed, ready to move on. I almost smiled; she was as uncomfortable with my mercy as she had been with the idea of my mother's justice.

My grandmother was a woman who would never be satisfied until she let herself be satisfied, and even in the short time I had known her, I had a feeling she would never completely allow for that.

"I still have to coordinate information with Harshad," Lady Penelope said, "but we must start at the beginning."

I nodded. "I'm listening."

"You know as I have told you before that I was sent here by Queen Victoria," she began. "This region has experienced plenty of upheavals in the last several years, including the Revolution of 1848 and the polarization of the main political aristocracy. When there were several deaths of representatives, especially by those who favored working with Emperor Franz Joseph, it was a signal to Her Royal Majesty to investigate. She sent me and Harshad, along with our small team, to come here and assess the situation. She is further concerned that Indian leadership shows signs of destabilizing."

"I remember that part. You came to talk with Dr. Artha and found that he was murdered."

"Dr. Artha was an informant of mine, and one of the few in the region familiar the Order. He also knew of the League."

"You said before they were the same."

"They have the same goal," Lady Penelope said. "When it comes to much of our work, anyway. But there are some more nuanced differences. We have worked together in the past, but there are some personal issues that remain between us. When Dr. Artha sent notice to Tulia, I did not realize they were such close friends. He also sent notice, through Father Novak, to the Light."

Understanding dawned. "Lumiere."

"Yes. 'Light' is his codename." She nodded. "I was so caught up in Tulia's reappearance that I forgot all about him."

That was understandable; Tulia had worked with my mother as a nursemaid and companion, but she was also Jakub's half-sister. The surface animosity between Tulia and Lady Penelope was clear, even if I was uncertain at its depth.

"If Dr. Artha sent for Lumiere, I doubt Lumiere would be the one who killed him," I said.

"Dr. Artha was the one who knew of the Order, and he knew of the deaths of the politicians, and the others who were getting threatened," Lady Penelope reminded me. "He would have recognized the Order's poison where it was used. That is likely the reason he reached out to the League as well as the Order."

I did not know what to say. It was hard to remember everything that was going on. There were murders and threats, whispers of coups and now, Amir, whom I had believed to be my ally, was getting accused of betraying Lady POW.

Lady Penelope glanced out the window of the coach. "Lumiere is the son of Louis Valoris, now the Minister of the League. He and I have never been friendly, exactly."

"So he is working against you?"

"Likely." She snorted. "He was very good friends with Jakub, your grandfather. We were his closest confidants several decades ago. After our relationship soured and I escaped from him, Louis naturally blamed me."

I thought of what Harshad had told me before about Jakub. Harshad was the one who had really rescued Lady Penelope, even if she did not credit him.

Despite the seriousness of the situation, I smiled. Harshad had been right about Lady POW; they had known each other long enough to know they could never truly be friends.

My thoughts turned to Ferdy and the letter he had given me. If I let him help the Order, was it possible we would be the same as Lady POW and Harshad? Would we be unable to be friends through our lives, even if we were able to work together?

But Ferdy already has helped me. I curled my fingers around the letter again, thinking of the League.

"So Louis is trying to help Lord Maximillian and Karl restore the Bohemian monarchy," I said, "and he knows he can expect a fight from you."

"That is likely why Lumiere has come, yes." Lady Penelope gazed out the window. "Louis always romanticized power, but he was a realist about it, too. The most powerful position for him, in his estimation, was always to be at the right hand of the devil instead of the devil himself."

"I suppose he liked my grandfather quite a bit then, from your earlier remarks."

She smirked. "He did. Louis has a point; the one holding the title of power is easily different from the one actually in power, and it makes for a great excuse and disguise, in the event something goes wrong."

"Like the French Revolution."

"It's humorous that you should mention France. Louis always dreamed of helping Napoleon."

"Well, it's no wonder he didn't like you," I said. "Not after you married the Duke of Wellington."

Lady Penelope laughed, a crusty sound that emanated from deep inside of her, almost as if she had forgotten how to do it. "I married Arthur more to ensure my escape from Jakub, but you are right. It would have been something Jakub and Louis would have hated. They were already leery of my British heritage, even though the Order transcends nationalities."

"Why didn't you just marry Harshad?"

As soon as the question left my mouth, I knew I had overstepped myself. I hurriedly shook my head, but Lady Penelope did not seem to notice.

THE ORDER OF THE CRYSTAL DAGGERS

"Harshad was a merchant trader before he came to work with the League," she replied. There was a vague practicality in her voice that made me cringe. She had clearly thought through this possibility more than once.

Before everything else, I knew for certain that everyone lied about something. As I watched Lady Penelope recount her earlier adventures, I saw that she was lying to herself as much as others. I could not say if she knew the *real* truth or not, but she was certainly against admitting it aloud.

"Harshad suffered quite a bit when he went up against Jakub, freeing me and Eleanor from him. I left him thinking it would help him if I stayed away. He was upset with me for trying to protect him further, and once I was certain I was safe and in a position to resume my duties for the Order, I understood why. He loved Eleanor dearly, as his own daughter. Harshad is the only one who called her Dezda, and she called him 'Uncle' affectionately."

"I think he might have loved you, too." My voice was a whisper against the darkness of the carriage; my words seemed to echo past the windows filling the night sky with their heaviness while the stars twinkled.

Lady Penelope shrugged, letting me see only the smallest degree of doubt. It was possible she knew she was lying to herself. "It does not matter now. Relationships only complicate things, especially when you work in the espionage business. Harshad might have wanted me to stay, but I know I made the right decision. Later on, I was able to reach out to him and secure his position as an honorary member of the League. We began working together, and we have been the same ever since."

"If you were just trying to protect Harshad," I said slowly, "I can understand why you would distance yourself from him."

THE ORDER OF THE CRYSTAL DAGGERS

I did not want to tell her just how much I understood her decision, and how much I envied her certainty. Ferdy's face once more came into my mind. I knew it was only my concern for his safety, and possibly my pride, that kept me from seeking him out.

"Well, that does not matter so much now." Lady POW straightened in her chair. "Louis has found himself a puppet in Lord Maximillian and an ally in Karl, and Lumiere has been sent to prevent me from stopping him. Louis is likely behind the death of Dr. Artha."

"But Louis is not here."

"Logic, Eleanora. He has resources. There are any number of henchmen and mercenaries he could employ, such as the one who died the night the castle walls fell. I would not be surprised to learn he was acting under Lumiere's orders, even if he was paid by Lord Maximillian or Karl."

It seemed like years had passed since that night, when Ben and I were on the same team, fighting for our lives and the lives of others in the underground walls of the castle's wine cellar. I could only see a blurry face when I thought about the man who had died in the blaze.

Lady POW gazed back at me. "Now, it is your turn, Eleanora. Tell me what Amir has been keeping from me. I know he and Lumiere are old friends. How long has he been talking with him?"

I blinked. "Amir is friends with Lumiere?"

"You heard him in there," Lady Penelope reminded me. "He knew your mother and held her in high esteem. Of course he would have been friends with Amir."

"I didn't know about that." I felt my mouth go dry. Lumiere was the enemy, and Amir was his friend? It did not make sense in my mind. "I know he mentioned before he had

THE ORDER OF THE CRYSTAL DAGGERS

contacts with other League members, but I heard it straight from him, the same as you did, that day in the library."

"You're not cooperating with me. Don't lie."

"I'm not involved," I said. "He did not tell me about Lumiere. I've never met him before today."

That's not true. My mind conjured up the memory of seeing him in the Cabal, and I faltered as I tried not to show my weakness.

"I can tell you are hiding something. What did Amir tell you then?" Lady Penelope asked. "There must be something."

"He told me how he got his scar, the one on his hand," I admitted. Surely there was nothing wrong in admitting that. "He said his family tried to kill him and he would have died if it weren't for *Máma* and Xiana."

There were other things he told me, too. He told me the journal, the one my mother had kept during her last mission, was missing. He told me Lady Penelope was looking for my weakness, and she was putting pressure on Ben to find out my secrets.

I mentally ran through the list of things I had learned from him, only to realize Lady POW was still waiting for more of a response from me when I reached the end.

She looked at me, irritated and expectant. "What else, Eleanora? What else did he tell you about the scar on his hand? Did he tell you what it meant?"

Slowly, I nodded. "He said it was the mark of the *nassara*, the Christian converts."

"That's all he told you?"

"Yes. There was nothing else."

THE ORDER OF THE CRYSTAL DAGGERS

"You're certain? You were paying attention to what he said, correct?"

"Yes." I frowned at her, upset at her insinuation, and still sore at her accusation against Amir.

"What is it?" Lady Penelope asked. "Did you remember something else?"

There was one other thing I could remember.

Amir had mentioned the *noon*, the symbol of the *nassara*, when he told me about his scar. It was the mark on his hand, but it was also the mark on my mother's journal.

After he told me his story, the use of the same mark had not seemed so unusual, considering Amir and *Máma's* history together.

If Lady POW thought Amir was keeping secrets from her—secrets that would affect our mission—it was likely that it had something to do with my mother. And that meant that it was possible it was tied to even more of the past than I had originally suspected.

The coach pulled up to a stop in front of the manor a moment later. We were home, and I saw a way to get out from Lady Penelope's grasp.

"Eleanora." Lady Penelope's voice was impatient, but my resolve was firm and final.

I shook my head. "I have nothing else to tell you."

She snorted disdainfully. "We will see about that, won't we? Come. Join me and the others in the library."

Regretfully, I gathered my skirts, keeping Ferdy's letter wrapped in my hand. In some ways, I gripped it in hopes of comfort; I did not like the foreboding feeling suddenly unraveling in my stomach.

THE ORDER OF THE CRYSTAL DAGGERS

The thought of Amir working against Lady POW, of him betraying the Order in favor of the League—all of it seemed too impossible at first. But I thought through his disagreements with both Harshad and Lady Penelope, how he protected me against Ben, and how he found a way to befriend me despite our difficult beginning.

Was it possible?

I hated asking myself that question. I walked into the house, heading toward the library. It was here, I thought, that Amir had told me himself that he was Lady Penelope's most loyal ally. Had he been lying to me?

It was only when Harshad spoke to me that I awoke from my troubling thoughts.

"Eleanora, what is it? What is wrong?"

His voice seemed to call to me from far beyond me. When I looked up at him, he frowned. Before either of us could say anything—before I could answer his question or before he could ask it again—Lady POW interrupted us.

"Harshad, where is Amir?" Her voice was brittle and sharp, and even Harshad knew it was best not to keep her waiting.

He looked at me, somewhat apologetically, before he said, "He has already left for his rounds tonight. He will be back in the morning."

Lady Penelope narrowed her eyes at me before the two of them began to speak in another language. I listened closely, hoping I would discover some clues. I caught "Valoris" and "Amir," and even "Ben," but I was not able to deduce the meaning behind their words.

Quietly, I sighed and took a seat. It was going to be a long night.

THE ORDER OF THE CRYSTAL DAGGERS

220

THE ORDER OF THE CRYSTAL DAGGERS

14

The next morning my fingers were cold, even as I gripped the cup of tea in my hands. Mindlessly, I blew on the contents, watching as the force of my breath rippled across the hot drink and the steam wafted away from me. I did not know what else to do but sit there and stare off into space. It was too tempting and too easy to get lost in my own thoughts, jumbled as they were. Only one seemed insistent on repeating itself, and it was the one I hated the most.

Amir had not returned to the manor.

Harshad and Lady Penelope had discussed things long into the night, leaving me to sit on the couch, silent and watchful. I had fallen asleep, still in my evening gown, and it was only hours later when I woke up, alone and cold.

After trading my gown out for a housedress, I went to the kitchens for some breakfast, even though I could hardly eat. The events of the past evening were too mysterious. Between Karl's anger, Ferdy's determination, and Amir's disappearance, I was tired of trying to figure everything out.

All of a sudden, nothing in my life seemed to be the same.

"Nora."

I blew on my tea again as Ben came into the small kitchen behind me. He was wearing a loose-fitting pair of pants and a tunic, one of the many training outfits Harshad had ordered for him. He even wore similar shoes, I noticed, seeing the soft woven coverings on his feet.

"What is it?" I turned to him and tried to keep down a yawn. It was past the usual time I woke up when I was working with Harshad, but no one had come to get me that morning. At the sight of Ben, I wondered if that was the

221

reason he sought me out. "Have you come to get me for a lesson?"

With everything that was going on, I was hoping that the chilliness between me and Ben would disperse some. When I saw him shake his head, I felt the last of my hope shrivel and die.

"No." He moved around me, reaching for his own cup. I heard him sigh softly. "I heard what happened last night."

I said nothing, only taking a small sip of my tea.

"Lady Penelope and Harshad have been awake for hours. They've headed out of the manor, both of them, so they can go and see if they can find Amir," Ben said. He hesitated before adding, "I am not sure they ever sleep, to be honest."

I liked that he was trying to be nice, bringing me tea and speaking kindly to me, even though I was upset about Amir. "Have you heard anything?"

"He's not here."

"I know that much. Do you think he is in trouble?" I asked. "I know he usually comes home by the time we're working with Harshad."

"By the time *you're* working with Harshad," Ben corrected.

I decided to let his barb slide this time, especially when I noticed Ben's expression was grim. "What is it?"

"Lady POW and Harshad are upset," Ben said. "And I think they have good reason to be."

I frowned but said nothing.

"I have been thinking it over," he said slowly, "and after talking with both of them earlier, I think they are right to be worried about him."

THE ORDER OF THE CRYSTAL DAGGERS

"Why would you say that?" I asked. "I mean, I am worried for Amir, too. He could be in trouble, or there could be some information that is causing his delay. There is no real reason to question his loyalty to Lady Penelope over a delay."

"It's not a delay."

My skin chilled over at the edge in his voice as much as the condemnation in his words.

"I saw him last night," Ben said. "I saw him as I was watching Karl's movements last night."

"You were watching Karl?"

"Yes. Lady POW wanted me to find out as much as I could about him, and she thought sending me would be a good idea." Ben shrugged. "She said if he caught me spying on him, all I had to do was tell him that I was worried for you, as your older brother."

"Makes sense," I murmured. I thought about Ferdy last night. *Did Ben see him while we were at the concert?*

"I nearly missed Karl as he stormed out of the *Stavovské divadlo*," Ben said. "He was angry and upset. I followed him to a new address, and then I saw Lord Maximillian come with a stranger."

"The man from the Cabal. Lumiere Valoris."

"Yes, that's who it was," Ben said. "How did you know?"

"I met him last night. He was the one who interrupted the concert and made Karl so angry. Karl had arranged for the last piece of the evening to be a tribute to Bohemia, and Lumiere ruined it for him."

Ben did not ask for details on Lumiere, so I knew he had discussed him with Lady Penelope before. I wondered if she had told him the same things that she told me, or if this was another way to see if she could get me to reveal my secrets.

THE ORDER OF THE CRYSTAL DAGGERS

"Lumiere is connected to Lord Maximillian and Karl," Ben continued. "I know from Lady Penelope that he is a member of the League, but she doesn't trust him. When he was done with his meeting, Lumiere went back to the castle with Karl. I decided to follow Lumiere after that. I didn't know who he was at the time, but I felt like it would be good to have some information on him since he talked with both Karl and Lord Maximillian."

"That was a good idea," I said, making Ben smile.

"I thought so, too," he admitted. "He didn't get far before I saw Amir."

"So Amir was near the castle last night?"

"Not exactly," Ben said. "I followed the carriage as well as I could. It wasn't too hard, since the winter weather has kept a lot of people from heading out. Eventually, Lumiere stopped at the church where Father Novak was murdered."

"Our Lady of the Snows."

He nodded. "He went inside for just a few moments, and then Amir stepped out of the shadows and greeted him."

I thought about what Lady POW had said before. "I know they were friends when *Máma* was alive."

Ben wrinkled his nose. "It seems they are still quite good friends," he said. "Lumiere was ecstatic to see him. Amir got into the carriage, and then they rode together for a few blocks before Amir slipped out."

"What happened then?" I asked. "Did you follow Amir?"

Ben took a long sip of his tea before he shook his head. "No."

"Did you keep following Lumiere then?" I asked.

Ben was suddenly much more reluctant to talk. I saw him glance back at the kitchen door, nervous and bitter.

He wants to leave now.

Which meant he had done something.

I stood up and put my teacup down on the small table. "Tell me," I said. "I might be able to help."

"I doubt that," Ben muttered. "You're Amir's favorite. You don't think he's a traitor."

"Of course not," I said. "He told me before he was Lady Penelope's most loyal follower. Even Lady POW told us that she would trust him with her life."

"That's exactly what a traitor would want you to think," Ben said. "Come on, Nora. Think about it. Something's happened to us in the last few weeks. Amir has been causing problems between us."

"Amir?" I slammed my teacup against the table. "Amir is not the one who has been using you to try to find out my secrets."

"Are you really that blind? He's the one who made you suspicious of me in the first place," Ben insisted.

"You didn't help by going out and beating Ferdy up."

"I told you why I did that." Ben stood up now, too, only to look down at me.

"Please, Ben," I said, grabbing his sleeve. "Even if you think Amir is the one behind the trouble between us, you have to at least face the truth that it only remains there because you keep it there."

"That's not true."

"Yes, it is," I insisted. "This is the first time in weeks we've spoken plainly to each other."

"Because you won't tell me the truth!"

225

I was taken aback. My hand dropped from his arm. "Is that really what you think? That I won't tell you all my secrets? That you can't trust me?"

"It's true." Ben shook his head. "You know it's the truth."

I felt my heart clench. Once more, I was tempted to tell him. But the thought of Ferdy's safety, of how wrong Ben was about Amir, and even Empress Maria Anna's concern stopped me, and that was when I realized something important. I did not want my brother's ire, but I did want his trust. I would not always be able to tell him things. I knew he had secrets of his own from me, starting with his own feelings about our father playing favorites between us.

The same thing was true of Ferdy, of Lady Penelope, of Harshad and Amir and even Tulia. I did not need to know all their secrets. I just needed to know I could trust them.

Lady POW had been adamant before that it was necessary to know that people would fail me. She warned me that I had to be on my guard at all times, and that it was important to pay attention to everything so I would not be surprised at betrayals, and that I would be able to know how to manipulate people to do what I wanted and get the results I wanted.

I had balked at the idea then. I realized now that she might have had a point, but there was a price too great for me to pay.

I wanted to be able to trust people, so that even if we failed in the end, we would be together.

I did not know if that was more important or not, but it was important enough to me right now that I knew I had to say something to Ben.

"Some secrets are not just mine, Ben," I said. "I can't tell you everything. Other people are counting on me to keep silent."

THE ORDER OF THE CRYSTAL DAGGERS

"I knew you were lying before." He did not sound smug; he sounded relieved, which made me soften, even if I did not want him to worry about it at all.

"I'm sorry. I don't do it to hurt you. I'm trying to protect others. Maybe I'm even trying to protect myself," I said quietly. "But there are bigger things happening here, things that are bigger than you and me."

"I know that," Ben insisted. "I'm worried you don't."

"I do know it. I'm still trying to figure it out some, but I do know there's a lot at stake. But you do know I love you. And I would never want to hurt you." I looked up at him. His blue-green eyes were just a little lighter than mine, and for some reason, it was so hard to explain to Ben how much I did love him. He was my family, my only family, and someone who had suffered so much at my hand, yet someone who still fought to protect me. I sighed. "I guess it's unavoidable that I will hurt you, but I don't want to lose your love. Or your trust."

I looked down at the floor, unsure of what else to do. Ben and I had always had a common enemy with Alex and Cecilia, and we had always had a common dream in Liberté. This was the first time in recent years we had different loyalties and different pursuits.

Finally, Ben sighed. He shifted his feet and put his hands in his pockets.

"I suppose you're right." Ben's voice was more gentle this time. "We are going to have to trust each other if we're going to succeed. And that includes trusting each other with our silence as much as our secrets."

Hope renewed inside of me. I almost cheered at his reply, but I stopped myself. Ferdy's earlier restraint had clearly been against his wishes, but he knew he could only have my trust if he could earn it. I would do the same with Ben; I would have to wait to see that I had earned Ben's trust back.

At the thought of Ferdy, my smile brightened even more. I loved him, and I knew I could trust him. He wanted me to trust him, and he had earned it.

I nearly squealed with delight, thinking of the next time I would see him. There would still be trouble between us, but if we trusted each other, we could find a way.

Ben sighed. "I still think it is fair to question Amir's loyalty," he said. "I talked with Lady POW this morning after I met with him, and she's certain that he is working to betray her. And possibly us, too."

"You met with Amir?" I frowned and waited for Ben to provide further information. I could already guess what happened.

Ben had confronted Amir, wanting information on Lumiere, and Amir told him something that made Ben and Lady POW suspicious.

When Ben finished his story, I was disappointed with how much of it I had guessed.

"He said he had to go and take care of something," Ben said. "He said that Lumiere was his friend and he wanted Amir to help him with something. He said it had to do with Lord Maximillian and Karl, and that was all he could tell me."

"Did he say when he was coming back?" I asked.

Ben shook his head. "But it's not a coincidence, is it, that Lady Penelope thinks he's betrayed her? The timing is suspicious."

What could Amir be doing to help Lumiere?

I could not think of anything, but I also did not know why Amir would be helping Lumiere in the first place. I had seen

THE ORDER OF THE CRYSTAL DAGGERS

him myself, chatting with Lord Maximillian. He had talked of meeting him the night of the Advent Ball, of mending the issues between them. It did seem like Karl and Lord Maximillian had been fighting with each other, too, as I recalled what Karl had told me, and the other information Ferdy had given me.

"We can question Amir's loyalty," I said slowly, "but I think we need to question Lady POW's, too. She has reasons for her own feelings on this matter. And there is no denying her own secrets."

Ben sat down at the table again. His expression was remorseful. He picked up his cup and poured more tea. "That is fair, I suppose."

I grinned and sat down across from Ben. "If that's fair, we've found a good starting place to start asking questions."

Reaching into my pocket, I curled my hand around the letter Ferdy had given me. "I have a few more questions I'd also like to run by you, *brácha*."

"I'll see to the tea. Looks like we're going to need more."

Before I could show Ben the letter, Xiana appeared in the doorway. She appeared like a ghost, silently and gracefully, and in her dark robes, I almost felt it was too apt of a description.

"There you are," she said. "I have been looking all over for you."

"You have?" I asked, sad to see my time with Ben interrupted. It was nice to feel like his friend again.

"Yes. You've received a message," Xiana said. "It's from someone named Clavan. He says Zipporah will be able to meet with you this weekend, on Saturday night after the Shabbat."

THE ORDER OF THE CRYSTAL DAGGERS

She handed Ben the small scroll of paper. I watched as Ben read through the note, before turning to Xiana. "Have you heard anything from Lady Penelope or Harshad about Amir?"

Xiana shook her head. "No. But if I know Amir, I know if he does not want to be found, he will not be found."

"You don't think he will betray Lady POW, too, do you?" I asked, surprised.

Xiana's stoic face hardened, ever so slightly. "He is more than capable of betrayal. Remember, that is what he did to your mother." She shook her head, her long braid of hair swinging behind her. "And others as well."

Before I could ask another question, she excused herself. I watched as she left, my mouth hanging open in shock and confusion. I would not have said Amir betrayed my mother; he left her, and broke her heart maybe, but he did not betray her.

What did Xiana mean by that?

Ben, unaware of my thoughts, looked up from the note. "Eliezer's wife will have our herbs for Tulia this Saturday. That's a few days away yet. We'll have to question her carefully. I don't like the thought of getting Clavan and Jarl and their friends mixed up in our trouble."

I nodded. "I agree."

"Now we just have to get to Saturday," Ben said. He leaned back, stretching out some. "And then we'll have our answers."

"Don't forget, we'll be able to make an antidote to the Order's poison, and we'll find out if anyone else is making it, too." I took another sip of tea, then got up from the table.

Hopefully Amir will be back before then, and we can forget this betrayal nonsense.

THE ORDER OF THE CRYSTAL DAGGERS

"Are you looking for something to eat?" Ben asked.

"Yes."

"Get some for me, too."

I laughed. "I was planning on it," I assured him. As I searched the kitchen, I glanced back at the doorway where Xiana had disappeared. Amir had told before that he had made a mistake when he allowed my mother to leave. I would not have said he betrayed her, the way Xiana had.

I did not think he would betray Lady Penelope, either. Ben and I did not agree with our conclusions, but there was no point in fighting about it until we found him.

THE ORDER OF THE CRYSTAL DAGGERS

232

THE ORDER OF THE CRYSTAL DAGGERS

15

◊

Three days passed, and there was no sign of Amir. I did not allow myself to despair, because if I did, I would not just wallow in my sadness, I would go mad. While time seemed to move only slightly quicker than absolute stillness, I relived our conversations, running them over and over again inside my mind, turning them over and examining them again. There were so many, from the time I had met Amir on the streets of Prague, to the time he had carried me to the front parlor. I thought about meeting him in the library the second time, knocking him down with a punch, and practicing the waltz with him. I thought about his devotion to my mother and the changing mix of pain and pleasure in his gaze as he talked with me.

It had been a struggle to pay attention to anything over the past few days; even Harshad seemed to understand my distraction. He had Xiana review the basics of stance, footwork, and technique with me before dismissing me from my sessions. Harshad said I would be too distracted to fight well, and he was right.

Ben was allowed to roam the city, searching for any sign of Amir, while Lady POW herself went to lectures and socials with other older ladies. It turns out the elderly were a wealth of gossip and information, but there was no mention of a rogue Turk wandering around the town.

We could only wait, Lady Penelope had said.

Her words were a prison sentence to my heart, but I was comforted in that she did not seem to take her own advice. I saw her as she prowled around the manor at all hours of the day, and even when we came back from our outings, I would wake up in the middle of the night to find her pacing the hallways. I had no idea where Amir's room was, but I heard her steps pass down my hallway more than once as the night dragged on. Neither of us seemed to be able to sleep well.

It's a miracle that I am able to stay awake for this, I thought, looking around at the scene before me.

The *Nàrodni muzuem* was full of aristocrats and the political elite, but it was not much different from any other ball I had seen. A large crowd had gathered in the atrium, where Karl lorded over the room from atop a twin pair of grand staircases. *The place really is beautiful,* I thought, taking note of the gothic arches and the detailed metalwork. The marble floors reflected the warm lighting, sending a ripple of sparkles through the regal crowd.

It was a fitting metaphor, as the secret prince of Bohemia reigned over the room as its crown jewel. He had been invited to make a speech, and the one he was making was full of meaningful, celebrated pauses as he impressed the masses.

As his audience broke out in another sea of applause, Lady Penelope cleared her throat behind me. "Stand up straight, Eleanora. There are a lot of important people here. We wouldn't want to look sloppy."

"Of course we wouldn't." I struggled to keep myself from yawning.

"Why are you so tired? You already fell asleep on the way here. Goodness, your hair is a mess." Lady Penelope discretely tugged on the combs in my hair, and I waved her meddling hands away at once.

"Stop it," I hissed. "I'll get it."

I did not want her fussing over me. I was already under severe scrutiny, since I was not actually a member of the political elite even if I was welcomed by Society. Many of the lords and ladies looked me over carefully as we had entered the museum, and I knew they had a right to be curious. As

THE ORDER OF THE CRYSTAL DAGGERS

Karl continued to make his speech, I saw a wave of eyes turn to glance at me.

Lady POW huffed. "You should have checked yourself better before we came in."

"You should have said something sooner if they bothered you."

"Why are you even wearing these combs?" Lady Penelope asked. Her expression suddenly soured as she straightened the one behind my left ear.

I was wearing the combs Ferdy had given me. After the long days of worrying for Amir, the twinkling combs served as a talisman of sorts, with all their small emeralds, the brilliant sapphires, all decorated around golden *fleurs-di-lis*. Wearing them reminded me to remain steadfast in my determination, even if I did not feel like being brave.

And, if Ferdy did come and "rescue" me from here, he would know I had decided to trust him. I tried not to blush, thinking of the pleasure he would feel.

Lady Penelope cleared her throat. "Did Karl give you these?"

"What? No. There is no need to worry about them." I batted her hand away one last time, before twisting the combs once more into my curls. I winced at the pain, but I gave Karl my full focus. Secretly, I hoped that the rest of the room would follow my example and pay attention to him.

I already did not relish the thought of seeing Karl again.

"It's not my fault you are content to look like you've napped all the way over here," Lady Penelope muttered. "Even if it is true, there's no reason give it away."

The *Nàrodni muzuem* was on the far side of Prague from where we lived. I considered my nap a small repayment for the task I was about to face.

"I've been working with Harshad in the mornings, and I had more late nights now that we are moving in Society again," I reminded her, trying to mask my moaning. "Be grateful I do not look worse."

"I have had some late nights myself," Lady Penelope remarked, and I was amused that she would admit to her nightly discomfort. "There is no reason you should not be able to recover if I can."

I ignored her, yawning again, as Karl continued on with his speech.

He seemed very happy, much more energetic than me. His voice was booming and somewhat seductive as he heralded the courage of his fellow men and condemned the uncaring heart of the emperor.

"Ever since the disastrous fire at the castle, there have been no condolences from Emperor Franz Joseph. What can we conclude, except for the obvious?" Karl waved his arms around, exaggerating his facial expressions. "Bohemia is not his concern. Our pain is not his pain."

There were several murmurs of agreement, even if they were quiet.

"Are we not called to be free?" Karl asked, speaking with the easy grace of a practiced prodigy. "The Lord himself called the Hebrews out of Egypt, and I ask you, my countrymen, are we not in Egypt ourselves? Surrounded by an empire that is crumbling under the weight of bureaucracy, the decadency of dispassionate rulers, of taxation without representation or recompense?"

There were more cheers this time. I glanced over at Lady Penelope. She had an impressed look on her face.

"You're not agreeing with him, are you?" I asked.

THE ORDER OF THE CRYSTAL DAGGERS

She gave me her sadistic smile. "I can appreciate an honest attempt to manipulate the masses, Eleanora. That's his Oxford education coming through, right there."

"I am here to proceed over this dedication," Karl said. "But I do not want to dedicate our work to the greatness of the empire. Bohemia's greatness is in its people. We are the dreamers, we are the makers, we are the ones who carried and build greatness from the bond of our blood. We are the ones who are called to represent Bohemia to the world, and it is time we took a stand and demand that we be heard, as is our due. We are the ones who make this country great, and we deserve to be properly represented on the world stage."

"He is certainly a good orator," Lady Penelope murmured, as Karl began talking about taxes and tariffs and the empire's abuse of our people. "If what he was saying was true, he would make a good ruler."

"His rhetoric could be considered treasonous in some circles," I said.

"That is good politicking," Lady Penelope reminded me. She gave me a wry smile. "Speak, strike, redress. You will be surprised how politicians use language to get you to believe what you think they mean."

"Hopefully, that will change one day." I shook my head. "That is dishonest."

"People do not want the truth. People want to be the hero of a good story, and more often than not, they want to be the hero without doing any of the work." Lady Penelope nodded toward Karl. "He is giving that to them now, and they are responding as expected. We will have to be careful."

"Will this disrupt Queen Victoria's relationship with India?"

"The worst part is that I don't know if it will or not," Lady Penelope said. "As much as it pains me to admit, many leaders do not have everything figured out. We can only act in

THE ORDER OF THE CRYSTAL DAGGERS

the manner we see best, without knowing if it will work, or if it will be the best position to have taken in the end."

I knew she was talking about her own position as the leader of the Order, and I wondered if it was good for me to have doubts about trusting her. I could not seem to help my response when it came to Amir, but there were other areas in which I did not trust her.

For the moment, I did not say anything about that. "It seems there is a lot of guesswork in trying to change the future."

I gave her a response that was ambiguous and vague, hoping she would be pleased.

She nodded. "Especially for the better."

"Better for who?" I murmured, wondering aloud more to myself as Karl concluded his speech and stepped down. The audience clapped and cheered, and he waved gallantly to them.

Lady POW sighed beside me. "If he is not stopped," she warned, "he will be a formidable opponent for the emperor. He has already made some high-ranking people uncomfortable. Harshad received a message from one of our associates in Vienna that said Franz Joseph has been asking King Ferdinand for information."

"Did the king respond?" I asked as I kept my eyes on Karl, watching him grin as he met with other members of the Diet and those who were in attendance. He seemed much happier than he was the last time I saw him.

"No," Lady Penelope said. "The king and Empress Maria Anna have been ill the past few days. They have not allowed anyone to meet with them. Empress Maria Anna has canceled her plans to leave for their country estate, too."

"I have heard she likes to travel," I said, "but with Karl here, I would think she would want to make sure he was staying out of any trouble."

"Yes, I suppose. Family members do tend to make poor decisions because of love." Lady Penelope turned to me. "And while we are discussing that particular subject, there is something I need to ask you."

"What is it?"

Lady Penelope's eyes, so similar to my mother's and my own, pierced through me. "Are you falling in love with Karl? I need you to tell me now, Eleanora. This is not the time to remind you that there is no room for romance in the life of a spy, but I feel I must. I know you are worried for Amir, and I will be the first to admit that this is my fault. I thought he had forgiven me for the business with your mother."

"We don't know if you're wrong yet," I said, choosing to ignore, if only for the moment, how she downplayed my mother's unhappiness and Amir's regret. "He hasn't had the chance to explain himself."

"Either way, it does not matter now. I'm more worried for you. Falling in love has no place in this job."

"I am not in love with Karl."

"You have not been yourself recently. You have not been yourself since the concert, and it's not just worry for Amir. There is more to it, isn't there?" Her eyes darted up to my hair. "I know Karl had to give you those combs, Eleanora."

"I already told you he didn't," I hissed, suddenly afraid. I reached out and lightly brushed my fingers against the jewels of the combs. Ferdy had insisted I take them, and I wondered all of a sudden if he had tricked me.

THE ORDER OF THE CRYSTAL DAGGERS

I straightened my shoulders. I had to take care of one thing at a time, and Lady POW's temper was the more immediate. I could find a way to yell at Ferdy later, I decided.

"It does not matter now. I am not in love with Karl, and if you make me scream it, it might damage our cover."

I hoped she would not say anything else; Lady Penelope had a perfect hold on me. I had nowhere to run as we were surrounded by the public. If I left now, and suddenly, there would be whispers that could adversely affect our mission.

She glared at me. "Eleanora, don't be ridicu—"

"My lady."

I was never so happy to see Karl as I was in that moment. He came up to me, and even though I could not stop myself from wondering if Ferdy was going to follow him, there was nothing dishonest about my smile as I greeted him. "Mr. Marcelin, how lovely to see you."

I curtsied, and he bowed over my hand, kissing it reverently while I praised God for his providence in allowing me to wear gloves once more.

"I am so grateful to see you here today," Karl said. "Especially since I know our last meeting was marked with unpleasant circumstances."

"Oh, there is no need to worry about it," I murmured, hoping that Lady POW was not listening. When I saw one of her friends had come up to speak with her, I added quietly, "Unless there is some reason I should expect to see the other Mr. Marcelin here?"

This would be another event where Ferdy would be eager to "rescue" me.

Karl's smile dropped. "No."

Ferdy had said he was leaving for Silesia in the morning on the night of the concert.

But surely, he wasn't actually leaving? I suddenly wondered if he had been telling me the truth.

He did promise me before that he would not lie to me.

Carefully, I asked Karl, and he shook his head.

"Please, Eleanora," he said. "The rededication of the museum has been a lovely event, and I'd rather not discuss the tragic events of this week. Please, come with me. I will introduce you to my friends."

"Tragic?" I smiled. "I know you have your struggles with family, but tragic is hardly the right description for them."

"You haven't heard the news?" Karl sighed. He took my hand, mumbled off an excuse to Lady Penelope about taking me to see Count Potocki, and then led me toward the side of the room.

As we walked, I was suddenly overcome with a feeling of dread. My palms were clammy, and I felt sick in my stomach. "Karl?" I asked. "What is it?"

"My brother is dead."

Karl spoke quietly, wearing the same stoic expression Xiana had worn as she told me Amir was more than capable of betraying the ones he supposedly loved. I felt like I had to hear the words several times over, as if hearing them did not make sense at all. My hand covered my mouth in shock; the floor seemed to quake beneath my feet, and my whole body suddenly went numb.

Ferdy is dead? How can this be?

"I regret to tell you this now," Karl replied. "But this is a very important day. Today, I have drawn up a resolution for

THE ORDER OF THE CRYSTAL DAGGERS

Emperor Franz Joseph, and with the support here, he will not be able to—"

"I don't understand." My eyes were watering over; my nose prickled with pressure, and I felt lightheaded. I pulled free from Karl, nearly tripping over the length of my gown. "What do you mean, your brother is dead?"

"Please keep calm," Karl muttered, his eyes dark and dangerous. "He was killed by a foreigner as he was on his way back to Silesia two days ago. His carriage was attacked and then doused in fire. A nearby vicar witnessed the whole thing. He nursed the coachman in his final hours and sent word to my family of the incident."

My chest constricted, and my heart stalled. Karl tried to explain the rest of my possible questions, but all I heard distinctively was how it was clear Emperor Franz Joseph did not care about his citizens, if he was going to constantly allow foreigners to come and do what they pleased.

The memory of Ferdy's question hit me hard.

"Do I know that we will ever meet again?"

I had trouble moving; I had trouble breathing. I barely noticed we were still at the *Nàrodni muzuem*, surrounded by Karl's political allies, and everyone was looking to me to smile and dance and charm my way into their hearts.

"Eleanora?"

"What is it?" I gaped as I looked around, as if my existence had suddenly taken on a form too alien to even recognize.

I am not supposed to live in a world without Ferdy.

Karl sighed, trying to soften his expression. "I know the news is very sad, but there is nothing we can do now. My parents have taken to their beds this week, and I did not blame them. But I know I must be strong, and that is why I am so glad you are here with me. I need you to be strong for

242

THE ORDER OF THE CRYSTAL DAGGERS

me here today. Please, there is no need for you to feel badly for me."

Suddenly, I wanted to scream at him. I did not need to feel badly for Karl; I was too busy feeling bad for myself! I could not believe how selfish he was being, and how little he must have thought of me, thinking I would just take sad such news in stride.

And then there was the matter of Ferdy himself. *What could have happened? Surely he is not really gone.*

Ferdy promised me he would not lie to me, I thought. He was supposed to return to Silesia. I mean, I knew he never went, but what if he was on his way back when everything happened?

There was no denying that King Ferdinand and Empress Maria Anna had been missing their scheduled appearances, and they *had* canceled their travels. Lady Penelope had just said so.

The world swam before me, and I began to withdraw into myself.

I did not know if I could bear it if Ferdy was really dead. It seemed more likely that I was dead, and this was a preamble to hell.

"Eleanora?" Karl's voice called me again, and I had to shake my head.

"I don't know what to say," I finally managed. My voice was raspy and weak, and I felt my eyes start to water. "But I do believe I need to tend to a call of nature. Excuse me while I go to the ladies' withdrawing room."

"Ella, come back here. This is our moment, for Bohemia. I have the resolution for the Emperor to give us back our throne, since he will not bother to be crowned here. This is important." Karl reached out and snared my wrist, tugging

THE ORDER OF THE CRYSTAL DAGGERS

me back toward him. Immediately, I shoved my palm forward, slamming it into his nose.

My training had taken over before I realized it.

"Ow!" He wiped his nose, which had a small smattering of blood on it. I had hit him too hard, I realized. Fortunately, it was only a little, and he was able to clean a large amount of it off without others' notice.

"I'm very sorry, sir," I muttered, ducking around him. "I must excuse myself."

"If you leave me now and make me look like a fool," Karl hissed, "you will regret it."

His angry tone stalled me for only a second, but the viciousness in his voice was not enough to overcome my sadness. If I had been thinking more clearly, I might have realized that Karl's mask had slipped again, and his lies were beginning to fall away. He was worried about his appearance, he was worried about his reputation. He was worried about what the other aristocrats would think of him; he was worried about falling out of their good political graces.

He was not worried about me, or my distress.

Karl said he wanted Bohemia's freedom, but he really meant he wanted power. He wanted his throne back. This was just all part of his plan—me included. What better queen to rule beside him than the daughter of a man who saved the last king during a revolution?

But I was too upset and too distracted to care.

I walked out of the ballroom, brushing past Karl's friends and hurrying down the large set of stairs in front of the museum. The winter breeze was mellow but sure as I made my way down the streets.

There was no clear task in my mind, no clear place to go.

THE ORDER OF THE CRYSTAL DAGGERS

But I kept walking.

I did not know what I could do. Amir was gone, I had no idea where Ben was, and I needed answers. So I went to the one place where I knew I could get them.

I had already walked for blocks when I noticed I forgot my cloak back at the *Nàrodni muzuem*. All I could do was put one foot in front of the other as the winter weather joined me through the snow-spotted streets. My hands were numb but shaking, and my feet were pinched with cold pain. I was more grateful than ever I had worn my new kid boots when I reached the Cabal.

I entered in, still listless but somehow more settled.

"Ella."

Faye's voice called out to me in a friendly manner as I entered her family's establishment. There were a few other people around, a couple of regulars nursing their drinks. I was surprised, for some reason, to find myself here at all. A lady did not walk the streets alone, let alone to come to a publican house.

"You look lovely." As if she knew of my own confusion, Faye came up to me carefully. I wondered if I looked as terrible as I felt. I could see her hesitation in her slow approach. Her eyes were wide with concern. "Are you well?"

"I need to speak with your father," I mumbled, unable to say anything else. It was as if there were two versions of me living inside my body, and half of me was hiding secrets from my other half. I did not know when I arrived that I was supposed to come here, and I did not know I was looking for answers until I asked for Clavan. "I'm sorry, but it's imperative. I need to speak to him or Eliezer now."

"If you're waiting for Elie's wife, I am not sure she will come here tonight," Faye said. "But you're welcome to come in and warm up. Where is your cloak? You must be freezing."

I felt my chin tremble as Faye led me to a nearby table.

"I'll call for my dad while I get you some soup and tea," she said. "Please, sit here."

"Please, I just need information," I said, even though I sat down. I did not want to tell her I was not sure if I could handle any food at all. My stomach was empty and grumbling, but my nerves stole any trace of my usual hunger. "Please. I promise that's all I need."

Faye was clearly troubled by my expression, but she nodded. I was grateful for her poise, especially as I felt the fear inside of me start to multiply.

When Clavan appeared through the door a moment later, I was too grateful to hide my desperation. "Mr. Clavan," I sputtered, standing up from my seat. The urge to run over and collapse into his arms shocked me. It hit me hard, knowing how much I wanted a father's comfort.

He took one look at me and shook his head. He grabbed a nearby bottle and a set of cups. "Patience, Lady Ella."

He sat down across from me. "I'm not surprised to find you here," he said quietly. "I know Ferdy is quite stubborn at times."

"What are you talking about?" I blubbered.

"You're here because of him, aren't you?" Clavan calmly poured a drink for me. "You're dressed up for all of Society to see, but you're in love with him. I imagine it's quite distressing on your grandmother."

"How you know my grandmother?"

"I hear the gossip from all around." Clavan gave me a small smile. His ageless eyes twinkled behind the little round glasses. "Lady Penelope Ollerton-Wellesley has been known to chase fortune and drama all her life, and I see she has not changed a bit, even after entering your life. The rumors say she has been dangling your suitors along, especially that Karl Marcelin."

"That's not why I am here." I took a sip from the cup before me, surprised to feel the burning sensation of the liquid. "What is this?"

"It's best not to ask the questions that have troubling answers," Clavan said with a kind, teasing smile. "I assumed when you came in here, you were looking for Ferdy. I know it's been a while since he's been here, but he'll be back. He always comes back."

I swallowed hard. "I wanted to know something else," I managed to say. "I heard something happened a few days ago, outside of the city. There was an attack on a carriage that was headed to Silesia. I wanted to know if you heard about it."

He raised his brows at my question but gave me a thoughtful look. "Do you mean the incident with the empress's cousin?"

My heart sank.

"The empress's cousin?" I repeated carefully. That was one of Ferdy's covers.

"Yes." Clavan nodded. "There was a carriage with the coat of arms for the Duke of Silesia that was attacked by a Turk a few days ago. He got away, but apparently no one else survived."

A Turk.

THE ORDER OF THE CRYSTAL DAGGERS

My hands fell away from my glass as I felt my heart break into two.

"The news and a mix of the gossip said that there was a fire from something the carriage was carrying with it. The vicar who saw the whole thing said it was likely wine."

"Wine," I repeated the word, as though it was as foreign to me as any of the Arabic words Amir had carved on his dagger.

I thought of the wine from before, the wine which carried the power to bring down castle walls. I fell back in my chair as Clavan told me the rest of the story, about the fire, about the futile search for the villain.

Ben had told me that Amir had talked with Lumiere before, and how Lumiere was connected to Karl and Lord Maximillian.

Was it possible?

I did not want to think about it. The idea that Amir had killed Ferdy, the idea that Ferdy was dead—those were impossible ideas.

The idea that Karl was somehow behind his brother's death, of course, was more plausible. With Lord Maximillian helping him, and Lumiere, too, all of it came together in the worst sort of way.

"Ella?" I heard Clavan's voice in the small seconds before the rest of the world slipped away and everything went dark.

THE ORDER OF THE CRYSTAL DAGGERS

16

◊

"Ella."

If there was a big difference between getting knocked out and fainting, I was not able to distinguish it. I heard Ferdy's voice calling to me as he had last time, and I woke up in just as strange a place as I had when the castle walls had come crumbling down.

"Ferdy." I sat up and opened my eyes, already searching for him as I woke up. Once more, I found myself in a foreign room, one that was not my own, and I was alone. My head fell into my hands as I collapsed forward.

I ran my hands through my hair as I looked up again. The room was far less grand than Ferdy's room in the castle, but it was neat and orderly, from the worn copy of *Jane Eyre* on the table beside me, to the impeccably embroidered pillow behind me.

Ferdy was not there. No one else was around, either.

I was in a small bed, with thin sheets and an extra quilt tucked over my gown. Through the small window behind me, I saw the sky was still colored with the white-gray sheen of a Bohemian winter afternoon. I did not know if a lot of time had passed since I was talking to Clavan. When I tried to think about it, all I could remember was the feeling of a father's love as my body was carefully carried and set down.

The door opened, and Faye walked in with a tray.

"Oh, good," she said. "You're awake."

"I'm so sorry," I mumbled, embarrassed. "I didn't mean to cause trouble."

"This is a publican house," she reminded me. "You're not the first person to pass out here, nor are you first to get what appears to be the first decent sleep you've had in days."

I felt my shame further deepen as I looked outside. As Faye indicated, it was clearly late. I suddenly did not want to know how long it had been since I had collapsed.

"You might be one of the sober ones who did, but other than that, we're very familiar with what happens."

"Is that how you met Jarl?" I asked, trying to smile even though I was unable to find any strength in me.

Faye laughed. "Close enough." She moved her book and put the small tray down on the table beside the bed. I saw there was the warm cup of soup and a cup of tea she had promised me earlier.

"For a moment, I was worried the brandy my father gave you was too strong," she admitted. "But when I saw you barely had any at all, I knew you would be well with some rest. Luckily, you're close to my height, and Jarl's uncle Rhys came in as Dad started to move you."

I shook my head. There was a pounding feeling behind my eyes, a pressure from the Clavan family's kindness and my own despair at Ferdy's loss. "I don't feel well at all."

"I can see if Eliezer and his wife will come," Faye said. "They usually come to see us after the Shabbat is over and she finishes her other rounds, but I know she will make exceptions for special cases."

I shook my head. "Your family has done more than enough for me. I am already indebted to you."

"We take care of our own," Faye promised. Her eyes, a pretty hazel in the dim lighting, sparkled with a benevolent mischievousness. "And sometimes others as well."

"Thank you."

THE ORDER OF THE CRYSTAL DAGGERS

"Just rest for now," Faye said, fluffing the pillow behind me. "I've been checking in on you every couple of hours. My room is small, but it'll be good for you to stay for a bit."

"This is your room?"

She nodded. "It's likely a bit smaller than yours, but—"

"It's wonderful," I said. I looked down at the finery of my dress. "I wasn't always the kind of person to wear gowns and go off to parties. I was a servant for my stepmother after my father died. He was knighted by the king before the Revolution, so I might have been born into a world of riches, but I can promise you, I envy you for your family's goodness. You are much richer than I am."

"You still have your brother."

"My brother, and my faith." I barely choked out the words. Both had been tested of late, and it felt wrong to say something was true when it did not feel that way at all.

Before Faye could do anything other than pat my hand reassuringly, Helen called for her. She quietly excused herself, and when I was alone again, I curled my knees up under my chest, letting myself sink into the sudden loneliness of the atmosphere.

I hoped I did not make Faye feel awkward. I already felt badly enough.

I had felt just as terrible when I woke up after the Advent Ball. It was mortifying to know I had been blind, to have missed Ferdy's real identity before. Now, I felt even more foolish.

What is this, God? I wondered. To have Amir's actions and motives questioned, and to have Ferdy's life ended?

Did I not believe ardently enough? Did I do something to deserve such sadness? Was he punishing me for my mother's sins?

"Is this further proof I have failed you, Lord?" I whispered, daring to ask a question of God. I did not know how I would respond to any answer I would get, if indeed I received any at all.

All I knew for sure was that there was too much sadness and too many secrets.

So many secrets.

Much as I had the day I left the castle, I looked out the window. I saw the outline of the city beyond the buildings and across the river, acutely aware there was so much brokenness in the world.

I grew up in the church, where we learned about the fall of Satan and the poison of sin in this world. As I remembered Karl's earlier speech about Bohemia's damaged pride, I thought about the magic of the city and the power it held to withstand the various foes of this world. I thought about sin and the power it had to engulf so many hearts in despair.

How did it come to this? I wondered, still lost in the cityscape before me. How did so much pain and so much destruction manage to infiltrate this world?

As I climbed out of bed and hurried to smooth out my dress, pat down my hair, and put on a presentable face, I knew I had no real answer to that question, either.

I did get an answer of sorts when I walked down the stairs and entered back into the bar, though whether it was an answer from God or Satan, I could not say.

Lumiere was back, sitting at the same spot as before, accompanied by his companion at the bar, half-hidden by the shadows. From what I could see, he was relaxed and cheerful.

In the face of Ferdy's murder, I was more than ready to kill him.

THE ORDER OF THE CRYSTAL DAGGERS

"There you are, Lady Ella," Lumiere called. His bright blond hair was wild and despite his best attempts, I could see the lines folding under his eyes.

"What are you doing here?" I hissed, as I came up beside him. Didier, as if sensing my desire to do harm, moved to protect Lumiere, reaching inside his elegant coat with one hand. Before he could pull his weapon free, Lumiere stopped him.

"She's fine, Didier," Lumiere assured him in quieted tones. "She doesn't have her dagger on her. Do you, Lady Ella?"

I stepped back, realizing he was right; and then I frowned, suddenly aware there would be no pretenses in this conversation.

I frowned. "You have some nerve to assume things about me."

"I'm very well-practiced when it comes to assuming things, I can assure you," he replied with a smile. "But I do happen to know you quite well. I knew you were Naděžda's daughter right from the beginning, even if I had doubts about how much Pepé had actually trained you."

"Pepé?" I wrinkled my nose. "Why do you use that name for Lady Penelope?"

"She was the mistress of my father's best friend for many years, and he repeatedly referred to her as such when he wanted to blame her for all his problems. I can assure you, my father believed she alone was responsible for your grandfather's excessive drinking and his incessant need to meddle in chaos. I imagine your grandfather would have been a quite a solemn priest, content to bore himself into heaven, if he had never met her."

The biting sarcasm of his words almost made me laugh, before I remembered he was the one responsible for my pain.

THE ORDER OF THE CRYSTAL DAGGERS

I glanced back at Didier. Harshad and Xiana had taught me the basics, and I did not think that would stand up well against Didier or his revolver. I was also unsure if Lumiere was armed.

"I heard about your recent departure from Karl Marcelin's brightest moment," Lumiere said. "He was quite upset you left him there alone. He was hoping to announce your engagement with you by his side, although knowing him as I do, I'm sure he enjoyed having the spotlight all to himself. You should know the crowds cheered quite loudly at his announcement."

"But I never agreed to marry him," I objected, curling my fingers into fists. "My grandmother would never agree to it, either."

"*Au contraire.* She agreed to it after you left the museum," Lumiere told me with a smug smile, making me feel even more queasy.

What is going on? Karl and I are engaged? Why would Lady Penelope agree to this? She promised me she wouldn't do this to me!

"He will have to issue a retraction," I said, trying my hardest to maintain my composure as panic began to take hold of me.

All I needed to do was get to Lady Penelope, I told myself.

"Doubtful. He is very determined to marry you. Most ladies would be flattered. He is leading the charge for Bohemia to become its own nation, to separate itself from the Austrians and the Hungarians, and the rest of the remnant of the Holy Roman Empire."

"Well, I don't want to marry him," I snapped.

"I noticed that, *chérie,* just as I noticed it took quite a bit of acting on Pepé's part to make sure others believed you do,"

THE ORDER OF THE CRYSTAL DAGGERS

Lumiere said. "She even left with him. No doubt there is some sinister work afoot."

"Karl will have to make peace with my departure. I was … sick."

"Your grandmother is also quite upset. But then I would be too, if I was forcibly escorted out of a party I didn't want to leave," Lumiere cooed.

"You're the reason for it," I hissed.

"*Chérie*, I am not the one who is lying to Karl about wanting to marry him." Lumiere giggled. "And not to mention his brother is in love with you. I commend you on being brave enough to wear the royal combs. I'm sure Karl loved seeing them on you, especially since Ferdinand would be the only other person in the world who could give the crown princess jewels to you."

I reached up and touched one of the combs, then I felt another part of my soul crumble. I had unwittingly blown my cover; I heard the anger in Karl's voice as I left him in the middle of the room. He would know the truth about me now, for certain.

Just like Lady POW does. I thought about her strange interrogation earlier, after she noticed them. She had assumed they were from Karl, and that was how she knew I was keeping other secrets before, too.

Indignation briefly ran through me; if Ferdy was not already dead, I would have been tempted to kill him.

Ferdy gave me the princess combs for my hair, tricking me into taking them. Now as a result, I had revealed myself, and the Order's whole mission was at risk.

"No one else has seen Pepé either since then," Lumiere continued. "I do believe Karl has finally taken my advice. I did tell him to stop letting people walk all over him when it came to being in the criminal side of business. Begin as you mean to go on, I told him. If you want the crown, if you want to rule, you have to be relentless. But I do have to admit, kidnapping your grandmother was a stroke of brilliance. I just hope he can handle it. It's rather like watching a baby bird choke on snake. Ah, well, if nothing else, it is delicious entertainment …"

Lumiere rambled on, trying to be funny and provocative, but all I could think about was how Lady Penelope was now Karl's prisoner.

Or, I thought, with a perverse sense of pleasure, *he is hers.*

But still, everything seemed to spiraling out of control. Karl had announced our engagement at the party last night. He had managed to get Lady POW to agree to it, even to the point she worked to convince the crowds of its truth.

I was engaged. Karl knew my secrets. Ferdy was dead. Lady Penelope was captured.

I put my head in my hands. *Where did I go wrong?*

All I wanted to do was scream, but Lumiere distracted me as he raised his glass. "Ferdinand is an excellent match for you. He needs someone who will keep him grounded. Of course, Karl would prefer he was grounded in a different sort of way, if you would believe it."

Suddenly, there were no tears left. I felt the full measure of my temper burst free. "I knew you were involved in all of this."

"This what?" Lumiere batted his eyelashes at me, trying to look innocent. "I have no idea of what you're talking about."

"I might not know the specifics now, but I am sure Amir will tell me."

"Oh, please. Amir wouldn't tell you we were friends. You are too close to her, and he knows how Pepé feels about me, considering who I am."

"Oh? And just who is that?" I asked.

"I am the prince of secrets and shadows, of course," Lumiere said. "I am the son of Louis Valoris, the head of the League of Ungentlemanly Welfare, and heir to the power of the British and French Empires—and the Austria-Hungarian Empire, too, if my father gets his way."

Before I could respond, he guffawed with laughter. "Ah, it is so good to laugh, especially after such a trying week. Assassinations and betrayals and set-ups are all so tiring, and I've had to plan plenty in the last few days."

I blanched at his words. "You're a monster."

"Yes," he murmured, seeing my reaction. "Yes, I suppose you are right. But as my father always says, it is the mark of true power to operate in the daylight. Alas, I am not quite there, but I at least have enough power to tell you that I *am* involved in all of this, and I am truly sorry to distress Naděžda's daughter in such a way. But one day I will make it up to you, and this is my oath. Didier, take note of today's date and my promises to Lady Ella."

I clenched my fist. "I don't want your promises."

"You might one day, especially if a certain Bohemian prince is involved."

"Leave Ferdy out of this!"

"Well, you do have a point," Lumiere conceded. "After all, he is dead. It's not like there was a chance that he would survive an attack so stealthily planned by *moi*, would he?"

The last of my hope perished inside of me. "I'll kill you," I hissed, already leaping at Lumiere. Didier moved to block me as I raised my fist.

Before, I had been too conflicted to fight.

But Ferdy's fate, and Amir's role in it, and now everything else, had killed something inside of me. I was no longer bound to protect Ferdy in this world, and I owed loyalty to no one other than myself. In that moment, I lived only to inflict pain and torture on Lumiere.

Didier managed to grab a hold of me, but I heard him grunt as I hit him instead.

Before I could fight any further, a new voice called out to stop us.

"Yes, Lumiere, Miss Ella is correct. You are a monster, and you do not need to be here at all. I think it is time for you to leave."

Eliezer was suddenly standing beside me, reaching out to put a hand between me and Lumiere. I blinked at the sight of him as he appeared, and I took the time to make a second look as he positioned himself between Lumiere and me. He was not much taller than me, and I likely could have fought him and won. But there was a commanding presence about him, one that did not waver.

It was surprising to see him again, and even more to be on my side; I had never really talked to him, and he was always so busy with his listeners and other friends when I was at the Cabal. I would have expected him to ask what was going on, but as I watch his dark eyes narrow at Lumiere, I realized they had already known each other.

"Oh, look who it is. Little Eliezer, I was wondering when I would get to see you again. Imagine my surprise to find you here, and after the Sabbath has begun, too," Lumiere cheered. He ran a hand through his hair, pushing back the blond locks with a sense of showmanship and glee. "I have missed you terribly."

THE ORDER OF THE CRYSTAL DAGGERS

Eliezer wore a look of disgust as he faced Lumiere. "None of us have missed you."

"Now, now, falling leaves return to their roots." Lumiere pouted. "A Jew is always a Jew, even if he prefers the Catholic church his father raised him in. Certainly Clavan would agree with me on that, and he is the proprietor here, *non?*"

"That is not the issue. All are welcome here at the Cabal," Clavan spoke up, "but welcomes can wear out, Lumi, and you are better off leaving before yours does. We will not have you upsetting our Ella."

"Oh, such a bother." Lumiere sighed, before he stood up and bowed to me. "I was having such a lovely time, too. But then, I suppose I cannot blame you for your affections toward Ella. She is quite her mother's daughter."

Didier followed him, but instead of bowing to me, he reached for my hand to shake it. I was surprised, given my own violent response, but he gave me the same smile as he had before at the Estates Theatre. "I look forward to seeing you again soon, my lady. Perhaps even sooner than you realize."

"I don't know if I would be so delighted by our next meeting, sir," I replied. "If I have my way, our next meeting will be our last."

"With all due respect, I doubt that, my lady," Didier whispered. "But should you wish to come and find us, we are staying at the port on the *Salacia.*"

It was only when they were finally out of the door that I turned to Eliezer. The loops of hair at the side of his head were bobbling with unexpressed anger, and I could tell he had done himself a favor as much as he had helped me.

"Thank you, sir," I said, struggling to contain myself. I breathed in deeply, hating that I had been stopped even though I knew I would not have survived the fight had it been allowed to continue.

"You're welcome." Eliezer looked me over. "You should stay away from him, but I have a feeling you already know that."

"What do you know about him?"

"He is a proficient liar and good at making people believe what he wants them to believe. He is no friend of ours, even though he would like to be." Eliezer gestured to the Cabal. "He used to come here before with his father, when we were both younger."

I glanced over at Clavan. "How long have you been in business?"

"The Cabal has always been a place of entertainment," Clavan said. "My father fancied himself a performer, but thankfully my mother convinced him he should have alcohol readily available for his audiences. Our family was kicked out of the Jewish Quarter for that, but I am content to remain its neighbor. Elie has been a real help in turning it into a place of information rather than entertainment."

"Much to Jarl's displeasure, I'm sure," Eliezer said. He straightened the yarmulke on his head and excused himself as another man, one I assumed was Jarl's Uncle Rhys, called out to him.

Clavan came up beside me. "I hope you do not let Lumi's words bother you."

"It is not his words so much as his actions," I said.

The anger inside of me continued to burn without mercy, and I decided it was time to end the waiting. It was time to face Karl, Lord Maximillian, and Lumiere. It was time to confront them, to trap them, and to get them to confess to their treachery—anything to ensure that they were stopped. It

THE ORDER OF THE CRYSTAL DAGGERS

was too much to wait for them to give me their trust, to allow them the space to continue when I knew they were guilty, even if it meant revealing myself and the Order to Society.

What difference did it make in the end? I had already failed.

Ferdy was dead.

I decided to start with Lumiere. He seemed to be the most deserving of my anger, and I had a feeling that, with Amir still missing, I would have less trouble convincing Lady Penelope to act.

Faye appeared once more, this time with more blankets. She insisted I stay in her room for the night, and then I could go home in the morning. I agreed only because she wanted me safe, and it was true that I was in no condition to return home on my own.

The situation did press into me the resolution that I would never leave the house without my dagger again.

THE ORDER OF THE CRYSTAL DAGGERS

262

THE ORDER OF THE CRYSTAL DAGGERS

17

◊

The long hour of walking home did nothing to temper the storm inside of me. I burst into the manor, my boots covered in mud and snow, my gown and Faye's cloak flowing out behind me with a mix of wind and rage.

"Eleanora? Is that you?" Harshad called out to me, but I did not stop.

I was putting everything together inside my mind as I made my way to my room. I slammed the door shut and immediately began to pull off my clothes. I paused only for an extra second as I felt the thin fabric of Faye's cloak. I knew the material was cheap and the stitching was worn, but the friendship I had with her, and the other members of the Cabal, was not deserving of anything so fine. I knew this was true, even before learning she had slept in her parents' room, while Clavan slept in a chair.

If I died avenging Ferdy and condemning Karl, I hoped they would remember me fondly.

My stealth habit was tight against my skin as I finished getting ready. My hood was up, my mask was in place, and my dagger was at my side. I would find Lumiere, I decided, starting with his ship, the *Salacia*. Ferdy's letter had shown me that they were all working together, and Lumiere had confirmed it. All I needed was some physical proof. Maybe I could find more letters from Lumiere to Karl or Lord Maximillian, and then I could take it to King Ferdinand and Empress Maria Anna. Then, they could send it off to Franz Joseph, so he could see the degree of treachery involved by his cousin and his cohorts.

"Nora? Harshad and Xiana are waiting for us in the library."

Ben's voice was full of concern and a brotherly cadence I could only marvel at, especially in light of our recent troubles. It was as if he knew I no longer had to worry about dividing my loyalty between him and anyone else.

"I'm coming," I said as I hurried to fix my hair. I tugged at the combs Ferdy had given me, the ones which always seemed so innocuous. I paused in putting them away, taking a moment to study them, thinking of how Lumiere had called them the crown princess combs.

When I had woken up in the castle after the attack, only to find myself in Ferdy's room, I was conflicted over whether or not I wanted him to love me. He was a prince, even if he was kept a secret from the rest of the kingdom.

Now, as I curled my fingers around the combs, I only felt angry with myself. I was in love with a liar. Once more, Ferdy had put himself—and me, and my mission—in danger, all so he could keep a hold on me.

No wonder Karl had him killed.

Ferdy had finally pushed his brother too far. And since he was dead, it was up to me to fix things.

"Nora." Ben knocked on the door again.

At the sound of his voice, I jolted out of my pained reverie. "I'll be there in a moment," I snapped. I was glad Ben and I had resolved some of our differences, but I wanted only a few moments all to myself, to grieve and to plan my vengeance.

I put the combs down in my drawer, lying them next to my mother's locket and my father's pocket watch. Recalling Lumiere had a similar watch, I picked it up and opened it, marveling once more at the workmanship. A pattern of gold circled its way around the clock, twisting its finery around each of the numbers. It had been many years since I had

THE ORDER OF THE CRYSTAL DAGGERS

wound it to work, but I felt the comfort of my father's memory in just holding it.

Máma's locket also shimmered up at me, calling to me like a little child eager for attention. Opening it, I saw the small miniature of me and Ben on the one side, and my father's picture on the other.

From everything I remembered about her, I knew my mother loved me and Ben. I never saw her disagree with my father, and when they were together, I only ever saw her smiling. Ben had told me before she had suffered from periodic bouts of melancholy, and I supposed it was unusual to think of my mother as only ever happy. But with Ben and me, and our father, too, it was still hard to think we were not enough for her.

Studying my father's picture, I knew *Máma* had loved *Táta*. And whatever her past held, I could face it, knowing she had known true love.

I thought of Amir, and how my mother had loved him, too. He did not go with her when she wanted them to run away together, but she had loved him enough to ask.

I rubbed my thumb over my father's picture again. He looked so young in the picture. I wondered when it had been completed.

Curious, I pulled the picture out of its small frame. The miniature slipped through my fingers and fell. I was just about to reach for it when I realized it was not the only picture in the frame.

There was a smaller picture tucked away behind it, of a younger man with dark brown eyes and hair the color of a starless night. There was no mustache on his face, but I recognized him regardless.

Amir.

I pulled out his picture to study it, setting my father's portrait aside. He wore a military jacket of the Ottoman Empire, but no smile. His hair was parted differently under the strange cap. I looked it over and smiled; the picture was like a portal, linking me not just to Amir's past but a whole other person's life.

On the back of Amir's picture, I saw the same scraggly shape of his scar, next to a small drawing of a dagger.

My mother's dagger, and Amir's scar.

Beside it, there was a date listed: *April 25, 1847*. The date did not mean anything to me, but I recognized the importance of the drawings easily enough. Amir had mentioned before, I recalled, that love was connected to suffering. I could imagine my mother suffering as she held onto his memory, even as she embraced my father and their future together.

I looked back at the picture of *Táta*. Had he known of my mother's devotion to another?

Did my mother know of Amir's pain, to the point he would betray me and Lady Penelope?

After another long moment, I carefully tucked the locket and its hidden contents into my drawer, along with the combs Ferdy had given me. I loved them all—my mother, my father, and Ferdy. Yet they all held secrets, some of them I was still trying to discover.

Harshad was right, I thought. Some secrets are kept as a matter of trust, bringing two people closer, and some were destructive, forcing others apart.

I could not say which result was more true as I made my way down to the library.

As I entered the room, I was surprised to find the portrait of my mother hanging over the fireplace mantle. Lady

Penelope had promised me before that she would have it restored, but it was still a shock to see my mother's blue eyes staring down at me.

"There you are," Harshad said. He looked down at my outfit and nodded. "I see you have come prepared."

"I'm more than prepared," I insisted, pulling my dagger out. The violet-colored alloy gleamed a dangerous purple in the firelight.

"Excellent. But I am not sure you understand the gravity of the situation."

"Karl has captured Lady Penelope, and Lord Maximillian and his new best friend Lumiere Valoris are preparing an assassination, a set-up, or both," I said.

I was gratified to see Ben's eyes widen. Even Harshad seemed surprised.

"We know that," Ben said. "But how did you hear?"

"Someone told me," I said, ready to tell him what happened.

But Harshad interrupted me. "Do you also know that Karl is requesting your presence at the Potocki house this evening?"

I opened my mouth and then closed it. I sighed and shook my head.

It figures that Karl would complicate my anger. His brother had a knack for it, so I shouldn't be this surprised.

"After you left the museum dedication earlier, he found a way to convince Lady Penelope to grant his request for your hand." Harshad began to pace the floor, and I started to get worried. Lady POW was the one who paced incessantly, and for Harshad to be adopting her mannerisms likely meant he was more worried than he wanted to admit, possibly even to himself.

"If he thinks capturing her will convince me to bend to his will, he's going to be surprised," I recalled Lumiere mentioning something like that earlier, but I had been too upset to notice it. I tucked my dagger back into its sheath. "We'll get her back."

"He blackmailed her," Ben said.

"At his own peril," I asserted. "Lady Penelope would not allow herself to be manipulated like that unless she knew how to control it."

"She managed to buy us time by agreeing to his schemes, I am sure, but that's all," Harshad said. "We were just about to go search for you. Lady Penelope is only able to work as a member in the Order by maintaining her cover as a respectable dowager duchess. While money does have a tendency to silence people, Karl, as the secret heir to the throne and the leader of a growing nationalist resistance, has the power to damage our reputation and diminish our ability to protect others."

"She could just kill him," I said, unapologetic in my anger. "That would solve a lot of problems."

"The last thing Queen Victoria needs is a spy who killed the son of a ruler," Xiana said. She took a step out of the shadows, her calmness and power clear. "Her Majesty is already facing a large amount of problems at home and abroad. The Order was sent in to stabilize the area. This is not official Crown business, or the League would have been sent in. While it may be a quick solution to our troubles here, killing Mr. Marcelin is not advantageous in the long run."

I clenched my fists. One heir to the throne was already dead.

"Eleanora," Harshad said. "You will go to the ball at Count Potocki's house tonight. Karl will announce your engagement, and then, as you leave the ball, we will capture him. We can bring him back here, to your family's manor."

"Karl will likely be protected," Ben said. "If he knows about the Order—"

"He does," I said. "He likely heard about it from Lumiere. He knows Lady Penelope."

Harshad shook his head. "Lumiere has always been a problem, and he enjoys it. To a fault, certainly. I warned Amir not to trust him."

Hearing Amir's name, I whirled on Harshad. "Do you know where Amir is? The last time any of us saw him was after he met with Lumiere."

"Lumiere is a friend of Amir's," Harshad explained. "They used to work on missions and carry out tasks together with your mother. But people grow older, and loyalties shift."

"I don't think Amir's have," Ben muttered.

"But your mother's did," Harshad countered softly, making me jump. "She left the Order before, and it is entirely possible, especially given Lumiere's father and his long-standing animosity toward Pepé, that Lumiere's have also changed."

I looked back at the portrait of my mother, thinking of the picture she carried of Amir close to her heart all those years after she married my father. Her loyalties did not shift, I thought. She might have married another, but she never forgot about Amir.

As for Amir, I did not know what to say. It still seemed impossible that he killed Ferdy, especially under Lumiere's direction.

"Do you know where Amir went?" I asked. I glanced over at Xiana, her calmness almost unnerving, before turning back to Harshad for an answer.

"No." Harshad shook his head. "But Amir would not disappoint me, even if he has unresolved feelings toward Lady Penelope."

I thought about Lady POW's own feelings about Amir. It was possible, I realized, that she was the one who had the unresolved guilt toward Amir. I had known both of them for such a short time, but I did not see Amir as someone who believed in vengeance.

Lady Penelope was another story.

"He always returns to me," Harshad said.

My eyes watered. Clavan had said the same thing about Ferdy.

"For now, we will have to worry about Amir later." Harshad clasped his hands together.

"I agree. We are losing our focus," Ben said. "Nora, you'll need to get dressed up for the party tonight. You'll go in and dazzle Karl, assure him you don't know what he is talking about when it comes to the Order. Xiana and Harshad can look for Lady Penelope. Once they find her, they can work out a way to kidnap Karl as you leave, and then we'll have him."

"And then I will have him at my mercy," I muttered. I gripped the hilt of my dagger. "Good."

Harshad shook his head. "I do not anticipate killing someone will be necessary in this instance. Empress Maria Anna and King Ferdinand will be able to rein in their son."

"I don't know about that," I said. "They are upset right now, and they haven't moved to stop him yet."

THE ORDER OF THE CRYSTAL DAGGERS

"With Karl working with Lord Maximillian and the League, not to mention his own support from people like Roman Szapira and Count Potocki, they are unable to confront him," Ben said. "If we can bring him down, at least to the point where he can admit he is trying to take back the throne, they will be able to report him to Emperor Franz Joseph."

"The emperor was already alerted to the plot," Harshad said. "That is why he is calling a special council in a few months."

"A council?" I asked. "What kind of council?"

"Empress Elisabeth is sympathetic to Bohemia's desire to be its own country," Harshad said. "Emperor Franz Joseph has decided to call a tripartite council, to discuss the possibility of allowing Bohemia to be a full kingdom as part of the Empire."

"So it would be the Austria-Hungarian-Bohemian Empire instead," Ben clarified.

"Karl would love that." I pouted. He would love that, and then he would use it as a way to wedge the kingdom free from the empire entirely. "I have heard Empress Elisabeth agrees with the democratic notions of the West."

"She does, but she knows her power is little, especially in the Austrian courts. The Hapsburgs have never been kind to outsiders. Empress Elisabeth is an outsider in her own home, even if Franz Joseph loves her."

"But she is technically the emperor's second cousin," I said. "Doesn't that make her a Hapsburg, too?"

"Through her mother's side." Harshad frowned. "She has been treated better since her son, Rupert, was born, but Empress Elisabeth has gone against the royal family in getting closer to the Hungarians, and she seeks to help Bohemia, too. I imagine she is a little more hesitant, given King Ferdinand is still alive, and there is a growing Nationalist movement."

THE ORDER OF THE CRYSTAL DAGGERS

"So she is calling a council to give Bohemia more power?" I asked.

"She has convinced Franz Joseph to do so," Harshad said. "That does not mean it will come to be."

"Karl has gotten bolder with his speeches." I thought about how he had called for Bohemia's freedom the day before. I had to push back a lot of sadness to recall what he said, but I knew if there was a possibility of emancipation, his rhetoric would likely turn dangerous.

"Karl likely heard of their intention," Harshad continued. "That is why his speech yesterday was so important."

Ben chuckled. "And that's why, when Nora left, he was extraordinarily angry."

"I don't understand why," I retorted. "I'm not anyone important. I know Society enjoys me, but there are richer women Karl could marry, or even people like Teresa Marie, who has a connection to the throne herself."

"You might be a passing fad," Ben said, "but Lady Penelope's history and her money make you very interesting. The fact that you are so talented makes people excited. And to top it off, you are *Otec's* daughter."

I was surprised to hear Ben say anything about our father. "What does *Táta* have to do with anything?"

"He protected the King during a raid on the castle," Ben said. "*Otec* refused to leave the king's side when he was attacked with a knife. He nearly died because of his wounds. That was why the king was so nice to him, remember?"

I did not remember the exact nature of my father's duty. If I had ever heard the story, it had been a long, long time before, and I had forgotten the details.

"Adolf Svoboda's role in saving the king, even though the Revolution eventually succeeded, is remembered by those

THE ORDER OF THE CRYSTAL DAGGERS

who are upset by Emperor Franz Joseph's neglect of Bohemia." Xiana folded her hands together in front of her. "You carry bravery in your blood, Eleanora, and that is a legacy that Karl Marcelin seeks to preserve."

"And claim as his own." I wrinkled my nose at the thought of marrying Karl.

"We will not let him do so," Ben promised. "You're my sister, and this is exactly the sort of threat I am allowed to keep you from."

"Thanks." I did not want Ben's protection, but I was glad he was at least offering it. I sighed. "I suppose I better get ready."

"Yes," Harshad said. "I fear if we do not move quickly, we will fail to save Karl from Pepé as much as we will fail to save her from him."

THE ORDER OF THE CRYSTAL DAGGERS

THE ORDER OF THE CRYSTAL DAGGERS

18

◊

The city once more passed before me as we rode by in Lady Penelope's carriage. It did not look much different from earlier, when I had walked home from the Cabal, but I felt more tired as I looked at it. Not only was I still upset about everything that happened, but I was about to make things even more complicated.

We were on our way to Count Potocki's address, and the plan was in place. I fiddled with my skirts, ruffling the gypsy red silk with an unacknowledged wonder. I was on my way to announce and celebrate my engagement. If I was not secretly a spy trying to dismantle foreign dissents and a traitorous prince, I might have actually been excited. Assuming I would have been in love.

"Are you well?" Ben reached forward and gave me a quick pat on my arm.

Mindlessly, I nodded. I did not want to admit I was looking forward to the end of the charade.

Harshad was up on the box, disguised in a footman's livery, and Xiana was also hidden away. She had twisted herself up in ways I never imagined possible, before securing herself to back of the coach.

Ben was with me in the carriage. I appreciated his presence, even though I wished I had the time to myself. I gripped my dagger, slightly irritated it was buried underneath another one of the fine gowns Lady Penelope had ordered for me. Much like the other one, I could easily dismantle myself from it and resume my movements in my stealth habit. I was not nervous. I was out for blood.

I wanted the time to myself for other reasons. There was a wide chasm between justice and vengeance; one was a divine calling, and the other a sin. I did not want someone I loved as much as Ben to see my nature tainted, even if it was necessary to help preserve the world's good.

"Everything will be fine." Ben tried to reassure me once more.

I looked at him as he sat across from me. He was dressed in his normal clothes, the everyday clothes of a servant he had worn when Cecilia was in charge of our lives.

"I know that I can count on Harshad and Xiana to save Lady POW," I said. "What will you be doing?"

"While you attend the party at the count's house, I'll be heading into town," Ben said. "Clavan sent the notice that Zipporah would be coming into the Cabal tonight, and she has the herbs we ordered. Once I have them, I will come back to meet up with you and the others."

"Are you sure that it's a good idea to leave us?"

"I'm certain between you, Harshad, and Xiana, you will find a way to extract Lady POW from her captors," Ben replied. "Besides, we should get the herbs. Lady POW has wanted them since she came here. She wants me to find out the names of other buyers, and if Zipporah has had any trouble getting her supply."

"It seems unusual that you would worry about getting the silver thallis herb now," I said.

"Disappointed you don't have any to use on Karl?"

I snickered at Ben's teasing grin, but I had to admit he was the one who was more right between us.

"Either way, it can't be helped," Ben said. "We've waited this long, and Xiana will be able to make some of the antidote

THE ORDER OF THE CRYSTAL DAGGERS

for us. We might be able to save some of the people that are dying off."

"I haven't heard of any new deaths lately."

"If you ask me, I think Karl's too busy planning for your nuptials."

Karl had talked about marriage at every occasion we had together. It was part of his plan, I assumed; gain the approval of my following, use the power of the people as leverage, secure the Bohemian throne, and reveal himself to be the true heir to the kingdom. Then all he would need would be a family to inherit his legacy, and Karl would have everything he had ever wanted.

"I would have thought Lord Maximillian would be doing more of those," I said. "He has been remarkably silent in recent weeks."

"Karl seems to have made it pretty clear he wants to marry you, and even more so since the Advent Ball."

"Lady Penelope and I did run into him at the Estates Theatre," I said. I thought of Ferdy's letter again, the one where Karl offered Lord Maximillian a role as a counselor. "Lord Maximillian tried to threaten us there. He was more than polite about it, and he would be the first to deny it, of course."

Ben frowned. "Is he coming to the ball tonight?"

"I don't know." I sighed. "I'll keep an eye out for him."

"Be sure to watch yourself most of all." Ben gripped his fingers together in his lap. "I know you can take care of yourself, but I won't be around to help."

"I'll be in good company."

"I know, or I wouldn't leave you." Ben sighed. "Amir was right. You are a weakness of mine."

THE ORDER OF THE CRYSTAL DAGGERS

I smiled. "And you are one of mine. But we can work with that, and that's the important part."

"Amir is one of your weaknesses, too, you know."

My eyes met Ben's from across the carriage bench. "I am sure he is," I admitted.

Ben was different from me in that I had been allowed to consider my weaknesses thoroughly; I was given time to work on mine. Ben had to begin his struggle right away, with our father's dismissal of him after his injury, and then Cecilia's further harm. Ben was taught to hate weakness, to get rid of it, and to condemn it. He was morally tied to the destruction of his weaknesses, while I was largely ignorant of mine. When I thought of my love for Ferdy or my admiration for Amir, I could see it as a weakness or as a strength, and I was unable to dismiss it entirely.

I looked away from Ben, turning my attention back to the city streets before me, feeling the clatter of the wheels as they turned over the cobblestone streets. "You know, if things had worked out differently, Amir would be our father instead of *Táta.*"

Ben shrugged but he said nothing. I sank back into silence, too.

The coach slowed down as the traffic became thicker. The moon was just peeking out from behind the snowy clouds when Ben said his farewells and slipped out of the coach, heading off for the Cabal.

I envied him. Ben was going into a den of friends, while I was waltzing into the heart of darkness.

To be fair, it was a very grand-looking trap. Count Potocki's manor had the high arches of Gothic architect, with brightly patterned windows and elegant masonry. The coach stopped, and Harshad hurried down to assist me.

THE ORDER OF THE CRYSTAL DAGGERS

"Once you're inside," he whispered, "go and find your grandmother. Karl will likely want to rehearse his terms, so you will be able to give us time while Xiana and I look for a way to overpower any guards he might have."

"I will." I patted his hand as I stepped down. "Thank you."

His face was expressionless, but I thought I saw a twinkle in his eye as I headed toward the door.

I picked up my skirts, making sure I was able to leave my boots covered. Underneath my dress, I wore my stealth habit and the matching black boots Lady POW had ordered for me when we had set out to captivate Society. My dagger was tucked away at my side. I could grab it through a slit in my skirt, one that was usually reserved for pockets.

It was strange to think I was dressed for war, and that I was marching into battle wearing a gown.

I held my head up proudly. The fact that I was wearing a gown, yet still facing my enemy, gave me confidence. Warriors came in all sorts of outfits, and I had chosen to don a disguise worthy of a spy.

The fact that I was here to help my own grandmother, the spymaster who was tangled up in our adversary's grasp, was only slightly less relevant. Karl was not anticipating a fight, but he was going to get one.

Upon entering, a hand reached forward for my cloak. I took it off and handed it over, only to find I recognized my helper.

"Amir." His name escaped in a gasp as I stood there.

"Shh, please, Eleanora," Amir whispered, holding a finger up to his lips. He hurried to pull me off to the darker confines of the castle before anyone else noticed where we were going.

THE ORDER OF THE CRYSTAL DAGGERS

As we walked briskly through a darkened hall, I was admittedly disappointed; if I was going to be rescued from a ball, I would have preferred Ferdy had come to save me rather than Amir.

But considering Ferdy had been killed by Amir, I knew that was not going to happened.

At that thought, I tugged myself free from his grasp. "What do you think you're doing here?"

"I came to help," Amir said. "Lumi told me that Karl managed to coerce Lady Penelope into leaving the rededication ceremony with him before, but we have a problem."

Lumi. Amir called Lumiere "Lumi," as if he was a friend.

"You aren't really trying to betray Lady Penelope, are you?" I asked, suddenly very worried. I took a step back from Amir, unable to see how any of this could make sense. Was he here to finish her off?

I struggled to maintain my composure. "I didn't want to believe it when she said that was what you were doing, but I can't believe that you would consider Lumiere a friend!"

"Eleanora—"

I felt my heart clench, as if it was struggling to continue to beat. "He orchestrated everything, Amir. He made you kill Karl's brother."

"What?" Amir shook his head. "I didn't kill anyone, Eleanora."

"I know Lumiere sent you after the coach," I insisted. "Ben told me that you were talking with him, and then you left for days."

"I can explain that," Amir said. "But you need to calm down, please."

THE ORDER OF THE CRYSTAL DAGGERS

"Fine." I took another step back, digging my fingers into my skirt, reaching for my dagger. I did not want to pull it out entirely, but I needed to protect myself. "Tell me about Lumiere first, and why you would be friends with that vile creature."

"Lumi is an old friend of mine," Amir said. "He was the one who originally told me that Karl and Lord Maximillian were working together. He knew because they were also in contact with Louis, who is Lumiere's father and the leader of the League of Ungentlemanly Warfare."

"I know about Louis, and the League, too."

"Then you know Louis is dangerous," Amir said. "Lumi told me that Father Novak had sent word to him, and he decided to come, especially since his father told him Lady POW was coming to Prague."

"Lady POW said he was your friend, as well as *Máma's*," I said. "For all you are his friend, he was not very nice to me."

"He is an acquired taste." Amir smiled, unable to hide his amusement. "But I know I can trust him."

"Which is why you went to kill Karl's brother," I accused, my voice nearly breaking. "Karl and Clavan told me what happened. I know that there were witnesses to the attack on that coach heading for Silesia. You can't deny it."

"I did not kill anyone, let alone your beloved."

I went silent at his words, taking the moment to glance around to make sure we were alone. "How did you know?"

"Lumi is a friend of his, too," Amir said. "They met each other while Ferdinand—or Ferdy, if you prefer—was at school in Paris. Lumi met Karl at Oxford for his education, too."

Breathing seemed abnormally difficult all of a sudden. I felt my hand cover my mouth in shock, as my mind raced with the implications.

Ferdy? Friends with Lumiere?

Ferdy had told me before he knew of the Order and the League, and it looked like he had plenty of personal connections to the two of them.

"Your beloved has been keeping secrets, hasn't he?" Amir took a cautious step toward me. "And he has asked you to keep them, too."

"Not entirely." I sighed. "His servant did. Empress Maria Anna seems to remember *Máma*, and I did not want to disappoint her, either."

"That's why you haven't said anything, and that was what you were keeping from Lady Penelope, wasn't it? You knew Karl had a younger brother."

Frustration ate at me. "I haven't known for that long. I found out the night of the Advent Ball. Keeping silent seemed to be the most prudent thing to do. I didn't want him to get into trouble."

"It seems as though he has a talent for it, living on the streets." Amir suddenly let out a small laugh. "I'll commend him on his disguise, though now that I think of it, I should have seen it from the beginning."

"What do you mean?" I asked.

"No ordinary street urchin would just happen to know formal Arabic."

"Well, that doesn't matter now, does it? I heard about what happened. I know he's dead." I turned away. I did not want to face Amir. "And it's all your fault, isn't it?"

THE ORDER OF THE CRYSTAL DAGGERS

There was a long, uncomfortable moment of silence between us that told me everything I needed to hear.

"You said you heard the story about what happened," Amir said quietly. "It is true those men are dead."

The lump in my throat suffocated me. I ducked my head into my hands and slumped down against the wall. My gown fluttered out around me as my dagger leaned into my hip.

Amir telling me that Ferdy was gone was like losing him all over again.

"Please, believe me when I tell you I am not the true villain; I had to go to the castle and find a way to track down the coach, and then I had to catch up with it. I was warned that there was another henchman following, to ensure that everything happened according to plan. Lumi was right about that; a man attacked about half a day's journey from Prague, killing everyone in the coach. I had only managed to catch up when he attacked. Once he was finished, I saw him light the coach on fire, and a piece of luggage exploded."

"You were too late." My voice was scratchy as I looked over at him. "Did you go over to help? Is that why the story was changed where you were the one who was …"

I couldn't bring myself to finish the sentence.

Amir seemed to understand what I refused to say. "I changed the message before it was sent out."

"You criminalized yourself?"

"I had to," Amir said. "Once a nearby village saw the fire, others came to help, including a vicar. Some people noticed me, and they assumed I was the villain anyway. There is a reason I do not join you and Lady Penelope in Society, and that I am an honorary member of the League instead of a full one. My skin color cannot be changed, and others know of

THE ORDER OF THE CRYSTAL DAGGERS

my heritage just by looking at me. I know the assumptions that come with it very well."

I went silent at his sadness. I knew the prejudice that existed in the world, and given that Amir was armed, he would have been arrested on the spot.

"People would have contradicted the story if they heard I was actually trying to rescue them, and there was no proof I was not the villain. You know no one would have believed it then," Amir said. "So I adopted the villain's role as I headed home. I had to watch out for those who heard and avoid the gossip. That is the reason for my delay in returning."

I said nothing again, as I attempted to right myself. I did not want Amir to think I was weak, but I was. I was devastated.

I could see Ferdy dressed up in his princely attire, waltzing around Prague Castle's ballroom, confessing his love for me in a way that infuriated me as much as it captivated me. The first time I saw him, arguing over my mother's journal with Amir. All the times I had seen him in costume—so many costumes any regular person would have wondered which was the real Ferdy, or if he existed at all.

But I knew him. I could see him again in my mind, dressed in proper breeches and a formal shirt. He wore boots but no cravat, and his copper hair was tousled in the wind.

And then there was a blaze of fire, and he was gone.

"Their bodies have been salvaged as much as possible," Amir said. "The Royals have been informed of their son's passing. And it is likely, since he was the king's son, they will have a funeral for him, although a private one. The king never announced his birth to the kingdom, so he was not a prince of the nation."

"I don't want to hear anything else," I said, struggling to stand up. I had to force myself to focus. There was a reason I

THE ORDER OF THE CRYSTAL DAGGERS

was here, and it was not to worry about Ferdy. I could no longer worry about him. I had to let him go for now.

"I'm so sorry, Eleanora. I know it does not mean much, or even anything to hear, but if I could do anything to save him for you, I would."

Amir's apology hung in the air between us as I waited for myself to accept it.

I did not want to accept it.

It seemed like a long time later when I breathed in deeply, wiped my eyes clear of any tears, and stood up tall. "It's too late to do anything else. We're here to save Lady Penelope, and Karl's expecting me."

"Please, listen. Lumi sent me to stop Ferdy's assassination from happening," Amir said. "He also told me that Karl cornered Lady POW after the rededication ceremony and forced her to leave with him."

"So?"

"So Lumi is on our side."

I wiped my running nose unceremoniously against my shoulder. "I do not believe it."

"The information he has given me is correct."

"It is also possible he's lying, and you're too close to him to see it." I crossed my arms. "Is he a weakness of yours, Amir?"

Amir grimaced. "This is getting us nowhere. Right now, we have to find your grandmother."

"That's the only reason I am here. Although I would not say no to killing someone right now."

Amir ignored my anger. "Lumi told me Karl wanted to offer a future to the nation, especially given his age, so that is why you—as the daughter of Adolf Svoboda, the former king's most loyal servant, with your charming innocence and the wealth from your dowager Duchess grandmother who is a close friend of Queen Victoria—play such a key role in his plans."

"Good to know I'm worth something to someone." I huffed.

"Considering who we are dealing with, I would not feel bad for being a pawn if I were you." Amir's expression softened. "It does nothing, but I can tell he does genuinely like you. He could have had Lady Teresa Marie as his bride if he did not think you were the better gamble."

"Well," I said, "Karl's about to find out that sometimes when you gamble, you lose. Once I find Lady POW, I will make sure he pays for his duplicity and treachery."

Not to mention his heavy-handedness. I gripped my dagger again, remembering his warning to me back at the museum.

"That brings us back the problem we now face. Lady Penelope is not here. I have been watching for you for the last hour, trying to intercept you. You will gain nothing if you confront Karl tonight without her here."

"Where else would she be?" I asked, perplexed. Amir was right. Even with as little I did know about Society, I knew if Lady POW was not here to protect me, Karl would have an easier time getting me to agree to his terms.

"Lumi told me that she was with Karl earlier," Amir said, "but that's clearly changed. She could be anywhere. If we are going to stop Karl, we will have to find her quickly. If you do not show up here, he is in a position to use her life as leverage."

I still had trouble imagining Karl as one who would take an old lady hostage, but I had no trouble considering that Lumiere had men who would do it for him.

THE ORDER OF THE CRYSTAL DAGGERS

The whole plan we had conceived earlier was for naught. If I was going to save my grandmother, I would have to find her before Karl was able to get away from his own party.

"Do you have any thoughts on where he might have taken her?"

"Karl is staying at the castle," I said. "Is it possible she is in the dungeons there? It seems like if he was going to coerce her, he would likely find a way to make sure she stayed where he put her."

Amir nodded. "It is a logical guess."

"Where do you think he would hold her?" I glanced around. "Are you sure he's not keeping her here, in some locked room, far away from the crowds?"

"I have been here for hours," Amir said. "I have examined the servants and walked through the majority of the house."

"Harshad and Xiana are also here, looking for Lady POW," I said. "Should we try to help them before we leave?"

"You need to leave right now." Amir took my hand again and started walking down the hall. "There is a servant's entrance here. You'll be able to wait for a lull in their movements and sneak out. Once you're out, find a way to get a ride on a departing coach and head for the castle."

"If I get there, I will be able to see the former empress," I said, suddenly dreading the encounter. Empress Maria Anna had entrusted her younger son's protection to me, and I had failed her. "She will recognize me and be able to tell me if Lady Penelope is there."

"It's the best bet we have right now," Amir said.

"What if she is not there?"

He shrugged.

THE ORDER OF THE CRYSTAL DAGGERS

"If you stay here, Harshad and Xiana might be able to help you capture Karl as he is leaving still," I suggested.

"I'll go and find them, and we will work out a plan. Either way, we will meet you at the castle."

"Are you sure they will believe you?" I asked. Was I able to believe him, too, then?

In the end, I decided that I could trust him for now. It was true that Amir had kept Ferdy a secret before, and he had apologized for failing to save him. And it was nice, I had to admit, that he wanted me to leave the ball. As majestic as Count Potocki's manor was, I eagerly embraced the chance to escape.

"Give me a moment." I stopped in my tracks and pulled out my dagger.

Amir looked at me curiously, unmoving, and I wondered if he thought I was going to attack him. It might have been tempting if I did not believe him, but instead, I ran the sharp and ancient edge through the side of my gown's bodice, cutting the outer layer of my fancy clothes. When I was done, I shed the outer layers and stood ready in only my stealth habit. The dark fabrics, overlapping each other across my chest and down my legs, allowed me to sink into the shadows like an agent of the devil himself.

Amir raised his brow.

"There's no use for me to wear the gown now," I explained. I tugged my hood over my hair and pulled my mask to the bridge of my nose.

"I see your argument," Amir said, "but you should still wear your cloak on the way out. There's no need to freeze, even if you will be able to maneuver through the streets with much less notice."

THE ORDER OF THE CRYSTAL DAGGERS

It was an easy choice for me to grant his wish. I pulled on my cloak, letting the fine fabric conceal my costume.

Amir squeezed my hand before we departed. "I know we have little time, Eleanora, but I have one last question for you."

"What is it?"

He looked down at me intently. "Did you tell Lady Penelope about anything that I said to you?"

"She thought you told me more, but I only admitted you told me about your family and your scar." I looked down at his hand, where in the dim lighting, I could still see the heavy outline of the *noon* above his knuckles. "That was it."

"Did she ask about Nassara?"

At the tone of his voice, so hollow and detached, I frowned. "I did not tell her about the journal, if that's what you mean."

Amir patted my hand and stepped back from me. "Thank you, Eleanora. I appreciate your silence on the matter. *Allah yusallmak*, and I will see you later."

At the sound of the foreign words, I suddenly had a new question for him. "Amir? What did Ferdy say to you the day we met in that alleyway?"

"After he understood the problem between us, he offered to trade your life for his," Amir told me. "He said he wanted to keep you for himself."

I did not know what to say to that. Amir had always known I had a beloved. I never thought it was strange how well he seemed to know until now.

"Thank you," I mumbled, before I turned and walked away. I held my dagger tightly as I left, grateful that even if Lady

THE ORDER OF THE CRYSTAL DAGGERS

POW was nowhere to be found, I would find a way to end everything soon.

THE ORDER OF THE CRYSTAL DAGGERS

19

◊

I was halfway to the castle when I realized I had forgotten something very important.

"*Merde*," I hissed at myself, stopping short as I passed by Old Town Square. "I forgot about Ben."

I glanced at the castle in the distance. The towers and walls of the ancient structure gleamed ghoulishly in the moonlight, backdropped against the dark pleasures of the city nightlife. I turned back toward the bridge, looking down the Vltava to see if I could estimate how far away the *Josefkà* was.

Should I alert Ben to the change in plans?

He was meeting with Zipporah tonight, getting herbs, including the silver thallis herb that the Order required for our special elixir. He was supposed to go over to Count Potocki's when he was finished.

It was uncertain if he was even still there, I thought. But surely it wasn't that unlikely? After all, I had left Karl's party much earlier than anticipated, and he had gotten off the coach several blocks away.

Ben would be upset with me if I did not include him, I reasoned. I remembered Lady POW telling me that she was not sure if she should allow him to continue helping out, and I made my choice.

No, I thought. *I cannot leave him out of this.*

Besides, if Lady Penelope was not at the castle, Ben and I would have a better chance at fending off Karl, in the event he came after us.

I slivered in and out of the shadows, heading toward the Cabal.

291

As I made my way through the cluttered streets and the alleys, I wondered if it really only had been less than a day since I had seen my friends at the Cabal. But, I figured, if the last weeks felt like a lifetime, it made sense that my temporal facilities were considerably off.

Keeping my cloak firmly against my skin, I slipped up beside the entrance to the Cabal. The wind blew my hood down, but I let it go. Without it, I could watch through the window as Ben talked with a comely woman near the bar.

At first look, I knew it was Zipporah. Eliezer's wife was nearly exactly the way I had imagined her to be. She had hair that was dark and curly like my own, though hers seemed thicker. She was considerably shorter than me, and she wore the proper clothes of a mother and caretaker. I saw her apron strings sticking out from underneath her coat and almost smiled at the gentle, delicate picture she made. Everything about her suggested that she was a perfect match for her short but commanding husband.

I watched as Zipporah handed Ben a small drawstring bag, one that was puffed out and full. He offered her coins, and I was surprised at the amount, before I thought about Amir. He had managed to work his way into Count Potocki's manor, and it was likely he had bought the silence of the staff in the process.

Bribery is a trick Ben has no doubt learned from Amir. I tried not to laugh at the thought of what Lady POW would have taught him to do. She would have told him it was acceptable to rob Zipporah at gunpoint or use a weapon to inspire fear. Xiana would have used her stealth to steal it, and Harshad …

I paused, suddenly stumped. *I do not actually know how he would go about getting the herbs if Zipporah was not a friend.*

After a few moments of consideration, I could see where Harshad would pay her, too, but I did not think he would retrieve the herbs himself. As a foreigner from the East

Indies, he would want to send someone with more anonymity to retrieve them—someone just like my brother, as a matter of fact.

"Miss Svobodová? Is that you?"

Hearing my name nearly made me jump. I grappled my cloak's ties, hoping against all hope the newcomer would fail to notice I was not wearing a gown.

I turned to see Madame Balthazar, one of the merchants I used to trade and do business with before Lady Penelope freed me from Cecilia's grasp.

"Madame." I greeted her as politely as I could, given that a small curtesy was all I manage without exposing my legs.

"I thought that was you," she said. Her mouth curled into a slight pout of disapproval. "What are you doing here? This is no place for a lady such as you to be."

"I am not here by myself. I was actually looking for my brother. I had only just lost him when you called to me," I lied.

"Oh, that makes sense." She looked relieved. "For a moment there, I thought you were in trouble. This is not a pleasant part of town, what with the Jews all around."

I pursed my lips and said nothing. I did not trust myself to respond in a way that did not end with me attacking her in some way, but thankfully, she kept talking.

"I wouldn't be here myself if it weren't for the fact I am desperate," she said. "I've been told that there is a midwife around here, and I need to speak with her at once. My daughter just had a baby a few weeks ago, and he has developed a terrible cough."

I was about to tell her Zipporah was inside the Cabal, but she kept fretting.

THE ORDER OF THE CRYSTAL DAGGERS

"I wish I had been able to find someone to send instead," she said. "It's so cold out tonight and I haven't had a bit of luck in finding her. Aren't you freezing, Miss?"

"I honestly did not notice."

She did not seem to hear me. "I should have called for that messenger boy. You remember him, don't you? Ferdy, that was his name. He always seemed so eager to pick up work, but not as much in recent days."

"It is probably the weather," I said softly. I did not have time to get caught up in mourning his loss anymore, and I really did not want to hear what Madame Balthazar thought of his passing.

"Perhaps, but not likely." She huffed. "I know for a fact he's been fighting again. There is a mission house that feeds those in poverty at the docks where a friend of mine works, and she says he's been causing trouble for the last few days."

I did not hear the rest of her words, as she complained about everything from the weather to the trouble that beggars and urchins caused. All I could hear was my heart beating between my ears while my skin started to prickle. I felt numb to the world, as if I had been shocked out of time's pull and then smashed back into it.

Was it possible Madame Balthazar was right? Ferdy was alive?

"You said he at the docks?" I repeated. The words tumbled off my tongue, thick and cluttered together, as though I was suddenly speaking a foreign language.

"Yes. Otherwise I would have sent him to find the midwife, of course."

"Nora? Is that you?"

THE ORDER OF THE CRYSTAL DAGGERS

Behind me, Ben appeared in the doorway. He had a confused look on his face, but I was at too much of a loss to say anything coherent.

Ferdy could be alive.

My mind reeled, first with unbelievability, and then broken with bursting, unbridled hope. It hurt to think that it could be wrong, but there was nothing I wanted to be true more ardently in that moment.

"Which dock is it?" I asked, turning back to Madame Balthazar. "Tell me where he is."

She looked shocked at my impropriety. "What? Why would—"

"Just tell me, please." I did not mean to sound like a desperate beggar, but there were any number of thoughts and feelings jumbled together inside of me, and everything from Karl, to Lady Penelope, to Lumiere and the mission— everything was lost as I suddenly had hope.

"He was at the Port of Prague, down by the riverfront." Madame Balthazar gave me the direction, and I hurriedly thanked her.

Before I could head toward the port, Ben came up beside us. I remembered the reason I had come, and hurried to usher Madame Balthazar toward the Cabal, telling her that Eliezer's wife was the midwife she needed.

The second Madame Balthazar was inside the Cabal and out of earshot, I grabbed a hold of Ben.

"Nora, what's wrong?" Ben asked. "What was that all about? Why are you here?"

"Things have changed. I need you to go to the castle," I said. There was too much to tell him, and I felt the words surge out of me like water from a broken dam. "Amir came back, and Karl is keeping Lady POW prisoner somewhere. Harshad and Xiana will be there shortly."

"What are you going to do?" Ben asked.

I was already moving as I hollered back to Ben. "Just go. I'll meet you at the castle. I have to check on something first."

"Nora!" Ben called back to me, followed by murmurs of sentences dotted with garbled phrases. Other than my name, I was not certain of what he said as I sped away.

It was likely something I ultimately did not want to hear. I knew I was already running behind schedule by stopping off to get Ben, and anything he said might have convinced me to stop my sudden quest.

But I had to know if Ferdy was alive.

The Port of Prague was not welcoming to any aristocrat at night, let alone a lady. I was glad I had shed my gown earlier; I could move more freely. I even managed to use some of the stealth techniques I learned from Xiana and Harshad as I made my way through the loading port.

Weaving through the tight spaces and the winding walkways, keeping as much to the darkness as I could, I tried not to think about the passing time. I could only be grateful I had sent Ben. He would be able to help the others in my place, and that gave me a little time to pursue my own interests.

I tried not to cringe at the thought; Lady Penelope would chastise me for sure, and I would further fall from grace. It did not take much for me to imagine her boxing my ears for

THE ORDER OF THE CRYSTAL DAGGERS

this, especially since the last time I went looking for the younger prince of Bohemia, I had gotten caught up in the partial collapse of the castle.

But this is worth it.

If he was here, everything would be worth it.

But, I thought, it would still be better if I could take care of this business quickly.

Fortunately, it did not take me long to find the warehouse Madame Balthazar spoke of. I crept up to the backdoor from the outside, surprised to find it was unlocked.

As I stepped inside, a flickering light whispered at the intrusion. I could feel the cold of winter much more sharply, and I held my breath as I acclimated to the putrid smell.

"Oh my, what is that?" I whispered, struggling not to choke. I had hoped the sound of my voice would comfort me, but I barely heard myself as the growing jeers and cheers from the other side of the hallway suddenly escalated.

I pulled my hood up more tightly to my face, and I secured my mask while I walked toward the sounds. I was able to see through the small sliver of the doorway.

For all the good it ended up doing.

The only thing I could see was a crowd of dock workers, many curled up in shabby clothes. Several were smoking cigarettes, and I briefly wondered if Jarl would be impressed or appalled at their choices.

After a silent, desperate prayer—was there any other kind I was offering to God of late?—I slowly opened the door and slid into the shadows.

No one noticed me on the outskirts of the crowd, and I relaxed to the slightest degree.

Until I saw why everyone was cheering.

THE ORDER OF THE CRYSTAL DAGGERS

There were two men, shirtless and covered in sweat, throwing punches, fighting with a force that shook me as I watched.

It was only as I watched the one fighter take a direct hit to the side of his torso and fall back that I recognized him.

Ferdy.

20

◊

It seemed to be a combination of shock, anger, and joy that stopped me from moving. From breathing, really.

He is alive. Oh, thank you, Lord, he is alive!

Never had I ever been so happy. Ferdy was alive and well, even if he was trying to dodge the fighter in front of him. I watched as he ducked down in pain at the blow to his side and then reached out and grappled with his opponent. I saw his hands were wrapped in leather, not unlike the ones Ben and I had used in Harshad's lessons.

I also had a really hard time ignoring his physique. Sweat rolled down his back as he moved, falling down the toned muscles. He had a very nice body, and I was not able to keep myself from blushing any more than I was able to look away.

It was only after he took another hit to the side that reality set in, and I realized he had lied to me—again.

Again!

He had lied to me about leaving for Silesia, and now he was in the middle of a needless, frivolous fight. All this while I was suffering at the thought of his death.

To make it worse, he must have known about the incident, too. And still he was here, saying nothing, reaching out to no one. Even his friends at the Cabal should have known he was here.

Were they lying to me, too?

I can't believe this! I had just decided to trust him, too.

That was the worst of it, I decided. I was in love with this selfish, privileged fool, someone who was content to waste his life on fights at the docks while his brother tried to murder him and seize the kingdom. Someone who seemed almost eager to run through my heart and make me question every decision I had ever made and every person I had ever trusted.

I watched as he feinted forward, making his opponent angry. The other man grunted loudly as he flung forward into the crowd. The men cheered even more as they pushed him back out.

Ferdy waited for a moment before the man raised his fists again. He was still his usual self, allowing even his enemy to have dignity. I saw him say something to the man, and the man shrugged it off and then spat. The wad of saliva hit the floor between them, and I could see he was more upset than anything else.

"Ew," I murmured as I tried to move closer. Ahead of me, off to the far side, there was a small gap between the front lines of the edge of their adapted boxing arena. I slipped in where I could, and if others paid me any mind, it did not stop their enthusiasm for the fight.

I will never understand men. I shook my head as another round of cheers filled up the room when Ferdy landed another punch, and the man fell down.

Another man came forward to check the man, who was struggling to get up. He seemed to be the referee, and he held up Ferdy's arm.

"Our winner for this round," he called, setting off a mix of booing and applause, along with the people calling on each other for bets to be settled.

Ferdy did not seem to care much. He nodded toward a couple of others, brushing off their comments. He was breathing hard and someone tossed him a towel.

That was when I noticed his opponent was getting up. His eyes were red, and he wore a cross expression.

He jumped up and steadied himself, wiping his long hair back from his face.

Before I knew it, he was running toward Ferdy, his fist balled and ready to attack.

And then, suddenly, I was leaping forward, entering the match grounds and bracing myself for impact. I ducked down and held my breath as he ran toward me.

I only briefly registered the man's shocked look as he tripped over me. My cloak tore free and fluttered to the ground as he went flying over my back. The fabric rolled over on the man, briefly trapping his arms as he flopped onto the ground.

The entire room was suddenly staring at me, including Ferdy. I straightened up and stared back at him. There were calls from the crowd for the man to be removed, but I only saw Ferdy's eyes widen and then narrow suspiciously.

Just like that night, I thought. It was the same look he had given me the night of the Advent Ball, when he recognized me as a member of the Order.

"It's a woman," one of the men shouted, and immediately the bets were announced again.

I finally glanced around, and my divided attention caught me.

My knees were swiftly knocked out from under me by my fallen foe. I tumbled down, feeling the sudden pain of a real fight at once as I landed on my back.

The man lunged over, trying to pin me down. My training with Harshad kicked in, and I hurried to block as I twisted out of his range. I rolled to my feet and held up my fists, surprised to see Ferdy with a headlock on my opponent.

"What are you doing here, Ella?" he called over the sounds of the crowd, as the room echoed with their overindulged pleasure.

"Trying to protect you!" I yelled back. I still did not know if I was more angry than relieved. "For all you deserve it, clearly."

The fighter elbowed Ferdy in the side, breaking free. He came running after me, and I used his focus to twist out of his reach. The second he ran past me, I lashed out a sidekick. His momentum carried him to the end of the arena, where the crowds were still cheering him on even as mud scrapped into his face.

"I'd like to think I deserve a better quality of protection than you can offer," Ferdy hissed as he came up beside me. From our sudden closeness, I could smell him, the faint scent of lavender and mint buried deeply under the aroma of ash and sweat. "I heard what happened."

"I did, too, and that's why I thought you were dead." I crossed my arms as I stared at him, furious.

"Why would you think I was dead?" Ferdy seemed surprised.

"You told me you were leaving for Silesia at the concert," I snapped. "What was I supposed to think?"

While I was distracted, our opponent came back up behind us. Ferdy pushed me out of the way as he threw out a hook. I could hear the *crunch* of the impact, and I watched in horror as the man flopped down onto the ground and stayed there.

Behind us, the crowd cheered again.

"Take a bow," Ferdy said, grabbing my arm and holding it up like the referee had done to him only moments before. "And then you and I are going to talk."

"Fine by me," I shot back. "I have plenty to say."

THE ORDER OF THE CRYSTAL DAGGERS

"I imagine you do." Ferdy rolled his eyes, and the two of us bowed. I had to stop myself from curtseying.

After that, Ferdy hurried to usher me out of the room. One of his friends tossed him a shirt, and he grabbed my dirt-splattered cloak on the way out. We headed back the way I had come, toward the other room in the warehouse. Once there, he found a smaller room, one I assumed to be an office, and shoved me in.

I stumbled forward, only stopping as I came up against a wooden box. There was a large pile of rope on the floor next to it. It was not an office we had entered, but a supply room.

Immediately, I whirled around to face Ferdy. I pulled down my mask and watched him lock the door. "Ferdy—"

"Shh." He glared at me in the poor lighting, listening at the door as some of the men walked by, talking loudly and possibly drunkenly about the fights.

I realized at once why Ferdy wanted me to keep silent. My eyes widened at some of their language; it was crude and coarse, enough to make even Lady Penelope blush—possibly.

When they were gone, and another round of fighting had commenced, Ferdy slipped into the shirt someone had tossed him. I was glad when he left it unbuttoned, even if I forced myself not to think about that.

"They're distracted now," he said, as another round of yelling and cheering resounded from the adjacent room. "I don't think they know we're in here."

"They seem very eager to be distracted."

"Poverty has its price. The entertainment here is brutal. I suppose you noticed that when you decided to make a spectacle of yourself. You shouldn't have done anything back there."

"That man was going to hurt you," I insisted. "It was the right thing to do, to stop him. Even if you deserved it."

"The men are just going to want more women boxers in the future after this."

"Maybe I'll give it another try after I'm done with you." I put my hands on my hips as I tried to make out his features in the darkness. The evening hours had arrived, and there was only a trickle of light coming in from the hall as we stared at each other. "Tell me why you're here in the first place, besides the fact that you've clearly gone mad."

"If I am mad for being here, what do you think that makes you for coming?"

I would not allow him to intimidate me. No matter what he had just done to that man. "You know why I'm here. I'm here for you."

"I'm not sure how your betrothed would feel about that."

I bit my lip, realizing why he was upset. Ferdy had likely heard the rumors, especially since he was taking care to watch his brother now. "I'm not going to marry Karl. You should know that. I told you before it was all a lie and part of my cover."

"Well, the morning papers are a little different," Ferdy snapped. "And besides, I didn't lie to you about Silesia, and *you* should have known about *that.*"

"You told Karl that you were leaving in front of me!"

"You're lying about how you feel about him in front of me," Ferdy pointed out. He pushed back the sweaty locks of his hair. Even in the poor lighting, I could see it was still wet from his recent fight. "Why wouldn't I lie about my travel plans in front of him as well?"

"You could have told me you were lying when we met outside the theatre." I felt a rush of embarrassment, realizing

THE ORDER OF THE CRYSTAL DAGGERS

he was right. But I was not going to admit it. Not now, not after I had discovered he did nothing to tell me he was alive when I thought he was dead. "At least I clarified my lies."

"I promised you I would not lie to you again," Ferdy said. He leaned back against the wall, and for the first time, I noticed there was an ugly bruise appearing on his right side, just under his ribs.

That has to be from Ben's attack. It had gotten worse with all the fighting.

"I know that I have kept important things about myself from you, and I wanted to make up for it. That is why I made you that promise—so you could trust me again." Ferdy looked disgusted. "I should have asked the same of you, but I didn't."

I crossed my arms. "If you wanted my trust, you should have told me that you were alive after the carriage exploded."

His fist lashed out, hard and quick, denting the wall behind him. I flinched but said nothing.

"Do you know what happened?" Ferdy asked, his voice slightly raised. I realized then how hard he was trying hard to keep himself together. "They killed Philip, and my other friends. They thought they were killing me, but they didn't."

My nose prickled with unshed tears, and my cheeks burned at my foolishness and shame as I thought about Philip and the others. Ferdy would have been devastated to learn what happened. And I was, too. Philip had taken such good care of me for him.

And my pain was only a pittance compared to Ferdy's, I thought. He had known him for years. Philip had been trusted with the kingdom's most precious secrets. My gaze lowered to the floor, thinking of the ones I loved and lost.

THE ORDER OF THE CRYSTAL DAGGERS

I already knew I could say nothing to make his pain go away.

"You know what the worst part of being a prince is?" Ferdy asked, his voice full of stinging bitterness. It was a complete departure from his energetic irreverence, and I lost all my hostility at his pain.

"No," I whispered. "Tell me."

"Other people feel the need to die for you." Ferdy narrowed his gaze at me. "People feel they need to lie to you. They feel so noble and justified in keeping secrets from you. All in the name of protecting you."

"I know that's frustrating." I knew from my own experiences with Lady POW and the others that I had plenty of others who were content to do the same thing to me.

"Damn it all to hell, of course it's frustrating." Ferdy punched the wall again, before he gripped his fist in pain. "I'm not special, Ella. No one should have to die for me."

I hurried forward and clasped my arms around his neck, holding on as he flinched. "I wouldn't die for a prince," I told him quietly. "But I would die for you."

I thought about telling him how much I wanted to kill for him, too, to punish Lumiere for his plans and Karl for his deviousness. But before I could think anything else, Ferdy reached up and pushed back my hood.

And then all of a sudden, his mouth was on mine again, and nothing else in the world mattered.

It seemed the storm inside of me was only matched by the one in him. His fingers were scratched and bloody as they tangled themselves in my hair, but I did not care. His kiss was rough and heavy, nothing like any other we had shared before. I could feel the frustration inside of him, along with

THE ORDER OF THE CRYSTAL DAGGERS

the anger, but I knew it was the uncertainty that drove him to seek the solace of truth.

I was breathless as he pulled me closer to him, and then pressed into me. My back came up against the wall he had hit in frustration moments earlier. I might have been afraid, but I was too overwhelmed.

His hands were suddenly on my hips, the heat of his body burning against mine. My hands gripped onto his shoulders before slipping under his shirt, eager to feel the strength of him I had witnessed earlier, desperate to soothe the ache of his bruise. My fingers trailed down his side, seeking out his injury. I felt him shiver at my touch and I was about to ask him if I had hurt him when he pressed his hand over mine, flattening my palm even more ardently against his bruised rib. The slickness of his torso was oddly irresistible.

"Tell me what you want, Ella."

I already had my answer. "I want you to keep me," I whispered, clinging to him even more tightly as I drew his lips to mine again.

It was all too much to have him with me again. The taste of him, the feel of him—everything rushed at me all at once, and I did nothing to stop it.

I used to think being free meant an escape; I thought it meant I would be able to move away from authority and addiction, to be still against the forces of time and space. But as he held me there, pushed up against a wall, I knew freedom was not an escape, but a coming home; it was a place to run to, a star to guide all other forces of life and light, pushing back against the darkness of hopelessness and sin. Embracing it meant I was loved and cherished as myself; I could be who I was, and even more of who I was meant to be.

THE ORDER OF THE CRYSTAL DAGGERS

Ferdy's breath was ragged as he finally pulled his mouth away from mine. "This is madness."

"I thought you said it was magic before." My voice was shaking and hoarse as I whispered into the darkness.

Ferdy laughed and kissed my neck, letting the shy stubble on his cheeks rest against my skin as he caught his breath. "There is nothing magical about me wanting to make love to you inside a warehouse."

I stilled at his words, suddenly very aware we were too close. I slid away from him, only a little, but he stepped back as well. "You're right about that. Lady Penelope says there's no room for falling in love in the life of a spy."

He leaned in and kissed me once more, softly and slowly, before resting his forehead on mine, just as he had that day I woke up in Prague Castle. "You are more than a spy, just as I am more than a prince."

There was no trace of jesting or mockery in his voice. This time, he was only sincere and succinct, and if I had not fallen in love with him already, I would have done so in that second.

"What does your grandmother think about a spy getting married?" Ferdy asked.

It was too hard to tell if I was more hopeful at the question or dumbstruck at the possible answers. Lady POW had not married except to ensure her survival, and none of her other team members were married, either.

But my mother got married.

The safest answer was the one I gave him. "I don't know."

"Well, I guess we will find out when I meet her, won't we?" Ferdy took my hand and brought it to his lips, lacing his fingers into mine.

I froze. The thought of being with Ferdy no longer seemed so impossible; if death was no longer between us, I did not see why social order and kingdom security would stop us from being together. But I was genuinely unsure of what Lady Penelope would say, and I did not know if I could bear her refusal, or what we would do if she denied us.

"I'm glad you came to find me," Ferdy whispered. There was still a hint of sadness in his voice, but he seemed more hopeful than before.

"Me, too." I barely remembered what a marvel it was, that I had been able to find out about him at all. If miracles happened enough, it was too easy to see them as normal and take them for granted. I was not supposed to even be near the port, nor was I supposed to go to the Cabal, or run into Madame Balthazar …

I am supposed to be looking for Lady Penelope and stopping Karl from announcing our engagement.

"What time is it?" I looked around and saw nothing to indicate how much time had passed. There was not even a window around to let me see if the moon had risen. "I have to go."

"Already?" Ferdy gave me a small smirk. "I thought you were going to see about another round of boxing?"

"If I do, my opponent is going to be your brother," I said. "He kidnapped Lady POW and he's holding her somewhere. That is the only reason the papers published the news about our engagement."

"Karl kidnapped your grandmother?" Ferdy frowned. "That doesn't sound like him."

"That reminds me." I scowled up at him. "He's working with your so-called friend Lumiere. He was the one who organized the attack on your coach."

THE ORDER OF THE CRYSTAL DAGGERS

"That does sound like Lumi. I wonder if he knew it was really me or not." Ferdy muttered a curse or two under his breath, and I immediately felt better. Lumiere likely wanted Ferdy to be his friend the way he wanted me to be his friend, and there was no way I could ever see that happening short of a miracle or two. "I'll have to ask him. He is very clever, but it would not be the first time his plans went awry."

"I can't believe you even would give him the benefit of the doubt there," I scoffed. It was true that I felt deeply empathetic for Ferdy and his loss, but it was no help to be ignorant of the facts.

"I did not say I would only ask him questions." Ferdy gave me a wink as he buttoned up his shirt. "I'll likely intersperse them with a few punches."

I nodded approvingly. "I would love to join you. Before we can take care of him, I need to find Lady POW."

"We can do that. What is the plan?"

"What?" I blinked up at Ferdy. "You're not part of the plan."

"I never was, *chérie*, but here I am. Are you really going to let me loose on the streets of Prague again without worrying for my life and safety?"

"You should be more worried about your life and safety if you think you're going to trick me into letting you help with my mission," I said, suddenly remembering Ferdy's other mischief. "Karl found out about us all because of you."

"What? I was extremely discreet when I came to visit you at the concert."

"It wasn't that. It was the hair combs you gave me before. He saw them."

Ferdy's hand gripped onto mine more tightly. "You mean you actually wore them out in public?"

THE ORDER OF THE CRYSTAL DAGGERS

"I didn't know they were the princess combs!"

"You really don't know anything about your kingdom's history, do you?"

"One does not need to know the history of a nation while working as a maid," I snapped. "Besides, knowing you as I do, I would say you didn't think I would recognize them. That was why you offered them in the first place."

"If Karl does know about us, that makes more sense as to why he kidnapped Lady Penelope and sent the notice to the papers," Ferdy said, clearly ignoring my point. "He had to force her hand because he knew I was pursuing you."

"You *were* pursuing me." I glanced around again, gesturing to the warehouse closet where we were located. "Or maybe I should say you were making *me* pursue you?"

"Let's call it even." He gave me a quick smile before his expression turned dark again. "Do you know where he's holding Lady Penelope?"

"Not exactly," I said. "I thought he would take her to the castle, since he's staying there, and he would be able to have someone watch her while he was busy with other things."

"I can help with that. My parents live there, after all, and all the servants are under orders to listen to me."

"I don't want you to get hurt." I hugged him close, looping my arms around his waist. "I already thought I lost you once."

"You couldn't lose me if you tried," Ferdy insisted. He tucked a stray curl of my hair behind my ear. "I am too clever for you, even if you are a spy for the Order."

"I've only just forgiven you for lying to me about being alive and blowing my cover, and you're comfortable enough to insult me?"

THE ORDER OF THE CRYSTAL DAGGERS

"They made your mission about me when they decided to try to kill me, remember?"

I was losing the battle, if I had not lost already.

"Consider this a matter of efficiency. And speaking of which, we should head out to the castle now," Ferdy said as he took my hand and opened the door. "If we're going to stop my brother, we'll need to … "

Ferdy's voice trailed off as he stopped. I glanced over his shoulder, only to see a small group of shadows stationed at the exit.

The shadows were attached to men, and all of them stared at us as we stood there. They seemed to be waiting around for something. I yanked my mask up over my nose, afraid they might have been looking for me. Ferdy inched in front of me; the same thought was likely running through his mind. He stepped forward and stretched out his arm, as if he was going to exchange greetings, but one of them pointed to Ferdy. "The boss was right. He's alive. Get him!"

Before I could do anything, Ferdy tugged me around and began running the other way. "Other way out."

"Well, hurry it up, you lazy thugs! Go get them." Another voice spoke up, and I struggled to keep running as I thought I recognized it. As carefully as I could, I turned to see the leader of the small group. While Ferdy and I had been preoccupied inside the supply closet, other lamps had been lit.

I gasped at the sight, my suspicions confirmed.

It was my stepbrother, Alex.

THE ORDER OF THE CRYSTAL DAGGERS

21

◊

The warehouse was much bigger and more complicated on the inside than what I had anticipated. Still stunned at the sight of my stepbrother, I was glad Ferdy was able to lead me through the makeshift arena and the labyrinthine halls connected to it. He would join me on my mission for sure now, but I was here to protect him as much as I was out to destroy Karl now.

We raced through the crowded halls, jumping through another round of fighters, before bursting into another storage area.

"Is this where you've been sleeping?" I asked Ferdy, looking around at a few shoddy makeshift beds and poorly constructed tents. There were several other people scattered throughout the warehouse halls, some of them sleeping, several of them smoking cigarettes, and many huddled together in close circles for extra warmth.

"It's not as bad as it looks."

I thought back to the days where Ben and I would sleep out in the barn, just to get away from Cecilia and her tyranny. Ferdy was likely right, but it did not make me feel any better. "I'm sorry."

"I could be dead," Ferdy reminded me.

"Apparently so, since there are still others trying to kill you." I glanced back to see the men were struggling to follow us. I saw them get caught up in the same crowds as we had. "My stepbrother is their leader."

"Your stepbrother?"

"Yes, Alex."

313

"How did he get involved in all of this?"

I was not even sure if I could describe what the whole situation was. I knew that Alex, along with the rest of Cecilia's household, had disappeared weeks ago without a trace. Now that I saw he was after Ferdy, it could only mean one thing: he was working with Lord Maximillian.

"Cecilia's a distant cousin to Lord Maximillian, the one who wanted to secure the throne for Karl," I said. "He purposefully broke off his daughter's engagement to Alex so he could get her to marry Karl."

"And then Karl suddenly decided he wanted you."

I blushed. "So did you."

"If you think my interest in you is sudden, you haven't been paying attention."

"You saw me more than ten years ago," I said. "I can't imagine that made any lasting impression on you, at least to the point you wanted to marry me."

"There are a few other times I've seen you in the city," Ferdy admitted. "But I still hold to my story. Something about my life changed when I saw you all those years ago."

"I appreciate that, I really do." I was panting hard as we ducked around a corner and pushed through a door. The bite of the winter night was harsh, catching my throat. "But this is not the best time for this."

"True."

"Even if your interest is not sudden, Karl's is."

"I doubt it. He knew of our father's admiration for yours," Ferdy said. "And he might have known of my feelings toward you, too."

I was panting too hard to respond.

THE ORDER OF THE CRYSTAL DAGGERS

Ferdy led me around several crates. "Stay down," he ordered, before glancing back. "I'm going to monitor them from over there."

"Be careful." I pulled out my dagger, hoping Alex and his cronies would have the good sense to give up.

"Hopefully they will lose us out here. The docks are dangerous, but especially at night," Ferdy said. "Stay here."

It was not the best time to argue with him, but I grimaced as he began issuing orders. He was the one infiltrating my mission, after all. If anything, he should have been taking orders from me.

Yards away, I heard some grunting mixed in with Alex's voice.

"Put your pistol away," I heard Alex say. "Max wants him alive. If we're going to correct the wrongs we've been dealt, we can't kill him."

It was not easy to picture Alex as I remembered him, with his bright hair brushed back and his fancy clothes, as the ringleader of mercenaries. But his words did make more sense; Lord Maximillian had hired him to find Ferdy.

Which meant that he knew of both the secret heirs of Bohemia. I was horrified to think what he would do to Ferdy if he got a hold of him. With Karl engaged to me, he might be looking for a way to usurp Karl's leadership.

A hand came down on my shoulder, and I jumped.

"It's me," Ferdy whispered. "Come this way. I think I found a way we can go around them."

"Where are we going?"

"To the Cabal. Jarl and his family are more than able to help, and Elie and Clavan might have more information for us."

Ferdy took the lead, and we began winding our way through the various lanes of shipping supplies, crates, and machinery. We were almost back on the cobblestone streets when a shot rang out behind us.

"Hurry!"

Ferdy did not need to tell me twice. I went running, recalling how Harshad had warned me before, in one of our various lessons, that it was unwise to get into a gunfight without a gun. Pistols had their drawbacks, but there was only so much I could do if I was shot.

Ferdy suddenly pushed me to the side. "You go that way," he said, pointing to a crossroad ahead of us. "I'll try to draw them back to the port."

"No," I objected. "No, you're not leaving my sight."

"It's a tactic, Ella. Divide and conquer."

I did not have a chance to point out that if we were splitting up, we would be doing their work for them. Ferdy turned around and headed for them.

"Ferdy!"

He did not pay any attention to me, and I skidded to a halt, ready to follow him. He was much quicker than me, and he turned down another lane before I could catch him.

I heard Alex call out to his men, telling them to separate.

"No," I huffed, still struggling to catch up. That was when one of Alex's henchmen began to run toward me.

A rush of fear propelled me to the side, away from where Ferdy went, and I found myself at the side of a smaller warehouse building. I could just hear the others as they cried out, and I did not know if Ferdy was able to fight them off or not.

Why in the world did he think it would be a good idea to leave me?

THE ORDER OF THE CRYSTAL DAGGERS

"Because he wanted to protect me," I realized, suddenly upset with myself. But Ferdy was not doing me a favor by endangering himself.

The henchman who followed me appeared, just yards away. I raised my fists, ready to fight.

"You're trapped now," the man said, lunging forward. "Nowhere else to go."

As I did my best to block his attack, I saw he had a handkerchief in his hand, one that held a sickly, sweet aroma.

Chloroform.

I had only ever smelled that once before, when Cecilia cut herself after yelling at one of the cooks about a year ago. She had to send Alex out for the doctor at once, while I watched from the shadows, both fascinated and horrified as she bled. When the doctor arrived, it was not long before he used chloroform to knock Cecilia out while he stitched up the gash on her leg. I would not have blamed him if it was to keep her quiet as much to keep her still, but he finished much more quickly with his work while she was unconscious.

I gulped, pressing my lips even more tightly together as we began to circle each other.

A few blows later, I was able to relax, if only in the slightest. The henchman was not as skilled as me as a fighter, but he did have a distinct advantage when it came to strength. And while I was surprised at the difference between fighting a real enemy as opposed to Harshad or Ben, I kept my focus clear. I had to get back to Ferdy.

Brushing off my blows, the man grabbed me and trapped me from behind.

He laughed, his chest rumbling with delight as he held me. "The boss will be happy to have an extra," he said as he laughed. "Might get paid more if you prove to be amusing."

THE ORDER OF THE CRYSTAL DAGGERS

I squirmed but said nothing; I did not know if he knew me or not.

The chloroform grew stronger. I held my breath, grabbing for my dagger.

My fingers looped around the hilt, and I pulled the blade free. Squeezing my eyes shut, I stabbed him in the thigh.

He screamed and let me go, just as I felt a sense of lightheadedness take over. I pulled my weapon free from him, noticing that in the moonlight, the dagger glowed a vicious purple.

There was blood dripping down the tip now. I knocked the man down to the ground and held him there, placing the blade at his throat as I stuffed his handkerchief into his face.

"I'm sorry," I whispered as his body went limp. I slowly stood up, using my skirt to wipe the sweat off my face. Glancing around, I saw I was alone.

I wiped my dagger on the man's coat, cleaning off the blood, silently thanking my mother for her help in protecting me. I knew I still needed a lot of work to master the skills, but I was glad to see I was able to hold my own against an attacker, even if my stomach twisted at the thought of harming him.

I looked down at my hands for a moment, wondering if the man's injury would lead to his death. The sickness inside of me burned even more, but I had to push it aside.

It had never bothered me to hurt Alex. He was the one who was terrorizing me, and it was worth it to hurt him in order to protect myself.

I was worth it. And so was Ferdy.

I hurried back to where he had left me—only to see the rest of Alex's crew carrying a limp form between the three of

THE ORDER OF THE CRYSTAL DAGGERS

them. I slammed myself back around the corner, my hand pressed into my racing heart.

"Ferdy."

In the background, I thought I heard the city clocks chime, ringing with an ominous delight as the last of the evening passed away into night.

"Help me, Lord," I whispered. Praying was the only thing I was certain I should do at this point. Karl would be unhappy with me for failing to show up at Count Potocki's, Lady Penelope was still missing, I had no way of contacting my other colleagues, and the man I loved was in the hands of my wicked stepbrother.

Whether I was prompted by the divine or not, it took me less than half a second to follow after the men. I did not know if I could free him on my own, but I could not handle losing Ferdy, not after I had found him again.

Lady Penelope and the others would just have to wait. And if Karl did anything to any of them, I would make him suffer so much, he would wish he had never been born.

I made that silent vow as I hopped across the lane, hurrying after Alex and his minions as they made their way down toward the docks.

The men were loud and boisterous, and it was so evident I was certain that it was part of their plan. They appeared to be just another group of friends, carrying the one who managed to drink himself into a stupor.

The one carrying Ferdy on his back grunted as they began walking toward a ship. "What're you going buy with your cut, Will?"

"He can't afford to buy anything, not with his gaming habits," another man said, sending the rest of the group into a round of laughter. I could see Ferdy's body shake in their grasp, his copper hair glowing in the small sliver of moonlight.

Their banter angered me as I trailed after them. All of them, save for Alex, of course, eagerly continued to discuss what they were going to do with their reward. None of it would be appropriate in any context I could imagine. It also saddened me that, when Alex finally asked about their friend, the one I had managed to fell, the rest of them shrugged and immediately cut him out of their payment.

So much for honor among thieves. Lady Penelope had said before that everyone had their own system of honor, but she had yet to meet these people, clearly.

I looked up at the side of the ship and choked.

The name on the bow read *Salacia.*

Lumiere's ship. I pounded my fist on my chest, trying to swallow the rest of my coughing. *I should have known.*

"What was that?" A new voice from Ferdy's group of captors crackled against the calm night.

I sucked in my breath quickly, nearly sending myself into another coughing fit at the chilly air. It was much cooler down by the water. I put my hand over my mouth, noticing that my fingers were slightly numb from the cold.

"Stop getting distracted. You'll have your money soon enough," Alex said, his cultured tones much more distinct as he ordered the men onto a gangplank.

I watched as they boarded the ship, praying they would stay at the port. I did not know if they were there for long. Given my own mixed signals with Lumiere, the sense of urgency never left me as I scoured the deck, hoping to see a way to climb onboard.

As Ferdy's limp figure disappeared onto the *Salacia*, I closed my eyes and fell forward, dropping my head into my hands.

THE ORDER OF THE CRYSTAL DAGGERS

Could this night be any worse? I wondered.

Lady Penelope's sharp voice, the part that had made itself home inside my head, answered me.

It might be worse than you wanted, but you're not making it any better by standing there, moping.

I sighed as I straightened. She was right about that. It was not the time to indulge in my hopelessness.

"What would Lumiere want with Ferdy anyway?" I wondered, trying to think through everything clearly. Lumiere had told Amir he was friends with Ferdy, but Ferdy did not seem as agreeable.

I thought about Alex. His reappearance was strange and worrisome, but only because I had no idea his role in this whole situation. Glancing up at the ship's name, so proudly carved into the bow of the ship, I frowned.

"Why would Alex be helping Lumiere?" I pushed back my hood, letting my loosened curls flutter freely.

As if to provide an answer, I felt a pinch on my shoulder. There was someone else standing next to me, someone I had not noticed.

Immediately, I had to muffle a scream. My mind went reeling, wondering if I would be knocked out and taken aboard, or if I was lucky enough that Ferdy had managed to wake up and escape on his own.

Since I knew chances of that happening were nonexistent, I was in trouble.

"Who are you?" I demanded.

There was no answer as a hand reached out for mine, grabbing my wrist. But when I felt the familiar pattern of wrinkled flesh, roughed with scars and patches of peeling skin, I realized why the stranger had failed to reply.

THE ORDER OF THE CRYSTAL DAGGERS

"Tulia?" I whispered, astounded.

Immediately, I got another pinch from her other hand. As she held onto me, she moved her fingers to spell out a snarky welcome.

"Oh, thank God it's you," I said, reaching out into the darkness and hugging her. "I was so worried for you."

She patted my back patiently before I slipped free and took her other hands. I jumped eagerly, like a little child happy to be back with her mother. "I'm so glad to see you again," I said before I snickered. It was impossible to make out any of Tulia's features against the night.

She grabbed my hand again and asked me a question.

Is it?

"Of course," I said. "I thought you …"

Then it hit me; Tulia was here of her own free will. She was well enough to move, even if she was older and still recovering from the burns she had sustained before.

Tulia was here by choice—working with Lumiere. She had been called for, by Dr. Artha and Father Novak. Lumiere was here for the League. He was here to help Karl and Lord Maximillian.

Tulia was working with the League.

I backed away from her, and she followed me out of the shadows.

I saw her face highlighted in the dim lighting. Her eyes were dark as she shook her head. Her fingers flicked across my vision briefly.

I'm sorry.

THE ORDER OF THE CRYSTAL DAGGERS

And then I felt her hand around my neck, an impossible amount of pressure. I thought about screaming, but my cry was cut short as I fell into darkness once more.

THE ORDER OF THE CRYSTAL DAGGERS

324

THE ORDER OF THE CRYSTAL DAGGERS

22

◊

"Psst. Ella. Can you hear me?"

The sound of my name seemed to come from miles and memories away, but I jolted awake at the familiarity. I lurched forward, accidentally slamming my face into the floor. "Ouch!"

I did not have to open my eyes to know I was not at home. From the slight bow in the floor and the dry wood, I had a feeling I was on the *Salacia*, and I could only hope we were not heading out for open waters.

"You need to keep your voice down." This time, the voice was clear. "Someone might hear you."

"Ferdy?" My voice was low and quiet, but my relief was blatant.

"I'm here," he said, talking to me from the far right. "Over this way."

"I'm so glad you're here." I tried to rub my eyes, but I found that my hands were tied together. From my position on the floor, I could see a small window on the opposite side of the room. It allowed in enough light that I could just make out my surroundings.

"I'm glad you're happy now, because you likely won't be for long."

Using my shoulders and legs, I twisted around and sat upright. All of those hours sitting with Harshad going over stretches seemed much more useful. In the dim lighting, I saw Ferdy was sitting on the floor not far from me. His hands were tied behind him, too, but he was also tied to a pole behind him.

325

"I'm glad you're willing to get us in trouble, all for the sake of teasing me," I replied, scooting over on my knees. I grimaced as they pounded against the coarse, unforgiving floor, but I forgot all about that when I arrived in front of him.

The ropes around him were thick and rough, no doubt similar to the ones binding my hands behind my back, but I did not pay them any attention as I leaned against him.

"I'm glad you are awake," Ferdy whispered, lying his head on top of mine. We were unable to embrace, but just having him beside me was enough of a comfort for me. "I was worried when they brought you in. I wasn't sure how long it would be until the chloroform wore off."

"I wasn't knocked out with chloroform," I said. "Tulia did something. She grabbed me by the neck and that's all I remember."

"Tulia?" Ferdy pulled back and looked at me. "Your companion?"

"Yes." I groaned. "I had no idea she was on Lumiere's side. But I guess it makes sense, in a way. Father Novak was murdered after he reached out to her and Lumiere."

"How many murders are we dealing with here?" Ferdy frowned. "I remember you were interested in that doctor's death before."

"I'll tell you all about it," I promised, "but it will have to be later. There's just too much going on. Right now, we need to get out of here. You're not safe here."

"*We* are not safe here, Ella."

I barely heard him as Lady Penelope's training, coupled with Harshad's lessons and Amir's insight, began to take over, and I started to make a plan.

THE ORDER OF THE CRYSTAL DAGGERS

The first thing we have to do is get out of our ropes, I thought. I cheered at the thought of using my dagger. It was sharp, and I knew just how sturdy it was now, since I had used it to protect myself.

Guilt seeped through me as I struggled to reach for my blade. I had to push off the guilt of killing a man, especially since he would have easily killed me, too.

Or maybe he wouldn't have killed me, I thought. Maybe he and his friends would have brought me here with Ferdy just the same.

Either way, I have to stop this. Feeling bad won't change things.

I had been worried before, when Ben started to sound more like Lady POW; hearing my own thoughts echo her reasoning, I was even more frightened.

But, like my guilt and everything else, I would have to worry about it later. I had Ferdy to rescue.

I began to shuffle around the pole where Ferdy was tied. "We need to get out of our ropes. I'm going to move into a position where you can get my dagger out of the sheath. Can you feel it?"

"I can feel plenty," Ferdy replied innocently. I made a mental note to hit him later as he playfully felt around my waist and hips before latching onto the hilt of my dagger. "Got it."

"Good. Now pull it out and hold still. I'm going to rub my ropes against the blade. You have to hold it tightly, or one of us could get hurt."

"I know."

"Well, good. Then I know for sure that it'll be your fault if I cut myself." I tried to give him a warning look, but he only raised his brow at me.

THE ORDER OF THE CRYSTAL DAGGERS

A few moments passed as I pushed my bindings against the blade, sawing up and down, glad no one could see me. No doubt, I looked like a clumsy fool. It did not help that I felt like one, too.

"There." I cheered as the ropes fell from my wrists.

Gratitude poured out of me, thankful for my mother's protection once more. As I rubbed the feeling back into my wrists, I glanced down at the sharp blade, wondering all over again how it was that I was here. If my mother had lived, if she would have taught me how to wield the weapon of an Order member, or if she would have dedicated herself to being a true lady in Society's eyes?

I also wondered why I had my weapon in the first place. It struck me as odd, as I held it, that I still had it on my person. Tulia would have known about it, and it was not hidden from sight as I wore my spy costume.

Either way, it is better I have it, even if I do not understand why it wasn't taken.

I shook my head to clear my thoughts, hurrying to cut Ferdy out of his bounds. The ropes fell easily at the dagger's cut.

"Thank you, Ella." He embraced me quickly, giving me another kiss.

"We don't have time for this," I warned him, already softening against him.

"I told you when we met again, I would allow us to have a proper reunion."

I laughed. "This is hardly what I'd call proper."

"When our lives are at stake, there's nothing more proper than a man telling his beloved how he feels."

"But not at the cost of our lives."

THE ORDER OF THE CRYSTAL DAGGERS

"Better my life at stake than my heart," Ferdy argued, but he allowed me to step away from him.

"I should have known you would say something like that." I headed for the door, pressing my ear to listen. There were plenty of sounds that grew louder as I concentrated on them; the sound of soft footsteps, the movement of men as they hoisted goods aboard. I heard the clatter of dishes and the different calls of seamen between floors. Cautiously, I tried to turn the knob. It was locked.

"I've never been on a ship before," I admitted to Ferdy. "I've never had to escape one, either."

"We're likely in a spare cabin," Ferdy said, glancing around at our surroundings. He walked over to a desk, one that was tucked away in the corner of the room. "This would be one of the servants' quarters."

"Are you sure? It seems large for a servant's room." The window caught my attention again. Swiftly but silently, I walked over and examined it. It was not big enough for us to escape through.

"Lumiere has expensive tastes, but he is actually quite generous. He would keep his crew in good order." Ferdy picked up a bag from under the desk. It was full of what looked like dark-colored balls; when he pulled one out into the moonlight, I could see it was a coconut. "Especially since it seems he's been visiting the Hawaiians."

"How do you know for sure?" I asked. "It could be from the Caribbean colonies."

"There's also a wedding announcement from a few months ago." Ferdy picked up a scroll of stationary. "Archibald Cleghorn and his bride, Miriam Likelike."

"Who is that?"

THE ORDER OF THE CRYSTAL DAGGERS

"She's a princess of Hawaii," Ferdy said. "I've never met her, but I know of her. She's just a little younger than you. I'm not surprised that she invited Lumiere to her wedding. They're both rumored to be very conscious of fashion."

I thought of all the exotic dressings and decoration of Lumiere's performance at the Estates Theatre. Were those flowers and clothes from Hawaii? I decided it seemed likely, but there was something else I wanted to say. "Ferdy?"

"Yes?"

"Please don't say things like he's someone to be admired." I wrinkled my nose. "He made the arrangements to kill you earlier. I don't think I'm going to like him, even if you are friends with him."

"I would not say we were friends. I met him in Paris, in a gaming club, if you must know."

"Somehow I am not surprised."

"You don't need to be so prudent all the time," Ferdy teased. "We were playing against each other in a card game, for high stakes, and in the end, when he won, he would take none of his winnings. He said he played for the game, not for the prize."

"He was more likely playing, so he had a chance to talk to you."

"You're right—that was his real gamble, and he took it." Ferdy smiled. "Just like I took a gamble in saving you from that thief when we first met."

"If you credit Lumiere for allowing us to meet, I think I might beat you. Does it not mean anything that he is the one responsible for Philip's death, and that we're being held on his ship as captives?"

"It means a lot to me," Ferdy replied, his voice soft and deadly. "But I'm only pointing out that Lumi has his weaknesses. And we can use them to our advantage."

"Unless we're going to play cards, I'm not sure how we can use that information."

"We aren't playing cards, but we are gambling with our lives." Ferdy glanced back toward the door. "There's no chance we can get through the window. It's too small. Now that we're free, we will have to find a way to sneak off the ship."

"I wish Ben was here," I admitted. "He would know how to pick the lock."

"We could always wait until someone comes to see us."

I arched my brow. "Do you think someone will come?"

He shrugged. "They've got to feed us, don't they?"

"What if we're out to sea before then? What if they just let us starve here?"

"We could try something else." Ferdy thought for a moment before he chuckled. "Though I guess it's not likely you will be able to escape using the withdrawing room excuse."

Despite the dread growing inside of me, I giggled. "If Lumiere is working with Karl, he's likely not going to believe me if I use that one."

"Quiet." Ferdy held up a hand, and for a moment, I thought he was upset at the mention of his brother. But as we stopped talking, I realized he was paying more attention to the window. The sound of hooves accompanied with the clacking of wheels called to us.

We both pressed our noses to the glass. Through the darkness, I saw there was a grand carriage coming down the narrow lane of the docks. I tried to see if there was a crest on the coach, but there was nothing I could see that would identify its passenger.

A click of keys clattered behind us as the door opened. Ferdy and I turned around just in time to see Alex's shadow fill the entrance.

"What are you doing here?" Alex stared at me, before a sadistic smile crept on his face. "Well, if it isn't my favorite little sister. Max told me that you had to be involved in all of this, but I must confess, Eleanora, I didn't think you had it in you."

"We're not family," I objected, but he ignored me.

His hand reached into his coat and he pulled out a pistol. "You always cause more trouble than you're worth."

A renewed sense of fear tingled down through my body.

Ferdy, on the other hand, leaned back and yawned. "I don't know why you'd even bother with us. We're not worth any trouble, especially if we're only going to give you more."

"My cousin says differently," Alex said, shifting his attention to Ferdy.

"Is that who just arrived?" Ferdy nudged me with his foot, carefully, waving his arm toward the window to further distract Alex. He wanted me to move.

I did not know his game, but I followed his silent orders. I stepped to the side carefully, making it only seem I was shifting my stance as Alex continued to focus on Ferdy.

"He says you're the younger prince of Bohemia," Alex continued, "and if we're going to secure the throne for our family, we have to kill you."

"I fail to see why," Ferdy said. "My own cousin holds the throne. Karl and I have no legitimate claim to it."

THE ORDER OF THE CRYSTAL DAGGERS

"Not yet," Alex grumbled. "I've come to take you to my cousin."

"I'm not going with you."

"I didn't ask," Alex snapped, and even in the dim room, I could see a flush across his pale cheeks. "I'd hate to kill you first."

"If you're going to kill me, you might as well do it now," Ferdy said. "So go ahead. Shoot."

I felt the blood drain from my face as Alex raised the gun. Before I could think through it, I stepped in front of Ferdy. "No."

"Ella, get back," Ferdy ordered. "He can't do it. I was calling his bluff. You really don't know anything about gambling, do you?"

"Apparently, she doesn't."

I glanced back to see Alex was watching us, and I could almost see his mind putting the pieces together.

"You're in love with her," Alex said, and I knew we were doomed. He turned the gun at me, a new perverseness on his face. "Excellent. If you don't do what I want, I'll kill her instead."

Ferdy's jaw hardened. Before I could assure Alex that Ferdy meant nothing to me, that such a prince would never fall in love with a former servant girl and current spy, Ferdy held up his hands in defeat.

"I will do as you say," he said. "But you must guarantee her safety."

"I swear on my life she will live," Alex assured him. "Now, come to me, Eleanora, and give me your weapon."

It was against everything inside of me to put one foot in front of the other and approach Alex. Slowly, I held out my

333

THE ORDER OF THE CRYSTAL DAGGERS

dagger, and he took it from me. His pistol remained pointed firmly at Ferdy as he tossed my dagger to the far side of the room. He grabbed my arm and thrust his gun just under my chin. I silently sent my mother an apology for letting go of her dagger; I had a feeling she would forgive me, knowing it was to protect Ferdy, but I felt her loss all as Alex held his weapon steady.

My nose twitched at the smell of gunpowder mixed with the metallic heat. The barrel jutted into my skin as my heart began to race in terror.

I was further alarmed as Alex locked his arm around my neck and clutched me against his body. "You always were too alluring for your own good, you know," he hissed, breathing in my scent deeply.

"Get away from her!" Ferdy yelled as he stepped forward, angered by Alex's attention to me.

"I said I wouldn't kill her, but I never said I would keep myself from her." Alex laughed, drawing me even closer to him. I began to resist, but the gun barrel dug further into my neck. I struggled to breathe at the pressure.

"You're here for me," Ferdy reminded him.

"Then let's get going, shall we?" Alex twisted his fingers into the ends of my curls, clearly enjoying his time incensing Ferdy as much as he was pleased to have me beside him. "It would be a pity to shoot such a pretty lady at such a close range."

Ferdy glared at him, his eyes never leaving Alex's as he walked toward us. I silently pleaded with him to do something, but I knew Ferdy would not risk me.

It is up to me, I thought. I scrambled to think of something, anything at all. I was not sure if any of the fighting techniques I knew would work.

And then a new idea struck me. I did not have to fight Alex. All I had to do was get him to think he had lost his advantage.

I gasped for air one last time, loudly, before I closed my eyes and allowed my body to go completely limp. Alex buckled under the sudden pressure of supporting me, and I felt the gun slide away from my skin.

"Hey!" Alex wrestled with the sudden extra weight, and Ferdy did not fail me. I heard his quick steps and a strange *crunch* as something flew through the air and hit Alex.

When I opened my eyes a second later, I saw a coconut rolling on the floor in front of me. I pushed out of Alex's grip and used the momentum to slam my fist into his nose. Ferdy came up beside me to further force Alex onto the ground.

I hurried over to where Alex had thrown my dagger. I'd just picked it up when the gun went off, and I heard Ferdy's cry of pain.

"No," I yelled, watching in horror as Ferdy fell back. My heart stalled at the thought of losing him. When I saw him grip his arm, gritting his teeth and struggling not to cry out in pain, I knew we had to finish this battle.

I gripped my dagger and used the hilt to bludgeon back of Alex's head. I did not feel any remorse as the dagger hit him, nor did I feel any sadness as I felt the shock of bones cracking and blood vessels breaking.

"Damn you." Alex's voice was slurred as he struggled to remain conscious, only to collapse onto the floor a second later. His breath came in uneven stints, but I was too concerned with Ferdy to care.

"Ferdy." I knelt beside him and carefully put my hands on his arm where the ruby red of his blood was leaking through his shirtsleeve.

THE ORDER OF THE CRYSTAL DAGGERS

"It's not bad," Ferdy insisted. "It was a graze, that's all."

"Let me look at it." I gently peeled his fingers away before tearing at the sleeve. A large gash, from the middle of his arm to the edge of his shoulder, glowered up at me. From what I could deduce, I agreed with Ferdy; it was a surface wound, though it looked like it had burrowed several little chunks of skin off from his arm.

"We need to get this cleaned," I said slowly.

"Just tie it up for now," Ferdy said. Sweat ran down his face as he gritted his teeth, determined to keep me from knowing how much pain he was in. "Tear some strips from my shirt. Once we get out of here, we can take care of it."

"I don't want you to be hurt."

"It's too late for that." He tried to give me a smile but was too pained for me to say anything.

I hurried to bind up the wound as he instructed, praying every step of the way he would be fine until we managed to get back to the Cabal, or even the manor. *Amir will be able to take care of this, surely.*

"Don't cry."

"Huh?"

"I can see the tears in your eyes, Ella," Ferdy said. His smile was much less pained this time. "Don't cry. You did well, especially handling that beast of a stepbrother you have."

We both glanced back at Alex's body. He was still breathing, but there was some blood coming out of his head.

"I'm glad he'll be in pain for a while," I said slowly. I did not admit the terrible truth, that I did not actually want him to die.

Well, that was not true. I did not care if he died, but I did not want to be the one who killed him.

THE ORDER OF THE CRYSTAL DAGGERS

Ferdy squeezed my hand tightly. "You can't trust someone like him to keep his word. He was going to kill you after he was finished with me."

He carefully stood up, and immediately I ran my hands down his back, clutching him. "I'm so sorry. I didn't think he would shoot you, I swear."

"It's fine, as long as you're safe." Ferdy wrapped his good arm around me, while his other bled freely. I felt him flinch and I knew he was trying to hold back his complaints as he held me. Another layer of guilt pressed into me, and I struggled not to cry at his pain. I leaned up and kissed him. I had no words that would suffice for an apology that could be accepted, but I wanted Ferdy to know I would be there to comfort him.

"I thought you said we didn't have time for this," he murmured against my mouth.

"I will never have enough time to love you properly," I whispered back. "Especially with people like Alex trying to kill us, it seems."

"Ella." His breath tickled my ear as I burrowed into his chest, losing myself in him.

When the castle walls had collapsed, I embraced him then, too. My kingdom of illusions and innocence had fallen, and I was crushed by its destruction. This time, as Ferdy held onto me and I clutched at him, I no longer felt the same sadness. My world before had been beautiful, but with very little to offer in the way of reality. Now, having been through the darkness and having seen the meanness of this world, I knew what true beauty and virtue meant. With Ferdy beside me, we could rebuild what had been burned down, and together with the others I loved, we could strengthen every good thing for the future.

A future where we are together.

THE ORDER OF THE CRYSTAL DAGGERS

"Well, what a lovely and touching scene this is."

Ferdy and I looked over at the door simultaneously. Lumiere stood there, lounging in the doorway. I pulled out my dagger, and Ferdy balled up his fists, while Lumiere only laughed.

"There's no need to jump the gun," Lumiere said. He nudged Alex's fallen body with his toe. "I trust my associate here did not give you too much trouble?"

"I'm going to kill him after I kill you," I promised bitingly.

Lumiere shook his head and tiptoed around Alex, picking up the gun Alex had dropped during our scuffle. "*Tsk, tsk,* Lady Ella. There's no need to be so hostile. I understand you are my guest, and you have been upset with your treatment while you have been here. But please, allow me the chance to properly rectify this situation before you rob me of all ability."

Before I could ask what he meant, he held up Alex's gun and fired.

My body reacted to the movement before my mind did. Ferdy and I both grabbed onto each other, the two of us trying to shield each other. I told Ferdy before that we were both determined creatures, and it seemed we were both determined to stay in this world or leave it together.

I prayed for deliverance and squeezed my eyes shut as the shot crackled like lightning and thunder, the smack of its force whipping past us.

But when the echo of the gunshot faded, Ferdy and I were both still standing.

We had not been shot.

"What did you do?" I asked Lumiere, before I saw my answer.

Down in front of us, Alex's body was no longer twitching. It was deathly still, as a puddle of blood began to bubble up on his back and pool out from underneath him.

Beside me, Ferdy gripped onto me even more tightly. I welcomed his strange comfort as a reminder that I had to stay composed, even at the gruesome sight.

"There," Lumiere said, tossing the derringer aside once more. "I've taken care of the situation. I can assure you, *chérie*, such a grave offense to your person will never happen again from this pathetic creature. Now, I must insist that you both come with me. And, if you do not want to end up like this vile mess, you will be silent."

He paused for a moment, before looking to me. The green of his eyes seemed to glow as he gave me his cocky grin. "I suppose I do not have to warn you. I know if you truly are Naděžda's daughter, your curiosity will keep you quiet."

I gripped my dagger in my hand, ready to tell him that my mother would be upset at his treatment of me, and I refused to believe that she would be friends with him, either. But then he nodded toward my weapon, waving his gun around in a dismissive movement. "I would also tuck that away. You will not need it to get the answers you seek."

THE ORDER OF THE CRYSTAL DAGGERS

23
◊

I was telling Ferdy the truth when I said I had never been on a ship before. Ever since *Máma* had been lost at sea, I did not like the thought of traveling by boat. It always loomed inside my mind like a shadow, and I did not think I would ever be comfortable sailing.

As we made our way through the small hallways of Lumiere's ship, I was further convinced my instincts were right. The deck beneath my feet tipped slowly from the right to the left, and then back to the right. My legs felt the strange pressure, almost as if walking onboard was an exercise Harshad would prescribe.

Ferdy walked behind me, and Lumiere behind him. My dagger curled into my side, further tucked into the small leather skirt of my habit.

When we immerged from the bowels of the ship and onto the upper deck, I saw there were torch lights glowing as workers hurried around, cleaning the deck and preparing to set sail. The workers were all clothed in masks, but I recognized the blond curls of a short figure as we headed toward the bow.

Betsy!

As if she heard my silent call, her eyes widened as they saw me, filling with hope and then fear. Before I could say anything, Lumiere cleared his throat behind me, and I had to refrain from action—for now.

But I knew, in seeing Betsy, what had happened.

Tulia and Lumiere had coordinated with each other, stealing away the household workers from my father's manor. They were now working on Lumiere's ship, which was kept far enough away from the dock that they risked drowning if they attempted escape. Lumiere kept them from leaving, and Alex worked for Lord Maximillian.

Did that mean Cecilia and Priscilla were also onboard? I wondered if that was possible, given Prissy's high standards and Cecilia's arrogance. My stepsister would not be willing to stay on a boat because of the lack of luxury, and Cecilia would be reluctant to do so without commandeering the captain's authority.

I glanced back at Lumiere for a quick second, and he continued to stare straight ahead. He did not seem like someone who would let another person hold power over him, no matter what Ferdy said about his card game.

"Ella."

Ferdy whispered my name and grabbed my hand. I was worried that Lumiere would not allow me to keep a hold on him, but when I looked forward again, I suddenly realized that Ferdy was the one who was worried.

Karl, Lord Maximillian, and a dozen of their bodyguards and runners stood in front of us. Karl saw me, and I blushed as he scowled. There was no hiding myself from him anymore.

"Gentlemen," Lumiere cooed. "I must apologize for the delay."

"What is going on? Where is Alexander?" Lord Maximillian's voice was harsh against the darkness. The rustling river below harmonized with it, adding an eerie quality to the atmosphere.

"Unfortunately, there was a bit of a scuffle, and I am remiss to have to announce he has passed from this world," Lumiere said. "Next time you're going to send someone after a member of the Order, you might want to consider sending

THE ORDER OF THE CRYSTAL DAGGERS

someone more experienced. Or at least someone who wouldn't get shot by his own gun."

I noticed Lumiere did not tell Lord Maximillian who it was that shot the gun in question.

"I see. Yes, that is unfortunate." There was nothing in his voice to suggest that he was upset at Alex's loss, other than a minor inconvenience. "Such a shame, too. He had promise."

"As what? A mercenary?" I snapped, and Lumiere nudged his gun into my shoulder. I knew he was unhappy at my outburst.

Lord Maximillian's heavy brows furrowed as he looked at me. "So, the rumors are true. Lady Wellington is a spy, and she has trained her granddaughter in the art. I must confess, I did not think you were capable of pulling off such an elaborate ruse."

I blushed at his cutting remarks. Ferdy squeezed my hand more tightly, likely pleading with me to abstain from commenting back.

Lumiere stepped forward. "She has her charms. And that helps blind us to her, shall we say, more egregious faults, perhaps? Isn't that right, Prince Karl?"

It was Karl's turn to turn red. He opened his mouth to say something, but Lumiere cut him off.

"Maybe I should have phrased it differently. I meant to say, 'Wasn't I right when I told you that your beloved Ella was secretly in love with your own brother?'"

Karl straightened, tightening his cravat around his neck. "You have made your point, Lumiere. You have my trust."

"I should think so, and I am appalled that you should have questioned it in the first place after all we have been through," Lumiere snapped, and I saw that he was genuinely upset at having to prove himself. He ran his hand through his hair, irritated, and then smiled brightly. "But, considering it is Ella, I am more understanding. I can see why you would want to marry her."

"Yes." Karl frowned. His eyes moved away from mine, following their way down to my hand in Ferdy's, before he focused on his brother. "What a pity it is, that she does not seem to share the same opinion on that matter."

Ferdy moved to stand in front of me. I could see a line of blood dripping from his arm, but the slow trickle did nothing to deter him from facing Karl. "I would apologize for my deception on the matter, if you hadn't called for my death, brother."

"As usual, you don't understand what is at stake, Ferdinand," Karl snapped. "Your selfishness was what nearly got you killed before, not my desire for vengeance. You were interfering with my affairs, and I will not have you continue to be my stumbling block."

"You would have killed your own brother for the kingdom?" I was finally free to ask my questions, no longer bound to the silence due to my disguise.

"He was actively plotting against me and the future of Bohemia, Eleanora." Karl groaned. "Please don't tell me you foolishly believe his lies, too. Ferdinand would gladly see the people of this country rule it by mob force. That is all direct democracy is, you know, when you allow the people who have no formal education or even reading ability to help determine law. Do you want such savagery to ravage our nation? Wars among our neighbors have already done enough damage."

I said nothing, and Karl only shook his head. "When we are married, I will have to see to your education."

"I'm not marrying you," I snapped. "No matter what the morning papers say."

THE ORDER OF THE CRYSTAL DAGGERS

"You *will* marry me, Eleanora," Karl hissed. "You've humiliated me enough, both in my own family and among my friends." At his grimace, I wondered if he was thinking of earlier when I left Count Potocki's ball before making an official appearance. "It is clear you will have to learn your place in this world."

"Why would you want to marry me anyway? I don't want to marry you."

"Your actions in Society have failed to suggest otherwise," Karl accused. "Even if I failed to see through your lies, no one else needs to know. We can still marry and free the kingdom from the empire."

"You can't force me to."

"I won't let you, either," Ferdy said.

Karl scowled. "Well, I can readily believe that, *brother.* You have never allowed me any happiness, have you? Especially not when it was convenient for you. This is no exception, I see. It is the same as when you did everything you could to become our father's favorite. You stole his love for me away, and now you have Eleanora's, too. But she is mine. My plans for the kingdom are too important for Bohemia. If you do not stand down, you will be put down."

"Karl, if you don't stop, you will be the one who is stopped," Ferdy told him. "The people don't want you as their king."

"They seemed plenty happy about my decision to pledge for Count Potocki's position once he steps down. Not that you would know that, since you missed the ball."

"I told you Eleanora was there," Lord Maximillian interrupted. "She left early, which is why I had my suspicions and had her followed."

"Yes, that is true," Karl muttered, clearly upset he had been interrupted only to be corrected. "I suppose I owe you for bringing my wayward brother back to Lumiere's. I am grateful for Eleanora's return, too, even though I am surprised she did not come to see me. I would have thought her grandmother's life was more important."

I felt my breath leave me at the thought of what Karl had done to Lady POW. "I swear this now, I will pay you back for every bit of pain you inflict on her."

"What an insolent girl." Lord Maximillian sniffed, his thick salt and pepper mustache fluttering the darkness. "I told you my daughter would have been a better pick, Karl."

"And I told you both, I would take care of the two of them for you," Lumiere said, stepping out in front of Ferdy and me. "Obviously, both of them are harder to kill and persuade than we originally planned, but what is the fun in doing an easy job? I happen to like harder jobs myself."

"What do you want now, Lumiere?" Lord Maximillian turned to face him, clearly irritated.

"Need I remind you I require payment, your grace?" Lumiere shook his head. "We all must pay for our pleasures. And as I enjoy seeing to my own pleasure, I must insist you compensate me for my trouble."

"I hardly think this was any trouble for you," Lord Maximillian muttered, but he called forth one of his servants, who brought forth a large bag.

Lumiere smirked. "It was trouble enough for you to be searching for the rumored heir of Bohemia for the past several years. The fact that you failed to contact my father before wasting so much time speaks to your weakness, not mine."

I glanced at Ferdy, and I suddenly wondered what Lumiere was doing, treating Lord Maximillian with such disdain. He

THE ORDER OF THE CRYSTAL DAGGERS

gave him a mocking bow as he took the bag, quickly opening it. By the light of the fires, I could see several hundred pound notes inside.

"I trust it is to your satisfaction?" Lord Maximillian asked.

"Why are you paying him?" Karl asked, his voice impatient. "I told you it was taken care of."

"Prince Karl, *mon ami*, you should know that my satisfaction can always grow," Lumiere replied, giving him a quick wink. "One only has to ask Didier if there is any doubt."

I glanced around as Lumiere continued to shuffle through the bag. Where was Didier? I wondered. I had never seen him far from Lumiere's side. Ferdy gave me a questioning look, no doubt wondering if I was planning something.

I did not know where to begin, but if we could do something, now was the time to do it. Lumiere was distracted, engrossed with his payment, and I was armed. I reached for my dagger, catching Ferdy's eye. I did not know if I could get the two of us out of there without his help, but I did not want to make his injury any worse. From the paleness of his face, I already knew I only had a little bit of time before I would have to find Amir or see if Zipporah was still at the Cabal.

Ferdy tensed up but shifted his feet, ready to pounce along with me. I took a deep breath and then stepped forward.

Only to be sidetracked at once, when Lumiere let out a stream of curses in French.

"*Mon Deus*, where is my letter, Max?"

I tripped forward as Lumiere began arguing with Lord Maximillian.

"You know I need that letter," Lumiere hollered. His face, always so serene and easy-going, was taut with boiling rage.

"My father is the ambassador to the French empire, not me. I need my diplomatic immunity!"

"It is in there," Lord Maximillian argued, stepping forward. "I signed and sealed it myself."

"I *need* it, Max, I need it so badly," Lumiere bemoaned. "Otherwise everyone will know about the information from my father regarding the Order of the Crystal Daggers. How I have helped smuggle your special wine across Bohemian hills and mountains, and I have delivered to you both the second heir to the throne and ensured the proper queen would ascend to the throne."

"Calm down!" Lord Maximillian shouted, surprising me with his stern tone. "Surely it is in there. You can't find it when you're throwing a hissy fit."

"I do love a good hissy fit," Lumiere yelled, "but not when so much is at stake."

"Ella," Ferdy whispered. "Look."

I turned away from Lumiere and Lord Maximillian, only to see the familiar gleam of a purple blade as it moved behind Karl. Several moving figures slipped onto the deck behind it, and I grinned.

Lumiere slowly looked up around us. He had noticed the new arrivals, too. "Well, it seems we have some more visitors here, your grace."

"Intruders!" One of Alex's henchmen cried out as he was cut down and tossed overboard. Squinting, I saw Ben was the one who had felled him, and my smile only grew wider.

"I hope you will excuse our tardiness. The traffic between here and the castle is quite awful." Lady Penelope's voice was scratchy but certain as she called out her wry greeting. "But I am pleased to say we made it just in time for Lumiere's confession and your agreement."

THE ORDER OF THE CRYSTAL DAGGERS

24

◊

Lady Penelope had never looked deadlier as she stared at Lord Maximillian. Dressed in men's clothing, with the fitted pants and the dark jacket, she had come prepared for battle. I watched with pride and terror as her eyes narrowed in the moonlight. At her side, I saw Amir appear from the other side of the ship, and together, the two of them were focused on their foe.

I was relieved to see that they had put their differences aside. At least, they did so long enough to make sure I was safe.

From the other side of the deck, I saw the shadow of Harshad's form, and I heard him call out for Ben to follow. My friends and family were all here, and I felt an enormous wave of relief break through me.

They are all here. They've all come to rescue me.

I suddenly groaned at the thought. While I was happy to see them, I did not need another reason for Lady Penelope to think I was incompetent.

I felt even worse as I realized my cover was blown. Karl, Lord Maximillian, and everyone else knew the truth of who I was, and who I worked for. There would be no more gallivanting around Society now, and I would be shunned by the crowds, if not driven out of the city for my indecency.

Ferdy took my hand again, and I glanced at him. He gave me his cheeky smile, and I nodded.

He might have been a prince among men, I thought, just as he was the prince of my heart.

349

I still had to focus. There was no use worrying about Lady Penelope's disappointment and Society's rejection if I was silly enough to die tonight. I gripped Ferdy's hand in mine, resolved, even if I was still ruffled by the future's uncertainty.

Ben appeared, hopping over the side of the ship. "You're lucky we managed to find you."

I smiled brightly at the sight of my brother. "Ben."

There was a bit of swagger in his step as he greeted me. I was glad to see he was here, not only because I knew I could count on him to help me, but because I knew it meant a lot to him to be included in our mission.

"You've missed a lot of action, Nora," Ben said. "Harshad, Xiana, and I met at the castle, and Amir came, too, as we were rescuing Lady Penelope from the dungeon. Amir had a message to come here for you."

He tried to explain everything to me, but Lady Penelope quickly became the center of our attention as she came up beside Karl.

"It is lovely to see you again, too, Mr. Marcelin," Lady Penelope said, giving Karl a mocking curtsy. "Let me take this quick moment to tell you I have decided to withdraw my own agreement for Eleanora's hand. It seems she is already engaged."

I glanced over at Ferdy with a raised brow, watching as he swallowed a laugh.

"I forgot about that," he said.

"Forgot about what?" I asked.

"I talked to my father about marrying you. All I needed was your approval."

"And my grandmother's." I looked back up to Lady POW, watching as she took her dagger out and pointed it at Lumiere.

I did not think it was time to ask her about it. Not when she had her intended prey nearly at her mercy.

Lumiere only laughed. "Madame, you never fail to delight me in your own right."

"Surrender, Lumiere," Lady Penelope ordered. "You are surrounded."

"We might be surrounded, but we are far from outnumbered. Remember the old adage for retirement? Death or defeat, and we fight only to the death aboard this ship, Pepé!" Lumiere pulled out his gun and fired out several shots wildly into the air. "Attack, men!"

The remaining guards, still a little confused, jumped into action. Lady Penelope and Amir quickly came to each other's rescue, fighting back to back as they were repeatedly charged.

"Ready, Ben?" I asked, glancing over at him as I widened my stance.

"It's about time we can practice Harshad's lessons in real life." Ben stepped up beside me, while I saw Karl duck where he stood as swords came out. He hurried toward the side of the ship, but a few of his guards, keen on fighting, blocked his way.

Ben and I stood back to back, while Ferdy tapped Ben on the shoulder. "May I join you?"

I grinned, but Ben frowned. "This isn't a game of cards," he snarled.

"Ben, stop harassing him," I muttered.

THE ORDER OF THE CRYSTAL DAGGERS

"He's been lying to us this whole time about who he is," Ben argued, before his gaze turned dark. "But then, I suppose you knew that."

I blushed, grateful another guard came up to attack me. After a few well-placed kicks, I was able to reply. "Just since the Advent Ball."

"If he wanted nothing to do with us then, he's lucky we're even here to help him now."

"I can assure you," Ferdy said as he flung another fighter away from our group, "I am happy to see you. And I apologize for my deceit. It has been a lifelong burden for me. And my brother, too, though his reasons for hating our requested silence are far different from mine."

"Which one of you had the reasons that included seducing my sister?"

"Ben!" I nearly hit him at his impropriety. He was fortunate we had other enemies that required our attention.

"I would have said romancing," Ferdy said, trying to coax a smile out of Ben. "But yes. You should know I'm in love with her, just as I know you can't blame me for it."

"Believe me, I'm more than content to blame her," Ben muttered.

I did not know if I preferred it that way or not, but before I could respond, Harshad leaped down from the upper deck. My mouth dropped, gaping as he landed squarely on the shoulders of a guard, and I could barely believe my eyes as I watched him. For a seventy-two-year-old man, he certainly had a lot of agility.

"You need to focus," Harshad said. "Lumiere is distracted. Use it to your advantage."

I did not know what he expected of us. While Lumiere was close by, we still had a few of Lord Maximillian's guards to

THE ORDER OF THE CRYSTAL DAGGERS

consider. "Well, at least we've stopped fighting each other when it comes to Ferdy, and we're fighting with him beside us."

"That's not going to change my mind about him," Ben replied.

"Can I just say, I'm happy to have the chance to defend myself?" Ferdy gave Ben a quick pat on the shoulder. "And you never know. You might change your mind about me."

"You mean like how you might change your mind about Lumiere?" I asked.

"I told you, he's overstepped himself," Ferdy replied. "Badly, too, this time."

Before Ferdy, Ben, and I could argue more, I heard Lord Maximillian cry out in frustration. "What do you think you're doing? You set us up!"

He was yelling at Lumiere. For a few short seconds, I watched as Lord Maximillian pushed against Lumiere, forcing him back several steps.

With a frustrated look, Lumiere stumbled back but quickly found his balance. It was then I noticed there was an envelope in his hand.

"A setup? I am appalled by this accusation. Is this really how you would treat me, when I am saving your life?" Lumiere pushed him, handing him his gun as he took the letter. "You're lucky I can be bought, Max! Now, go and take your prince. I'll hold them off while you escape."

"No," I cried, jumping in front of Ferdy. I pulled out my dagger, ready to defend him from anything, at any cost—only to find there was no threat.

But Lord Maximillian did not pay any attention to me. Ben rushed forward. "Watch out, Nora."

THE ORDER OF THE CRYSTAL DAGGERS

Ben raced toward us, heading for Lord Maximillian. A gun gleamed in his hand, and I worried he would take a shot at Ben.

Everything seemed to happen all at once. I saw Lord Maximillian's finger tighten around the trigger. I saw Ben running toward him, oblivious to the danger.

There was no way to stop the gun, but I knew I could stop Ben. I jumped forward, hitting Ben hard as he passed us. He wobbled as I fell over, while the momentum of our impact pushed him over the railing of the upper deck.

"Ben!" I shouted, just as the gun went off. The bullet missed both of us, but I scrambled to see where my brother had gone.

I heard his scream—almost the exact same terrible scream I had heard before, all those years ago, when he fell off the barn roof—and I froze.

Every moment of my life from the moment of Ben's first accident to this one collapsed inside of me, and I felt the pressure crush me. Tears started to form in my eyes as I realized, once more, that Ben was suffering, and all because of me.

"Ella," Ferdy called from behind me, and I barely managed to turn around to make sure Ferdy was safe, too. Lord Maximillian was heading toward him.

"No." The word rushed out of me, and I began to panic—until I saw Lord Maximillian pass Ferdy and head for Karl, grabbing him and guiding him off the ship.

"Keep holding them off," Lord Maximillian called back to his guards.

At that moment, I realized why Lord Maximillian had been required to pay more. He had not come to the *Salacia* to get Ferdy. He had Ferdy and me captured in order to get at Karl.

THE ORDER OF THE CRYSTAL DAGGERS

"Prepare to set sail!" Lumiere called, and his crew members appeared in their heavily cloaked forms.

I glanced back at Lumiere as he tucked the envelope he had in his hand into his jacket pocket before turning his attention back to the bag of money. Seeing he was sufficiently distracted, I took the moment to head toward the stairs.

"Where are you going, Ella?" Ferdy called after me.

"I have to get Ben."

"What about my brother?"

"We will have to get Karl later." I was just about tell him that since Lord Maximillian had confessed, we could have him brought to the castle for a trial. Everything was nearly over, as long as we caught him.

But that was when Lumiere appeared in front of me, blocking me from the stairs, blocking me from Ben.

Anger filled me at the sight of Lumiere, coupled with the fear I felt for my brother's life.

As if he knew of my struggles, Harshad called out to me. "I'll see to Ben, Eleanora."

From where I was, I could see the top of Harshad's head, his white hair a crown around a small bald spot. He knelt in front of Ben, who was still whimpering in pain, while Lady Penelope swooped down a nearby railing to help.

I said nothing in reply, but I was eternally grateful in that moment Ben had someone to help him. I breathed out a quick sigh of relief, my breath forming a cloud against the lights along the port.

It was then that I noticed the ship was sailing away from the docks.

What is he planning for us now?

THE ORDER OF THE CRYSTAL DAGGERS

Lumiere was still onboard. He might have been buying time for Lord Maximillian to escape with Karl, but he was still stuck with us and the guards.

"You must be exhausted from all the failing you've done tonight," Lumiere said, as if to confirm my losses. I turned my attention away from the river, ready to face Lumiere at last.

Ben was injured, all because of me. We were trapped on the ship, Lord Maximillian was gone, and there was no way for us to keep up with him as he carried Karl off.

"Eleanora," Lady Penelope called. She stared up at me from beside Ben's fallen form, and it seemed hard to believe that I had forgotten how imposing she could be in the last two days. "Get to work. If he wants a fight, don't just stand there."

"I've been assured by many of my lovers how much work I can be," Lumiere warned me playfully, as Lady Penelope took off again. "Are you up for the challenge of fighting me?"

To answer him, I stepped forward with my dagger stretched out. It was true that I had failed tonight, but I was determined to see to the protection of those who were mine, and if Lumiere did not let me see my brother, I would force him out of my way.

He twirled away as I attacked, but I anticipated his movement. My dagger was high and dropped down swiftly, allowing me to cut through his coat.

The fine fabric spliced open with a loud rip, and while I did not think I drew blood, I had a feeling Lumiere was just as upset as he would have been if I had.

"This is French," he shouted, holding up the ends of his coat, clearly upset. "There is no fixing this!"

"I agree," I said, charging him again.

THE ORDER OF THE CRYSTAL DAGGERS

This time, he was more eager to engage. He grabbed my arm and elbowed me. I cried out in shock more than pain, and nearly dropped my dagger. I fully expected him to hit me; he had no weapons on his person that I could see. I was preparing myself for the eventual blow when Amir stepped in between us, pulling Lumiere away from me.

"Enough, Lumi. Leave Eleanora alone."

"Amir!" I cheered at the sight of him. "How is Ben?"

He shook his head. "I cannot examine him now, but I promise I will take care of him, right after I interrupt your fight with Lumi here."

I watched as Lumiere smiled. "I just need to occupy her attention for a little while longer, *mon frère*."

"Why don't you fight me instead?" Amir offered. "It has been ages since we last sparred."

"Don't you have more amusing targets to chase?"

Amir sneaked a quick glance over at me, one that was strangely entertained, before looking back at Lumiere. "How could anyone be more amusing than you?"

Lumiere grinned. "I've always loved your wit. A Turk with a sense of humor is indeed rare in this world."

"As is a Frenchmen with a sense of honor, if we're going to go by stereotypes."

"Ha! Honor is for those who see good and evil, not for those of us who only want to win. And I happen to like stereotypes. Personally, there is nothing quite as thrilling to me as putting someone in a box and then watching them cut their way out of it."

Despite the tension, Lumiere did not look insulted. He was talking with Amir the way that Clavan and Jarl often did, using the language of old comradery and respect, despite disagreements.

Amir slid his dagger into his sheath and took up a fighting stance to match Lumiere's. "I'm still waiting for an answer, Lumi."

Lumiere ran his hand through his hair, brushing back his ruffled locks. "You have a fight on your hands, then."

The two of them began to fight, and it was hard not to stare at them. It was a violent form of waltzing, where Amir would bob and duck and Lumiere would jab and cross.

"Ella." Ferdy appeared at my side, nearly out of breath. The bandage on his arm was leaking blood, but he seemed determined to ignore it. "That's the Turk who robbed you before. What is he doing here?"

"He's on our side," I said, as I caught sight of the new layer of sweat that had appeared on his forehead. I put my hand on his brow, discouraged to find he was terribly hot. "You need to be careful. That earlier wound is still causing you pain."

Ferdy gave me a weak smile. "I'll live. If for no other reason than I'm hungry."

His wry humor was comforting in that moment, and I could only hope we would be able to escape. While Ferdy wanted to get dinner, I just wanted him to get his arm fixed.

"Eleanora."

There was something so painfully distinctive in how Lady Penelope said my name as she appeared beside us.

"What is it?" I asked, turning to her. "Is it Ben?"

"No. No, he'll be fine, eventually. His leg is broken again."

The world went out from under my feet as all I could think was that it was my fault—*entirely* my fault. My hand went over my mouth in shock, but Lady POW did not seem to notice my dismay.

"There aren't too many guards left, but if you're just going to stand here and let other people fight your battles, I have a task for you."

I frowned at the accusation. Amir and Lumiere seemed to enjoy fighting each other. "What is it?"

"We have to stop the ship," Lady Penelope said. She pursed her lips as she nodded toward Ferdy. "See if you can get the other Mr. Marcelin to help with that, perhaps? If he does not feel like too much of a prince to help with such a lowly task?"

The bitterness of her voice was clear. She was more than a little upset with me, and possibly with Ferdy, too. I knew if she was fighting alongside Amir, she would not let her anger at us interfere with the mission, but it was only a matter of time before she said something.

"How?" I swallowed hard. "How—"

Lady Penelope shook her head. "There was a reason Karl was comfortable taking me to the castle dungeons. He accused me of the murder of his brother. At those charges, even Empress Maria Anna wanted nothing to do with me."

"I apologize if my mother has said or done anything improper," Ferdy said as he kicked at another guard, preventing another attack on us. He hurriedly wiped his hands off on his pants and extended one in greeting to Lady Penelope. "It is lovely to finally make your official acquaintance."

"The feeling is not quite mutual," Lady Penelope said, eying his bloody knuckles with a raised brow. "But if I can curry favor with the royal family, especially one who is supposedly deceased right now, I will take it."

"You can have all the favor you want, if I can only keep Ella."

"I've already figured out your earlier attempts, Prince Ferdinand, and I do not much appreciate them, given that I was put in jail because of them." Lady Penelope frowned. "But right now, I will excuse you, since we have a ship to stop and villains to catch."

"Yes, Madame." Ferdy looked more than a little deflated.

Lady Penelope paused and rolled her eyes. "If you are willing to prove your worth, help Eleanora stop the ship."

Ferdy brightened, but I only balked. "How do we do that?" I asked.

"Figure it out yourself," Lady Penelope said. She brandished her dagger in one hand while she pulled out her pistol in the other. "But try not to hurt the crew. We can use them for information later."

"That's even more difficult—"

"Just find a way to do it. I'm going to help Harshad with the last of the guards on the bow."

With that, Lady Penelope sped off. I watched as she headed for a trio of guards, firing shots and using their sudden movements to attack with her dagger.

"Come on," Ferdy said. "We've got to go."

"Go where?" I asked, looking at the port. We were already floating toward the middle of the Vltava, heading down the riverway. I wondered where Lord Maximillian had taken Karl.

"We have to stop the ship first," Ferdy said. "That means we have to get Lumiere."

He wants to get to Lumiere so we can get the rest of the crew to stop the ship.

THE ORDER OF THE CRYSTAL DAGGERS

"You're a genius," I said, following after him.

"Of course I am. I told you I was smart enough to outsmart you."

I felt irritated by his remark, but I decided not to say anything as we turned our attention back to Lumiere and Amir, who were still fighting. Ferdy and I agreed to barge into the fray from opposite ends.

But as we circled around, I stopped when I heard my mother's name.

"Naděžda would be proud of your little Eleanora," Lumi said, wiping a small amount of blood off of his lip. "She's just like her mother."

"There's no need to taunt me by mentioning Naděžda." Amir stepped back and they began circling each other again. "If you have to resort to such lows to win, it only means you lack the skill."

"It is not the individual skill that decides the victory," Lumiere argued. "It is the sum of all skills, and that should include mockery, ridicule, and insult."

They exchanged a few more blows before Amir landed another punch to Lumiere's side, driving the hilt of his weapon into Lumiere's rib. He bowed over in pain.

I met Ferdy's gaze, and between the two of us, we knew it was time. We would follow Amir in delivering the final blow, and then use our opening to capture Lumiere.

Lumiere seemed to know he was about to fall himself. His smile left his face, and he glared at Amir as a hint of genuine animosity finally came through. "Besides, Amir, if I wanted to render you helpless, we both know that Naděžda is not your greatest weakness."

"Is that so?" Amir asked.

He nodded toward Amir's hand, the one that was marked. "All I have to do is mention Nassara."

Nassara?

Amir's face suddenly contorted in the worst sort of anger. I watched as his chestnut eyes darkened with blood and rage, as his mustache twisted along with his mouth into the deepest frown. His heavy brows slanted downward. His dagger was suddenly out again and flying through the air.

That's the name of the Christian converts in the Ottoman Empire.

It was also the meaning of the symbol on Amir's hand and the inscription on my mother's journal.

I did not know how badly he did so, but it was immediately clear Lumiere had miscalculated. Lumiere fell back hard as Amir tackled him, holding his blade at Lumiere's neck hard enough to draw a fine line of blood.

Ferdy motioned to me, but I shook my head. We could not let him continue. We had to stop Amir from killing him—though I do not know if I would have objected—if we were going to use him to stop the ship.

"Amir," I said, coming up and grabbing his wrist. "We need Lumiere to live for now."

"Well, I am certainly glad to see you again, Ella." Lumiere's eyes were still wide with fear as he attempted to add levity to the situation. "I will be ecstatic to help you, if you would only tell Amir to get off of me, please."

Amir did not move. He seemed to be in shock.

Ferdy shook his head as he struggled to pull Lumiere free from under Amir. "Good God, what did you do to him, Lumi?"

THE ORDER OF THE CRYSTAL DAGGERS

Lumiere's smirk came back as he looked at me. "I suppose you'll have to excuse him, *chérie*. It has no doubt been many years since he's thought of Nassara."

Amir dropped his dagger and ducked his head. When he looked back up, there were tears in his eyes, and grief was written all over his face. "Don't mention her to me. You dishonor her like this."

I felt terrified. Even as my lips formed the question, I did not know if I wanted to know the answer. "Who's—"

"How did you know?" Amir asked, his voice cracking as he held Lumiere by the collar.

"Naděžda told me, of course," Lumiere said. "I came to see her along with my father when the League was last in Prague. She told me she lost the baby, and that was the reason why she wanted to stay with her Dolf when she wound up pregnant with their son. That is also why she decided to protect the empress."

"Baby?" My voice was a whisper, and I did not have to ask any further questions.

I could see it all play out inside my head. Amir and my mother grew up together, and then they fell in love. Lady Penelope objected to the union. My mother had been pregnant, and then she miscarried the baby.

Nassara.

The baby had been another little girl, I realized. My mother had another child before Ben and me. Amir's child.

Xiana's words to me when she arrived made much more sense. *"How wonderful it was that she was able to keep you."*

My mother had been able to keep me, after losing her previous daughter.

363

And when *Máma* tried to convince Amir to leave the Order with her, to start a new life, he said no. And so she left him.

The fighting and everything all around me went numb as I watched Amir wrestle with his pain. Lumiere, no longer struggling, was trying to shrug it off. It was Ferdy who reached out a hand to Amir, breaking the spell that seemed to capture the rest of us.

"If you please, sir," Ferdy said. "We need you to move. We need Lumi to order the crew to stop the ship. We can still hold his life hostage, but we need him to live."

"For now," I muttered darkly.

Amir allowed Ferdy to help him up, and I kept my guard on Lumiere.

"They already have their orders," Lumiere said to Ferdy as he stood up and began adjusting himself. "They'll finish them, and then evacuate."

I frowned at him, holding my dagger up to his face. "Evacuate?"

"Watch where you hold that thing, Ella. I don't need you ripping up my coat even further." Lumiere shook his head, running his hands through his hair again to smooth it over and flick it back in his stylish way.

"Just tell us what you've planned," Amir said. The anger was gone from his face, while the shadow of sadness remained.

"If you know me so well, you know it'll be a blast," Lumiere said with a small chuckle.

Not one of us—Ferdy, Amir, or myself—appreciated his attempt at humor.

Lumiere rolled his eyes. "Didier's been loading them into another boat, back by the stern," he explained. "I've already

THE ORDER OF THE CRYSTAL DAGGERS

dislodged the anchor, so the ship is not going to stop. Besides, I've already shot through the sails, remember?"

I thought about his temper tantrum earlier, as he was calling Lord Maximillian's guards to attack. "Why did you do that?"

"For show, of course. There's no point in committing acts of high treason without some fanfare. I might as well get caught at gunpoint or go into a dark room and hang myself." He shuddered, appalled at the thought. "It's such poor showmanship, in the end."

"You're worried about showmanship?"

"I told you he was big on fashion before," Ferdy whispered. "It's not so hard to believe."

I glanced around. Harshad and Lady Penelope were still fighting. The crewmembers, true to Lumiere's assertion, were gone. They had their orders, they carried them out, and it was time to leave.

"We need to get everyone off the ship then," I said. "We will have to see if another ship can haul it in."

"No one will want to," Lumiere warned. "There's plenty of gunpowder and explosives down in the cargo holds."

Ferdy groaned. "It was a literal blast you were talking about."

"Did you think I was being facetious?" He gave Ferdy a grin. "Well, if that's all it is, I think I will leave it to you, won't I?"

Lady Penelope appeared beside us. "No, you won't. You're coming with us."

"Since I am the one who is in charge of the crew's rescue, don't you think it should be that you're the ones who are coming with me?"

Lady Penelope grabbed him and hauled him over to the side of the ship. "It would be a shame to toss you in, especially in your fine clothes, Lumiere. I know you would sink to the bottom from the weight of your jewelry alone."

Lumiere tried to fight her off. I took a step forward to help her, but Amir stopped me.

"Let her handle it now, Eleanora," he said. "Lumiere's rigged the ship to explode. It's better if it's in the middle of the river for that. We need to make sure the rest of the crew is off the ship first though."

"Can't we stop the explosion?" I asked.

"Lumiere has grown up working with the French and the Chinese," he said. "They have some of the best and most potent gunpowder in the world. If we can save everyone, it will be better. That will also get rid of Lumiere's ship, and that will force him to stay here. And we can definitely use that to our advantage."

I took his arm. "If you say so. Ferdy and I will go and check the ship."

"Stay away from the cargo hold," Amir said. "You don't want to set it off. I will go and see to it that Lumi does not escape. I have some more questions for him, it seems."

I nodded but paused before I left. A half a second later, I reached around Amir to give him a hug.

Amir stiffened under my embrace. I could not blame him for the surprise as I held onto him tightly. Rationally, it was a silly choice; we were in the middle of a fight, and there was so much at stake. We did not have the time or the luxury to console each other on our losses.

But he had lost a daughter, I had lost a sister, and we had both lost my mother. What else could I do?

THE ORDER OF THE CRYSTAL DAGGERS

"I'm so sorry," I whispered. I did not know what else to say, and honestly, I did not know if I could have said anything else. Amir's kindness to me took on a new light as I thought about how much pain he must have felt in seeing me. It was not just my mother he had lost. It was a daughter, one who would have been only a little older than me. Considering my initial hostility, and even our acknowledged silences and shared stories, I was a poor replacement for a future I knew he feverishly wanted.

"Thank you." He patted my hair, reminding me of my own father in that moment. "But you have to go. We can talk later."

I nodded and swallowed hard. I let him go and reached for Ferdy, who seemed to understand my heart was broken at another's anguish.

"Let's start down and work our way back up," he said, grounding my attention in the moment.

"Good idea." I rubbed the last remnants of tears from my eyes, using his words to focus. "I'll lead the way."

THE ORDER OF THE CRYSTAL DAGGERS

368

THE ORDER OF THE CRYSTAL DAGGERS

25

◊

Together, Ferdy and I ran back through the galley, heading down into the lower decks of the clipper ship.

"How are you feeling, Ella?" Ferdy asked, as we made our way down a stairwell.

"As well as can be expected." I did not sound vague intentionally, but as I thought about it, I wondered if I was still trying to figure out how broken I was. "How about you? How is your wound?"

"The bleeding seems to have stopped," Ferdy replied. He plucked at the crude bandage, trying not to wince at the resulting twinge of pain. "It still hurts to move it, though."

"I hope you haven't made it worse by all the fighting up there."

Ferdy gave me a rueful smile. "It would be considerably worse if we were dead. I can handle fighting with my left hand for now."

"Please just be careful. I know Amir can take care of it, once we get back to the manor."

"Amir is the Turk who was fighting Lumi out there, I presume?"

Quickly, as we methodically made our way through the ship, I told Ferdy about Amir. When I finished, Ferdy nodded. "I see. What a tangle, fate is."

"I'm surprised you recognized him," I said. "I did not think you would remember him after all this time."

"There are not many Ottomans in Prague. My Arabic instructor was from the Arabian Peninsula, where there are plenty of smaller coups rising up against the sultan. He taught

369

me a lot about their culture. When I saw you that day in the city, I was worried for you, since I saw he had been branded. They brand thieves and other villains."

"Amir told me what you said to him." I stopped for a moment, glancing into a small room, similar to the one we had been held in earlier, looking for any sign of Lumiere's remaining crew. "He said you told him you would trade your life for mine."

"Of course I would, *chérie*. I told you before, I do not deserve you."

"I still say you have it wrong." I cupped his cheek. "I am the one who does not deserve you."

It was hard to believe I deserved anything. I had forgotten Lady POW in search of Ferdy, I had caused Ben more agony, and I had dismissed Amir and Harshad over various causes, some of them imagined and others misunderstood. And I had even thought I could abandon Ferdy if my duty called for it. It was only after I thought he was dead that my heart revealed the truth.

"It is possible, you know, that we do not deserve each other. In that case, we are perfect for each other," Ferdy said.

I smiled as he kissed my palm and took my hand in his. Maybe that was the true miracle of God in a fallen world. There were things in this world that were able to be so true that they were more than real, and when I lost my footing, I could still use them to find my way back to where I needed to be.

"Come on," I said. "Only one more level to check, and then we can get off of this ship, too."

We quickly resumed our task. It was only a matter of moments later when we came to the next floor, and I heard a small, familiar squeak. I turned and saw the same figure I had seen earlier, when I was walking on the top deck.

THE ORDER OF THE CRYSTAL DAGGERS

"Betsy!"

She was curled up behind the stairs, sitting with her knees up to her chin. She looked so small and childlike in her uniform, even though her face was gaunt and fearful. When she saw me, she stood up and hurried to embrace me.

"Nora!" she cheered. "Oh, I never thought I would see you again. And when I did, I was certain that you were going to be killed."

"What's happened to you?" I asked, watching as she pulled her hood down. "You look like a nun."

Betsy giggled, some of her girlishness coming back to her fraught face. "You look like an Amazon."

"I'm sure that's some of the inspiration." I glanced over my shoulder. "Ferdy, this is my friend, Betsy. It's a long story, but she was taken here with the rest of my stepmother's household."

I made quick introductions. Betsy was clearly tickled as he bowed and kissed her hand, just like the gentleman I knew he was.

"Can you tell us what happened? How did you get here?" I asked.

"Yes." Betsy nodded. "That man, the tall, blond one with the demon-green eyes, he came and took us the night after the Advent Ball. He had several dark, scary guards with him, so we followed him without much hassle."

"Is Cecilia here, too?"

"Yes. But Lumiere got tired of her, and Miss Priscilla, too."

"I can imagine that."

Betsy smiled at my wry tone. "The day we got here, he gave them over to your old friend Tulia. I haven't seen them since she stuffed them in the cargo hold." She blushed, her heart-shaped face burning over red.

"What is it?" I asked.

"I've heard their cries from that room," she admitted. "But I did not bother to see if there was a way to help them. I figured it was them, and I rather liked that they were out of my way. It has made my chores much more bearable."

I could understand her decision in that matter, recalling my own hours working in the manor while Cecilia was busy with paperwork or while she was asleep from the late nights before.

For now, though, I did not have time to reminisce. I took Betsy by the shoulders. "I need you to go and get into the boat at the stern. Ferdy and I will see to Cecilia and Prissy."

Betsy nodded. "Please be careful, Nora." She smiled and bobbed a quick curtsy to Ferdy, and then hurried upstairs.

"I hope Lady POW is finished taking care of the others," I said. "I wouldn't want her to run into more trouble."

"From the sound of it, your stepmother and stepsister are all that are left to get," Ferdy said.

I was about to agree, before a hunched shadow filled the hallway before us. "Tulia."

Tulia signaled her hello, and I drew out my dagger. She rolled her eyes before tapping her finger to her head.

She did not seem hostile, but I was still hesitant to trust her. "I'm doing much better, from when you knocked me out before."

She frowned at my tone and shook her head at my reaction. She signed out a repentant response.

I said I was sorry. You were able to come onto the ship and keep your dagger.

THE ORDER OF THE CRYSTAL DAGGERS

The blade at my side did seem to confirm she had only been acting in my best interest. "We don't have time for apologies," I said. "We need to get Cecilia and Prissy out of here before the ship explodes."

This time, Tulia frowned. Her hands twisted fast as she clearly objected.

"What did she say?" Ferdy whispered.

"She said that Cecilia and Prissy should be punished for how they treated me and Ben all those years ago. She's not going to help us get them out, and if we don't leave, we could end up dying."

"So …what do we do now?"

Tulia pointed to the door, flicking her wrist and then shaking her head.

"It's locked, and Tulia won't give me the key."

In some ways, I appreciated Tulia's efforts to avenge me. She was trying to help by forcing me into making the only choice that seemed rational, all so the burden of their deaths would not rest on my soul.

But my eyes fell to my dagger, and I knew if I left them to die now, I would not be worthy of the Order. It was not, as Ferdy had repeatedly told me, an assassination group. We protected people, and even though I hated Cecilia's actions toward me, I did not want her to die with my stepsister, trapped inside a ship full of explosives.

I put my dagger in my sheath. "If she's not going to help us, we need to find a new way to open this door." I faltered as I stepped forward, wishing desperately that Ben was able to be at my side. He had always been the one who tinkered with machines and mechanical ideas. The thought of him lying unconscious on the top deck stymied me, and I had to

THE ORDER OF THE CRYSTAL DAGGERS

push through my sudden guilt and sadness to focus on the mission again.

Just get the mission done, and then you can tend to Ben.

Ferdy turned around and headed back down the hall. "There might be a spare key in the captain's room. I'll search around for one."

"Hurry!" I called after him, before narrowing my eyes at Tulia again. I studied the door, trying to see if I could fit the tip of my dagger in and break the lock. "Don't you do anything else."

Tulia only crossed her arms and began her silent tirade. Her hands flashed and fluttered, but I paid no mind to her. It was already tempting enough to leave Cecilia and Prissy, and if I could get away with it and not feel responsible for another person's death, I would have done so.

I knocked on the door, hard enough to bruise my knuckles. "Hello? Lady Cecilia? Priscilla?"

I waited a moment, before I heard some scurried movements on the other side. "Hello?" I called.

"What do you want?" Cecilia's voice crackled, and even from the other side of the door I felt her voice scrap at my patience and goodwill. "We're trapped in here, if you failed to notice."

"I'm trying to get you free," I called back. "Can you unlock the door?"

"What an egregiously unintelligible question. If we had been able to unlock the door, don't you think we would have left already?"

"Mother, be quiet," Prissy said. Her voice was weak and whiny, but I felt more compassion for her at once. After all, I would not want to be stuck in the cargo hold of a ship with my stepmother, either.

THE ORDER OF THE CRYSTAL DAGGERS

I examined the lock again. It was a metal one, so it would be hard to use my dagger to pick the lock. I did not have any pins in my hair, since it was tied it back with only a band.

I glared at Tulia again. "Why can't you just let me get them out?"

Why can't you just let them die?

Trying to reason with her was impossible. We went through several rounds—the Order was supposed to protect the innocent (*They are not innocent*), it was morally wrong (*It is morally wrong to let injustice remain*), they might be useful for information (*I can provide better information*)—before I was ready to give up and wait for Ferdy, hoping he would be able to find another key.

Tulia raised an eyebrow at me, her ancient face folding into wrinkled layers, and at her triumphant haughtiness, I tried again.

"It is not what my mother would want," I insisted.

You don't know have any idea of what your mother would have wanted. Tulia gestured to my outfit. *She would not have wanted you to join the Order.*

At that, it was just like before, when Ben had attacked me in Harshad's lessons. I froze, my heart aching at the stunning realization that she was right.

I had nothing to offer Tulia anymore. I shook my head. "You should go. I know Didier has the rescue boat near the stern. I have nothing more to say to you right now."

She shook her head sadly, but she left. As she walked past, I studied her features carefully. Tulia was my grandfather's half-sister, and I wondered if he had been just as unmerciful to Lady Penelope.

The moments passed, and I was stuck listening to Cecilia and Prissy's moans, repeatedly assuring them help was

THE ORDER OF THE CRYSTAL DAGGERS

coming. I did not know if they believed me, but I honestly did not know if I believed me, either.

It was only when Ferdy came down the stairs carrying a bag and waving a key in his hand that I felt any gleam of hope return to my soul.

"Oh, thank you, Lord," I whispered, hurrying to unlock the door.

"And me, too, right?" Ferdy joked. "There were a lot of interesting things in the captain's room. I brought a few things to see if you wanted to look at them—"

"Not now," I said. I barely heard him protest as the door creaked open, and I ran inside to see to my stepfamily.

Inside, the room was framed in crates marked with warnings. Cecilia and Prissy were both chained to the far wall. The smell of the room was awful, flooded with the singed smell of ashes and gunpowder. I did not want to look too closely at what Lumiere kept in the hold of his ship.

Cecilia sniffed, sticking her large nose up in the air as she saw me. "Well, I would say it's about time you came for us."

"Apologies, Madame," I muttered. I knew Tulia had good reasons for wanting them to die. It was fortunate that she had plenty of bad reasons, too, or I would have left Cecilia there at her sniveling.

Prissy was much kinder. She was tired from the lack of exercise, her skin was pale, and she seemed much thinner than before. I almost wondered if she was happy with the results of her imprisonment, even if she did not like the imprisonment itself.

"Thank you, Eleanora," she whispered to me, and I pulled her arm around my neck to help her as her legs buckled under the rocking ship.

I only nodded, but I was grateful Ferdy was willing to help Cecilia. She did not recognize him as a Prince of Bohemia, and even I had to smile as she called him "urchin garbage" as we made our way to the top deck.

Lady Penelope was waiting for us. Her gun and dagger were tucked away, and she was clearly in command of the ship. Lord Maximillian's guards, Karl's attendants, and even some of Lumiere's crew were scattered around the deck. I tried not to notice some of the blood dripping along the wooden planks of the ship's floor, but in the moonlight the crimson wash glimmered eerily.

"Excellent work, Eleanora," Lady Penelope said as we approached her. "You and your companion have done well."

Cecilia huffed. "I would beg to differ."

"I would love to see you beg to do anything," Lady Penelope snapped. "If I were you, I would keep from saying anything else until you are back at the manor, and even then, a vow of silence would be more than appropriate for you. After all, you would not want me to drag you to the castle to beg for forgiveness for treason, would you?"

Cecilia's lips opened and shut, and then she glared at Lady Penelope.

"Yes, Lord Maximillian confessed, along with the secret heir to the throne," Lady Penelope told her. "You can guarantee your name will be brought up, too. Especially since your son is dead."

"Alex?" Cecilia's voice cracked before she began to sob.

For the first time in my life, I felt truly sorry for her. I felt even more sympathetic as Lady POW waved her aside and told her to take Prissy and get off the ship before she was killed, too. There was nothing remorseful in my grandmother's gaze as she issued her commands.

THE ORDER OF THE CRYSTAL DAGGERS

Cecilia, without another word, did as she was told.

Lady Penelope turned her attention to Ferdy. "Well, Your Highness, it looks like I owe you my thanks."

Ferdy bowed his head. "Please, Madame, call me Ferdy. I would have us be friends."

"And here I thought you were more concerned with being family." Lady Penelope's tone was cool, but she seemed pleased by Ferdy's response. "Well, then, we will talk business later. Right now we have to leave."

"Is everyone else off the ship?" I asked.

She nodded. "Including Lumiere. I have him bound and just for the fun of it, gagged. He told me he would enjoy it more that way, likely thinking I would not agree with him. But I can tell you for certain, I enjoy it more."

I did not want to ask her about Ben. Lady POW was not the most compassionate of people. I worried she would tell me that he would be useless and cut out of the Order's future missions.

Ferdy took my hand as we boarded Didier's small boat. I could barely see it, tucked away in the shadows of the *Salacia*, with no lights on to show its presence. There were several others on the small riverboat, including Amir and Harshad, but no one—not even Cecilia—made any noise as we pushed away from Lumiere's sinking, demolished clipper.

It was only as we began to disembark back onto the docks that I heard a series of loud noises, all rippling out from the bottom of the boat. We all seemed to turn back at the same time, watching as an explosion ripped through the *Salacia*, setting it on fire.

A large spray of water washed over us, soaking us with the icy waters of the Vltava. Beside me, Ferdy laughed, while I heard Lumiere, already free of his gag, complain that his residence was gone—it was his own fault!—and Ben let out another groan. Harshad began to call for assistance, and Lady Penelope began rehearsing threats under her breath.

"Time to go home," Ferdy whispered behind me.

I reached up and hugged him, careful to watch his injured arm. I was surprised to find he had the bag from the captain's room on his back, but I said nothing as I held onto him.

I held onto him, and he held me back. It was enough.

I was with him, and it was enough.

THE ORDER OF THE CRYSTAL DAGGERS

THE ORDER OF THE CRYSTAL DAGGERS

26

◊

I do not remember much of the trip back to my father's manor. Harshad and Lady POW, as always, seemed to have the situation under control. We were able to hire several coaches to carry us back, though some of the servants, having nowhere else to go, decided to walk. Harshad issued instructions for a few of the men who were willing to give us information. With the members of the household, Lumiere, Cecilia, Prissy, and the rest of us, I imagine we could have been something out of the Wild West in America, like a kind of traveling caravan.

Ferdy tried to stay awake for as long as possible, looking to find ways to make me smile. He kept asking about dinner, wondering aloud if Clavan would be willing to send some of Helen's stew to the manor. Before I knew it, and likely before he did, too, he was leaning on my shoulder, silent at last.

I watched Ferdy sleep for several moments, thinking how serene he looked. With his jaw relaxed, the lines of his face eased into slumber, he seemed much younger. I missed the sparkle of his eyes, but as the moonlight clung to his skin, I could not stop my smile.

Even in his dirty rags and covered in blood, he was a prince.

Because we were all drenched, I curled up against him and tried to fall asleep, too. I managed to doze off and on, unable to stop replaying the scene in my mind where Ben had gotten hurt, and all because of my mistake.

My only comfort was knowing Amir was tending to Ben's leg as best as he could while we were on the road. I was glad I was not in the same curricle as they were; I did not want to hear Ben's moaning in real life any more than I knew it would haunt me inside my mind.

I helped everyone inside as we arrived. I let Harshad and Lady POW deal with the main villains of our night. Her footmen were up and ready to take care of guarding them, and I was content to know I had a break from seeing either Cecilia or Lumiere, even if it was only for a short while.

Once everyone was settled, including Ferdy, Amelia came to help me clean myself up. I was able to wash up and change, getting rid of the chill in the air.

After I finished seeing to my own care, and sending Amelia away, I made my way back to Ben's room, where Amir had gone to tend to his broken leg.

I opened the door, and Amir did not look up at me as he spoke.

"You don't have to be here, Eleanora."

I watched as he pulled out a bag that I had never seen before, one that was full of medical tools and other supplies. Amir reached inside and searched for something. A moment later, I saw he held up a syringe and a small bottle.

"I know I don't have to be here," I whispered back, trying not to cringe as Amir filled up the needle with the bottle's contents and injected it into Ben's thigh. "I just ..."

My voice trailed off, and I could not say whether it was because my reasoning was too embarrassing or because I knew Amir would not agree with me regardless.

As if he sensed my thoughts, Amir shook his head. "I know why you came, and I can tell you, punishing yourself will not make Ben's leg heal faster. And if you are here to see if he will forgive you, you might be waiting for some time. The drug I gave him on the way over won't keep him asleep for

THE ORDER OF THE CRYSTAL DAGGERS

lcng, but I can say for certain he does not want to talk to you tonight."

"I know that, too," I said. "But I want to be there for him."

"He has a long road of recovery before him," Amir told me. "I did everything I could, but there is no way to know this will not get worse yet."

"This can't possibly get worse."

Amir sighed. "I am hoping I can set and wrap it without waking him. You might as well go and get some sleep."

My brother had fallen asleep during the ride over, and I doubted Amir wanted him to wake up any more than I did.

"It might make him feel better, though," I retorted, though I did not want Ben to wake up only to curse me out.

"That won't make him *be* better in the end, either."

The fire was bright in his room. Lady POW's seamstresses apparently doubled as a small band of nurses, as they all bustled around his room while Amir worked.

"What happened, Nora?" Marguerite asked, her pretty young face worried as she looked down at Ben.

I shook my head and said nothing. I did not want to tell her that I had caused this. I might have saved him from a worse fate, but it was because of me he felt the pain of a broken leg, and it was possible he would face the life of an outcast once more.

I did not dare ask Lady Penelope if Ben would have to quit the Order. I knew it would be too painful for him.

Amir waved them away, quietly dismissing them. He did not seem eager to talk with me while they were there, and when they were gone, Amir put aside his medical tools to focus on me. "I finished sewing up Ferdy's arm for you. He's resting now in the room beside yours. He's a good patient,

THE ORDER OF THE CRYSTAL DAGGERS

despite the pain he was in. He was eager to talk with me in Arabic, if you can believe it."

"I can believe it." I smiled ruefully. I wondered if most of those Arabic exchanges involved foul language or curses. "Thank you."

"He should be the one to thank you, for taking care of his wound as quickly as you did. It was good to get it wrapped up quickly. I didn't see any infection or pus, but we will have to watch it to see if there's any part of the bullet still in there."

I nodded. "I'm just glad he will be well."

"And you?"

"I don't have any injuries."

"Your heart is still tender from the many things we experienced tonight," Amir replied quietly. "You should go rest."

This time, I shook my head. "I don't think I can. I feel so terrible about what happened. If I had done things differently, Ben's leg wouldn't be broken again."

"He will likely be angry with you for a while yet, but he still loves you. He told me about how it broke the first time. I know from my own experience that the heart will win out in the long run."

I wondered if he was thinking of Nassara, or if he was thinking about my mother.

"Everything in your life will circle back around to what you love," Amir said. "Even if you deny your heart, your heart does not go away. That is why everyone lies, everyone has secrets, and everyone has regrets."

"I certainly have regrets today."

THE ORDER OF THE CRYSTAL DAGGERS

A moment passed before Amir took my hand, holding my palm against his scar. "Listen to me, Eleanora. Your mother left me, and it broke me."

The spell of my own sadness shattered as Amir knelt before me and his eyes met mine.

"I'm sorry," I said. "I'm sorry she left you. Even if I am only here because she did." I tightened my hands around his, wishing I could will away the scar on his hand and the deeper scars on his heart.

Amir surprised me by shaking his head. "No," he whispered. "I deserved it. She was right to leave me. I loved her, but I was not worthy of her. I did not stay by her side when she needed me the most—when she needed me to stand up to your grandmother."

"You don't have to tell me this," I said, unsure of how this related to anything at all.

"I am telling you this because I know Naděžda wanted a different life for you and Ben. She wanted to quit the Order and have a family and a chance at a normal life."

"That is not what happened."

"No. Your grandmother strongly objected to our relationship. She was quite furious with me for a long time." Amir looked away again. "We only reconciled after Naděžda was lost at sea and we could finally lay the past to rest and attempt for a separate peace between us."

"She still thinks you're only here to betray her." I thought of that night in the carriage, before Amir had disappeared after Ferdy's traveling coach as it made its way to Silesia.

"Lady POW has trouble when it comes to her own heart. I don't imagine that feeling of hers will ever go away. I'm telling you to go and tend to your heart now partially because

THE ORDER OF THE CRYSTAL DAGGERS

of her. I think her heart has been broken quite a bit, and I do wonder sometimes if she prefers it that way."

He patted my hand. "I do not want to see that be your fate, Eleanora. And I know for certain your mother would not want that, either."

My mother apparently would not want me in the Order at all, from what I knew. I had chased her memory, only to find myself disappointing it.

I was not the only one who had disappointed her, I thought, looking back at Amir. I did wonder why he had refused to leave the Order with her, especially given how much he clearly still loved her.

"What is it?" Amir asked.

I squeezed his hand back. "*Máma* would have been happy to meet Nassara."

Earlier, I had seen Amir fight and take down enemies, but when I said his daughter's name, he crumpled. He buried his head in his hands for a long moment. When he looked up, he was mostly back to his usual self, aside from the swelling tears in his eyes.

"Your mother wanted a different life for her children," Amir said. "She did not want to be a part of the Order. Lady POW reminded her before she went off to Prague that death or defeat is the only true way to be free."

"But she found a way," I said. "She quit."

"As I said, where your love is, your life will follow. She met your father and they married, and Ben came shortly after." Amir's light tone hid the majority of his bitterness.

" Lumiere said she stayed with my father only because of Ben."

"It was likely the truth." Amir grimaced. "She had already lost one child. She did not want to lose another. But I doubt that was her only reason. From what I know of her, I would say she did love your father."

"She still missed you." I thought of the miniature portrait of Amir I had found tucked away in my mother's locket.

"One day I will see her again. And when I do, I would be remiss if I did not help you find the life you are looking for. Naděžda would be most upset with me, and her temper is worse than your own."

Amir's attempt at levity fell flat as I thought about Ferdy. The Order was nothing like I thought it would be, but if I was loyal only to the truth, then Amir was right. And the truth was, I loved Ferdy. I had tried to forget about him, I had tried to lose him, and I had tried to protect him.

"Everyone has secrets, everyone lies, and everyone has regrets." Amir put his hand on my shoulder affectionately. "But there are some regrets you can live with, and others you can't."

He nodded toward the door. "Love is always a risk, but I don't believe you should step back from embracing it. It is a regret you will never forgive yourself over. Now, please go and tend to your beloved. It will help heal the wounds in your own heart."

He was speaking from his own experience, and I knew that in offering me the lesson of my mother's life, Amir was trying to protect me, too.

"You're right. I have to go," I said. "Excuse me."

After one last look at Ben, watching him sleep so uncomfortably in his bed with his leg wrapped up. I hurried away, allowing Amir to resume his work in peace.

387

THE ORDER OF THE CRYSTAL DAGGERS

He is a good doctor, I thought. A good doctor for the body as well as the soul.

I headed across the manor with quiet steps, feeling the angst in my chest. It seemed to grow and then shrink, before it dissolved and only my resolve was left behind.

The door to the room beside mine clicked gently as I opened and closed it. For a small moment, I stood there, with my back against the door as I looked at him on the bed.

He was flipping through a book, sitting propped up with a stack of pillows. He had been given a new set of clothes, and it was likely he had been able to wash up, too. His injured arm, wrapped up in thick bandages, was resting off to the side, almost as an afterthought. At my arrival, he turned to face me, giving me the same old flippant grin. "Ella."

And then, all of a sudden, I was running to him.

I nearly fell into his lap as I climbed up next to him. My lips found his as I carefully, desperately clung to him.

Ferdy responded to me at once; he wrapped his good arm around me, keeping me close as I braced my hands on his chest. His body was warm beneath his shirt. As my fingers curled into crisp fabric, I thought I could hear his heart begin to pound.

I felt him flinch as he moved his injured arm, but his mouth never left mine as we kissed, over and over and over again. For long moments, we stayed there, reveling in the certainty between us, marveling at the undeniable longing and irresistible response.

"Ferdy." His name escaped me between breaths as I pulled back from him. For a silent second I felt him still, and I could almost hear his mind wonder if I was going to pull away from him again, as I had so many times before.

Instead, I leaned into him even further. I would not leave him. I would not be able to bear that regret, and I knew it. I could no longer lie to myself about that.

"I love you," I whispered.

"I love you, too."

The wanting I had felt before, the ache I had for him, instantly transformed into need. I needed to feel the warmth of his skin, to taste the wonder of his kiss; my body shook with tension, forced between forbidden desire and moral constraints. As each second passed, I found myself drowning in flames, and more convinced I would enjoy such a fate.

It was only when Ferdy cupped my cheek, and I felt the wetness of my tears between us, that he eased back from me.

"Ella." Ferdy's voice was husky with passion as he whispered my name. "Everything is well now. We are safe. You saved us."

"No," I choked. "No, you are the one who saved me."

"I don't know if I would call getting kidnapped the same thing as saving you."

"No, that's not it." I lowered my eyes, letting my gaze fall to his bandages.

"What is it then?"

"I thought, in joining the Order, I would do something worthy. It was something my mother did once. I wanted to be free, but if I couldn't be free, fighting for her was something I could stand for."

Ferdy held on to me tightly as I continued to ramble, trying to put my muddled thoughts into a decipherable manner.

THE ORDER OF THE CRYSTAL DAGGERS

"My mother resigned from the Order because of love. I joined the Order for her, to make her proud, and to protect others."

"Which you have done," Ferdy said.

"But …" I sighed. "If I truly want to honor her, I should leave, as she did."

My eyes met Ferdy's in the dim light. I leaned in and kissed him again, tasting the fun and freedom I had found before, even as it was buried underneath the memories of our evening and hints of lavender and mint.

Ferdy's lips grazed my neck as his hand slid down my body before resting on my hips. As the heat simmered between us, I knew why my mother left the Order. She had wanted her freedom, but she had wanted love more. My father was not her first love, or even the most passionate. But he was the one she chose. She wanted to be with him and start a family with him, even if that meant forsaking her mother—and her mother's expectations.

I pulled back from Ferdy again, panting as I struggled to catch my breath. "Now all I want is to be with you, Ferdy. I don't want a life where I have to give you up."

"That's not true."

I stilled at his comment. "What do you mean? Of course that's true."

"Ella, *chérie*, please understand. I am flattered, but I know you want more than that. You honor your mother by choosing to follow your own heart. There is no need for you to live her life for her. But I know you want to protect others. I know you want to be there for your brother and your other friends."

"Not if it means losing you."

THE ORDER OF THE CRYSTAL DAGGERS

His fingers traced my lips tenderly. "You are not the only one that must make a sacrifice when it comes to love."

He kissed me deeply, letting his lips slide over mine once more. "Let me be with you. Let me make that sacrifice, and we can be together."

"What are you talking about?" I asked, inexplicably overwhelmed.

"I love you, Ella. I can't remember a time when I haven't. I've wanted to be with you for the longest time. Let me stay with you and keep you as mine."

"I couldn't leave you if I tried." And that was true. I had tried, and I knew it was hopeless. The days of distancing myself from him, trying to forget him, were over, like a bad dream.

Despite his injury, Ferdy bounced beneath me. "Excellent. I was legitimately worried I would have to fight Karl for the right to marry you."

"Marry me?" My mind was still full of passion's fog as Ferdy arched up against me. I gasped at the sudden movement.

"Of course I will," Ferdy said. "As soon as possible."

I held onto him. "Are you sure you want to?"

"I'm sure I want you." He cupped my cheek again, wiping away another stray tear—a happy one this time. "I want you most of all. Why do you think I've been asking if I can keep you?"

And then he kissed me again. I lost myself in it, and in him, as time slipped by in slower seconds. I barely recovered as Ben burst into the room.

THE ORDER OF THE CRYSTAL DAGGERS

At the sight of my brother, barely recovered from our earlier battle, balancing on his new crutch with his broken leg in a thick cast, I practically flew off of the bed.

"They're coming for her," he said. "They're coming for Lady POW."

Hurriedly, I smoothed down my hair and straightened out the wrinkles in my dress. "Who? Who's coming for her? And why are you out of bed? Your leg—"

"I can walk with crutches. The medicine still prevents me from feeling a lot of pain," Ben said. "This is an emergency, Ella."

My brother calling me "Ella" said everything to me about how he felt. He was upset with me, and I was unable to do anything to rectify our relationship now. Before I could say anything else, Ben glared at Ferdy.

"Your castle guards are here," Ben said flatly. "The police came too, and now they want to take her to the king. She was fighting with them when Xiana came to get me."

Ferdy sat up with a sigh. "I guess I have to give the news of my surprising return and Karl's disappearance to my parents anyway."

I nodded quickly, hurrying to grab Ferdy's coat and prepare myself. As we headed out, Ben grabbed Ferdy's injured arm.

"You can explain yourself on the way there," Ben growled.

Ferdy twitched in pain but gave my brother a smile. "*Absolument*, my good sir."

"Ben, let him go. That's where he got hurt," I said.

"He knows," Ferdy told me. "But it is better for me to forgive him. After all, we are going to be sharing a lot of adventures together from now on, *mon frère*."

THE ORDER OF THE CRYSTAL DAGGERS

Ferdy gave me that smile of his—reckless and risky, ever the irresistible man I loved. "Isn't that right, Ella?"

Ben rolled his eyes. "Just hurry up. I have to tell Harshad. You'll meet Amir and Lady POW at the stables."

Ferdy waited until he was gone from the hallway before he chuckled. "Well, I knew that wouldn't be easy. But I bet I'll still have an easier time winning him over than your grandmother."

Despite everything, I laughed. The sound was still echoing in the halls as Ferdy leaned over and kissed me again, allowing me one last reprieve from reality before we set out to face the world's trouble once more.

393

THE ORDER OF THE CRYSTAL DAGGERS

C. S. Johnson is the author of several young adult sci-fi and fantasy novels, including *The Starlight Chronicles* series, the *Once Upon a Princess* saga, and the *Divine Space Pirates* trilogy. With a gift for sarcasm and an apologetic heart, she currently lives in Atlanta with her family.

THE ORDER OF THE CRYSTAL DAGGERS

AUTHOR'S NOTE

Dear Reader,

As always, I am deeply touched by the time you pour into reading through my work. *Prince of Secrets and Shadows* is the second book in this trilogy, and in many ways, it took even more time to write than the first book; the theme of freedom I used as a starting point for Book 1 is a much bigger question than I thought it would be. So much about freedom is universal and personal at the same time. Working through this book, it was clear that freedom is tied to so many other ideas that it relies on, especially as it moves toward the personal side of application. So much of our freedom is only capable if there is truth and goodness, and maintaining freedom requires moral checks and balances.

With regards to this book, freedom and truth—and the trust required for it—is at the center, especially when it comes to identity. Who do you really trust? What do you really believe in? Which values are the ones that you are advocating for, and why? Such questions can be terrifying, especially if we do not want to examine our answers too closely. While Eleanora struggles with Ferdy and Ben over who she is and who she could be, she comes to face the reality of life in a fallen world, learning that sometimes people do bad things for good (or not so good) reasons, that bad things can still bring about good results, and that not everyone will agree on what is good or bad in the end.

That is a hard lesson to face on a more practical level. I'm not sure that a lot of people have truly learned it, including myself.

Freedom, truth, identity and morality. All of it matters, and all of it comes crashing together in the seconds between the choices we make when we choose to answer the question of how we should then live.

THE ORDER OF THE CRYSTAL DAGGERS

As you can see, there's still much to look forward to in Book 3! I am hoping that it will be easier to write, now that I have my sights set on the end.

Thank you again once more for joining me in this novel's adventures. I hope you will stay on for the ending of this series in the next book, *Heart of Hope and Fear*, where the fate of the empire—and the future of Eleanora and her companions—will be decided.

Until We Meet Again,

C. S. Johnson

THE ORDER OF THE CRYSTAL DAGGERS

SAMPLE READING

Chapter 1 *from*

NIGHT

of

BLOOD and BEAUTY

A COMPANION NOVELLA TO

THE ORDER OF THE CRYSTAL DAGGERS

featuring Amir and Naděžda's story of falling in love …

◊　　◊　　◊　　◊

C. S. Johnson

397

398

1

◊

"Miss Eleanor."

The desperation in his voice was only matched by his irritation, and the moment he said anything, Amir feared he had inadvertently given himself away.

The sapphire eyes he had come to both love and hate twinkled mischievously at him. "Why, Mr. Qureshi, I do believe you're quite flustered. Especially if you're going to use your manners. Where are those mongrel ways of yours? I might mistake you for a real gentleman with such a formal tone."

Her lyrical, teasing voice did nothing to lighten his mood; rather, it plucked at his heartstrings with a bittersweet twang, and Amir had to force himself to remain still as he stared down at her.

It would do nothing for his case if he showed any further sign of compromise, especially now that his partner sensed his weakness.

"It is only proper I address you as such, Miss Eleanor," Amir said, keeping his voice stripped of all his conflicting emotions. "Your mother, Her Grace, would be the first to agree with me."

At the mention of her mother, her gaze only grew bolder. "We both know my mother's favorite thing in the world is being a hypocrite," she said, crossing her arms and tapping her toe. "Call me Naděžda, as I've told you to before several times now."

Inwardly, Amir groaned. He should have known better than to say anything. If there was anything Eleanor Naděžda Ollerton-Cerná excelled at—and there was plenty—it was

399

arguing with him. And while there was enough wrong with that in itself, it unnerved him how often he found himself losing those arguments.

"Miss Eleanor, propriety demands—"

"Is this my punishment, after all these years, to have you give me the same lecture I gave you when we first met, Amir?" Naděžda asked, arching her brow as she pouted.

Amir hated how he stared at her mouth. His Abba had always been so concerned about him looking into a woman's eyes that Amir never realized how sinful looking at a woman's lips could be. Even beneath her *yashmak,* the transparent veil worn by women on the streets of Constantinople, seeing Naděžda stick out her bottom lip was like watching a rose bloom under misty moonlight.

He was secretly relieved when she crossed her arms and let out an indignant sigh, turning her face to the side; her patience was dwindling as quickly as his resolve.

All I have to do is outlast her. Amir relaxed in the slightest degree; it was always easier to outlast her than it was to outwit her.

"If I didn't know you better, I would question your intellect," she said.

"What is stopping you? You've questioned it often enough in the past several months we've been working together on the Order's missions." Amir frowned, his own patience wearing thin. "Unless, of course, you have good reason to agree with me in this case?"

"I fail to see why finding a way to engage the target would be a mistake. He's old enough to be more patient with someone of my age."

"He's old enough to see you as a nuisance."

THE ORDER OF THE CRYSTAL DAGGERS

"Doubtful. He's likely no more than ten years older than I am, probably married with a wife and an heir at home. A little flirtation from someone like me will make him feel like a young, attractive, appreciated hero. We've followed him long enough to know he's a soft touch."

Amir frowned. "Now I really don't like your idea. He could fall in love with you on sight."

"What better way to get him to slip up?" Naděžda sneered. "If anything can ruin your life, it is love."

He hated both her tone and how much he agreed with her. "Spies are not supposed to fall in love."

Though his tone did not betray it, that reminder was one that was burned into him daily, often multiple times as he worked with Naděžda.

She was a member of the Order of the Crystal Daggers, an ancient group of spies and assassins, specializing in political security and clandestine reconnaissance missions. Naděžda's mother was its leader, and Lady Penelope took great pride in her responsibilities, with an unrivaled, orderly fervor. While their adventures varied in location, task, and time, Amir always embraced the chance to work beside Naděžda. While he was not a member of the Order, he was a medical adviser and companion on many of their assignments.

Above all else, he sought to honor that trust. That was why he had to keep Naděžda safe—perhaps despite her wishes otherwise on such matters.

Amir cleared his throat cautiously. "Right now, it would be an unnecessary complication, especially if you are right about the wife and nursery at home."

"But it would be so easy." She clasped her hands together. "He's drawn to books. What better way to get his attention and earn his respect than engaging him at the book vendor?"

"No matter how much he loves books and no matter how much charm you throw his way, the Bohemian ambassador is not going to discuss business with the likes of you."

Amir glanced back at their target. They had been following him for hours now, ever since he walked through the construction site where the sultan's new Dolmabahçe Palace was being built.

Considering the crowded streets of Constantinople, and the finer points of the Bohemian's diplomacy, finding him was a miracle more than anything else. Amir did not want to lose him, and Amir especially did not want to lose him because he was too distracted from arguing with Naděžda.

And over such nonsense, too.

"I should go anyway," Naděžda murmured behind him, just loudly enough he knew she was angry enough to be serious. "You never let me do what I want."

"That's enough," Amir told her sharply. "The ambassador is the one who is supposed to meet with the merchants from the Haberecht Shipping Company, and we need to find out where they are located and why he is meeting with them. Her Grace says the company has rebellious sympathies. She suspects they could be behind the missing shipment themselves, rather than the Ottomans who supposedly took off with it."

"King Ferdinand is not concerned about the rebels. He just wants the weapons for himself."

"A king is allowed to protect his own country."

"Yes, but how can he protect himself from his own country? There is trouble brewing in Bohemia, just as there is trouble in Italy, Germany, and other Austrian principalities."

"That is why we need to find out where the shipment went."

THE ORDER OF THE CRYSTAL DAGGERS

Naděžda wrinkled her nose. "My father would likely know. If we really wanted to find out, all we would have to do is ask him."

"You know how Her Grace feels about that," Amir said quietly.

"She probably thinks he is behind it, given his own history with the League of Ungentlemanly Warfare. That's likely the main reason the Order is here, isn't it? There is nothing my mother would love more than to strike out against my father, especially now that she has the full weight of the British Empire behind her as a League member herself."

"Even if he's not behind it, we need to find the truth. Those weapons could unwittingly cause a lot of trouble for the people, even if they are the ones who end up wielding them."

"I suppose that is true," Naděžda agreed, her voice full of sad resignation.

Amir fell silent. He did not know what to say, especially since, from what he knew, Naděžda was likely correct. Ever since her parents' tumultuous affair and failed partnership, there was nothing but enmity in Lady Penelope's eyes at the mention of him.

Naděžda sighed. Seeing the soft vulnerability in her features made Amir want to reach out and comfort her.

Instead, Amir turned away, allowing her privacy while she grappled with her family's brokenness. A long moment passed in silence between them, before Naděžda sighed.

Amir took it as a sign she was ready to move on. "Right now, we just need to find the actual destination of the shipment."

"It could have been easily dispensed on the black markets already."

THE ORDER OF THE CRYSTAL DAGGERS

"That's true, but you said it yourself. This is something that is tied to the unrest in different countries, and we need to be prepared if fighting breaks out."

"Yes."

"So we need to follow the ambassador now, not flirt with him."

Naděžda whipped out a small fan from underneath the embroidered shawl she carried, fluttering it playfully in front of her half-covered face. "Well, my dear, you wouldn't be the one flirting, would you?" She straightened herself, drawing herself up to her full height, just shy of meeting him at eye level. "That is my area of expertise."

"You needn't remind me." The words came out softer much more husky, more provocative than he had intended. There was a quick, fearful gleam in her eye, and he saw she was uncomfortable, too.

She quickly played it off, snapping her fan shut and brushing off the billowing folds of her striped walking gown.

"Goodness, do all the women in this town have to be so covered up? I'm dying in these multiple layers," she said.

"The privacy of women is sacred here," Amir reminded her, more than grateful for the change in topic. "When something is sacred, it becomes law, and as such, modesty is the law of the land."

"There is no tyrant quite like one in place for one's own good, is there?"

"You should appreciate it. Wasn't your mother in Her Majesty Queen Victoria's court this past month?" Amir could not resist provoking her. "And even now you're wearing the bustle that's *à la mode*, and that seems much more troublesome than a veil."

THE ORDER OF THE CRYSTAL DAGGERS

The large, bulbous bump at the back of her gown twitched as Naděžda huffed.

"I might as well wear the Western fashions. I'm not going to blend in here," Naděžda insisted. "Even with the veil."

She was right about that, Amir thought to himself. In all the years since he had known her, she had never fit into any aspect of his life comfortably. Being so close to his childhood home, he was disheartened to see she never would.

He studied Naděžda out of the corner of his eye as she stood next to him in the small, dark corner of an alleyway. They were just outside the Court of the Mosque of Sultan Ahmed I, where tents poured out into the middle of the crowded streets and shops were tucked away behind them. The bright wooden buildings bordering the streets were interspersed with lattice-covered windows, hinting at the private sitting rooms afforded to women, allowing them a safe escape from the surrounding world of men and their markets.

Yes, Amir thought, Naděžda was indeed out of place. But knowing her as he did, he also knew she was accustomed to the experience.

"It's so hot." Naděžda waved her fan distractedly. "I'll be lucky if I don't die out here."

"You get used to the dry heat after a time," Amir told her. "And it is not all bad. It allows you to taste the salt in the air from the Bosporus, once you're close enough to the harbor, and you feel the full blessing of Allah from the wind."

"You could also assume that the heat was flying up from hell itself," Naděžda murmured, and despite his better judgment, Amir smiled.

Not one of his family members would approve of Naděžda in the slightest. She was everything he had been taught to abhor in a woman—outspoken, brash, impatient, stubborn,

THE ORDER OF THE CRYSTAL DAGGERS

and at times domineering. She had an enormous awareness of propriety, if only because she learned how to break it so beautifully. Many times they had fought, on everything from customs to food to manners, to religion and politics and family.

Given his own upbringing, he should have hated it. But Naděžda was smart and passionate, and he almost always enjoyed fighting with her just to see that spark of challenge light up her eyes.

Almost always.

"As I see it, the faster we get the information we need, the sooner we can head back to the ship and report back to Uncle," she said, gathering her skirts. "Talking with the ambassador would save us time."

"Mr. Prasad would not approve of your methods," Amir countered, thinking of his mentor and sponsor.

If there was ever a man he was indebted to, it was Harshad Prasad, and he would not see Naděžda come to ruin for anything. Part of the reason Harshad insisted they work together was so Amir could protect her. With the medical training he had received as a doctor, both from his father and Harshad's patronage, and having the benefits of understanding Western and Eastern cultures, he was more than capable of seeing to Naděžda's safety as she worked for the Order of the Crystal Daggers, especially in places such as Constantinople.

In theory, anyway.

Naděžda pursed her lips, reminding Amir of her mother, and he groaned. The newly proclaimed leader of the Order, Lady Penelope Ollerton-Wellesley, the dowager duchess of Wellington, was a force of nature, and she had taught her daughter to wield chaos just as skillfully than she did, if not more so.

THE ORDER OF THE CRYSTAL DAGGERS

Queen Victoria was no doubt very fortunate to have Lady Penelope's loyalty, Amir thought. The Order of the Crystal Daggers was an ancient society, one that was originally established to protect and maintain peace in Constantine's empire. When the Empire fell, the Order remained, quickly aligning themselves with those who were able to protect and assist them.

Which is why Harshad was here, Amir recalled. They had arrived with Harshad on the *Splendor*, one of the teak clippers from the East India Company. As an honorary member of the League of Ungentlemanly Warfare, Harshad was overseeing the fulfillment of the Treaty of Nanking, ensuring Chinese were complying with the terms of their loss. He would report back to Queen Victoria and the House of Lords when they returned to London.

It was fortunate Harshad was here, too, or they might never have realized a shipment of weapons intended to go to Prague had gone missing, or that the Bohemian ambassador had arrived for unexpected meetings with the Sultan and the Haberecht Shipping Company.

Naděžda cleared her throat, drawing Amir back to the moment.

"Are you sure it's Uncle who would not approve of my idea, Mr. Qureshi, or is it just you? Because I do believe Ambassador Svoboda would approve of me, and his approval is more important."

"What are you saying?"

Naděžda leaned toward him, batting her eyelashes flirtatiously. "I do believe you're jealous."

"Why would I be jealous?" Amir frowned, suddenly defensive. "This has nothing to do with that."

"Is that so?"

"Yes, and it never would," Amir insisted. He immediately regretted the sharpness in his voice.

Naděžda smiled bitterly, her eyes suddenly much sharper than before. "Well, then, as long as you have no claim on me, I'm overruling your order, Amir, with the stern reminder I am here as your partner, not your associate and certainly not your underling." She flipped her shawl over her shoulder proudly. "If anything, you are here under *my* seniority, given that I am the one in the Order, and you are merely here at Uncle's wishes."

"Miss Eleanor." This time, his voice came out as a hiss, but it was too late. She feinted and sidestepped him, before bustling out into the sunlight of the street, where the bazaar was full of mid-morning shoppers.

THE ORDER OF THE CRYSTAL DAGGERS

AUTHOR'S ACKNOWLEDGEMENTS

EDITOR

Jennifer C. Sell

Jennifer Clark Sell is a professional book editor and proofreader. She works from her home in Southern California. With her years of professional and personal experience, she offers several quality packages for authors. Find her at https://www.facebook.com/JenniferSellEditingService.

Photo Credit: Savannah Sell

AUTHOR'S ACKNOWLEDGEMENTS

COVER ILLUSTRATOR

Amalia Chitulescu

Amalia Iuliana Chitulescu is a digital artist from Campina, Romania. Raised in a small town, this self-taught artist has a technique which is delineated by the contrast between obscurity and enlightenment, using dark elements in a dreamy world. Her areas of expertise include the use of theatrical concepts to create a macabre and surrealistic world that still maintains a highly recognizable attachment to reality. Bridging a diaphanous environment with light elements, an eerie view, she creates a dream world of dark beauty, done with a blend of photography and digital painting. Find her at
https://www.facebook.com/Amalia.Chitulescu.Digital.Art

Photo Credit: Amalia Chitulescu

Thank you for reading! Please leave a review for this book and check out www.csjohnson.me for other books and updates!

412

THE ORDER OF THE CRYSTAL DAGGERS